A Virtuous Death

A VIRTUOUS DEATH

A Lady of Ashes Mystery

CHRISTINE TRENT

KENSINGTON BOOKS
www.kensingtonbooks.com

KENSINGTON BOOKS are published by

Kensington Publishing Corp.
119 West 40th Street
New York, NY 10018

All Kensington titles, imprints, and distributed lines are available at special quantity discounts for bulk purchases for sales promotion, premiums, fund-raising, educational, or institutional use.

Special book excerpts or customized printings can also be created to fit specific needs. For details, write or phone the office of the Kensington Special Sales Manager: Attn. Special Sales Department. Kensington Publishing Corp., 119 West 40th Street, New York, NY 10018. Phone: 1-800-221-2647.

Kensington and the K logo Reg. U.S. Pat. & TM Off.

eISBN-13: 978-0-7582-9327-5
eISBN-10: 0-7582-9327-5
First Kensington Electronic Edition: November 2014

ISBN-13: 978-0-7582-9326-8
ISBN-10: 0-7582-9326-7
First Kensington Trade Paperback Printing: November 2014

10 9 8 7 6 5 4 3 2 1

Printed in the United States of America

For Anthony Papadakis
Brother, Confidant, Friend

Our conversations are like fine wine:
They improve as we age.

ACKNOWLEDGMENTS

All of the usual suspects helped me bring this book to fruition, from plotting to editing: my mother, Georgia Carpenter; my brother, Tony Papadakis; my friend Diane Townsend; and, of course, my beloved husband, Jon.

My sister-in-law, Marian Wheeler, provided valuable input to the manuscript and is a constant source of spiritual comfort and support.

Mary Russell has been my best friend for over twenty-five years and provides me with much-needed writing breaks of shopping and dining.

Dr. D. P. Lyle, M.D., quickly—and graciously—answered my questions concerning the manner of death for my victims. He is an amazing resource for mystery writers. I have no idea how he gets anything done beyond responding to badgering authors.

I am appreciative for the grace and expertise of my new editor at Kensington Books, Martin Biro, whose love for mysteries shows in his careful editing of this book.

My thanks to Regency romance novelist and mystery enthusiast Emily Hendrickson, for encouraging my career and being such a lovely correspondent.

Beth Rockwell at Turn the Page Books in Boonsboro, Maryland, is the best of booksellers, and I am grateful for her enthusiasm and promotion of my books.

Gloria in excelsis.

CAST OF CHARACTERS

VIOLET HARPER'S FAMILY AND FRIENDS

Violet Harper—undertaker
Samuel Harper—Violet's husband
Mary Cooke—mourning dressmaker and Violet's friend
Harry Blundell—fellow undertaker
Will Swift—co-owner, with Harry Blundell, of Morgan Undertaking

THE ROYAL FAMILY

Queen Victoria—Queen of England
Albert Edward (Bertie)—Prince of Wales and the eldest of
    nine children
Alix of Denmark—Princess of Wales
Princess Helena—Victoria's fifth child, dowdy and double chinned
Prince Christian of Schleswig-Holstein—Helena's indolent husband
Princess Louise—Victoria's sixth child, outspoken and unsentimental
Prince Leopold—Victoria's eighth child, sickly and weak
Princess Beatrice—Victoria's youngest child, shy and serious

SERVANTS AND STAFF

John Brown—the queen's ghillie, or outdoor servant
Owen Caradoc—Beatrice's art tutor
Reverend Robinson Duckworth—Prince Leopold's tutor
Reese Meredith—footman to Lord Christie, the Earl of Baverstock

ARISTOCRATIC FRIENDS AND ENEMIES

Sir Charles Mordaunt—cuckolded member of the House
    of Commons
Lady Maud Winter—friend of Louise's
Charlotte Tate, Lady Marcheford—friend of Louise's
Ripley Tate, Lord Marcheford—Charlotte's husband
Lady Hazel Campden—friend of Louise's

THE MORALISTS

Josephine Butler—moralist dedicated to women's causes
Lillian Cortland—an associate of Mrs. Butler's

THE DETECTIVES

Magnus Pompey Hurst—detective chief inspector at Scotland Yard
Langley Pratt—second-class inspector at Scotland Yard

If thou art rich, thou art poor,
For like an ass, whose back with ingots bows,
Thou bear'st thy heavy riches but a journey,
And death unloads thee.

—from *Measure for Measure*, 1604
  William Shakespeare, 1564–1616

You colliers lift your hearts on high,
To God, Who rules the earth and sky.
He only can defend your head,
While toiling for your daily bread.

—from an old English coal-mining song

Prologue

Leeswood Green Colliery, Flintshire, Wales
June 2, 1869

"What's wrong with that little urchin over there?" Samuel Harper asked from his elevated viewpoint atop his mount. He pointed to a spot near one of the coal mine's many tunnel entries.

Eustace ap Llewelyn, Samuel's guide he'd hired in Cardiff, looked in the direction where Samuel indicated.

"Ooh mean that girl there with the bald patch on 'er head?" he said in his thick Welsh.

"That's a girl? Impossible. She's just a mite, couldn't be more than eight years old." Bald patch? The child looked as though her hair had been snatched out in great clumps before a hawk had begun clawing at the top of her head, so scabbed and misshapen was it.

"Nooo, I'd say she's round twelve. Children aren't as big and lusty 'ere as I hear they are in America."

The girl reached out her hand to a boy—presumably a boy—and led him away from the entrance toward an area where other children sat in a circle, slurping a stew from tin plates. The boy wore a chain around his waist, the tail of which dangled behind him along the ground. He resembled the girl—less the bald patch—so Samuel assumed they were siblings.

All of the children were scrawny and vacant eyed, eating in silence as though talking might require too much energy.

"You don't mean to tell me it's legal for young girls to work in coal mines?"

"Nooo, it's been against the law since '42." Eustace shrugged. "But they need work. They'er families need money, else they'll all starve to death, so mooost folks turn a blind eye to the law."

Samuel shifted the reins of his horse from one hand to the other as he considered this. Working in a coal mine was probably better than being in a workhouse, as his Susanna had been many years ago.

"Why is her head so mangled?"

Another shrug. "She's probably a hurrier. The boy sitting next to 'er with the chain—he's 'er partner. On 'ands and knees he's attached to the front of a cartload of coal and he crawls up the tunnel, pulling it behind 'im. She gets behind the cart and pushes, mooostly with 'er 'ead. Once they get the cart to the surface and see it emptied, it's back down to the bottom of the mine for another load."

"Why don't they use ponies or donkeys for the work?" Samuel said.

"Children are cheaper. And smaller. Those tunnels are less than three feet high. Can't get an animal in there."

"Why don't they make the tunnels larger?"

"Och, man, are youer not listening? It costs money and time to make a tunnel big enough for a beast of burden to get through. Child-sized tunnels are moooch easier to dig."

Sam nodded from his vantage point as he watched the children finish off their scant meals, give the tin plates to a man wearing an apron, and return to their duties. The bald girl took the chain-wearing boy's hand again in a protective way, leading him back to the tunnel's entrance. She attached the trailing end of his chain to an iron clasp on an ore cart and patted him on the shoulder.

With the cart behind the boy, he dropped to his hands and knees and crawled back into the tin entrance, the cart squealing in protest. When the cart was almost entirely inside the tunnel, the girl also dropped to her knees, grabbing the top edge of the conveyance with her hands and pressing her head against the metal.

In seconds, the bizarre little chain of children and cart disappeared into the bowels of the mine.

How far would they travel on their scabbed knees for their next load? A mile? Perhaps more?

Sam urged his horse away from the colliery. "I've seen enough here. If we don't get to Mold soon, we'll miss our train to Pembrey."

"But I thought youer wanted to see 'ow they planned to open up the new shaft."

"I've seen enough to know it won't be as effective as dynamite. Let's go." He turned without checking to see if Eustace was following him.

Having turned in their hired horses, Sam and Eustace sat in The Three Pits, a tavern a couple of blocks from the Mold train station. Remains of sausages, mash, and peas lay on their plates like swirled bits of ash left behind from a dampened coal fire.

Sam spoke little during their meal, planning in his mind his upcoming meeting with Mr. Nobel. He'd originally met Alfred Nobel at his home in Sweden several weeks ago and was enthralled with the man's demonstration of dynamite, immediately realizing the impact it could have on the opening of the many gold and silver mines springing up in the American West, places such as Nevada, California, and his home state of Colorado.

Nobel, however, was having a difficult time selling his brilliant invention in Europe, particularly in Great Britain. Most governments feared the destructive power of dynamite, despite Nobel's assurances that it was, in fact, much safer than other methods of removing rock.

Buoyed by Sam's enthusiasm, Nobel had asked the American's help in persuading the Welsh government to let him start a dynamite factory in Wales. Samuel had been a member of a diplomatic corps in London during the American Civil War and had distinguished himself there.

Samuel might not be Welsh or even British, but he had a few connections left—he hoped—and could perhaps help the heavily accented Swede achieve some acceptance for his invention.

Sam's head swirled with the potential of it all. Start a dynamite factory in Colorado? Start one in Great Britain, supplying it out not only to Welsh mines, but to those in the States? Labor was certainly cheaper here in the queen's realm.

He paused as the specter of the young hurrier rose in his mind.

Sam put that thought aside as he took a final swallow of his ale. He wondered how Violet was faring. He missed his wife terribly, but it wouldn't be much longer before—

"Mr. 'arper, I think we 'ave some troooble." Eustace nodded at the window, an ancient piece of glass, pitted and wavy and rendered nearly opaque by years of cigar smoke and neglect.

Near the entrance to the train station, it looked as though several police officers were escorting two men in iron manacles.

"Why should there be trouble? They look well secured."

Eustace shook his head and said nothing.

A grimy boy burst into the inn, his eyes wild as he spewed out an urgent concern in Welsh, so rapidly that Sam couldn't catch a word of it. Eustace, though, nodded grimly, and other patrons abandoned their glasses and plates and headed for the door.

"What I figured. Come on, then." Eustace stood and Sam followed him as the guide explained.

"There's been bad doings 'ere as of late. The new pit manager, an Englishman named Young, 'as been a hound from hell on the miners. First he prevented them from speaking Welsh while underground. Then he began impooorting English miners and giving them the best jobs. Even wooorse, he announced a cut in wages. Stupid whelp. Green behind the ears and black as coal between them.

"A groooop of miners held a meeting and decided to show Young the error of 'is ways. Swatted 'im about a little, frog-marched him to the police station, then went back to 'is house and hauled all of his furniture back here to the rail station, in hooopes of sending 'im off for good."

Outside, a crowd was gathering around the police and their captives, stalling their progress.

Someone shouted, "'Tisn't fair. Should be that black'art Young in chains!"

Others murmured in agreement. Most of the crowd appeared to be miners, from the smallest boy to the largest man. Their eyes were bleak beneath layers of black dust settled into the lines and crevices that adorned their faces, and they all bore expressions of fury.

A few women were among their number, as well. Women who were not working in the mines, like the children supposedly were not? The group must have been exceedingly angry to have abandoned their work for the day, which at the least would result in docked pay, but more than likely a firing.

"Several men were arrested for attacking Young, and ooordered to stand trial today," Eustace continued. "Those two, Ismael and John Jones, were just sentenced to a month's 'ard labor at Flint Castle."

"Brothers?"

Eustace stopped and eyed Sam pityingly. "Don't know moooch about the Welsh, do ooh? Every other man's name is Jones." Eustace looked beyond Sam. "More townsfolk coming. Best to get to our platform a bit early, if you see my meaning, Mr. 'arper."

Sam turned and saw an indistinguishable mass of dirt-streaked faces, all scowling and muttering.

By this time, the entry into the train station was blocked by several miners. One shouted at the police, "Ooh'll not be putting our friends on the train to the castle. They done nothing wrong!"

Sam and Eustace would have to wait until the disturbance was over to leave. "Let's head back to The Three Pits while this blows over," Sam said.

"Won't be that easy," Eustace said, pointing.

To Sam's dismay, a group of soldiers, as determined looking as the miners, approached, their rifles ready to inflict damage.

Far from intimidating the crowd, the soldiers' presence served only to infuriate them more. There was a simmering blend of miner hatred and supervisory indifference here that reminded Sam of a Civil War skirmish he'd been in, involving a cocky young factory owner's son who'd bought himself a commission and thought that soldiers were the equivalent of factory workers—who were no better cared for than Southern slaves.

The situation before him would go no better than what happened that day in '64, when three other soldiers lagged behind their commander and shot him in the back in unison in the heat of battle. The three had gone on to meet their ends that day at the tips of enemy bayonets, so there was never a need to report it, but Sam never forgot the treachery, nor how easily it was inspired.

His military instincts took over now and he surveyed the land around them.

Tapping Eustace's arm, Sam said, "Look over there. A patch of high ground. Let's see if we can make it over there to wait until some kind of order is restored."

The two men waded through the morass of rough, blackened fists waving in the air and the shouts of people who were feeding off one another's frustrations and weariness.

Several other townspeople had the same idea of seeking safety on the little rise of terrain not far away. It was just high enough that nothing was built on it.

Sam's old leg injury throbbed by the time he and Eustace—and dozens of others—had reached the hill. He despised the reminder that he wasn't as vigorous as he'd been before his time in the Civil War.

He stood next to a young woman whom he would have guessed to be about fifteen, but based on his earlier inability to guess, perhaps she was as old as twenty.

Dressed in a prim gray uniform that told him she was not attached to the mine, the girl turned fearful eyes to Sam and let out a barrage of Welsh.

As near as Sam could tell, the girl was simply on an errand in town for her mistress and had stumbled into this mob, just as Sam and Eustace had. Concluding her unintelligible tale, she hugged herself, shaking her head as she watched events unfold.

More miners and townspeople were filling the area. Sam estimated there to be hundreds of people witnessing the two convicted men being escorted to the train for their sentence at Flint Castle jail.

The scene violently escalated as a couple of bystanders flung stones at the police and soldiers. One missile struck an officer on the forehead, drawing a bright trail of blood down the side of his face and eliciting a cheer from the crowd. Even one of the manacled prisoners smiled at the policeman's injury, although it may have been combined with relief that the stone had missed the prisoner's own head.

The successful hit inspired others in the street to pick up small, sharp stones from the road and add them to their taunts.

Sam was more concerned by the expression of the soldiers' faces, visible even where he stood. Their narrowed eyes and compressed lips were indicators of how badly this might go.

The mob, enchanted with its own temporary victory, was oblivious to the men with guns.

"I think we need to move farther—" Sam started, but was cut off by the precision firing of rifles. With fluid repetition, the soldiers lifted their weapons to their shoulders, shooting upward with little aim in an effort to frighten the crowd.

It didn't work. The deafening cracks stopped the people for mere moments before the mob took steps even closer.

A man moved as though to grab the rifle of the soldier nearest him.

"Fool," Sam hissed. The maid turned curious eyes to him.

"You never attempt to disarm a man who—" Sam's words were cut off once again as the soldiers, losing all control of the situation, lifted their rifles and fired into the crowd again, this time with aim and intent.

Sam touched the elbow of the maid, urging her to step backward with him, but she was rooted to her spot in morbid fascination.

That was the trouble with fear. It didn't always cause you to run to safety. Sometimes you became powerless to what was going on.

Pop! Pop! The guns fired again as more stones and street debris were lobbed at the soldiers and police, some of the projectiles even hitting the manacled men the mob wanted freed.

"Miss, please." Sam tugged at the young woman's arm. She turned to him once more, but this time there was pure confusion in her eyes.

"Are you unwell, miss?" Sam asked, knowing she probably couldn't understand his American English any more than he could understand her Welsh.

In response, she looked down. A scarlet stain was spreading across her midsection. Without thinking, Sam easily scooped the girl up in his arms and ran farther away from the chaos, assuming Eustace was following, toward a chapel whose steeple beckoned.

By the time Sam reached the rear door of the church, a place he deemed far out of reach of the soldiers' weapons, his leg was violently rebelling against the activity and he was gasping for breath.

The interior of the building was deserted, and his footsteps echoed loudly against the stone walls and arched ceiling. He propped the girl up against the lectern, which was heaped with sermons and other papers, trying not to consider the irony of someone bleeding and suffering beneath a stained-glass rendering of the Crucifixion.

"You'll be fine, miss; we'll get you some help," Sam said as he tore off his jacket and pressed it against the girl's stomach to staunch the flow. "You don't understand a word I'm saying, do you? Eustace, we need a doctor. Can you find one?"

Sam's guide loped off without a word. Heaven knew where the nearest hospital might be.

The girl's eyes were glassy and she was shivering. Sam eased himself as close as possible and wrapped his arms around her. "Now don't you worry. Samuel Harper doesn't leave anyone behind on the battlefield. I'll stay with you until the doctor arrives and you're fixed up proper."

In the distance, the sound of gunfire had been replaced with the screams and confusion of a complete rout. No doubt others were shot and possibly lying in the street in front of the train station. That was the way disorganized attacks on disciplined fighting men usually turned out. Were the convicted men also suffering wounds . . . or perhaps dead?

The maid tried saying something, but she was shaking so violently now that her teeth were chattering.

"Hush now. Eustace will be back any min—what's that?" He leaned closer to listen.

It sounded almost as if she'd said, "Find another piece," but he'd never know, because her body stilled in his arms.

Sam didn't react but just continued holding her, even after her body grew cool to the touch and her mouth hung open in the lifeless pose he knew too well. He'd seen many men die of battle wounds, but never a woman. What was wrong with men who thought it was acceptable to point a rifle at a defenseless woman?

How senseless.

1

Buckingham Palace, London

V iolet Harper had never been inside Buckingham Palace before. Her work for Queen Victoria had always taken Violet to either Windsor Castle or Osborne House, as after her husband's death the queen had retreated from Buckingham Palace to both of these places that held such fond memories of her marriage.

Lately, though, the queen had slowly returned to life, which meant she was taking more interest in political affairs and in her residences that had seemed destined for dusty cobwebs and faded draperies.

Buckingham Palace was so neglected that a wag had once posted a sign at the gate: "These commanding premises to be let or sold, in consequence of the occupant's declining business."

Now, however, as Violet was ushered through wide corridors and past elegant state rooms, it was obvious that the palace was coming to life again in richly colored wall coverings and sparkling chandeliers. The number of ballrooms and dining rooms suggested to her that the queen and prince consort must have entertained lavishly while he was still alive.

Violet's mind was not entirely on the state of the palace, though. The queen's summons gave no indication of why she wanted to see Violet. From experience, Violet knew it could mean anything from a death in the family to hunting down a killer.

Thus prepared, what actually awaited her inside the queen's private sitting room two floors up was disconcerting.

All of the pale blue drapes were pulled closed, despite the sunny day, and candles set in sconces decorated the fireplace mantel and every available table surface. The gas lamps in the room were extinguished, so that the room had an eighteenth-century glow to it.

Queen Victoria, dressed in her customary black, sat on a blue and gold settee across from her favorite outdoor servant, or ghillie, John Brown. Between them on an ottoman lay a familiar spread of cards. Standing behind the queen and observing what was going on was a girl, maybe twelve years old, with long, straw-colored hair flowing wildly down her back and pulled off her face with a simple red ribbon. Pearls swayed from the girl's ears in equally simple gold settings as she intently watched as the queen's personal servant gathered the cards back up, shuffled, and redistributed them facedown in a formation resembling a cross with four additional cards lying in a vertical row to the right of the cross.

"Ah, Mrs. Harper, you've finally arrived," Victoria said. "Dear Mr. Brown is about to do another reading."

Violet rose from her deep curtsy that the queen seemed not to have noticed in her thrall of the cards. "Your Majesty, did you summon me to attend—"

"Please sit, Mrs. Harper. Mr. Brown's readings have been exceedingly significant lately. He is having difficulty interpreting the cards, and since you share our passion for the afterlife and things otherworldly, we thought you would be interested in joining a reading."

"Your Majesty, I'm an undertaker, not a spiri—"

"We also thought you might try your hand at interpreting the cards, since you have an affinity for those that have passed into the Great Beyond."

Violet sank into the plush peacock-blue chair that the queen had indicated. "Yes, but my affinity is merely—"

"You haven't met our daughter Beatrice. She, too, is very spiritual in her nature. Sweetheart, this is Mrs. Harper, the undertaker we mentioned."

Princess Beatrice raised large, soulful eyes at her, eyes that seemed to render Violet completely transparent to the girl's penetrating stare. Violet shivered. Perhaps the princess was the one Victoria should consult with on spiritual matters.

Violet rose from the chair and sank into another curtsy, unsure what the proper etiquette was with such a junior member of the royal family.

"I am delighted to make your acquaintance," Beatrice said in a solemn, flat voice. Violet took that as a signal that she could rise and sat back in her chair again.

The queen reached down and tapped the back of one of the cards. "We haven't seen you use this deck before, Mr. Brown. It is lovely."

Brown swatted the air around the queen's hand. "Ach, wumman, don't touch them. You'll disrupt the aura surrounding them. I had these cards imported from Italy."

"Oh dear." The queen pulled her hand away.

Beatrice leaned farther forward over the back of the settee in order to get nearer to what was happening. It almost looked as though Victoria had two heads, so close was daughter to mother. Victoria impulsively brought a hand up and patted the girl on the cheek, and Beatrice responded with a kiss to her mother's ear.

"With Baby here, and you, as well, Mrs. Harper, we will undoubtedly reach an answer together, won't we, Mr. Brown?"

"I am confident of it, ma'am." Brown turned over his first card, which lay over a hidden card in the center of the cross. "Yes, the two of pentacles."

The queen brought a hand to her mouth. "Ohh. Again, Mr. Brown. It's a two of pentacles each time."

The servant had turned over a card that showed a man in medieval peasant dress, his back to the viewer so that one could only partially see that he was holding some sort of puzzle knot in his hands.

Brown dropped his voice low. "As you know, madam, this card represents your current situation. Our young man in the picture is trying to balance two ends of a very big knot, which tells us that you have a very difficult problem before you, one that is hidden from your view."

He divined that much from a card mass-produced on a printing press?

His voice dropped even lower. "Now let us see what the near future holds for Your Majesty."

Brown flipped over the card that had been underneath the first one. This one featured a man holding three swords, with two more at his feet, as he looked sadly over what appeared to be a burning village.

The servant shook his head. "This represents your near future. Desolation and loss, I'm afraid." He sat back and closed his eyes, spreading his hands out, palms up, in supplication.

"Yes, I feel intense suffering for Your Majesty. It is almost as if—oh!" Brown dramatically clutched at his heart with one hand. "The pain is almost unbearable."

"What is it? Will we be ill? Is it our heart? Oh, we've felt such palpitations lately."

Brown spread his hands out again and breathed deeply. "No, it is not disease or illness."

He opened his eyes again. "Let us look further at what the cards tell us." He rapidly turned over the remaining cards, each bearing a figure in some sort of pose, surrounded by numbers and words such as "pentacles," "cups," "chalices," and "wands."

"Look at this card. It represents Your Majesty's hopes and fears, and is the tower, from the major arcana. It speaks to me. It speaks of arrogance, and ruin, and of someone's downfall. In fact, I see death."

The queen gasped, and even Violet recoiled at what the ghillie had just said.

Brown waved his hands over the cards as though he was absorbing thoughts or feelings from the miniature artwork, although Violet couldn't imagine how the cards might be telling him some sort of story.

"There are secrets in the palace, ma'am. Someone within the palace walls is plotting a dangerous scheme. Someone has dark secrets, black as coal. The cards, they are afraid to speak directly to me about this very serious matter. They say there is someone else to whom they will reveal the truth. Someone who comes out of blackness."

Eerie silence descended on the room as Brown let his words settle on the women like coal smuts on a freezing cold morning.

"What does it mean, Mama?" Beatrice asked.

"We don't know. If only your father were here, he'd know. Perhaps we need a séance to communicate with our dear prince, so that he can relay the meaning. Don't you think so, Mr. Brown?"

"Yes, ma'am, we can certainly summon the spirits to seek your dear husband's advice, but I believe the cards are pushing us in a specific direction." He closed his eyes briefly and opened them again.

"Out of the darkness the answer will come. No, wait, someone dark will provide the answer. No—" Brown took a deep breath and blinked rapidly for several moments as he held his hands over the cards again. "Ah, the cards speak more plainly now. Someone in black will divine the solution."

Victoria looked down at her dress, which made her look like a roosting crow. The severe color was relieved only by a cream lace collar and a matching lace cap on her head, as well as a gold mourning brooch that contained curled locks of Albert's hair.

Now it was the queen's turn to take a deep breath. "Surely the cards do not suggest that the Queen of England traipse the streets like a Wilkie Collins character, poking about in dark alleyways for clues."

"Mama, the plot is inside the palace, not in St. Giles or Whitechapel."

"Still, Baby, it is unseemly for the spirits to demand this of us. Surely they mean someone else, Mr. Brown?"

"Perhaps, good lady, perhaps."

"Why do you look at Mrs. Harper so curiously? Surely you don't think . . . but perhaps you are correct. Mrs. Harper, you dress in black regularly for your profession, don't you? And with your love of the occult, why, you must be whom the spirits want as their medium. Mr. Brown, perhaps the spirits led us to call Mrs. Harper here for today's reading."

A slow smile spread across Brown's whiskered face. "You may have the right idea of it, Your Majesty."

Violet was horrified. Wander about Buckingham Palace's corridors hoping to meet with either a horde of specters or a confederation of traitors?

"Your Majesty, my husband will be returning soon from Wales, and—"

Victoria waved her off with royal aplomb. "He will certainly understand that your queen needs you to perform this small service."

Violet had learned that services for the queen were never small, and they had resulted in Violet's near demise on more than one occasion.

"Yes, Your Majesty."

With an enthusiasm incongruous to her black garb and the dire warning her servant had just pronounced, Queen Victoria clapped her hands together. "So we shall have our own mystery here at Buckingham Palace, and the undertaker shall solve it. Is that not frightfully amusing, Mr. Brown?"

"Quite."

"Mrs. Harper, you are permitted to roam our palace at will, as long as you do not disrupt any official or family affairs. Please remain at St. James's Palace while you investigate."

Violet had been installed at St. James's while helping the queen on a peculiar situation involving a murdered viscount that had been resolved recently, and still retained her quarters there.

"You are very generous, ma'am, but perhaps I am not the best—"

"Mr. Brown will be happy to do more readings for you, to help you get more in touch with the spirits."

"I'm sure that won't be necess—"

"Mama, I want to help discover the plot. We must prevent any deaths from occurring." Beatrice's eyes flared with anticipation.

"Now, Baby, don't you want to stay by your mama's side? We have so much correspondence for which we need your help addressing envelopes, and you told Mr. Caradoc you were ready to start your painting lessons."

As quickly as it was ignited, the light in Beatrice's eyes was extinguished. "Of course, Mama."

"Mrs. Harper, we will await your findings."

This was Violet's cue to leave. "Thank you, Your Majesty."

Violet backed out of the room, bewildered by the task she had been assigned. Did this just amount to a game Mr. Brown was playing to entertain the queen, or was it possible that there was some sort of treasonous plot being contrived in whispers and secret rendezvous inside the queen's own residence? He didn't actually mean to imply there would be a murder within the safety of the palace walls, did he?

Violet sighed heavily as she made the short walk from Buckingham Palace to her quarters at St. James's Palace. How had she just gone from royal undertaker to royal snoop?

Winterbourne Manor, Wiltshire

Reese Meredith poured out some more neat's-foot oil on his cloth and applied it to the brass-studded leather harness. He rubbed it in, darkening the rich brown leather.

Setting it aside for the moment, he picked up another harness and applied more oil to it. Reese had learned to leave the harnesses to sit for some time before buffing them out. Lord Christie was exceedingly particular about the condition of any of his property viewed by the public, and everything having to do with his horses and carriages was prized. It required only one spittle-filled lecture and cuff on the ears by Mr. Parks, the stable master, to ensure Reese never presented a ride for Lord Christie that wasn't gleaming, sparkling, sleek, brushed, and burnished.

Reese put the second harness down, picked the former back up, and applied a new cloth to it, rubbing with vigor. When he was finished, the leather was smooth and supple and he could nearly see his reflection in the brass.

Mr. Parks couldn't have any complaint today.

Reese sat straight on his stool and put a hand to his lower back. *Och,* how it hurt to sit here for hours. Being in the saddle was much better, even if it was in the form of hanging on to the back of a carriage as a groom.

He supposed he couldn't complain about the job, though. After service to the Crown in the cavalry, fighting in China ten years ago to legalize opium trade and open all of China to British merchants, he'd come home to find few positions for a man of his considerable military skills.

Reese had been lucky to find this position as groom to the Earl of Baverstock. The pay was terrible and the hours long, but Reese was used to that.

He picked up a third harness. Five more to go.

No, what had surprised him was that his employer had as little respect for him as the army officers had. Punishments were the same, too: docked pay, bread-and-water rations, and the occasional cuffing.

Reese's military training and exploits made him a quick learner, though: Keep your head bowed, obey without question, and don't do anything too stupid, unless you thought you could pull off something glorious and worthy of reward.

"Meredith, did you see today's paper?" Kip Runyon, a fellow groom who enjoyed lording his literacy over Reese, casually sauntered in with the folded paper under his arm. Reese wasn't completely ignorant; he just didn't have as much learning as most. Runyon, though, believed himself to be a better man because he could read and do sums faster than men such as Reese.

Reese snapped a strap of leather. It cracked loudly inside the small room attached to the stable.

"No, been too busy. Can't put my feet up on a stool all day long the way you do."

Not rising to the bait Reese tossed out, Runyon instead smirked in his usual irritating way. "I s'pose those of us with more than porridge between our ears end up with leisure time. Look there, a bit of manure on your boot. Won't want the master to see that."

Reese looked down. There was indeed some crusted dung on his toe. "They isn't my riding boots, numbskull. You too busy with newsprint to notice even the simplest things about your job anymore?"

Runyon didn't reply and instead leaned against the planked wall and began speaking about the article he was reading. "Ah, a fire over in Trowbridge. Burned down some lord's house and stables. Four Welsh cobs and two Cleveland Bays lost. Shame about the beasts." He flipped the page and scanned some more.

"Some chap named Sainsbury has opened a fresh foods shop in London. Promises perfect quality and lower prices to all shoppers. Sure, no chalked milk or coppered pickles from him, eh?"

Reese ignored Runyon, picking up another harness and pouring out more neat's-foot oil.

"What else do we see here? Hmm." He turned another page. "What's this? A riot over in Wales, in Flintshire. That's where you're from, isn't it?"

"Yes, what of it? You think I had something to do with it?" Reese had worked hard to eliminate his Welsh dialect, but somehow people always discovered where he was from.

"Don't be so tetchy. Nobody's accusing you of anything. Where was I? Yes, here it is. Yes, very interesting. That will ruffle a few feathers in London, won't it, now? So much terrible destruction."

God, but Runyon was irritating. How was such a horse's rear Mr. Park's favorite? Reese considered planting his manure-covered toe firmly up that rear but didn't think the docked pay was worth it. He wiped down the harness in his hands a few more times, then let out a beleaguered sigh.

"So, Runyon, won't you tell me what the article says?"

The other footman deliberately raised an eyebrow.

"Please," Reese said through gritted teeth.

"Sure, happy to help those less fortunate than me. A couple of days ago, two colliers were sentenced to jail for attacking their pit manager. Townsfolk didn't like it and attacked the police escort. The pit manager must have been one mean buzzard, eh? Soldiers were brought in, and they shot and killed several people."

Reese frowned. "Does it say who was killed?"

"Let's see, yes, two colliers, Robert Hannaby and Edward Bellis, were both killed. A local maidservant, Margaret Younghusband of Chester, was shot and killed. And the wife of a collier was also killed. Shot in the back, she was. Now that's just not proper. These soldiers get worked up and think they can just—what's wrong with you, Meredith? You look green."

Reese tried to maintain his balance on the stool, but everything was spinning and he knew he'd soon be sharing the straw-covered floor with the remaining dirty harnesses.

He swallowed and licked his lips. "What was the name of the maidservant again?" His voice came out as a dim croaking in his ears.

"Margaret Younghusband. You know her?"

Reese took a deep breath, trying to get some semblance of control over his racing heart and the endless swirling of mental images adding to his unbalance. "What? No. Her name sounded familiar, but I'm sure I don't know her."

Och, Margaret, what happened? What were ooh doing there?

He ignored the trickle of sweat trailing down past his ear. The room was coming back into focus again. "What else does it say? Has the queen or Parliament made comment?"

Runyon scanned the article again. "No, no proclamation from Buckingham Palace. I guess the queen's too busy getting her children married off to the crowned princes and princesses of Europe to be worried about a few grubby Welsh coal miners."

"Right," Reese said. *Margaret, I'm sorry I wasn't there to protect you.*

"Well, back to work. Lady Christie wants to go into town and won't be kept waiting, will she, eh?"

With Runyon gone, Reese savored the silence as he mechanically returned to his work, unsure what else to do. Questions of *Why?* and *What happened?* were swirling around inside his throat, choking him, like the dust that billowed from the thundering of horses' hooves on a dry road.

He gathered up the harnesses and staggered to his feet, still not quite sure he'd heard aright. *A local maidservant, Margaret Younghusband of Chester, was shot and killed.*

Swallowing to keep his stomach from lurching the contents of his boiled egg and cold ham breakfast onto the tack room floor, he focused on hanging each harness on its proper hook. Saddles, harnesses, and stirrups were all identified by the specific riders for each animal at Winterbourne Manor. Woe betide a footman or groom who got them mixed up.

That done, he stumbled out of the room and into the stables themselves. No one there; good. Finding an empty stall, devoid of a horse that must be now carrying Lady Christie on her errand, he huddled in a corner where no one could see him.

He knew he'd end up covered in straw that would never come out of his clothes and it would undoubtedly earn him a cuff or two, but it didn't matter for the moment.

As a member of the King's Dragoon Guards, Reese had witnessed plenty of death during the opium war, all of it sickening and much of it committed by him. He'd hacked at men from atop a saddle while sloshing through disease-infested waters, even as horses were cut out from under him. He'd severed, stabbed, and shot dozens in the name of queen and country.

He'd also seen his fellow cavalry members destroyed before his eyes. Being on the receiving end of a friend's intestines after he was sliced open next to you was enough to make any man cower in terror.

But not Reese Meredith. He barely noticed any of it. After years of working in the grimy, brutal conditions of the coal mines, war was almost a relief. At least it was all conducted outdoors, instead of underground.

But this, *this,* was cracking his heart like a pickax against a coal face. He covered his face with his hands. *Margaret, was this my fault for leaving you behind?*

After several minutes of heaving and sobbing, with no one to hear him except a few mares, snuffling anxiously at the sounds, Reese wiped his face on his sleeve—also cuff worthy—and reined in his thoughts. In time, he heard the telltale clopping of horseshoes. Lady Christie had returned and Runyon was bringing the horses back.

Reese slipped out of the stable stall before he was caught. As he returned to his duties, he decided upon one thing.

Someone should pay, and pay dearly, for murdering his sweet Margaret.

2

Two letters awaited Violet at the palace, one from Susanna and one from Sam. Violet set Sam's aside to savor later and opened the one from her daughter, which was full of newsy tidbits about her work in Violet's undertaking shop in Colorado during her absence. Susanna left the most important news for the end.

> *. . . I know Papa has told you everything, so it will be of no surprise to know that Ben Tompkins and I are now engaged. Isn't it wonderful? I know I should have waited for you, but I was so excited that I visited Mrs. Perry on my own. She has the most marvelous silks, imported here from Provence. And yards and yards of different laces. I can't decide between Chantilly lace and the lace being produced by some of the Indian tribes here. I wish you were here to help me. You will be home soon, won't you? I cannot bear the thought of waiting to get married, but I also cannot bear the thought of getting married without you and Papa here.*

Violet couldn't bear the thought of missing her daughter's wedding, either. To think that she would be delayed in order to chase filmy spirits up and down parquet hallways was beyond mortal comprehension.

It had been months since she'd left Colorado, yet she had to admit to being happy back in London. Despite the fog swirling in the streets, the smuts blackening the air, and the dark alleys inhabited by thieves, prostitutes, and worse, London had always been home to her. She'd learned her trade here, and she'd embalmed hundreds—perhaps even thousands—of its citizens, making her part of both the city's present and its past.

So although she missed Colorado's blue skies, the grandeur of its mountain vistas, and its sense of endless possibilities, it was good to be in London, especially since Sam was with her. Well, he was in nearby Wales, but only temporarily. If only Susanna were here, instead of thousands of miles away . . .

Violet also had the Suez Canal ceremony to consider. After the last service she had performed for the queen, Victoria had given Sam and her a royal invitation to attend the opening of the Suez Canal in Egypt. The waterway was scheduled to be opened in November. It was now June. How could she ever possibly discover the plot at the palace, return to Colorado for Susanna's wedding, and then rejoin the entourage in London and head to Cairo before November?

It wasn't likely.

She sighed in frustration. It was difficult to be in service to the queen, since the queen's demands came before everything else, including a husband and daughter to whom you wanted to devote much time.

This was probably why Victoria was usually highly incensed when any of her palace staff had the desire to marry. The very audacity of it!

Violet put Susanna's letter aside. This decision would require discussion with Sam. Perhaps he could head back to Colorado for the wedding. She imagined the scene at the church, with her spot in the pew empty, and felt a nervous flutter in her stomach.

It just wouldn't do. She had to resolve the queen's problem, created by Mr. Brown for unknown reasons, and return home to Colorado as soon as possible. Besides, she'd purchased Susanna a beautiful pair of dolls, wearing exact replicas of the wedding garb worn by the Prince and Princess of Wales for their wedding six years ago. Susanna had to have the dolls in time for her wedding.

*　*　*

Sam's letter was equally newsy but more disturbing than Susanna's. In it, he told of a terrible incident whereby he witnessed a revolt that resulted in several town residents being killed, including a young woman who died in Sam's arms.

> *. . . Fear not, Wife, for I immediately knew what I must do. After my guide returned with a doctor, who immediately declared her dead, I sought out the girl's family. Her employer told me she had none, and, in fact, did not seem overly upset by her sudden death. I traipsed about until I found a local undertaker, and remanded her body to him, giving him payment myself to ensure she had a decent, Christian burial.*
>
> *Let us hope that the entire incident is finished and that there will be no more violence in the aftermath. I do not care to engage in any further battles or wars, especially ones having nothing to do with the United States.*
>
> *I am now in Pembrey, waiting for Mr. Nobel to arrive from Stockholm. He telegraphed me that his ship was delayed at the Norwegian port of Kristiansand prior to entering the North Sea. I expect him any day, and together we will meet with local authorities to discuss his idea for a dynamite factory here, although I cannot imagine why he wants this location. As far as I can tell, there are no diatomite reserves here, as most are in the north surrounding an old volcano. Diatomaceous earth is critical for making dynamite, so why does he desire this place? It is certainly marshy here; perhaps he suspects there is an undiscovered deposit. It also has good access to the Bristol Channel and so would facilitate shipping to the United States.*

Violet was still mystified by Sam's enthusiasm for this explosive dynamite. Both he and Mr. Nobel were convinced it was perfectly safe, but how could anything whose primary purpose was to detonate be safe?

Her anxiety over her husband's activities was tempered by her gratitude over his service to a dying girl. And the undertaker in Violet definitely fretted: Did the others who were slain also receive proper ministrations?

Violet wrote first to Sam, telling him about Mr. Brown's tarot card reading and her new assignment. She had difficulty explaining it all, since she wasn't sure she even actually understood it herself. She also expressed her turmoil over whether they should stay permanently in London. One of the owners of her old shop, Morgan Undertaking, had offered to let her buy back in. She wanted to do so . . . but was it the right thing for them?

To Susanna, she expressed her delight at the engagement, and her fervent hope that she would return before Susanna got too impatient and donned her veil without Violet's presence.

No, Violet wasn't entirely unhappy to be in London, but part of her heart was in Colorado.

Reese crumpled up yet another sheet of writing paper and shoved it into one of the side pockets of his groom's coat. Damned if he'd ask Runyon for assistance, though. He would muddle through this himself.

As he stood on the rear stand at the back of Lady Christie's carriage, he tried again, working as covertly as possible against the landau's roof. Fortunately, Lady Christie never went out with the top down, "to save her complexion," as she insisted. Runyon, today serving as driver, sat stoically on the box at the front of the carriage, not looking in any direction but forward, so Reese could work without notice by anyone except for the other aristocrats coming and going from inside the jewelers' shop.

Aristocrats were unlikely to notice much beyond the crest on the carriage and the white and green colors of the Baverstock livery, homage to the family's supposed connection to the Tudors. Lord Christie showed off his title well.

Reese drew a line through *not a speck of compashun in the harts of those who preetend to serve us*. Too harsh? After some more scratching and rewriting, he was finally happy with his effort. He glanced up to look into the jewelers' shop. Lady Christie was still poking through trays of baubles and probably wouldn't be done for a half hour or so.

Under his breath, he reread his letter to the *Times* editor aloud: "'Dear Mr. Walter, I know your readers will be as unhappy as I am to learn that many people are pointing their fingers at not only Parlemint but the queen herself as responsible for the trajedy at Mold that kilt a number of innocent citizens.

"'Is it not enough that the owner of Leeswood Green Colliery and his loutish, ruffian managers care noothing for the lives of their workers? Must the prime minister and the queen turn their backs on them, too?

"'There has been no apology from any of these black, evil parties who see young children booried deep underground sixteen hours a day and feel nothing about it. Or who witness starving miners having their wages cut without a thought about their families that will starve. And who also know that innocent young wimmen are being kilt in the streets to proteckt the sinful acts of vile men.

"'Is there no shame? Citizens of London, if this is happening in Wales, think you that it woun't happen in the match facktories and cotton mills in England? We must demand vengeance for these wroongs.

"'Will you stand up?

"'Yours and et cetera, A Citizen Concerned for Coal Miners' Rights.'"

At least, that's how he hoped it read. Reese knew it was badly misspelled and his written grammar probably bore no relation to his stampede of ideas, but certainly the newspaper editor would clean it up before publication, wouldn't he? The world needed to know what was wrong in Mold—and all across Great Britain—with these dangerous coal mines.

Reese needed to make an excuse to Runyon so he could jump down and post his letter. Once it was published, anger would surely erupt in London.

Anyone who knew darling Margaret would be outraged. Such an impish, round face, with auburn hair that tumbled wildly down her back. Her tresses were always in differing lengths because she was forever hacking at them to imitate the fancy hairstyles of the day that were popular, but never quite succeeded at copying any of them. Who could not love her, having known her for just moments?

Reese Meredith knew her better than anyone else on this cruel earth and would never, ever let the matter rest. He would have satisfaction for his half sister's life being so tragically cut short.

Violet returned to Buckingham Palace the next day and went looking for Mr. Brown. A servant suggested he might be in one of the stables, so she went there. Located about five hundred feet behind the palace, the mews was constructed of unremarkable beige stone. It was built around an open area where grooms were exercising several of the royal mares.

Because the building was a uniform, two-story square surrounding her, Violet wasn't sure exactly in which direction to go. A servant in livery approached her.

"Pardon me, there are no tourists permitted in Her Majesty's stables. You can see the Prince and Princess of Wales in their carriage when they depart today at half past five for the theater."

"No, you don't understand. I am Violet Harper and I—"

"Ah, yes, the undertaker on the queen's mission. How may I help you, Mrs. Harper?"

"I'm looking for Mr. Brown."

The servant extended his hand toward the center of one side of the mews. "If you go through the archway, I believe you'll find him in the stable there."

"Thank you." Violet started to walk away, but the servant stopped her.

"Please, ma'am, if you don't mind, the ground floor contains the horses and equipage and is open for you to inspect. The upper floor, though, is where all of the stable hands' quarters are, and it is private, if you don't mind not going up there."

"Of course." *What an odd request,* Violet thought as she made her way to where she hoped she'd find Mr. Brown. Why would servant quarters be of any interest to her, especially those located in the mews?

Just outside the stable, two footmen were busily digging through a carriage's hammer box, pulling out tools to repair an obviously broken rear axle. They ignored her presence.

Through the archway, she found herself inside the cleanest stables she'd ever encountered. Most of the stalls to either side of the wide corridor were full, with either a horse or a miniature children's carriage, yet there was almost no odor, nor did she see any manure droppings. Even the most freshly swept London streets still contained smears of manure that had been sloppily shoveled or stepped in by an unwary pedestrian or run over repeatedly by carriage wheels.

A monarch's life was certainly different from that of mere mortals.

She heard off-key humming, and, following the sound, found Mr. Brown outside a stall near the end of the building, personally brushing down the queen's favorite pony, Lochnagar. Violet had met this particular beast during one of the queen's afternoon rides many weeks ago. Other horses snuffled in their stalls nearby as though waiting for their own turns to be groomed.

"Mr. Brown, I should like to speak with you."

The ghillie turned around from what he was doing. "Thought ye might, lass. First, though, have ye considered wearing something besides that blasted black all the time? 'Tisn't good for Her Majesty to be encouraged by you to wear it herself."

"I am an underta—"

"Sure now, and I'm the queen's ghillie, but you dinnae see me got up in riding clothes all the day, now do ye?"

Violet took a deep breath. The dead were so much more agreeable than the living, especially when the living thought they were experts in all matters.

"Mr. Brown, I am an undertaker. As such, I never know when I may be called upon to serve a grieving family and I make myself ready at all times to manage death. Unlike yourself, who may be called upon to change clothes multiple times a day for such onerous activities as escorting the queen to another residence, or walking her on her pony, or sitting down to shuffle tarot cards. I suspect your hands are full in taking care of your own position, so I'll kindly thank you not to interfere with mine."

The expressions on Brown's face ranged first from shock, then to mottled fury, and at last to a begrudging respect. Finally, he burst into laughter.

"Yes, I suppose you're right, lass. I mean, Mrs. Harper. What ken I do for ye?" He turned his attention back to making long strokes down Lochnagar's side.

"What can you do—" Violet caught her anger. "I want to know the meaning behind yesterday's tarot card reading."

Brown kept his back to her and continued working. "Now that's something I cannae know, can I? The cards are mysterious."

"Are they truly? You have divined so many other meanings before, yet now they have suddenly closed themselves off to you."

The ghillie stopped what he was doing, much to Lochnagar's snorting displeasure. "I cannot control the spirits, madam. Sometimes they are agreeable, sometimes nae so agreeable."

Violet crossed her arms. "I wonder what it was about a mysterious plot afoot in the palace that made them so disagreeable?"

He leaned close, and Violet caught a whiff of liquor on his breath. Whisky, if she wasn't mistaken. She kept her face blank and pretended not to notice.

"This is what I ken tell ye," Brown said quietly. "There is something the queen needs to know, but the spirits say I am nae the one to tell her, lest she become . . . agitated. It must come through someone else. A wumman. She'll be less overwrought."

"But you've already stated that there is something treasonous going on at Buckingham Palace. What could make her more distressed than that? And how would details of a crime against the Crown be less upsetting coming from a female?"

He shrugged. "I dinnae know the motives of the spirits. But they brought ye here, so ye have started in the right place to uncover the secrets. Leave me now, Mrs. Harper."

With that, Brown hung the leather-strapped brush on a hook outside Lochnagar's stall, escorted the beast back in, and walked away.

Violet contemplated running after Brown but didn't want to make a scene in front of the servants outside. She stepped inside Lochnagar's stall and patted him on the neck. He rewarded her with a nuzzle at her cheek, then at her hand.

"Sorry, boy, I have nothing for you. Maybe next time?"

Lochnagar responded with a huff.

"I wish you could speak. Maybe you know what it is Mr. Brown is up to with his tarot card readings."

Mr. Brown was a scoundrel; of that much Violet was sure. But what, exactly, was he plotting?

"Mother, you are in entirely too high a dither over this."

"Why are we not surprised that you would take this so lightly?" Furthermore, why did Victoria continue to be surprised by Bertie's petulant behavior?

Bertie rolled his eyes and flopped down onto a settee. So un-princelike. "Mordaunt is just in a rage because his wife has confessed to bearing him an illegitimate daughter. That child has nothing to do with *me*."

"According to Sir Charles, that child may have everything to do with *you*, and half the aristocratic houses of England. Does Lady Mordaunt even know who the father is?"

Bertie stretched out casually, crossed his ankles, and reached to the table next to him for a cigarette, a habit he'd picked up from the Raybourn family.

"Freddy says it might be his."

"Sir Frederick Johnstone? Why do you associate with such low men? You will be *König*, King, of the United Kingdom, one day. You cannot have such stains on your reputation."

"Don't be dramatic, Mother. No one notices these things, and if they do, they are most forgiving as long as their prince delivers a healthy number of heirs. I have Albert Victor and George, and Alix may deliver me another boy yet." He blew a stream of smoke toward the ceiling.

"Bertie, you know we despise smoking in our presence."

"Only when it is me doing the smoking. Your Mr. Brown seems to have the privilege of doing as he pleases."

"Do not change the subject. We are discussing your appalling behavior with regard to Sir Charles."

Her son crushed his half-smoked cigarette out in the engraved brass ashtray she'd presented to Mr. Brown on his birthday last year. "Harriet and I were just having a bit of fun, Mother."

"Have you no conscience, Son? We don't know how you came by this . . . this . . . attitude. Your father would be so ashamed. He was so dedicated to his wife and family. There was never a breath of scandal around him—Bertie, stop rolling your eyes at us; it's very undignified."

"That's what this is about, isn't it? You don't care a fig for what goes on between Sir Charles and his wife. You've found another reason to blame me for Papa's death."

"Bertie, language! This has nothing to do with casting blame. You are the source of your own desolation."

Oh, there was that word Mr. Brown had used at the reading. Was Bertie the source of a plot the spirits spoke of? He was certainly her source of desolation and loss. She must mention this to Mrs. Harper.

He shrugged. "Harriet and I are simply friends; there's nothing to worry about. Sir Charles doesn't want the dragged-out court proceedings necessary to pursue a divorce. No doubt he'll come to an accommodation with her."

"What do you mean, an 'accommodation'?"

"I suppose he will either lock her away in one of his estates or else pick up with an inamorata of his own."

Victoria shuddered. What was wrong with this generation of youth that they thought nothing of humiliating themselves in society? Had he not died, dearest Albert would have eventually taken Bertie well in hand and Victoria would not have had to face this alone.

"You fail to understand all of the consequences at play, Son."

"What consequences? This is a storm in a teacup. Or should I say a storm in Sir Charles's bedroom? Hah!"

Would that God grant her patience when dealing with this impertinent little *Junge*. How could such a little boy be the inheritor of a kingdom on which the sun never set? It was enough to make her cry, if she thought he was worth expending tears upon.

"Let us discuss the possible outcomes. First, we desire to make a good match for Louise. It is her time to marry. What royal house will be interested in a girl whose brother is already proving to be an embarrassment and may continue to do so when king?"

"Oh, Mother, you're—"

"*Genug!* Hold your wicked tongue! Furthermore, you have a pregnant wife, who will deliver a prince or princess in a few months. What effect do you think this scandal will have on her? *Mein Gott,* what if she were to lose the child? It would be entirely your fault for running about with other women like some kind of wild dog." Whenever Victoria exchanged heated words with Bertie, she forgot all of her royal breeding and reverted back to Hanoverian German. Bertie's detrimental influence was boundless.

"Unlike you, Alix understands that I sometimes develop innocent friendships that mean nothing. You, of course, invent wild fantasies and use them to find me guilty of imaginary crimes. Perhaps if I open the door I will find a jury and executioner waiting for me."

Bertie yanked open the door to Victoria's sitting room. Behind it was Mrs. Harper, one hand raised as though to knock and the other carrying a newspaper. She looked from queen to prince. "Pardon me, Your Majesty, Your Highness, am I interrupting?"

Yes, praise God. "Not at all, Mrs. Harper, please come in."

"Yes, do. There is very little of interest happening here." Bertie swept his arm into the room. "I'm sure *you* will at least be welcome." As the undertaker entered, he turned and bowed gracelessly to his mother before exiting and shutting the door behind him.

Mrs. Harper curtsied and sat on the chair Victoria indicated. "I'm sorry to intrude, ma'am, but I thought that to determine which plot might be afoot inside the palace perhaps I should start by seeing what might be afoot elsewhere in your kingdom and in the world. I have been reading yesterday's *Times*, and found some interesting news items."

Victoria frowned. "In a newspaper? The spirits do not typically speak through the presses."

"No, of course not. I just thought it was another way to seek them out. If I discover the correct situation, the spirits might, er, find favor with my efforts and choose to reveal themselves to me."

"Yes, yes, that makes sense. And so what have you found?"

"There are several articles of interest. First, there is the Cretan revolt in Greece. It looks as though the Turks have put down the rebellion."

"Yes, Greece's King George is the Prince of Wales's brother-in-law. George has wanted to unite Greek lands into one nation for years. Bertie tried to convince the foreign secretary to intervene on behalf of the poor Greeks, but he refused. An embarrassment for Alix, I'm sure."

"An embarrassment for the Prince of Wales, too. Have you any Greek members on the palace staff?"

"What? Heavens, no. Everyone is of good British stock."

"Perhaps that isn't it, then." Mrs. Harper returned to the paper. "There is the Irish Church Act under discussion, which will disestablish the Church of Ireland, disassociating it from the state so that the Irish will no longer be required to tithe. There is much acrimony between the Commons and the House of Lords over it."

How irritating. "Yes, Mrs. Harper, we are fully aware of the act, since we are intervening personally in the situation between the two parliamentary bodies. We do not see how it brings personal desolation and loss to us."

"If I may be so bold as to suggest it, Your Majesty, perhaps what is agitating the spirits has to do with your realm and not your person. After all, you are the embodiment, and beloved treasure, of Great Britain."

"Mr. Brown did not say this was so."

"No, ma'am."

"If the spirits meant that it concerned our realm and not our body, he would have said so."

"Yes, ma'am."

"Was that all you had to show us?"

Mrs. Harper referred to the paper again. "There was one more item I wished to share with Your Majesty. It is back here and quotes from a Welsh border newspaper, the *Flintshire Observer*. . . ." She flipped through several pages, finally pointing to a small editorial.

"This is about the recent riots in Mold, a coal-mining town in Flintshire. Is Your Majesty aware of them?"

"Yes. There has been some bickering in Parliament about it. Some foolishness about the Welsh miners attacking soldiers simply because they were required to speak good English. What ruffians. We speak English even though it is not native to our family. If their queen does so, why can't they?"

The undertaker looked as though she'd eaten a spoiled egg. "There is more to it than that, Your Majesty. My husband was present for it, and told me that the miners also had their wages cut for no apparent reason. When I saw this article, I thought—"

"My dear Mrs. Harper, please content yourself with seeking out our spiritual difficulties."

"Yes, ma'am. If you will forgive my impertinence, it's just that what I read here is an indictment against the English government for oppressing the native Welsh people."

Violet read aloud: " 'The time has now come for the cessation of these stupid and blundering attacks. How can you turn a stream that has flowed so long? How can you transplant the feelings and impressions of one people into the language of another entirely a stranger to those impressions? Language is but the reflections of thought and you can no more dry up or write down every old language such as this than you could level the mountain or turn back the stream. . . . There is a great fault in the English character and it has been the secret of their want of success in attempting to rule all colonies subject to them.' "

"Mrs. Harper, if we cowered each time a journalist uttered a criticism, we would soon be a rabbit hiding inside its burrow. Those who did not understand our grief over Albert's departure wrote scathingly of us in print, yet we did not allow them to impact our necessary mourning."

"But this was not the writing of a journalist. These are the words of George Osborne Morgan, the member from Denbighshire in the House of Commons. If the ill feelings about the treatment of the Welsh has spread beyond the confines of local collieries and into the halls of Parliament—"

"This is quite enough."

"—then perhaps there is revolt, or worse, being festered in their minds. This might be the desolation and loss the spirits warn of, Your Majesty."

"But Mr. Brown was clear that the wickedness was for us personally. We believe it may have something to do with our wayward son, Albert Edward. You have read political meaning into it, Mrs. Harper. If it were political, the spirits would be warning Mr. Gladstone, would they not? We have so many worries on our mind, and now that the other world is attempting to reach us, we find it is impossible to find *appropriate* assistance."

She hoped her meaning was clear, but the undertaker's expression was inscrutable. Yet still the woman persevered.

"I'm sure I cannot begin to understand Your Majesty's feelings," Mrs. Harper said, although she didn't sound contrite at all. "Yet I do wonder if the situation isn't more far-reaching than the cards have stated."

Victoria was about to chastise Mrs. Harper for her impertinence when the door opened again.

"Mother, have you seen my writing box? I may have left it—oh, pardon me, I didn't realize you had a guest."

It was her daughter, Louise, the sixth of her children and her fourth daughter, and the one for whom a suitable marriage would soon need to be made.

Although Louise was not her favorite, Victoria still employed her as her personal secretary. She was capable enough, although Louise's lack of sufficient grief over Albert's death had always been like dust in Victoria's throat. Louise was by far Victoria's prettiest child, a talented sculptress, and appropriately polite, but there was something less . . . proper about her. Unlike darling Baby.

And what was this? "Louise, what has happened to your hair? It is quite untidy."

Her daughter reached up a hand to pat her tightly wound curls. "Forgive me, Mother, I was outside and the wind blew it about." Louise looked curiously at Mrs. Harper.

"Louise, this is Violet Harper, the undertaker who helped carry your dearly beloved father to his final resting place. She left England for the United States four years ago to marry an American lawyer, but she has returned to London and is assisting us in a spiritual matter."

Mrs. Harper curtsied to Louise, who nodded graciously back to her.

"There are my writing supplies," Louise said, heading over to a leather-topped knee-hole writing desk and picking up the silver-inlaid box that held her pens, ink pots, and engraved writing papers. "I've been through the day's obituaries, and there are several letters of condolence I need to prepare for you, Mother."

Victoria nodded approvingly. It was so heartwarming when her children were considerate of their mother. Louise might not be her favorite, but she was certainly better mannered than Bertie. Why, he could—wait, what was this?

"What is that clinging to your hem?"

"What?" Louise said, looking down. "Oh, it's nothing, just something I must have picked up in the garden."

Did her daughter truly think her mother was a simpleton? "It looks like straw to us. Why would you be cavorting about in the mews?"

"I wasn't cavorting about anywhere, Mother. You are mistaken. These are just a few weeds that have clung to my dress. I really should have some new walking gowns made that won't attract debris." Louise tossed the words off nonchalantly, but Victoria knew she was hiding something.

"Your hair is mussed and your dress bears the marks of you having been walking through the stables. We can only hope it was just walking. Will you confess to what you were doing there, or shall we make an assumption?"

Must all of her children bring such grief? At least she knew she could rely on little Beatrice.

"I've not been doing anything immoral, if that is what you mean to imply."

Victoria sighed. "And here we thought that Bertie would be the ruination of us all. You know suitors have been suggested for you from both Prussia and Denmark? Shall we send them each a photograph of you looking as you do now?"

Mrs. Harper's expression certainly wasn't inscrutable now. The undertaker's face registered wide-eyed horror at Louise's obvious indiscretion. At least Victoria knew she could trust the undertaker to be silent.

"We will speak later on this, Daughter. Go write your letters."

Louise fled the room, her face flushed with embarrassment.

If only the girl understood how often their mother had to manage embarrassment on behalf of others.

Violet left the queen's presence completely frustrated. Sam's description of the scene in Mold, combined with what was being said in Parliament, led her to believe that something terrible was brewing. And although Mr. Brown was a Scot, both Scotland and Wales had long chafed under English rule. Might not Mr. Brown be sympathetic to the Welsh problem and be trying in his own way to force the queen to address it? If today's reaction was any indication of Victoria's opinion, Mr. Brown might have been wise in cloaking everything inside a tarot reading.

But why so much subterfuge around Violet? Why did he not just speak plainly to her in the stable?

She walked back to her rooms at St. James's Palace and opened the newspaper again. Did the Mold riot really have anything to do with Mr. Brown's reading or was she just grasping at straws?

And what of Louise's apparent activities in the mews? Was she meeting someone there? A man? Surely the Princess Louise Caroline Alberta, daughter to the queen of the most powerful nation in Europe, was not debasing herself with a groom.

But what if it was someone else who had reason to be among the horses? Oh, surely not. The idea was preposterous. Mr. Brown was the queen's loyal servant; he would never . . .

Would he?

Why must all women be carping harpies? the man thought as he considered his options. From the lowest kitchen maid to the highest well-born woman, her heels clacking imperiously on marble floors, they had all given him no end of grief.

All except for one, of course. But he wouldn't think of her right now. Not when he was this busy, tenderly nursing his grudge and willing it to blossom into the purest form of hate and rage.

He would need that hate and rage for what he knew was eventually to come.

3

Half-irritated that the queen wouldn't listen to her and half-discouraged by the weak plan she had concocted the previous evening, Violet headed back to Buckingham Palace.

Today she planned to make Mr. Brown aware of her presence, then lurk about in corridors until he caused some sort of spiritual "appearance." She'd already had a message sent to him that she would be at the palace all day.

It didn't bode well that this was the best plan she had.

Only one servant stopped her as she made her way to the Ministers' Staircase, a rear passage leading up to the palace's private rooms. Violet intended to avoid taking the Grand Staircase or walking anywhere near the state rooms, which were simply overwhelming in their grandeur. She felt like an unwelcome intruder, furtively darting through in her black skirts.

She finally reached the queen's apartments, which were marked by less opulence and more warmth. As Violet stood in the main corridor, debating where to lodge herself, she was met by Beatrice, wearing a smock and carrying an armful of paints and brushes.

"Good morning, Princess," Violet said, executing a minor curtsy. The queen had nine children. At this rate, Violet would be bobbing up and down like a goose all day. "Are you working with oil paint today?"

Beatrice paused, giving Violet the full benefit of her intensely sad expression. "Yes, Mrs. Harper, my tutor is teaching me how to make eye portraits. Would you like to see what I've done?"

The princess's art room was as good a location as any to start. "It would be my pleasure to see your work."

Together they entered a room that was unmistakably meant for messy artistic work. Paint- and glue-spattered rags had been sewn together and were scattered across the expansive floor. The windows were so enormous that even with their draperies they allowed in a flood of light, which was nearly blinding as the morning sun's rays bounced off empty gilded frames and half-finished canvases. The air was heavy with a mix of paint odors and the smell of cleaning solutions.

"Here." Beatrice led Violet to a table, upon which sat a wood box with a self-contained easel of about two feet in diameter propped on top of it, with three drawers below it. On the small easel sat an oval piece of ivory, about the size used for mourning brooches.

"I am making an eye portrait of my father, the esteemed prince consort. My tutor is teaching me to work in watercolors for it, so I was just roughening the ivory with a pumice stone before you came, to ensure the paints will adhere. Mr. Caradoc says I should bleach the ivory in the sun to whiten it, but I prefer it in its natural state."

An open case containing slots filled with watercolor cakes sat waiting on the table next to the box. Beatrice opened one of the box's drawers and removed several brushes, all with very fine tips. "I am going to paint his left eye and part of his nose from one of our family photographs. Mama says Papa's nose was majestic."

"What is this?" Violet pointed at another, half-finished piece of ivory.

Beatrice picked it up. "It was one of my first attempts at Papa's eye portrait, but it wasn't very good, so I abandoned it."

Although not complete, the detailing of the pupil and eyelashes was astonishing, especially since they had been done at the hands of a twelve-year-old girl. Beatrice was surprisingly serious about her work for such a young girl. Violet imagined most girls Beatrice's age would be more interested in pet dogs and fancy hair ribbons.

"Your art tutor has taught you a great deal about painting," Violet said.

"Yes, Mr. Caradoc is very talented and intelligent, just like Mama's friend, Mr. Brown."

"Indeed. What is this?" Violet pointed to an array of photographs spread upon a table. Most were of animals: a caged ring-necked parakeet, a border collie, and a horse harnessed to a miniature carriage.

"They are photographs I have taken. Mr. Caradoc says I should concentrate on real art—painting and sculpture."

As if he had been summoned, a tall, thin, prematurely balding man entered.

"Mr. Caradoc," Beatrice said. "This is Mama's undertaker, Mrs. Harper."

Caradoc frowned in open puzzlement. "Pardon me?"

"What the princess means to say, sir, is that I am an undertaker doing work for the queen."

"Has someone died?"

"No, it is work unrelated to a funeral. Her Majesty wishes me to investigate some . . . possible funereal oddities inside the palace."

"I see." Clearly he didn't. "And to what do we owe the honor of a visit, Mrs. Harper?" He held out a hand and Violet shook it. Like the rags on the floor, it was stained in a variety of colors.

"I am just admiring Beatrice's work with the camera."

The art tutor barely glanced at the photographs. "They are a hobby, but not really an art form. I am trying to impress upon our princess that she must remain concentrated on *true* art."

He moved over to Beatrice's unfinished eye portrait. "Did she show you this? Not perfect, but she shows great promise. Now this is genuine art. Eye portraits went out of fashion forty years ago, but the queen has expressed interest in them, so we just might revive the art, eh, Princess?"

Beatrice nodded. "Mama would be so pleased if that happened, sir."

Caradoc smiled, revealing teeth with wide gaps between them. His expression was boyish, despite his balding pate.

"Have you any artistic ability, Mrs. Harper?"

"I'm afraid my talents lie only in the preparation of the deceased for burial."

"Ah, so you ensure the bloom of a cheek and a calm repose. Is that not art of a nearly pure form? Translating death into life? Yes, I imagine you have much artistic ability coursing through your veins. Perhaps someday you would like to share a lesson with Princess Beatrice."

For the first time, Violet witnessed Beatrice's face lighting up. "Yes, Mrs. Harper, we can work on easels side by side. I have an extra smock you can wear. Oh, but your dress is so long, we will need to tie it up so that it doesn't drag in any paint." The girl chattered on as Mr. Caradoc indulged her childish prattle.

"Can you come soon, Mrs. Harper?" he asked. "The princess is obviously beside herself over it, and I'd like to give you the lesson before I leave in a few days to visit my brother."

"I'm not sure I can paint more than a few rosy dots."

"Mr. Caradoc will teach you. I will send you an invitation straightaway." Beatrice reached over and grabbed Violet's hand.

This girl was a princess but was quickly reminding Violet of her daughter, Susanna, at the same age. Susanna was an orphan when Violet found her in her twelfth year, while Beatrice was blessed with eight siblings. Yet, ironically, this girl was just as desperate for companionship as Susanna had been.

Beatrice looked to Mr. Caradoc for approval. He nodded gravely. "There is much to do in preparation for Mrs. Harper's visit, isn't there? We'd best get to work."

Violet left them, saddened for Beatrice's solitary existence. Being not only a princess but also several years younger than her next sibling made for a lonely childhood. No wonder the girl clung to her mother.

As Violet paced through the hallways, waiting for either Mr. Brown or one of his spirits to make an appearance, she considered again something Beatrice had said, that she found Mr. Brown to be very intelligent and talented. Talented at what? Had she witnessed him at something besides horsemanship and tarot cards? Might she have valuable information? Was it possible that Beatrice knew more about Mr. Brown's readings than anyone might imagine?

Violet needed to question the girl more closely but needed to tread carefully as well. She had no desire to appear to be making friends with the vulnerable princess just to interrogate her.

Violet puzzled this out while walking through the corridors, waiting for a visitor, either an earthly one or a spectral kind.

She received neither.

Reese dug the newspaper out of a rubbish can behind the kitchen and scanned it. He might not be wholly literate, but he would know his own letter when he saw it.

It wasn't in today's paper, either.

What had happened? Did it not make it to the editor's desk? Had some lackey thrown it away?

Maybe it *had* made it to the editor. Perhaps the editor pitied the colliery owner, instead of the real victims. If he was rich, that was probably exactly what happened.

Reese crumpled the paper in fury and shoved it back into the bin. Not even the press cared about what happened to British subjects.

He ran a hand irritably through his hair, then pulled it away in disgust. How could he have forgotten about the Macassar oil all of the grooms now had to wear? The master thought it looked fashionable for all of the male servants to not only wear livery but also have matching hair.

At least they weren't required to wear wigs.

Reese pulled a scrap of the newspaper back out of the bin and rubbed his hand on it. Someone had ironed the paper to set in the ink, but it was no match for the oil, and now he had both oil and newsprint on his hand.

He rinsed his hand under the pump in the center of the kitchen courtyard. He was so distracted lately that he was forever doing something stupid. This was unnoticeable, though, unlike when he'd forgotten to have a carriage ready by ten o'clock one morning for the mistress and her snooty daughter to go round and offer sympathies to some family whose *tad* had died. Reese knew how difficult it was to lose your father, but the rich had plenty of money to comfort them.

Forgetting the carriage had been a bad mistake. Mr. Parks had cuffed him good and docked his pay. Worse, Runyon had laughed on it for days.

Curse them all.

Reese returned to the stables to check on a horse suffering from thrush. He scrubbed the infected hoof, then soaked some clean rags in iodine. As he stuffed the iodine rags into the hoof's clefts, his anger grew until he could nearly taste bile in the back of his throat.

Reese and Margaret were examples of how little the English cared about the Welsh, and she had died as proof of it. Except that it was the aristocracy—those who held china cups in their hands and vile thoughts in their heads—who were truly responsible, for they were the only ones who could truly fix things.

The queen perched herself at the top of this revolting heap of people. Constantly mourning her long-dead husband, with not a tear to spare for those who lived . . . and suffered.

Perhaps it was time for Reese to take further action. First, though, he'd give *The Times* editor a tongue-lashing he'd not soon forget.

Once Reese's duties for the day were over and he'd crawled into his narrow bed around eleven o'clock that night, he lit his gas lamp to a low flame and sat beneath the coverlet with pen and writing paper. He'd be more careful this time, for the paper was consuming a lot of his pay, and if he got docked too many more times, well, soon the master would expect Reese to pay *him* for his work as a groom.

He slashed at the paper for nearly an hour before he was satisfied. There. The newspaper editor was not likely to ignore *that*. And if he did, there kindled in Reese the spark of an idea, ready to ignite in the murky, hate-filled reaches of his mind.

After two days of pacing and lurking in the palace's corridors, poking her nose into closets, and closely observing any servants she encountered, Violet was heartily tired of whatever it was Mr. Brown had divined. He hadn't responded to any of her messages, nor had he—or the spirits—made an appearance.

The servants seemed to be quite tired of Violet, too. In fact, they probably thought she was the spirit come to wreak havoc among them.

Perhaps it was time to tell the queen that this was a useless endeavor. Or, rather, it was time to *suggest* it to the queen. Violet would have to tread lightly given the high favor that Mr. Brown enjoyed.

She didn't look forward to that conversation.

She may as well have another look around. An elderly maid came around the corner and nearly ran into Violet. The maid squealed and dropped the stack of starched tablecloths she was carrying.

"Ma'am, you nearly frightened me to the grave just now."

"Pardon me—Rose, isn't it? Why, we are both named for flowers," Violet said as she bent to pick up the folded bundles and hand them back to her.

Rose wasn't impressed with their common floral bond.

Violet tried again. "Perhaps I can help you. Can I take care of some of these tablecloths for you?"

"I'm not sure it's proper for you to do so."

"No one will notice me shaking out a couple of pieces of damask. It's the least I can do for frightening you so."

Rose nodded, openly mollified by Violet's gesture. "These two go into Prince Leopold's bedchamber. Go to the end of this corridor, turn right, and the room is the first door on the left. You'll see the matching pair of tables where they belong. This red one with the gold fringe belongs in the prince's classroom next to his bedchamber. I'll lay the cloths on this end of the corridor."

Violet nodded and took the tablecloths from Rose. She quickly found Leopold's bedchamber and knocked quietly. Or was it proper to scratch at a royal's door? Fortunately, there was no answer, so she entered the room and billowed the tablecloths out over the tables. If she recalled correctly, the prince was about sixteen years old and the youngest next to Beatrice. He was nearly unknown in the public eye because of his frail health. A skin condition, wasn't it? No, wait, it was a blood disorder, hemophilia. The poor boy probably suffered from terrible spontaneous bleeds in his joints and other locations. Violet had once prepared a hemophiliac, a girl of about eight, who had bled into her own skull so much that her head was purple and misshapen.

Prince Leopold would be most difficult to prepare when he died, requiring vast cosmetic skills.

Violet immediately cringed at her own thought. She should be praying for the prince's health, not imagining his death.

As she closed the door to his bedchamber behind her, it occurred to her that poor Beatrice didn't even have the brother closest to her in age to play with. No wonder she was eagerly anticipating anyone willing to be her companion.

Deep in her own contemplations about the princess, Violet forgot to knock at the door of the prince's classroom, merely turning the knob and entering. Now it was her turn to squeal in fright.

Seated behind a desk at the opposite end of the room was a man exceedingly handsome except for his bulbous nose. That nose reddened in mortification by Violet's appearance.

It wasn't the man, however, who shocked Violet. It was the young woman perched at the edge of the desk, running the lapels of his jacket through her fingers. An intimate and inappropriate gesture.

Particularly for a princess for whom the queen was seeking to make a marriage.

Certain that her face was as scarlet as the tablecloth she held, Violet attempted to recover herself. She curtsied and said, "Your Highness, forgive my intrusion, I was just—"

"Why are you carrying linens as though you are one of the maids, Mrs. Harper?" Louise wore no expression of contrition or embarrassment. Instead, she was nearly defiant.

"I startled one of the maids in the corridor, so I offered to help—"

"You seem to make a habit of being in surprising places and startling others. Do you know the Reverend Robinson Duckworth? He is my brother's tutor." Louise slid off the desk gracefully in a single move.

Violet was too stunned to reply.

"I don't think I've had the pleasure, Miss, ah—" The reverend was stumbling, his face as pale as Violet's was red.

"Reverend, this is Mrs. Harper. She isn't in mourning, despite her clothing. Or, rather, you could say she is in permanent mourning, like Mother. She's the undertaker who prepared Father."

Duckworth nodded tightly, looking around the room as if he hoped he might find a hole into which he could disappear.

"Mother hired her to work on a spiritual matter. Perhaps she could use your advice, Ducky."

The reverend was now so bloodless that his lips were quickly fading into his skin. Only his nose remained scarlet.

"My assistance to the queen is of another nature than those concerned with God," Violet said. "As, I suppose, your assistance to the princess is." She quickly curtsied to Louise and turned to leave.

"Mrs. Harper, just a moment. I must apologize. This isn't as it looks. The reverend is merely a friend. We enjoy debating politics and religion. There's no harm in having a friend, is there? Mother tolerates so few of them."

"I suppose not, Your Highness."

"You won't tell her, will you? That Ducky and I are friends?"

Duckworth's eyes implored Violet as though he were a condemned man on the scaffold waiting for the king's grace.

"I am certain this is none of my business. I am, as you say, here for the queen's spiritual matter."

Louise's manner turned serious. "I do hope you are trustworthy, Mrs. Harper. Many lives would be ruined if Mother thought I was doing anything other than attending to her correspondence."

"Yes, Your Highness."

Violet fled the room before the princess said anything more. Why would any lives other than Duckworth's be ruined if the queen discovered Louise's affections for him? And did this explain Louise's mussed appearance and straw-embedded hem before? Was she trysting with Prince Leopold's tutor in the stables, his classroom, and wherever else she could find privacy?

Violet supposed that Duckworth's indiscretion with Louise could amount to some sort of treason, but surely this wasn't what

Mr. Brown knew and was afraid to tell the queen. Although, quite frankly, Violet herself trembled at the thought of having to share such news with Victoria. Perhaps it was best that she kept this to herself.

Winterbourne Manor, Wiltshire

Reese sat in the servants' hall, waiting for dinner to be served by Mrs. Welby, Winterbourne's cook. The kitchen maids were scrambling to put jugs of water and trays of turnips and potatoes on the long table, which had chairs lining the length of it on either side.

As backbreaking as his own work could be, at least he didn't work in the kitchens, where you served not only the master and his family but also the rest of the staff. Those poor girls probably only slept four or five hours each night.

Each new maid hired always flirted with Reese, hoping for his attentions, but he wasn't interested. His plan had always been to go home to Wales to marry and to give his half sister, Margaret, a place to live with him and whomever he might take as a wife.

Of course, everything about his life and plans was ruined now, wasn't it?

The head butler said grace and they tucked into Mrs. Welby's boiled beef. For a while, there was no sound except that of forks and knives scraping plates, but eventually Runyon, who loved nothing more than the sound of his own voice, broke the silence.

"Anyone read the paper today?" he asked.

Reese resisted the urge to throw his knife directly into the man's chest. Runyon knew that many of Winterbourne's staff could barely read. Perhaps he *should* aim it at the man's heart. He might even be cheered for it. *Huzzah, Meredith did away with the stupid scrut.*

Instead, Reese speared another piece of beef and ignored the other groom.

"You recall the story of the coal miner riots in Flintshire? That's in Wales, for those of you who don't know.

"Anyway, a coroner's inquest was held regarding the soldiers who fired on the crowd. Seems like the coroner was a doddering old fool, so deaf that he had to take evidence through an ear trumpet. Can you imagine? The jury turned in a verdict of 'justifiable homicide' on the soldiers, so they were let free. I expect there will be more riots. What's the matter with you, Meredith? You look like you've swallowed a toad."

Reese twisted the knife between his thumb and forefinger. "Nothing," he muttered.

Runyon turned his attention back to the rest of the staff. "But the news isn't over in Wales. On the tenth of June, there was an explosion at the Ferndale colliery in Rhondda. Fifty-three people were killed."

"Fifty-three!" Mrs. Welby said. "What a terrible shame. Imagine even wanting to work in one of those mines, deep underground. So very dark and dusty." She shuddered. "I'm glad I have my good place here."

"We all have good places, Mrs. Welby," the butler said.

Reese harrumphed, covering the sound with a napkin to his mouth.

Runyon picked up the story. "Rumor has it that the colliery owner hadn't implemented safety precautions after another explosion two years ago. Despite that, there won't be any criminal prosecution against him. The rich always have friends, don't they?"

"I'd like to be rich one day," Agnes said. She was the most recent housemaid hired and Reese remembered her cornering him at the door leading to the male servants' quarters one night. He'd had a hard time removing himself from her clutches.

"Sure you would, Agnes," Runyon said. "And I'm hoping to be the King of England one day, myself."

The maid blushed, and Reese almost felt bad for her having to endure the other groom's insults.

"May I be excused, sir?" Reese asked the butler. "I don't feel well."

"Yes, Meredith, you do look a bit green."

Reese fled the dining hall for his room. Once there, he went to his clothes chest and dug down into one of the drawers, his fingers searching for a particular scrap. Ah, there it was. He pulled it out and sat on his bed, lighting his lamp against the fading daylight so he could see it better.

It was a sketch of Margaret that she had made of herself when they were still children. She'd had remarkable talent, even then, but of course her destiny would never have been anything more than that of a servant.

The picture was amateurish, but still he could make out her lovely, rounded cheeks and full lips, her wild, untamed hair and pearly teeth. All of which now moldered in the earth in who knew what sort of anonymous grave.

Which reminded him that his second anonymous letter to *The Times* still hadn't been printed. Certainly it wasn't lost a second time. No, he was being deliberately ignored. That proved that the editor was just another rich society member, eager to protect the aristocrats above him.

How bitter was the herb of realization that people like him and Margaret were as nothing, just beef bones to be tossed to the dogs. His stomach burned at the thought.

With burning, though, came clarity. As the night grew black and still, Reese's mind glowed with activity. By sunrise, he knew with certainty that something must be done.

Some action that would make the nation take note, to force a halt to the careless treatment of his people.

Someone must be held to account.

It was of no use to appeal to newspapers. They were his enemies, too. No, he had to act against those at the top of the aristocratic pile.

He nodded grimly to himself before finally rolling over to sleep.

Yes, it was the queen and those who surrounded her who were the ones responsible. They would be held to account.

Scotland Yard, London

Detective Chief Inspector Magnus Pompey Hurst had just returned to London from a visit to Brighton and was eager to get back to his duties at Scotland Yard. His visit had not been fruitful, and he wanted nothing more than to forget about it. For although he'd told everyone that he'd gone there for rest and relaxation along the seaside, the true mission of his visit had been to find a wife.

He'd carefully considered what he was doing. It was June, so all of the society misses would be in London for the Season. They were out of his class—and who wanted a spoiled brat, anyway?—so he figured that the unattached women left would be a more appropriate field of choice. Brighton was his selected locale, since it was such a popular seaside spot for holidays.

He'd prided himself at the time on how his analytical skills had enabled him to make such a clever deduction. Unfortunately, he'd forgotten his own qualities in his cerebral reasoning and it turned out that very few unattached women were particularly interested in a giant bear of a man entering his fifties who had little to offer except vastly superior skills of deduction.

One had even laughed when he introduced himself to her, calling him the Centurion.

No, the visit had been very unsuccessful, so now that he was back in London he would throw himself back into his work. It was where he belonged. What was he thinking, trying to charm women when his days were typically filled with browbeating criminals?

During one of his most recent murder cases, he'd even found himself bullying a lady undertaker, not that the woman had put up with much of it.

Anyway, his interlude at Brighton was best forgotten. That particular case was not only closed but also sealed away in a vault. It was good to be back to the frantic pace of Scotland Yard, and if Commissioner Henderson's dour look was any indication, he was about to hand Hurst and Second-Class Inspector Langley Pratt a very interesting assignment. The two of them sat down expectantly across from Henderson's desk.

"Inspectors Hurst and Pratt, I've received some rather curious information from Mr. Walter over at *The Times*." Henderson scratched at his side-whiskers, which gave Hurst the uncomfortable desire to scratch at his own. "He's received some rather unusually threatening letters."

"He's a newspaper publisher," Hurst said. "I imagine he receives them all the time."

Langley Pratt, Hurst's junior by fifteen years, silently nodded in agreement.

"Yes, but these have concerned him enough to come to us. I've told him you would visit him at his offices this morning to discuss the situation."

"Why Scotland Yard? Why can't the police handle this?" This assignment wasn't interesting at all.

"Because Mr. Walter is concerned that the writer is a madman, who just might be targeting the queen herself."

Well, *that* would certainly be an interesting case. Suddenly Magnus Pompey Hurst's outlook brightened considerably.

Printing House Square, London

The Times's offices rattled and hummed above the basement filled with printing presses, which must have run day and night, spewing out copy after copy on a single day's news, while the paper's editor sat upstairs completing his daily tasks.

If the number of paper piles on a desk was any indicator, John Walter III was a busy man. And although he was a busy man, he was never too busy for tidiness, for the piles were arranged neatly by size. Just as neatly as he maintained his own clothing around his portly figure.

Walter had inherited *The Times* from his father, John Walter II, and Walter fully expected his own son, also John, to run the concern one day.

A profitable concern it was. The paper had been ahead of all other London newspapers for many years now, which most people attributed to John Walter III's conscientious character.

Even *The Times* building, with its rows of ordered windows and finely manicured lawn behind a wrought-iron gate, reflected the mind of a highly principled, scrupulous owner.

Each paper was printed in rolls on his newly invented Walter press, each roll nearly four miles long and with about thirty rolls used each day. Circulation was well over thirty thousand.

Above all, John Walter III enjoyed order, religious study, and the smell of hot black ink.

A breathless assistant entered Walter's office, carrying a stack of mail. Walter preferred to go through citizens' letters to the editors personally, and there were typically dozens to go through each day.

Reading the concerns of his fellow Londoners not only gave him an indication of what stories the paper should be covering but also assisted him in his role as the member from Berkshire in the House of Commons.

Walter put on his wire-rimmed glasses, so unfortunately necessary these days to read anything. As he carefully sliced open the envelopes with a brass letter opener, he started two new piles on his desk. To one pile he would place letters he deemed Publishable, and to the other would be consigned letters that were Unpublishable.

Today's collection had the usual assortment of people either praising or condemning various politicians, expressing concern over the Princess Alix's delicate condition, or postulating Christian views over prostitution, drunkenness, and other social woes. It was this third category of letter he liked best, but in any case, only the most civilized letters would be printed.

He'd recently received a couple of letters where the sender had so badly mangled the spelling of the newspaper's address that it was a wonder it had even arrived. Ink blotches suggested the writer was not used to managing a pen, either.

They were missives from "A Citizen Concerned for Coal Miners' Rights," and they were as poorly worded and spelled as their envelopes and made nearly illegible from ink smudges. However, the thrust of the letters declared outrage over recent events at a colliery in Wales.

Walter was well aware of the situation, having listened to George Osborne Morgan rail about what was going on with his countrymen in Parliament.

Walter had considered printing the letters but, upon closer inspection, realized that "Citizen" was throwing blame for the Mold riots at the queen, demanding that she publicly apologize for her foolish, senseless, and stupid treatment of the Welsh.

This had made *The Times* publisher bristle with indignation. Queen Victoria was a deeply religious woman, sharing many of his own views. There was much to admire in a woman who had done her duty to her people by not only producing many children to carry on the royal line but also constantly desiring to always do *good*.

The implication that she was less than upright in her dealings with her people hadn't sat well with him. He reread the jumbles of words and thoughts and decided that the letters sounded as though they were from a madman. A madman bearing wild and illogical grudges. Undoubtedly he was from Wales. Were all of the Welsh this deranged?

Walter had added the letters to the Unpublishable pile each time they had arrived. Eventually, though, his conscience began bothering him. What if this fool intended to do something? Walter had finally decided to send word to Scotland Yard about it and was now waiting for two detectives to arrive.

An assistant rapped on the door. "The two gents you said were coming have arrived, sir."

Walter checked the neatness of his paper piles one last time before going to greet the detectives.

"How do you stand the noise?" the one named Hurst asked Walter as he and his junior colleague followed him back down the corridor to a door with a glass inset stenciled "Mr. Walter, Publisher" on it.

"What noise do you mean? That of the presses? I stopped hearing it long ago. Besides, that is the sound of news being created, for consumption by anyone who can read. It is a marvel!"

Inspector Hurst clearly had no appreciation for the newspaper industry, for he replied with, "Yes, quite. Commissioner Henderson says you have information about a possible plot against the queen?"

Walter lifted a packet from his desk and opened it. "I've received two very disturbing letters from someone who calls himself 'A Citizen Concerned for Coal Miners' Rights.' They are poorly worded, practically illiterate, but he is very passionate on his topic." Walter went silent as he began rereading the correspondence.

"And this topic is . . ." Hurst prompted.

"Yes, the man—I am quite certain it is a man, as a woman would be incapable of expressing such stark and unadulterated rage—is obsessed with the recent coal miner riots in Wales."

"Permit me to interrupt, Mr. Walter. We have witnessed women committing unspeakable acts. In fact, just recently a nurse named Catherine Wilson was terrorizing certain parts of England, killing patients after convincing them to write her into their wills."

Inspector Hurst was proving quite tiresome. Did he believe that in his years in the newspaper industry he'd had no experience with the evil desires of both sexes? "Of course, I submit to your greater knowledge, Inspector, but I have been reading letters to this paper for many years, and I am quite confident these are from a man."

"Maybe they were written by a man but dictated by a woman," Pratt said.

"Don't be helpful," Hurst said. "Go on, Mr. Walter, what do the letters say?"

"Would you care to read them for yourself?" He passed a letter to each of the detectives.

Hurst glanced at the letter and blinked at the abomination of misspellings and spidery handwriting. He handed it back to Walter. "I think we will rely on your translation, sir."

Pratt returned his letter, too. "All I can make out is the 'Citizen Concerned' signature."

"The writing is, obviously, rambling and incoherent," Walter said. "I've seen many of these sorts of embittered letters before, but these two are particularly . . . virulent. From the cadence, I'd say the writer is a Welshman. I am fairly certain the author is outraged over the Mold riots that have taken place recently, and somehow blames our gracious queen for them, as well as every member of the peerage. It would seem that the fires of hell are the least of the punishments that should be meted out upon them all."

Walter put the letter down. "His tone was inflamed enough that I became concerned that he truly means to do something drastic. I thought it imperative that I contact the authorities."

"You were quite right to do so," Hurst said.

"Yes," Pratt added. "I remember when I was a bobby working in

Hackney. A man left anonymous, threatening letters with a book-seller for supposedly inserting indecent prints inside women's ro-mance novels. We managed to—"

Hurst cut the junior detective off with, "Have you a department that handles the post? Does someone there know whether the let-ters were hand delivered?"

"Yes, we do have a specific department to handle each day's post—which runs into hundreds of letters and packages, as you might imagine—and the boy who received both letters remem-bered that they came via the post. I did question him closely, and he specifically recalled them because of the atrocious handwriting on the envelopes."

"I appreciate your diligence, Mr. Walter, although we'd like to question the boy ourselves."

"Of course, Chief Inspector." Walter rose and spoke through a tube jutting out from the wall, and soon an escort presented him-self at the door to take the inspectors to the mailroom. Before they left, Walter said, "Gentlemen, if I may. I have had extensive con-versations with most of my employees, and I don't believe you will gain anything of use there. May I recommend that you investigate hotels around Buckingham Palace, to see if any Welshmen have recently checked in for extended stays?"

Hurst gave him a thoroughly exasperated look. "Why do all of London's tradespeople think they need to tell me my business?"

But Walter noticed that as they departed Hurst was already in-structing Pratt to visit several hotels around Belgravia and West-minster.

Violet was still pondering Louise's curious summons as she once again entered the Buckingham Palace mews, the place where Louise wanted to meet her. Violet stood in the courtyard, undertaking bag in hand per request, not sure where to go, since Louise hadn't been specific about where to find her, only that she must come immediately to see about a death.

The area was bustling with its usual activities—carriage mainte-nance, horse exercise, manure hauling—and, in the distance, Violet heard the snorting of horses and clipped commands of trainers working with them. Yet there was no sign of the princess.

A young groom with closely cropped dark hair approached Violet, holding the reins of the horse who obediently clopped behind him. "Help you, miss?" he asked.

"I'm looking for the Princess Louise."

"She isn't scheduled to ride out for another half hour. Besides, she'd be picked up at the palace; she wouldn't come here. What is your purpose here?"

"My name is Violet Harper and I—"

"You're that undertaker everyone talks about. You're planning to perform an exorcism or some such for Her Majesty."

"No, no, that isn't my purpose at all."

He eyed her bag suspiciously. "Do you have potions and crucifixes in there?"

"Of course not. This bag contains my—never mind. I just need to find the princess. She asked me to meet her here."

"Here? Are you sure? This isn't a fit place for a member of the family."

"Nevertheless, I must wait for her here."

At that moment, Violet saw Louise emerge from one of the many doors leading to the stable workers' quarters. What was she doing up there? The princess came down one of the rickety iron staircases as elegantly as she could, giving Violet a wave as she did so.

The groom was nonplussed. "Now that's strange," he muttered as he took leave of Violet with his unsaddled horse following amiably.

Louise was breathless and flustered by the time she reached Violet, who dipped into a curtsy. "Please, no more of that, Mrs. Harper. I suspect that after today we shall be friends. Or, if not friends, confederates. Come, come, we must leave right away." She called out to the groom who had just questioned Violet, "A carriage to Gainsburgh House in Belgravia, right away. Nothing fancy."

"Yes, Your Highness. You'll not be wanting the other carriage, then?"

"No, I've changed my mind and wish to leave right away."

They waited as the groom hurried to do Louise's bidding. "You don't want Mr. Brown to escort us?" Violet asked.

"Absolutely not. What an idea. What made you think of such a thing?"

Violet shook her head. "I am perhaps mistaken in my thoughts. My apologies."

"My mother's . . . I don't know what to call him . . . is the last one I'd want to have word of this," Louise said as she was handed into the carriage with Violet right behind her.

"Word of what, exactly, Princess? All I know is it regards a death."

Louise looked out the window for several moments as the carriage made its way out of the mews and onto Buckingham Palace Road, heading south to wherever their destination was. People walking about near the entrance of the mews craned their necks to see who was inside the carriage and waved upon seeing Princess Louise. She graciously returned the waves. Once the carriage was clear of the mews and the onlookers, she turned back to Violet.

"It's my friend, Lady Maud Winter. She's the daughter of the Duke of Gainsburgh. She's dead." Louise said this flatly, as though she were referring to an expired pigeon found outside her window. Violet knew, though, that many people reacted in such a stilted manner when learning of a loved one's death, tending to deal more with the logistics of death rather than the emotions. It allowed them to swallow their pain until a more private moment.

"I am deeply grieved for Your Highness."

Louise pulled a monogrammed handkerchief from her sleeve and dabbed her eyes. "Yes, well, she was ill for quite some time. It is my wish that you prepare Lady Maud's body for burial."

"Pardon me, but won't the family want to call in their own undertaker?"

"I've already sent word that I was bringing the royal undertaker. They will be pleased to see you. Ah, we're here."

The carriage rolled to a stop outside a magnificent stone residence with pillars impressively reaching up four stories.

"There's just one thing you should know before you see Lady

Maud," Louise said as the door was opened and a gloved hand appeared to help her down the fold-out steps of the carriage.

"Yes, Your Highness?"

Louise didn't hesitate in her next statement. "Her family believes she died naturally; however, I know for certain that she was murdered."

4

Gainsburgh House was heavy with the air of grief. It was a combination of disbelief, anguish, and exhaustion that blended together into an invisible fog that permeated the corridors and stairways of any home that had experienced a death. Despite the tall painted and gilded ceilings of the duke's residence, it, too, suffered from the fog, which always settled down to the floor and wrapped itself around the feet and shoulders of the grieving, making their movements wooden and sluggish.

The duke and his wife attempted royal courtesies, but Louise stopped them by kissing them each on the cheek and hugging the duchess to her. The ducal couple looked almost alike in their bereavement, and both offered the princess sad, quivering smiles and murmured words of appreciation.

"We knew this would eventually happen, since she was so tender and fragile," Lady Gainsburgh said. "But this is so soon. I can hardly realize it."

The duchess dabbed at her nose with a square of lawn fabric that had been worked and worried into tatters.

As Violet stood by somberly, her bag in both hands in front of her, Louise directed the action.

"Your Graces, may I present Mrs. Harper? She is the undertaker who attended my father."

"Yes, right. I suppose you'll want to see my daughter straightaway?" the duke said.

"When you're ready, sir. I can wait."

"We may as well go ahead and—"

"Princess!" A young boy, no more than ten years old, bounded into the grand entryway from somewhere behind the dual staircase.

"Master Arthur," Louise said. "I've come to pay respects to your sister."

This caused him to frown. "Yes, Papa says she has gone to see Tubby, my old beagle. I wish she would come back soon. It will be dark and she won't be able to see."

The emotional fog grew thicker, as neither of Arthur's parents knew quite what to say to their son's guileless comment. In the end, the duke merely told the boy to go play and escorted Louise and Violet up one side of the staircase.

Violet was the first to enter Lady Maud's bedroom. The others held back as if waiting for a pronouncement from her. As was her custom, she first took a deep breath inside the room. It was fragrant, smelling faintly of rosewater perfume. Maud's death was indeed fresh, lacking the mustiness, and eventual smell of decay, that took over beginning a day or so after death, especially for those already rotting inside from disease and ill health.

Now it was Violet's turn to take command.

Lady Maud Winter lay on top of the bedcoverings, her hair long and loose and her hands clasped together.

With sensitivity toward the family, but mindful of Louise's concern of foul play, Violet said, "Your daughter passed in peaceful repose. Quite unusual." This elicited the response she hoped for.

"No, no, I moved her," Maud's father said. "She was on the floor when we found her. She never answered the call for breakfast, so finally our butler came up to check on her and found her . . . found her . . ." The duke swallowed, trying to choke down his misery, but was unable to continue.

"I understand. You've done a fine job with your daughter. She looks very sweet and dignified. May I suggest that I finish her preparations, then we can sit down and discuss her funeral?"

At the word "funeral," Lady Gainsburgh's eyes started watering again.

The duke took his wife by the elbow. "My dear, why don't we go downstairs and leave the undertaker to tend to Maud?"

As the young lady's parents departed, Lady Gainsburgh stopped. "Please, do as little as possible to our dear girl. We want her to remain as pure in death as she was in life."

Violet nodded. "You may rely upon me, Your Grace."

The ducal couple left, but Louise remained behind. "Do you see?"

"See what, Princess?"

"Maud was found on the floor, not in her bed as if she'd died in her sleep."

"Yes, but she probably arose to pour herself a glass of water."

Louise pointed toward a table by the carved walnut bed. On an ivory doily sat a full carafe of water and a glass, untouched.

"She may have also arisen to relieve herself in the middle of the night and fallen. Such a fall could have broken her neck or injured her head."

"Perhaps," Louise said. "I'll go down to comfort His and Her Grace. You'll watch for anything suspicious, won't you?"

"Of course, Your Highness." Although Violet couldn't imagine what could possibly be suspect about the poor girl's death.

Almost like a hesitant afterthought, Louise said, "Oh, and please clip some of Maud's hair. I've never made a hair brooch before, but as a tribute to Maud, I am willing to learn how to do it."

As the door gently clicked behind Louise, Violet turned to give her full attention to Maud Winter.

She dropped her undertaking bag several feet away to keep it out of view for what she planned to do next. Taking the girl's hands in her own, she spoke softly to Lady Maud.

"My lady, have no fear on my account. I will be here but briefly, and it is my honor to serve both you and the House of Gainsburgh. Illness has been kind to your features, a great blessing, so it will be a simple thing to honor your mother's request in preparing you."

Violet went about her ministrations, removing the girl's clothing, washing her down with a sponge and bottle of cleaning solution from her bag, noting no obvious superficial abrasions, then re-dressing Lady Maud in her sleeping gown, and finally replacing the girl's hands the way her father had put them and tying them at the wrists with string hidden under her nightgown sleeves. Violet made a mental note to ask the Gainsburghs if they had a special dress they wanted their daughter buried in.

Then, with scissors in one hand and a paper box in the other, Violet clipped several long locks of the girl's hair, taking them from the nape of her neck where their absence wouldn't be noticed. As she rearranged Maud's hair, her fingers brushed over something bumpy on the deceased's neck. Violet gently turned the woman's face to take a closer look.

There were two bite marks at Maud's nape. Something must have landed on her recently and feasted. Had the insect been poisonous? Had it hastened her death?

Now it was time for preparing Maud's face. Violet lifted her bag onto a chair and removed several cases of cosmetics. The deceased's skin was very pale, so Violet needed some rouge to bring some life back into it. She held up a pot and looked inside. "Medium Pink Number Four seems about the right color. Something similar for your lips, too. I think that—"

Violet's work was interrupted by a ghastly noise coming from the bed, that of someone coughing and gagging at the same time. The rouge pot clattered to the floor as Violet froze in place.

Am I working on a living body?

Her heart beating furiously and erratically inside her chest, Violet looked up at Maud. The girl was still at rest, except now her mouth was agape, a common occurrence as a corpse began relaxing in death.

Violet put a hand to her own chest, trying to control the wild thumping inside. "Lady Maud, you gave me quite a scare. For a moment, I thought you were still—well, never mind."

This bodily expulsion of air had only happened to Violet one other time, and it had frightened her just as badly. Preparation of a corpse usually involved total silence, so to have the body seemingly wake up as it expelled air was positively nerve-wracking.

Violet had heard other undertakers speak of bodies actually moving on their own—another rare but possible event—occurring from the body's reaction to embalming.

As much as Violet despised funerary trickery, such as coffins with escape hatches in case the deceased wasn't really dead, she did understand why family members would wish to purchase them. What if . . . ?

However, in all of Violet's experience, and despite Lady Maud's coughing, she had never known a dead body to return to life.

Her heart now beating normally, Violet retrieved the rouge, which had rolled beneath the bed. With the rouge pot and a paintbrush in hand, Violet went to apply color to the girl's cheeks but realized she had to address her open mouth first.

With Lady Gainsburgh's admonition in mind, Violet cradled the girl's cheeks in both hands. A bit of cord under the jawline and around the ears, then tied behind the hair, perhaps. If so, Lady Maud would need to be dressed in a gown with a particularly high neckline.

Violet frowned. What was this protruding from under Lady Maud's tongue? A scrap of paper. She pulled gently on the corner of it.

"Forgive me, my lady, for the intrusion, but this doesn't seem to be a normal part of your person. Ah, here we are."

It wasn't paper but a torn piece of muslin. Why in heaven's name would this be in the deceased's mouth? Was she chewing on fabric for some reason and choked to death on it?

Violet raised the cloth to her nose and sniffed tentatively but quickly recoiled. "Forgive me again, my lady, but that was a stench unlike any I have encountered in a long time."

In fact, she couldn't even identify what it was. There was the telltale pungency of death, for sure, yet there was more. Of course, Lady Maud had just expelled a variety of gases, so perhaps that was what made it so putrid.

The real question, though, was why the girl had fabric in her mouth to begin with. Sometimes the insane had strange habits that they managed to hide from others. Did Lady Maud count among their number? Did she have a nervous habit of secretly chewing on clothing and linens?

Violet shook her head. It didn't seem right. Surely Louise, as a close friend, would have noticed odd behavior, even if Maud's parents didn't. But if the girl was mentally unbalanced, she may well have managed to cloak it.

Just months ago, Violet had been pursued by a deranged killer who seemed perfectly normal. Who knew what lay in the minds of those who were cerebrally impaired? If this was true of the young Lady Maud, it was a tragedy, and it was pointless to draw her parents' attention to it. Violet tucked the scrap of cloth into her undertaking bag and returned to making Lady Maud as lovely as she must have been while alive.

Louise was on a settee, an arm around Lady Gainsburgh, when Violet descended the Grand Staircase into the front parlor. Lord Gainsburgh stood awkwardly at the fireplace, avoiding his wife's tearful glances.

"Your Graces, the Lady Maud is a picture of good health, her cheeks in bloom and her lips in smile. I believe you will be pleased. May I inquire as to whether you are ready to discuss her funeral?"

Lady Gainsburgh blanched, even as her husband nodded. Louise left the room and Violet removed her service book from her bag, flipping to the section marked "Titled."

They deliberated on the proper number of horses, ostrich feathers for the glass hearse, pages, coachmen, and attendants. Maud's parents also decided on a photography sitting for their daughter, asking Violet to place her in a crimson and cream gown that she'd worn for her presentation to the queen.

Violet now had everything she needed and promised to return shortly with a photographer. A maid escorted her back upstairs, where she quickly re-dressed Lady Maud; she then rejoined Louise for the carriage ride back to Buckingham Palace.

"So, what do you think?" Louise asked as soon as the carriage rolled away from Gainsburgh House.

"About Lady Maud's death? She was sickly, Your Highness."

"I know this. But I'm certain she didn't die of her consumption. She was being courted by Lord Effingham's son, and was quite happy about it. I'd not seen her look so, so . . . exuberant . . . in quite some time."

Violet doubted whether exuberant infatuation would prevent

consumption from taking its course but said nothing. The cloth she'd pulled out of Maud's mouth popped into her mind, but she decided it best not to share this discovery with Louise, lest the princess's mind wander even further down paths of treachery.

Besides, Violet hadn't even told the girl's parents about it. It would be unfair to share it with Louise first.

"Your Highness, is there something specific you wish for me to do?"

"Yes, find out how Lady Maud died, and who did it to her."

Like mother, like daughter, both assigning Violet with foolish, impossible tasks. Violet hoped the princess didn't notice the sigh of resignation that caught in her throat. Was Louise sending Violet on this chase as a distraction from her affair—if it had progressed that far—with Reverend Duckworth? And did this secret relationship have anything to do with Mr. Brown's spectral warnings?

Maybe there *was* something to investigate, but not what Louise had in mind.

Violet returned to Gainsburgh House several hours later with the photographer, Mr. Henry Peach Robinson. It was a silent ride in Mr. Robinson's photography wagon, for they'd argued heatedly inside his shop.

"My dear Mrs. Harper, you must understand that I am the expert in this situation, and it is my professional opinion that the ambrotype is the better way to capture the girl's image."

"That may be so, but I wish you to produce daguerreotypes."

The photographer gave her a withering look to ensure she understood his superiority in the matter. "Madam, the ambrotype can be tinted, a small service for which no doubt such a prestigious family would willingly pay. I can make their daughter appear to be in the bloom of health."

"Actually, Mr. Robinson, it is *my* responsibility to bring Lady Maud to the bloom of health. The tinting is unnecessary, and we both know the ambrotype process is weaker and the image will not last as long. It is, however, simpler, is it not, saving you from extra labors while charging my customers an extravagant price?"

Robinson tried a new approach as they climbed onto the driving box and he guided his team onto the street. "You are a business-woman, Mrs. Harper. You know that it is practice to charge accord-ing to what the classes can afford. The Duke of Gainsburgh can afford much."

"He just lost his daughter, which has already cost him a great deal," Violet snapped. "If you're charging a daguerreotype price, it is a daguerreotype you shall produce."

Silence descended on the driver's box as they rode the rest of the way without speaking. Violet vowed to never hire Robinson again. Unfortunately, Mr. Laroche, Violet's favorite photographer, was otherwise engaged and unable to accept this commission.

Once they arrived at Gainsburgh House, Mr. Robinson went to the rear of his wagon to gather his equipment, while Violet went up to check on Lady Maud. Two chairs had been pulled up next to the bedside. The duke and duchess must have spent time grieving next to Maud, perhaps even pouring out the contents of their hearts to a beloved child who would never respond to them.

It gave Violet an idea.

She pulled one of the chairs around to the other side of the bed. At that point, Mr. Robinson arrived and unpacked his black cam-era box, silvered copper plates, and a heating lamp. On top of this flame went a cup Violet knew was full of mercury, used to develop the daguerreotype pictures.

While he finished setting up his equipment, Violet had the duke's and duchess's presences requested in Lady Maud's bed-room.

Lady Gainsburgh had worked in the interim to improve her own appearance. She'd changed into a different, less-wrinkled, black dress and rearranged her hair. The duke still looked haggard and drawn.

Violet presented Mr. Robinson to Maud's parents, then quickly set up several poses. It was best to get photographs captured be-fore the family could dwell on what was happening and thus suc-cumb to grief during the session.

First, Violet did one with the couple on either side of the bed, each with a hand covering one of Maud's. Next, she had Lord Gainsburgh sit next to Maud and gently lifted the girl's torso and placed it against him. He naturally put his arms around his daughter, and Robinson captured the poignant moment.

Violet also arranged pillows behind Maud's head to push her forward and had Robinson do several photographs this way, as well as relaxing the girl's body down on the bed and having him take an image from the side, capturing Maud at rest with her hands over a Bible.

The Gainsburghs seemed pleased with the poses and left Violet and Robinson to finish their work. As Violet returned Lady Maud back to the supine position appropriate for visitors, she watched Mr. Robinson at work and had to admit that, despite their combative start, the man was efficient and able.

As he pulled each plate from his camera box, he set the exposed piece over the heated cup of mercury, and soon the latent image was developed by the mercury condensing on the areas on the plate where the exposure light was most intense and less so in the darker areas of the image. Once he was satisfied that the image was finished, he slipped the plate into a developing box to inspect the image through a special glass window to determine when to stop development.

Next, Robinson "fixed" the image onto the plate by dipping it into a saturated salt solution. After drying, the plate would be ready to be sealed in glass cases evacuated of air and filled with nitrogen to stabilize the photograph.

Violet gingerly held up a finished photograph by the plate's corners. The image was firmly defined, with Lady Maud's features clearly reflecting a very sweet expression. No wonder Lord Effingham's son was taken with her.

Violet nodded as she carefully handed the plate back to Mr. Robinson. "This is fine work, sir. I'm sure the family will appreciate seeing them in their cases."

Violet and Mr. Robinson's ride back together was much more pleasant.

*   *   *

Lord and Lady Gainsburgh decided that they wanted Lady Maud presented in grander fashion than in her bed, so Violet returned with undertaker Will Swift to remove the girl's body to a coffin they set up on a bier in the ballroom. Chairs lined the walls like somber sentries performing guard duty around the body.

Will Swift and Harry Blundell had acquired management of Morgan Undertaking from Violet when she moved to the United States. Prior to that, they had worked for her in the shop. Now that she had returned for a protracted stay in London, Will was pressing her to buy his share of the business back from him, despite Violet's previous insistence that she would be returning home to Colorado soon.

He brought it up again in low tones as they artistically arranged pots of lilies around the bier and draped a cloth embroidered with the ducal crest over Lady Maud's lower half. The coffin lid would be stored away until it was time to nail it down for the funeral itself.

"Mrs. Harper, Lydia is bent on my abandoning the funeral business to join her father's floral shop. Are you sure you aren't interested in purchasing my interest?"

"Of course I'm interested, Will, but it's still possible that I will be returning to Colorado soon, just as soon as Sam finishes up his work with Mr. Nobel and I complete a task for the queen."

Will nodded. "And as soon as you see another body interred. This is, what, your third funeral since you arrived?"

Violet thought about the mysterious deaths surrounding the Raybourn family she'd recently investigated. "I suppose this is my fourth one."

"Don't forget that you also have the Suez Canal opening ceremonies to attend in November."

"Yes, but that is positively the last thing keeping me here."

"Oh, most certainly that is true. Except that by then, the queen will have something else for you to do. Please consider my offer, Mrs. Harper. Talk it over with your husband."

Violet had already mentioned it to Sam, but they hadn't come to a decision yet. She promised to do so, and Will departed while Violet stayed behind to do some touch-ups on Lady Maud's cosmetics. The jostling caused by transporting corpses, especially on long flights of stairs, frequently marred their perfect composure.

Violet had just tucked everything away in her undertaking bag when the tall double-mahogany doors to the ballroom were opened by an unseen servant's hand. In swept a couple in their late twenties, probably a little older than Lady Maud. Violet stepped respectfully back into a corner, quietly setting her bag on one of the many ballroom chairs.

". . . and Lady Gainsburgh looks downright sickly, doesn't she?" the man said.

"Naturally, Ripley. Maud was everything to her." The woman was a petite and blond foil to the man's dark and towering presence. Both were appropriately dressed in solemn black, with an armband snug around the man's upper arm and gloves encasing the woman's hands.

"We can't be surprised by what happened to Maud, though, can we, Lottie?" Ripley dropped his voice to a hiss as they reached Maud's coffin in the center of the room. Both were oblivious to Violet's presence.

"What do you mean?"

"You know precisely what I mean. All of that . . . activity . . . you peahens are involved in. No wonder it wore Maud out until she finally just collapsed. It could happen to you."

"Don't be silly. Maud was always sickly. I've never been ill at all."

"Yet we have no child."

"This again? Ripley, it isn't for lack of trying. And anyway, this is a horrid time and place to speak of it. Poor Maud." Together the couple leaned over the coffin to look at her.

The woman called Lottie bent over and affectionately kissed Maud's forehead. Violet winced, for the deceased's cosmetics had just been freshly reapplied and were not yet necessarily set. It was difficult to know at Violet's distance whether or not Lottie's lips were stained with Porcelain Bisque Number Two.

"Farewell, lovely Maud," Lottie said softly, continuing to gaze at her friend.

"Don't be disgusting. I'll not have it said that my wife goes about kissing corpses."

"You are an ass, Lord Marcheford."

"You've been perfectly clear about your opinion on many occasions, my dear. Are we quite finished here? I want to escort you home so I can get to the club. Barton has a new Cabernet imported from Anjou that we're going to sample."

"You go on and send the driver back for me. I want to stay here with Maud a bit longer."

"Suit yourself." He kissed his wife on the cheek with all the enthusiasm of a fish having a hook removed from its mouth.

As soon as her husband departed, Lady Marcheford put her head down on her arm atop the edge of the coffin and sobbed, a sound that nearly split the room in half in its misery and wretchedness.

Violet knew what it was to have a bitter and thoughtless husband, having had one herself prior to Sam. Her professional instinct to remain quietly in the background was overridden by her female desire to comfort. She went to the woman and said as faintly as she could, so as not to startle her, "Lady Marcheford?"

Violet's peaceful approach didn't work. Lady Marcheford unsuccessfully tried to swallow a most unregal screech. "Who are you and where did you come from?" she said, a gloved hand flying to her chest. Her lips indeed had a smudge of cosmetic massage cream on them, but that was the least of Violet's concerns now.

"My apologies. I am the undertaker, here to care for your friend. I stepped back when you arrived, so as not to disturb your visit."

"You are the undertaker. How very curious. Actually, it's rather appropriate in Maud's case."

"Madam?"

"Never mind. Did you hear the argument the earl and I had?"

"No, madam. My attention is for the Lady Maud, and she no longer speaks."

The woman looked furtively at the door through which her husband had just exited, then sighed. "I suppose it is of no matter. It isn't as though all of our servants—and therefore half of London—haven't heard it before."

Violet cast her eyes down. "Yes, my lady."

She sensed that Lady Marcheford was about to unburden herself, and she didn't have long to wait.

"I am Charlotte Tate, the Countess of Marcheford. My husband is waiting impatiently to inherit the Marquess of Salford title, but his father has remained unforgivably healthy. Unlike poor, darling Maud."

Lady Marcheford bent down once more and stroked Maud's jawline as she continued talking. The cosmetic massage was rubbing off onto her glove, but she didn't seem to notice. "My husband's mistress is also unforgivably healthy. Maud had no idea how fortunate she was in her unwedded state."

"I understand Lady Maud had recently found love."

Lady Marcheford frowned and stood once again. "How did you hear this?"

"From the Princess Louise. She engaged me here on behalf of the family."

"I see. She shared such a personal detail about our friend with you?" Her tone was more curious than accusing.

"Her Highness has placed a level of trust in me." Violet hoped that sounded neutral enough.

"Did she tell you anything else about Lady Maud?"

"What do you mean, my lady?"

"Did she suggest our friend was in danger?"

Proceed carefully, Violet Harper.

"The princess very clearly loved Lady Maud very much and wants to be sure she had no . . . undue distress before she died."

"Cleverly said, little undertaker. Well, I wouldn't be surprised if harm had come to her, and she wouldn't be the only one in danger."

"Pardon me, madam?"

Lady Marcheford was unable to answer, for she broke into a coughing fit. She frantically reached inside the drawstring reticule hanging from her wrist and pulled out a handkerchief, which she pressed to her mouth. Once the coughing had subsided, she glanced at the handkerchief and tucked it back into her bag, resuming her conversation as if nothing had happened.

"No, there are others in danger. I do hope Louise is being attentive to others besides darling Maud."

"Do you speak of yourself, my lady?"

"Have you any idea what it is to be married to a man who is handsome, polished, brilliant . . . and thoroughly rotten in his soul?"

"In fact, I do."

"Does he approve of your undertaking?"

"He's dead."

"Ah, then you approved of his own undertaking." Lady Marcheford put the cosmetics-stained-gloved hand to her mouth to cover a weak smile. "Sorry, what a rotten joke. I mustn't be so boorish."

"It's quite all right, madam. My husband died long ago, and I have since made a much happier marriage."

"So it is possible then? To wait it out until His Rottenness comes to his own dreadful end and then pick up with someone kinder and more loving?"

This was an uncomfortable conversation. "My lady, I wouldn't say that I was waiting out my husband's demise, it was more that he . . . brought it on himself."

"If only Ripley would do so. The man is simply loathsome. Sometimes he frightens me. I've learned to stand up to his browbeating, but you never know when a man like that will shatter and embed everyone around him with shards of glass. I am prepared for it, though."

Lady Marcheford pulled open her reticule and held it up for Violet's inspection. Nestled inside was a pearl-handled derringer. "I nicked it from my father's collection. He has so many he doesn't even realize it's missing. I know how to use it, too."

She pulled the drawstrings tight once more and put the reticule back over her arm. "I hope it doesn't come to this between Ripley and me, but I'm prepared for him."

Violet murmured sympathies and quickly excused herself. Were

Louise and all of her set this irrational, or was there something to their fears?

Reese Meredith was amazed at his own good luck. It had been so long since he'd had any. Yet he'd managed to leave his position at Winterbourne Manor with a good character reference in hand and the amusement of having Agnes weep on his shoulder while Runyon glared at him.

That was a very satisfying moment.

Yet it was only a foreshadowing of what he would accomplish now in honor of Margaret's memory and to ensure there were no more Margarets being slaughtered in the streets of Mold and towns like it.

For now he had accomplished his first goal, which was to get near the queen and her family. How simple it had been. His experience in the cavalry, fighting for his country in Hong Kong and Peking, culminating in the assault and capture of the Old Summer Palace and thus concluding the Second Opium War, had duly impressed his new employer, resulting in an immediate hire.

Here Reese sat in a new servants' hall, with new companions and new routines to follow, but it was all irrelevant to him as he remained lost in his own thoughts while steaming bowls of potatoes, braised rabbit, mince pie, and peas with bacon were passed around. A new butler said grace, and a new cook blushed at the praise heaped upon her roasting talents.

Every house was like another, only some were larger than others.

Reese considered his plan as he scooped out a serving of peas for the simpering maid across the table from him. All of his movements must be just perfect. Any misstep would reveal his plan. He didn't care so much for himself, his own life, but it wouldn't do for him to be caught and thus foil his precisely crafted scheme.

What did he need to do next? Perhaps he needed an opiate of some sort. A woman struggling in his arms was so very distasteful, even if she was a member of the peerage. Yes, he must figure out how to procure something . . . soothing . . . to the fairer sex.

His ruminations were interrupted by a tidbit of gossip that floated above the rest of the nattering the servants were doing.

"What did you say?" he asked of one of the scullery maids.

"It's one of the Princess Louise's friends what died. Lady Maud Winter. The princess is all broken up. She even rode over with the undertaker. Imagine that, a princess of the blood being seen with an undertaker out in public."

"So from what did Lady Maud die?" Reese asked.

"They said she had the consumption something terrible."

Reese's lips carved into the first smile he'd had since before hearing of his sister's death. His new position at Buckingham Palace mews was already proving quite profitable.

5

Sitting before a large map of Great Britain were Detective Chief Inspector Hurst and Detective Second-Class Inspector Pratt. The two had worked for hours to diagram out where all of Great Britain's coal mines were. Although Mr. Walter was certain the writer was Welsh, given his language and his complaint about a Welsh colliery, it wouldn't be thorough to survey only those coal mines. You never knew with these unbalanced types. Sometimes they became aggrieved over situations having nothing to do with them. Or perhaps this poor fellow was from a coal-mining village to the north and wanted to give his fellow workers his undying support.

Pratt cleared his throat. "It seems to me, sir, that we should start with the obvious."

Hurst agreed, but wanted to test his junior protégé. "And what would be obvious?"

"That we should take the writer at his word, and go to Mold in Flintshire, where the riot was that he complained of."

Hurst nodded. "Quite correct. And if we get no satisfaction there, we'll head to the largest colliery on the map, and work our way down in order of size. Do you understand why we will do it that way?"

"Because they are easier to reach?" Pratt's voice was hopeful.

"Inspector, we do not order our work around what is simple, but according to what makes sense. Larger coal mines employ more people, making it more likely that we can find our man more quickly at one of them. We're going to stop this little fellow from carrying through on any of his blustering threats; this I can promise you."

Lady Maud's funeral was an elegant affair despite the rain and fog of the morning. The duke held up surprisingly well as he stood next to Maud's younger brother, who seemed completely baffled by the proceedings.

Fortunately, Violet was the only one who noticed that Harry and Will nearly lost their balance on the wet, slippery ground as they slid the coffin into the family crypt at the cemetery.

As was customary, Lady Gainsburgh remained at home, surrounded by female friends and family members, until the menfolk returned to report on the funeral.

At Louise's request, Violet returned to Buckingham Palace later in the day to help her make mourning jewelry to honor Lady Maud.

Violet sat at one of four round oak tables inside Louise's rooms while the princess and several of her friends, including Lady Marcheford, crowded around to watch her demonstrate. From among a collection of tools and supplies she opened a case full of empty crystal-topped brooches, rings, and lockets, all wrought in gold with fancy filigrees, knots, wreaths, and gemstone flowers adorning them. Violet had selected only the finest pieces from Morgan Undertaking's stock, knowing that the daughters of earls and dukes expected unique and fanciful jewelry.

Each woman selected an item or two of jewelry that she wanted; then Violet opened the paper box containing Maud's long tresses, each coiled into a circle tied with a ribbon on both ends. Gently removing one and unraveling it, she said, "This is the lovely Lady Maud's hair. I have washed, dried, and washed it again to remove any oils. However, as you can see as I remove one of the ribbons holding it together, when I stroke it the hair wants to fly away. Therefore we will lightly moisten the hair before working with it.

"There are three general ways you can create a memorial piece with hair: working the hair into a piece of jewelry, as I believe most of you wish to do; using the hair to paint a scene on ivory; and, finally, creating a multidimensional bouquet or tableau from the hair and placing it under a glass dome. I must be truthful, though, and tell you that I have very little skill with the tableaux; it requires someone with great artistic talent, and I am but an undertaker. Also, we would probably need the hair of several people and many months in order to make one of these dome scenes. Therefore, we will make tributes to the Lady Maud in either jewelry or painting."

"I should like to paint," said a pale woman, her eyelashes as blond as her hair. Neither of these features, though, compared to her plump figure, straining against her corset and threatening to disgorge itself. Violet noticed that the woman breathed in short, shallow breaths, probably because her laces were entirely too tight.

"My lady . . ." Violet began.

"I am Lady Hazel Campden. My father is Earl Littlebury."

"I am honored. First, you will need a little piece of ivory. What did you select as your jewelry piece? Ah, I believe a ring will be entirely too difficult. May I suggest this?" Violet pulled a large brooch, encircled with amethysts, from her tray. Lady Hazel nodded her acceptance.

"This ivory is slightly large for the brooch. Let me just . . ." Working quickly, Violet went through her slivers of ivory, selected one that was approximately the right size, and scraped along the edges gently with a metal file until it fit properly in the brooch. She slid the piece to Lady Hazel. The room was silent except for Violet's activity as the women watched, enthralled.

"You need some of this sepia paint. . . ." Violet selected a jar from her supplies and poured a bit out onto a small palette.

"It's just a drab, reddish brown," Louise said.

"Yes, Princess, made from the ink sac of the cuttlefish, then combined with gum arabic. It's a very popular medium. Leonardo da Vinci used it for his writings and drawings."

Louise frowned. "It still seems a bit dull."

"That is the exact point of sepia today. It gives the artwork a somber feeling, very appropriate for mourning jewelry."

Violet picked up the unraveled coil of Maud's hair. "Now I will snip just the barest amount from the end of this lock, and a tiny bit more, and again just as small a clipping as I can make." She did this over the poured sepia paint, then took a paintbrush and stirred the finely chopped hair into the sepia.

Sliding the brush and palette to Lady Hazel, Violet said, "You are ready, madam, to create your masterpiece."

Lady Hazel stared, dismayed, at what lay before her. "But what shall I paint?"

"I must confess, madam, that I am not much of an artist myself, but there are several themes that are popular. You might paint a crying angel, or an empty tomb to represent Lady Maud's ascent to heaven, or perhaps a weeping willow."

"What if I were to do all three?"

"Madam, if you are confident enough in your skill, then what you propose should result in a magnificent piece."

Lady Hazel began working and Violet continued her instruction.

"For those who would like to work Lady Maud's hair into jewelry, we will need this bottle of plain gum arabic, a pair of scissors, some wire . . ." Violet gathered all of the necessary tools. "I will also need the brazier."

The women stared at her.

"It contains several curling rods."

Still no one moved. Violet realized that she was instructing an aristocrat to do a task for her. She pushed her chair back to retrieve the brazier herself. Lady Marcheford giggled, and the rest of the women followed suit.

"Pardon us, Mrs. Harper. We are so accustomed to the brazier just appearing at our dressing tables and our maids preparing our hair that we weren't quite sure where to find it. I'll retrieve it." Lady Marcheford went to the fireplace.

"The gloves, my lady, the gloves!" Violet shouted. The woman was about to wrap her bare hands around the heated metal box.

"Oh, how very silly of me." Lady Marcheford stretched the gloves hanging next to the fireplace over her hands and brought the brazier to the table. Resting on a grate atop the box were several tiny, wood-handled iron rods, the iron made hot by smoldering coals resting below the grate.

Violet could only hope one of the women wouldn't end up with blisters upon her hands.

"First I will spread a small amount of gum arabic on the hair to help it stay together as we work with it." With another paintbrush, she dipped into the solution, then painted it onto the lock of hair. "Notice that I use just the sheerest amount of it, lest it make the hair sticky."

"Like the old wigs of the last century," another of Louise's friends said.

"Exactly, Lady . . . pardon me, I've forgotten."

"Julia Leventhorpe."

"Lady Julia's father is the Duke of Dunwall," Louise said. "Mother has been almost as interested in her marriage potential as my own."

"I see. Yes, Lady Julia, we don't want the hair to behave as was popular last century, what with bear grease used to stiffen and straighten towers of curls. We simply want to be able to work with it without it flying away from us."

Once she was satisfied with her application of the gum arabic, Violet snipped a six-inch length and painstakingly counted out sixty hairs. "Now we will make what is known as a Prince Regent's curl." She wrapped the top half of the hair around one of the thin iron rods. A puff of smoke gently drifted upward. After a few moments, she gently slid the rod out. The result was a tightly coiled end, making the hair resemble a letter "b."

"That's all?" Lady Julia said with a sniff. "That doesn't look like much."

"Ah, but we aren't quite finished. Who would like to donate some of her own hair to our final creation?"

"I'll do it," Lady Marcheford said, quickly undoing pins in her own coif, reaching for a pair of scissors, and clipping a lock of her own blond hair. It had coppery tones to it and was therefore darker than Lady Maud's.

"Lottie, you're so brave!" another girl said.

Lady Marcheford shrugged indifferently. "My hair is neither admired nor cherished. I much prefer to see it resting with Maud's.

Besides, Maud always appreciated unique artwork. I remember her once dabbling in china painting."

Violet nodded. "We don't have time for multiple washings, but I can see that your hair is quite clean, so we will continue with the same process." Violet clipped the correct length, applied gum arabic, counted out strands, and curled the hair on the iron rod.

"I now have both the Lady Maud's curled lock, as well as Lady Marcheford's donation. Watch." The women eagerly bent forward over the table nearly in unison. Atop another piece of ivory Violet laid out Maud's lock and carefully spread out the curled ends, so that they overlapped one another at an angle to the left. With Lady Marcheford's hair, she did the same thing, only in reverse, so that the curls pointed to the right.

"It looks like a plume of feathers," Louise said. "My mother has one of these made from my father's hair."

Violet quickly tied a thin piece of wire around the base of the two locks of hair to hold them together. From a capped jar she counted out three tiny seed pearls. "These represent the tears you shed for your dear friend."

Violet laid the pearls across the joined locks of hair where the wire was, to cover it. The gum arabic on the hair would adhere them. "There is much more you can do: Add a dried flower that was a favorite of Lady Maud's, or use a larger iron to make bigger curls, or add in a hair ribbon. Anything that makes it feel special so that you can hold her near to your heart."

Violet placed a thick piece of creamy writing stationery over the curled hair, then placed a thin block of wood over that, followed by a piece of metal that looked like a miniature brick. "We shall weigh this down for several hours; then it will be ready to be placed under a crystal top. Is everyone ready to try for herself?"

The women started their projects with great enthusiasm, although Lady Julia became quickly frustrated when her curled section of Maud's hair quickly frizzed from being wrapped around the iron too long.

"Please do not worry, my lady. You may try again from another lock of hair, or consider using the frizzed part in this manner." Violet worked the hair with her thumb and forefinger and laid it back down on Lady Julia's ivory.

"It resembles a bouquet of flowers," Lady Julia said. "Could I place pearls on the curls to represent their center pistils?"

"I think that's a wonderful idea."

Despite her chubby fingers, Lady Hazel showed remarkable talent wielding a paintbrush over the miniature surface. Already her ivory showed a clear outline of an angel facing left, bending and weeping into a cloth. To the right side of the angel was the narrow trunk of a tree, with leaves yet to be painted, and to the left side was the outline of a Gothic-style tomb. It looked nothing like the Gainsburgh family crypt, but Lady Hazel wouldn't know what it looked like, since she would have gotten no further than the chapel service, only departing before the men handled the actual interment. The bits of hair mixed into the sepia added depth and dimension to what she was creating.

"My lady, I am no expert, but I believe your work to be exquisite."

The young woman pinked even as she struggled to breathe. "My art tutor once told me . . . that if I wasn't destined . . . to make a great marriage . . . I might have been a great artist."

"Your future husband will be depriving the world of the next Leonardo da Vinci."

Lady Hazel blushed again and returned to gasping and painting.

As the women chattered and worked, periodically crying out triumphantly or groaning in despair at their efforts, Violet moved around their tables, offering suggestions and mentally totaling up what they were using in supplies and jewelry. As she came around to Louise's spot, the door opened and the queen's favorite dog, a border collie named Sharp, pranced in, followed closely by the queen herself.

The chattering stopped as the women jumped up to curtsy. Violet joined them.

Victoria gave a rare smile over their mourning activities. "We see you are making remembrances over your dearly departed friend. So poignant and so worthy. Louise, you are finally showing the sentimentality you lacked when your dear papa died."

"Yes, Mother," Louise said mechanically, returning to her work. The other women also went back to their seats.

"Mrs. Harper, a word?" Victoria passed back into the hallway, Sharp at her heels. Violet followed her and pulled the door closed behind her.

"How may I help you, ma'am?"

"We approve of what you are doing to assist these young ladies in their grief. Losing a loved one is so very difficult, is it not? You expect that he will be there forever to hold your hand in his dear, strong one, and then one day the one we all loved is gone to his Maker."

"Yes, Your Majesty."

"These little remembrances make the loss easier to bear." Victoria tapped her own mourning brooch. "Did you know that Beatrice is making an eye portrait of her darling father for us?"

"Yes, Your Majesty, she has considerable talent."

"She is without equal among my children. A rare orchid. So sweet, so agreeable. However, what we wished to discuss with you concerns the cost for their mourning jewelry. Kindly send the entire bill along to my lord chamberlain for payment. We shall pay for it from our personal purse."

"That is very generous, Your Majesty."

"No cost is too great in honoring those who have passed before us, Mrs. Harper." The queen swept away with Sharp, who offered Violet a happy farewell bark before leaping ahead of his mistress down the corridor.

As Violet turned back to Louise's rooms, Mr. Brown stepped out from the shadows. Once again, Violet was startled nearly witless, although the appearance of the Scottish ghillie wasn't nearly as frightening as a dead girl coughing.

"I've been searching for ye, Mrs. Harper."

"Indeed?"

"Sure, and I've been wondering if you've discovered what the cards mean."

"Actually, Mr. Brown, I've been a bit too preoccupied with

Lady Maud Winter's death and funeral to be concerned with your roving spirits."

Brown seemed to take no offense and instead nodded his head slowly. Once again, she caught the faint whiff of spirits—the liquid kind. "Aye, and there might be a connection between the Lady Maud and the spirits, dinnae ye think?"

"A connection between a consumptive young woman and the game of cards you're playing? I can hardly see what it could be."

"'Tis not a game, Mrs. Harper; 'tis a very serious matter. I see that we must have another reading."

"I hardly think another card reading could possibly—"

"I'll suggest it to Her Majesty. Expect an invitation." Brown sauntered off down the corridor.

In total exasperation, Violet pressed her head to the door before reentering the room to attend to the mourning jewelry.

Not again.

She sighed to exhale the dread that now overcame her each time she encountered the queen's servant, and turned the knob, returning to the world of hair jewelry, weeping angels, and mourning clothes, the world where she belonged.

Normally, Violet had little patience for spiritualists and mediums, but at the moment she sincerely wished she knew one who could convince Mr. Brown to fling himself from a window. The queen's servant sat once again before the ottoman in the queen's private sitting room, dealing out cards in the form of a cross.

Besides the queen and Violet, both Beatrice and her sickly brother, Leopold, as well as Bertie and his wife, Princess Alix, sat watching. Bertie's expression was one of utter boredom, something Violet felt but hoped her face didn't express. Leopold watched quietly, as if evaluating what was happening, whereas the other women were enthralled.

Even in the shadows of the dozens of candles Mr. Brown had arranged, which Violet had to admit lent a certain heightened atmosphere of expectation to the proceedings, she could see that Leopold was a very ill boy. He was supposedly sixteen but looked younger. His skin was translucent and papery, as if the slightest touch might tear him into pieces.

His hemophilia was not going to permit him a long life.

She shifted her attention back to Mr. Brown, who bade Victoria to touch the deck after he shuffled, then turned cards over while nodding gravely. For heaven's sake, if there was something the man wanted her to know, why not just say it and be done with it? Why the subterfuge? What was so fearsome he couldn't speak of it before the queen? And, if it had something to do with Lady Maud, how could it possibly have been so fearsome that he wouldn't risk a tongue-lashing in order to save the girl's life?

These questions gnawed at Violet as Brown examined the cards. "Look, wumman," he said. "Death in position five, which represents one possible outcome of events."

The queen gasped.

"Yes. Death, the Reaper, *La Mort*, as the French say."

"Oh dear," the queen said. "What do you think it means, Mr. Brown?"

"It may refer to Death himself, or that which surrounds death. Funerals, grief . . . undertakers." He had a mournful expression. "I believe the spirits grow anxious, dear lady."

"Anxious for what?"

"For the lady in black to find them."

All eyes turned to Violet.

I don't need a medium. I should just push him out the window mys—

"Mrs. Harper, have you been contacted yet?" Victoria asked.

"I'm afraid not, madam, although I have spent considerable time waiting. Of course, I have also been distracted by the funeral for—"

"Mr. Brown, our lord chamberlain has received notice from Scotland Yard that they are concerned about an evil presence, as well, just as you have been saying. Perhaps the spirits would speak through the cards and tell Mrs. Harper where she can find them."

"An excellent idea ye have. I shall gather them and reshuffle as such, yes, and now lay them out again." This time, he had the queen touch individually each card he'd dealt. As Brown was flipping over cards, he said, "Ah, most interesting, yes, most interesting. I feel . . . I feel . . ."

Alix spoke for the first time. "Yes, what do you feel? Is someone here?"

"No. The spirits are leading me on a merry chase through the palace." Brown closed his eyes and leaned back. "Through Her Majesty's state rooms, up the Grand Staircase, down the Grand Staircase, through the green drawing room, the throne room, gliding above the picture gallery. It's too fast; I cannae see it all. Slow down, spirits. Where are you really taking me?"

"To the refuse pile," Bertie muttered, which earned him a sharp look of disapproval from his mother.

"I am outside the palace now, hovering over Her Majesty's guard, now back over the rooftops. I see into rooms. I see Her Majesty sitting before a spread of the tarot, surrounded by her beloved children. . . ."

Bertie rolled his eyes as Alix leaned forward, breathless and both hands across her gradually swelling abdomen.

"Now we fly away from the palace—but to where, spirits? Nae, it cannae be! Why this? Why here?" Brown shook his head in wonder. "The stables? What is there to see here? A stall here, a trough there. What of it? Wait, 'tis nae fair, spirits, to darken the scene. Ye must return. What? What?" Brown's eyes fluttered open. "What happened? Your Majesty, you cannae imagine what just happened to me."

"But I can, Mr. Brown! I witnessed it for myself. Through your words, that is. The spirits took you all around the palace."

"Yes, that's it."

Bertie snorted. "Yes, that was certainly it."

"Dearest—" Alix said.

"Yes, yes, I know. I must behave myself. I'll hold my tongue, but only for you, Alix."

Brown turned to Violet. "And you, Mrs. Harper? Did you read anything in what happened?"

"I believe I'm beginning to understand what happened."

"Did you also sense the spirits, Mrs. Harper?" the queen asked. "We knew you were very spiritual."

"Yes, Your Majesty."

"Soon we shall all know what horrible thing surrounds us. We wonder, Mr. Brown . . . We wonder if the spirits are cautioning us about our upcoming Drawing Room event."

He nodded sagely. "If anything should happen at the Drawing Room, it would be personally devastating to ye."

"Oh, then perhaps we have solved the mystery of it all. Mrs. Harper, you must see what the stables have to do with our Drawing Room next week."

With the queen's eager blessing, Violet departed for the mews. She was halfway down the staircase when she heard a noise behind her. It was Beatrice on the top landing, staring at her with those serious eyes.

"Yes, Princess?"

"I should like to accompany you."

"You would? But why?"

The girl shrugged. "It would be interesting."

Violet doubted she'd find anything more interesting than a few broken horseshoes to step around, but it certainly wouldn't be dangerous. In fact, Beatrice might be useful. "Do you know of a rear exit from the palace to the mews?"

Beatrice nodded.

"Come along, then. Show me."

As the two walked to the stables, Violet took the opportunity to ask Beatrice questions about Mr. Brown, hoping she was being tactful and subtle.

"I can see that you admire Mr. Brown, Princess."

"He is Mama's special friend."

Violet nodded. "He seems to know a lot about the tarot."

"Mama says he is very gifted and very spiritual."

"I wonder if he knows secrets beyond the tarot."

Beatrice stopped to ponder this and shook her head. "Mama has never said so."

Violet realized that Beatrice's admiration of Brown was solely a reflection of the queen's adoration. The princess didn't know anything valuable.

Once again, Violet entered the Buckingham Palace mews, except this time with a twelve-year-old princess in her wake. Stable workers quickly dropped into poses of respect for Beatrice as they walked past. Assuming that Mr. Brown was guiding her to where they had met once before, she led Beatrice through the courtyard to the familiar row of stalls.

The princess was oblivious to what was probably a serious breach of etiquette—a member of the royal family stomping through straw and inspecting horse stalls, with an undertaker, no less. Instead, Beatrice seemed delighted with her role as Violet's assistant.

"Mrs. Harper," she said. "Do you suppose that, rather than looking for someone or something, we should let whatever it is find us?"

"An excellent idea. Where shall we wait?"

Beatrice shrugged, her shallow well of ideas now dry.

"What lies behind that doorway?" Violet asked, pointing to the other end of the long stable building.

Beatrice stared at her blankly, causing Violet to suppress a laugh. "Sorry, Princess. Of course, how would you know the layout of the mews? Let's go see."

They walked beneath the wide, curved arch that led them into yet another long building, this one containing a variety of small coaches for children, including a brightly painted snow sled, as well as some finer coaches with emblems, crests, and plumes decorating them.

It was, however, the coach in the center of the building that caused Violet to come to a standstill, with Beatrice nearly colliding into her.

Dominating everything else was a magnificent carriage, larger than any other she'd seen before—not counting public transport—whose ornate carvings gleamed in bold relief. It dwarfed everything else in size and pure ostentation.

"What is this?" she asked.

"The state coach," Beatrice said. "Mama rode to her crowning in it."

"How do you know? You weren't born for nearly twenty years after her coronation."

"Everyone in the family knows this. My brother Bertie will ride in it one day."

"It has no use other than to carry a king or queen a few blocks to Westminster Abbey to be crowned?"

"Mama doesn't like it. She says it has distressing osh-cu-lay-shuns."

"Oscillations?"

"Yes, that's it."

It was hard to imagine such an impressive work of art would be thoroughly uncomfortable to ride in.

Violet realized they'd been standing next to the state coach in solitude for several minutes, soaking in the resplendent grandeur and the history in which it had participated.

"Princess?" she said.

"Yes?"

"The spirits haven't visited us. I believe it's time we returned to seeking them out."

Beatrice nodded and followed Violet back through the buildings and into the courtyard. As they stood there, amid the commotion of wheels and hooves under a bright and cloudless sky, Violet had an idea.

"Princess, follow me." Violet headed for the staircase that Louise had stepped down recently. What had she been doing up in the stable workers' quarters that day? Violet had forgotten all about it in the tumult of Lady Maud's death.

"Madam, stop! You cannot go up there!" A stable worker scurried over just as Violet was putting her boot on the first step. She turned to face him and saw that he had dropped into a bow before Beatrice.

"I cannot do what?" Beatrice said.

"Pardon me, Your Highness, I did not realize . . . I mean, I only saw the undertaker. . . ." The man rose, and Violet realized it was the same groom who had stopped her the last time she was here.

Another groom sauntered up to see what was the matter. "Need help, Teddy?"

"No, Meredith, mind your business. You're new here and have no concerns with the princess."

"Doesn't mean I can't assist two lovely ladies." Meredith winked boldly at Beatrice.

"Go on with you. Back to whatever stall you were mucking."

The other man smiled and walked away as casually as he'd come.

Teddy scratched his cropped head. "Forgive me, Your Highness, but might I inquire as to what you need from our quarters? I'm happy to get whatever it is for you."

"Actually," Beatrice said in a tone of authority that suggested she might have been the queen herself, "we are meeting with the spirits and they may be waiting for us there."

The groom blinked in astonishment. "You plan to . . . ghosts . . . meeting with them . . ." The poor young man was stumbling again.

"What the princess means to say is that we have business upstairs that is quite secret. Can you keep a secret—Teddy, is it?"

"Yes, ma'am, of course, ma'am."

"Then tell no one of our visit here. It's vital that no one knows the Princess Beatrice was in the mews."

He straightened up. "You can rely on me, ma'am. I'll make sure Meredith and the other boys keep their yaps shut—pardon me, I mean that they keep quiet about your visit, too."

"The princess is grateful." Violet nodded at Beatrice, who took the undertaker's cue to offer him her hand. The poor boy nearly fell over in awe but composed himself enough to take it and bow over it.

Thus freed from the attention of the mews workers, Violet and Beatrice crept upstairs to see if anyone—or any spirit—awaited them there. The rooms up here were hidden behind nondescript doors every few feet, all along a catwalk above the courtyard. Should they knock on doors? Simply enter them?

"Why don't we walk along slowly? Perhaps we'll hear something."

"What kind of sounds do the spirits make, Mrs. Harper?"

"Oh, I imagine they'll sound very close to human."

They walked along the catwalk slowly, with Violet tilting her ear toward the doors and Beatrice trailing her fingers along the metal handrail. At the end of the row of doors, Violet stopped before the last one, hearing voices. She frowned. It couldn't be.

"What do you hear, Mrs. Harper?"

Violet put a finger to her lips. Beatrice nodded. She and Violet were not the only females in the stable workers' quarters, as unmistakably female voices floated out through the door. She bent to listen, and Beatrice joined her.

". . . if they think they can stop us—" This voice was familiar, but Violet couldn't place it.

"Why isn't Mrs. Butler here?" A different voice.

"She has gone to see Dr. Garrett." Yet another woman speaking.

". . . intolerable. They will have to realize that we won't permit this situation to continue."

At this voice, Violet jerked upright. Beatrice, too, must have realized who it was, for she gasped and covered her mouth.

It was Princess Louise speaking. What did she find intolerable, and to what would she resort to stop it?

"Princess," Violet whispered. "I think we've found Mr. Brown's spirit."

The continued conversation behind the door was too garbled to understand, so Violet signaled that they should leave.

As they reached the bottom of the stairs, the groom named Meredith was waiting for them. "Your Highness, do you need a carriage made ready for you? I would be pleased to drive you."

"No, I don't leave the palace without my mother."

"And yet here you are. Maybe you'd like a visit to the confectionery or doll shop?"

Beatrice slipped behind Violet, whose maternal urge began coursing heavily through her veins. "Thank you, we do not need passage anywhere, we'll just be returning to the palace. All we need is for our path to be cleared."

Meredith stepped back and swept an arm to indicate the walkway. "As you wish," he said.

Violet had seen her fair share of insolent and disrespectful household servants, having never been able to successfully manage them herself, but this young man was different. It was as though he was practically mocking her and the princess.

How had he ever been hired to work in the queen's palace?

Violet had no time to wonder about it, for the more troubling question was whom Louise was associating with and what sort of activity she was involved in.

Pray God it wasn't treasonous.

As Beatrice and Violet neared a rear entrance to the palace, she said, "Princess, I think we should keep what happened today between us."

"Oh yes." Beatrice nodded her understanding with a wisdom beyond her years. "Mama would never forgive Louise for being in the stable workers' quarters unaccompanied."

That, Violet feared, was the least of Louise's troubles.

Reese Meredith's luck was holding. Only at Buckingham Palace just over a week and already he'd met a member of the royal family. It was just a girl, not the queen, but who knew they would deign to crawl around the mews? He'd seen one of the elder daughters also wandering around recently.

But who was the woman in black? A governess? A spinster relative, one of those poor-cousin types who rely on the charity of wealthier family members? Maybe she'd been recently widowed. She was far too familiar with the young princess, and far too well dressed, to be an ordinary servant. She was also far too haughty.

No matter. What was of concern was that she was very protective of the little princess and seemingly in her company with some regularity, which made Reese wonder if the woman also spent time with the queen.

The woman in black would bear careful watching. If she was an aristocrat, she'd learn only too well what happened to them.

Violet regretted that she hadn't gone straight to the queen with her minimal knowledge of Louise's activities, for here she was, riding in a carriage with the queen to Cumberland Lodge. This residence, located on the grounds of Windsor Castle, was home to Victoria's twenty-three-year-old daughter, Princess Helena, and her husband, Prince Christian of Schleswig-Holstein.

The queen's latest idea was to have a tarot card reading at Princess Helena's home, not only to "further explore the spirits' meaning" but also to entertain the sickly Helena, who Victoria said was having a relapse of her "malaise."

If only Violet hadn't decided to keep things to herself for the moment. Without full knowledge of what Louise and her compatriots were discussing, though, it seemed rash and premature to report it to the queen. What would she say? That Louise was gossiping with friends in the grooms' quarters at the mews? And what could be the possible repercussions? Beatrice's prediction of unforgiveness? Not exactly a conclusion to whatever evil might be lurking about the palace.

Not only that, a report like that to the queen would earn Violet Louise's enmity.

No, despite a ride to yet another tarot card reading, one that she was now certain was an ongoing fraud Mr. Brown was perpetrating and that he was not a genuine seer, it was better to endure another one of his sessions than to risk unnecessary condemnation.

For heaven's sake, she wasn't even sure what she was looking for yet.

The queen had been chatty on the train ride to Windsor, discussing the foibles of her children and her now growing bevy of grandchildren, with a particular emphasis on Helena.

"Helena," Victoria confided, "is a bit *too* sickly. Complains about this condition and that disease, but we believe she really suffers from hypochondria. Nothing whatsoever really wrong with her except boredom. Now, when our dear prince, Albert, was still alive, it was obvious that he genuinely suffered. . . ."

Violet sought haven in her own thoughts as Victoria waxed on about Albert's virtues, which surpassed those of all his children combined.

After the train ride to Windsor, the groom named Meredith handed them into a carriage and drove them from the palace to Cumberland Lodge inside Windsor's Great Park. The queen was finally changing subjects.

"Tell me, Mrs. Harper, is your husband still involved in that distasteful dynamite business?"

"Yes, Your Majesty. He is currently in Wales with Mr. Nobel, trying to convince the authorities there to allow for a dynamite factory."

The queen shuddered. "If it happens, we shall have to avoid any visits to Wales. We could not risk the danger to our person."

"I don't believe that any factory would be located near the center of a city."

"Nevertheless, it seems an unpleasant sort of affair. We warn you, Mrs. Harper, that terrible things will come from your husband's involvement in it."

"Yes, Your Majesty."

As Meredith handed the queen out of the carriage at Cumberland Lodge, she turned back to warn Violet once more. "Mind you, it would be wise for your husband to abandon his plans for a dynamite factory."

"Yes, Your Majesty."

Meredith gave Violet a peculiar stare as he handed her out, as though he, too, was offended by Sam's investigation into a dynamite factory.

Violet was overwhelmed inside the grand Tudoresque home, not by the architecture or luxurious furnishings but by the gathering. Whenever she encountered a finely dressed group of people, it was typically for a funeral and she was in charge. Here she was completely out of place. At least everyone else was also wearing black, although whether this was for the queen's benefit or their own private grief Violet couldn't tell.

Louise was there, standing next to Lord and Lady Marcheford, whom Violet recognized from Gainsburgh House. She assumed the dowdy-looking woman and grizzled man next to her were Princess Helena and Prince Christian. Heavens, Helena was only twenty-three, so her husband looked an aged uncle standing next to her. Meanwhile, Mr. Brown sat at an impressively large, round mahogany table surrounded by nine other chairs, shuffling cards and ignoring the royal presences.

Violet was introduced and made her curtsies, and she could see the curiosity in everyone's face except that of Lady Marcheford, who complimented Violet's expertise in making mourning jewelry and pointed to the brooch on her bodice.

"Of course, it's nothing as brilliant as Lady Hazel's miniature painting."

Violet agreed. Lady Marcheford's hair collage was done competently, but her friend had shown considerable talent with a paintbrush. "Your brooch is very lovely, and something I'm sure would bring tears to Lady Maud's eyes."

Charlotte's own eyes watered, but she sniffed back her grief. "Yes, if only she could see it."

As the others stood talking in their own private groups, Violet turned to Louise. "Your Highness, are the Prince and Princess of Wales to be in attendance?"

The princess laughed. "You must be joking. Alix at Cumberland Lodge? It will never happen."

"Pardon my intrusion, but why is this?"

"She never approved of Helena's marriage to Christian. You see, Helena and her husband are actually third cousins in descent through Frederick, Prince of Wales, in the last century. Christian is also a third cousin to Alix through Frederick the Fifth of Denmark. We royals cannot stop marrying each other, although I don't plan to follow suit in all of this foolishness.

"Anyway, Alix thought Christian was entirely too closely related to too many branches of the tree, so to speak, and was vocal about her objections. My mother, though, had already approved the union, and was quite put out to be challenged by a daughter-in-law. To maintain peace, Alix and Bertie avoid attendance at most events involving Helena and Christian, and my mother pretends she has forgiven Alix for her impudence."

How utterly complicated royal lives were.

Mr. Brown cleared his throat, his signal that the reading was to begin. The tarot reading room was brightly lit and a large, ornately framed photograph of Albert resting on a floor easel dominated the room. Victoria put her fingers to her lips and then delicately to Albert's face as she walked past it to the table, and so the others followed suit, Violet included.

The reading began like the others, with Mr. Brown arranging the cards in a cross formation, with a column of four cards next to it. This time, though, he asked the queen to place her hand over the cards in the center of the cross. "To bless the spirits, Your Majesty," he said.

Victoria tittered.

To Violet's surprise, though, today's reading was actually different. He presented the usual statements of evil lurking about, then went in a different direction. "Ah, a two of pentacles," Brown said, flipping over the sixth card in the cross pattern. "Notice that he walks upon a rope. He is pulled in many directions. He walks a fine line between good and evil, happiness and anguish. This represents the near future, dear lady, so let us see what the remaining cards have to say about the outcome, and the hopes and fears that will influence it."

Brown quickly flipped over the remaining cards and studied them, nodding and sighing. "Yes, someone in this room is bound to come to grief for his foul actions . . . or perhaps they are the actions of a woman."

"A woman? What a thought!" Helena said, wagging her head. "Next thing you know we'll be accused of starting wars and murdering vagrants. Can you imagine me lopping heads off, my love?" Helena brayed loudly and turned to Christian, who grinned back stupidly through his gray beard and mustache.

"It is hard to imagine you involved in anything underhanded, my pet, my little Lenchen, although if you have learned to use a hunting rifle, I could use you on safari."

Husband and wife found his statement uproarious, while the rest of the table remained silent.

Mr. Brown ignored the interruption and proceeded with his reading once more. "What is being done must be cut off, and be done no more."

"If they think they can stop us—" Lady Marcheford said.

"Lottie, hush," Louise said. "I'm sure we'll know more when Mr. Brown is finished with his reading."

"What are you talking about?" Lord Marcheford demanded. "Are you up to something untoward again, Lottie?"

Charlotte's face flamed at being openly castigated by her husband in front of the queen. "No, no, I was just thinking of . . . ah . . . the little party we had to make mourning jewelry for Maud."

Violet was still, certain the color had just drained from her face. Lady Marcheford's was one of the voices she'd heard in the mews. Was it a coincidence that she and Louise were meeting so soon after Lady Maud's death? Was it her death to which they referred? Violet tried to remember. Wasn't there mention of a doctor, a Dr. Garrett? Perhaps the women were investigating Lady Maud's death on their own?

If so, then what did it have to do with Mr. Brown's conjuring of mysterious spirits who were revealing a treasonous evil within Buckingham Palace? Had the Lady Maud indeed been murdered, as Louise claimed?

Moreover, was Brown aware of their meetings and trying in his own way to stop them? If so, why didn't he merely speak up? Why did he see it as Violet's responsibility to interfere?

Whether or not Lady Maud was murdered, Violet was beginning to see that there was something afoot at Buckingham Palace, and she planned to make a point of discovering what really lay beneath the tarot card readings.

"So, Inspectors, what did you discover?" Henderson said, scratching at his side-whiskers, a habit that Hurst had adopted more than a year ago, much to his own chagrin. Why was he imitating his superior's nervous quirks?

"First, Commissioner," Hurst said, "we assessed what exactly had happened. Sometimes the newspapers muck the story up to suit themselves, as you know, sir. We know for certain that the drawings regarding the incident in the papers were wholly inaccurate.

"We conducted numerous interviews." Hurst nodded to Pratt, who held up his battered leather notebook. "We worked with local constabulary to find as many people as possible who were present at the riot. We focused especially on the family members of those who died, either at the hands of the soldiers or in the general melee. Most were cooperative; some were not."

"Yes, and?"

"There was only one victim for whom we couldn't talk to a family member. It was a young woman, aged nineteen, name of . . . what was it?"

Pratt flipped through his notebook. "Margaret Younghusband."

"Right, Margaret Younghusband. She was one of the first shot. Someone saw her rushed off in the arms of a stranger, to the nearby Free Church on Tyddyn Street. She died there, and was later buried at the back of Mold Parish Church in an unmarked grave. Locals told us that she had a half brother by the name of Reese Meredith. A few years older than Margaret, he started off as a wagon driver for the Leeswood colliery, then went off to fight in the Second Opium War ten years ago. Since then, his whereabouts have been sketchy. Most people assumed he would come back to take care of Margaret, since she was all alone except for him. Her parents—his father—died in a typhoid outbreak several years ago. They have as many outbreaks among the poor as we do here in England. Meredith was taking care of her, and managed to see her into service with a wealthy family, rather than see her turned into a mine rat."

"Good brotherly love, that," said the commissioner.

"Yes. He returned briefly after he was released from Her Majesty's service, then disappeared. There were occasional letters from various estates where he obtained employment, but they'd stopped some time ago. Last anyone knew, he was working on a Cornish estate."

"Why so much interest in him? Is he just a lost brother?"

"Maybe. Everyone else we interviewed seemed clear to us, but what we heard about this Meredith fellow, well . . ."

"Well, what?"

"Looks like he had a bit of a temper. Once got in a row with a man in a pub over a game of skittles. Nearly choked the other man to death. Most people figured it was due to Meredith being affected by the war, but it shows he is prone to violence. I'm not comfortable with the thought that we don't know where he is."

"Why don't you start looking for anyone named Reese Meredith living in Great Britain?"

Hurst tried not to show his annoyance. As though this were his first case and he would have never considered such basic investigative work. "Yes, sir, we are working on that. It's not an easy task."

Pratt spoke up. "There must be hundreds of birth registries listing a Reese Meredith, sir. It's a common name."

Henderson nodded. "Excellent."

"Yes," Hurst said. "We also propose putting police on duty at *The Times* offices, in case Meredith comes along, looking for Mr. Walter."

"Very good. What next?"

"We'll comb through whatever exists of Her Majesty's records of men who served in China. They're usually disorganized and confused, with little relation to who really served where, but we'll make our best attack at it, so to speak. Reese Meredith won't get away with anything while we're after him; you can be sure of that, sir."

He waited patiently on the servants' staircase, off the corridor near Lady Marcheford's private rooms. She'd be home soon from whatever excursion of shopping for fripperies and baubles she was on. In her thrall of her purchases, she wouldn't notice him; she'd be too busy counting gemstones and adding another piece of Wedgwood to her collection.

He smiled as he contemplated what was to come next, his only companion the sound of a grandfather clock ticking somewhere. All of the servants were out; he'd made sure of that. No, nothing could possibly interfere with his task.

Tick-TOCK-tick-TOCK.

He'd been looking forward to this. She deserved it, pathetic creature that she was.

Tick-TOCK-tick-TOCK.

To occupy his time, he rummaged through his case of tools, to make sure everything was there. Of course it was. He knew what he was doing.

Tick-TOCK-tick-TOCK.

A door opened and shut, and he heard Lady Marcheford call out for her husband. She wouldn't find him waiting in the parlor today.

Finally, her dainty steps made their way up the main staircase.

He crouched lower, although it was impossible for her to see him where he was. Once he heard her enter her rooms and the door click quietly behind her, he stood erect and took a deep breath for the necessary undertaking that lay before him.

Hah, undertaking! Charlotte would need an undertaker soon. Which reminded him of that curious woman in black. Who was she, really? Why was she so cozy with the royal family?

He strode to the eight-paneled door and placed his hand on the polished brass knob. Power surged through him as it always did, his sign from the heavens that he was to be successful.

Some might have said that this was the devil's work, but then, those weren't people who'd felt the apexes of joy and the depths of despair he had, who had experienced the vagaries of life the way he had.

He turned the knob and entered.

Lady Marcheford was arranging gloves—shop tags still dangling from them—inside boxes. Funny, that was something she should have saved for her maid to do. She looked up at him in surprise. "What are you doing here?"

"I've been waiting for you."

"Why would you be wait—" She stopped, speechless, as he opened his case, pulled something out, and showed it to her.

"Be calm, and all will be over soon," he said.

But she was not calm, no, not at all, and he soon realized that she would be much more difficult to subdue than her friend was.

6

"Now do you believe me?" Louise said, her eyes wild with grief.

Violet stood in Lady Marcheford's bedchamber with Louise and Lord Marcheford. Charlotte lay slumped over the bed, her feet trailing on the floor. A bloodstained handkerchief lay next to her, and more than a dozen pairs of newly purchased, boxed gloves were scattered on a table. It seemed an extraordinary number of them for a single day's shopping. Violet's overall impression of the room was that it was . . . unsettled. As though there had been a disturbance in the room and someone had quickly cleaned it up. The room was tidy, and yet it was unbalanced.

The same could be said for Lord Marcheford. His clothing was impeccable, as though he'd just dressed for an evening out, but he was nervous and jittery.

"I don't know what to think, Your Highness. My lord, you must be very grieved. Would you like to step out while I examine your wife?"

Ripley's eyes darted to and fro, as though he wanted to avoid what lay before him. "No, no, I'm fine. It's best to know what happened."

Violet sat on the bed next to Charlotte and stroked the woman's hair. "Dear girl, what happened to you? Did you fall ill, or was this something else?"

Violet looked around the girl's body and picked up the handkerchief, which was brown and encrusted with blood, presumably Charlotte's. She opened it, examining it closely; then she folded it in such a way as to concentrate the dark stains in one location of the cloth.

"It looks as though Lady Marcheford may have coughed this up. Was she ill, sir?"

"A little. She didn't complain much of it, though. She was too preoccupied to be much worried about illness." Ripley gave Louise a dark look.

Although she was eaten up in grief from the death of two friends, his comment caused Louise to raise an eyebrow, giving her the haughty expression that only royalty can wear well. "I'm sure *you* were much too preoccupied to worry over her illness."

The battle between grieving friends and relatives was one Violet had witnessed many times, and one in which she always stepped in to conciliate. "May we conclude, then, that Lady Marcheford suffered from the initial stages of consumption, or some other lung disease?"

"Perhaps," Louise said. "But that doesn't explain why she is fallen over her bed."

No, it didn't.

"Can *you* explain it, Marcheford?" Louise demanded.

"I cannot. But I can guess that you overworked the woman to death."

Violet stepped in again. "I think we might get to the bottom of the matter if we discuss this together, rather than accusing one another. Let me ask some more questions. First, who found her?"

"Killigrew, her lady's maid. Killigrew was out visiting her sister, and when she came back to attend to my wife's clothing for dinner, she found her like this."

"She has not been moved?"

"I don't think so."

"I see. And what was Lady Marcheford doing earlier in the day?"

"She went shopping, as she always does."

Louise spoke up again. "You say this as though it were merely to destroy the Marcheford fortune. You know fully well that everything she purchased went to—" She stopped.

Lord Marcheford pressed her. "Go on, say it, Princess. All of it—including this sprawling collection of gloves bought from my own allowance—goes to those despicable friends of yours."

What were these two talking about? Whatever it was, Violet wouldn't have it conducted before Lady Marcheford. "I believe you are both in too delicate a condition to remain while I examine her in detail to determine how she died."

Violet knew that she should draw in Scotland Yard, but not before she had a chance to look things over. Otherwise, her talents would be dismissed and she would be relegated to counting floral urns.

"How will you know by looking at her?" Lord Marcheford asked.

"She will tell me."

"She will tell you? You're beginning to sound like the Scottish Sage, Mr. Brown."

"Mr. Brown and I each have our own techniques. Now if you will both be so kind . . ."

The princess and Lord Marcheford left, renewing their argument as they went. Violet returned her attention to Lady Marcheford, gently squeezing an arm in several places. "This is not a good time for your rigor mortis to be setting in, my lady. I ask that you be done with it quickly. May I turn you over?"

In her current position, Lady Marcheford was difficult to move; however, with some acrobatic skill, Violet managed to push Charlotte forward and get her feet on the bed. That done, Violet turned Charlotte over.

And gasped in shock.

Beneath the woman's body lay her open reticule. In one hand, she gripped the derringer she'd shown Violet. The one she'd purchased to protect her from her husband.

Why was it in her hand? If she'd drawn it out, it must have been because she'd felt threatened. Was Lady Marcheford indeed forced to use it against her husband? Obviously, her murderer was able to overcome her before she could use it. Violet gently removed the gun from the woman's hand, also a difficult task, since rigor mortis was stiffening her hand into a claw around the weapon.

Once Violet disengaged it, she tucked it back into Lady Marcheford's reticule and hung the bag by its drawstring around the doorknob. She then worked to place Lady Marcheford in an elegant position against her pillows.

Violet was sweating by the time she'd laid the woman out properly on the bed.

She sat at the edge of the bed next to Lady Marcheford and put a hand to the dead woman's face. "My lady, you will need some work to bring your face back to its state of beauty. Let me get my—" Violet sniffed the air.

What was that? It wasn't the stench of decay, Lady Marcheford hadn't been gone that long, but it was . . . strange. Sensing the direction from which the odor was emanating, Violet slipped to the floor and looked under the bed. Her hand touched a damp, wadded-up cloth, and she pulled it out, bringing it to her nose. It was sharply acrid . . . and familiar. It didn't have the odor of death attached to it, but it was strong with the underlying stench of what she'd smelled before, on the scrap of fabric she extricated from Lady Maud's mouth.

Well, here was one connection between Lady Maud and Lady Marcheford. Was there another?

Violet quickly searched Lady Marcheford's neck but saw nothing. "Were you bitten elsewhere?" she asked, running her hands up and down the countess's arms. Nothing there. Violet expanded her search over Lady Marcheford's body.

"Ah, what have we here?" Violet felt the same bumps behind Lady Marcheford's left knee. "A clever little wasp to sting you back here. Were you allergic, my lady?"

Now there were two connections between Lady Maud and Lady Marcheford, but what did they mean?

Violet couldn't understand the association, but there was one thing she knew for certain. It was time to bring in Scotland Yard.

Violet sat once more before Commissioner Henderson, privately discussing recent events. She'd first met him during the investigation over Lord Raybourn's death, and he had been a friend when others in his department had not.

". . . so you see, sir, although both women were ill, and neither one came to any sort of obvious bad end, the Princess Louise is understandably nervous, since both were her friends. She is concerned that someone may be after all of her associates, or perhaps even the princess herself."

"You say you tended to these bodies, Mrs. Harper. Did you notice anything peculiar about them? Strangulation marks? Any blood whatsoever?"

Should she mention the bite marks and the foul-smelling cloths? The apparent bite marks may have been just that, a stinging from an angry wasp, or the attack of a determined horsefly. As for the fabric, well, it would be humiliating for the Gainsburghs to hear that their daughter may have been chewing on cloth scraps.

Violet pulled the cloth she'd found under Lady Marcheford's bed from her reticule. "I did find this in Lady Marcheford's room."

"It looks like a lady's handkerchief."

"Smell it."

Henderson took it, raised it to his nose, and looked at her, puzzled. "I smell something faint on it, perhaps an old perfume or maybe something it rubbed against in your bag."

"What?" Violet took the cloth back and sniffed it again. The strong odor was nearly faded.

"Are you having a bit of fun with me, madam?"

"No, to the contrary. This handkerchief had a very peculiar smell. It was quite pungent, unlike anything I've smelled before."

"Yes. Did you notice anything else?"

"Well, yes, actually. When I rearranged Lady Marcheford, I found a derringer tucked in her hand."

Henderson sat straight up. "She was holding a pistol? Had it been fired? Were there any blasts in the wall?"

"No. I doubt it had ever been fired."

Henderson relaxed again. "It's quite fashionable for women to carry them. So she was in some sort of delirium and she began brandishing her derringer. Or she carried it about in a pocket and it fell out as she lay dying of her illness."

"Yes, perhaps. As I said, the Princess Louise is quite upset. Could you provide some protection to the queen's Drawing Room, being held in three days? There will be many young ladies there, some of Louise's acquaintance. If there is indeed something amiss, it would make everyone feel safer if you had men there."

Henderson considered this. "Actually, your request is more fortuitous than you think." He leaned back, his chair creaking beneath his shifting weight. "There is another case I have Inspectors Hurst and Pratt working on that makes guarding the queen a timely occasion."

"Do you believe the queen to be in trouble?"

"No, no. Everything is fine. But we are interested in taking precautions where we can."

Violet left Scotland Yard, nervous and even looking over her shoulder at imagined shadows as she walked through St. James's Park to her rooms at the palace. Whatever it was that Mr. Brown was trying to convey, there was no doubt that something was very, very wrong within the royal family.

That woman again.

Hurst crossed his arms as he and Pratt sat across from the commissioner again. "Do we really have to work with her again?"

Hurst heard the whiny sound of his own voice and cringed. Had his trip to Brighton turned him from a man into a child?

Henderson had little sympathy. "You've worked with her before, and quite successfully, I might add."

"Mrs. Harper figured out what happened to Lord Raybourn," Pratt offered.

"Yes, well, she needed our help for it. We would have gotten to the answer sooner except for her nagging."

Pratt turned back to the commissioner. "A very interesting profession she has, sir, caring for the dead and all. She truly enjoys it."

Hurst snorted. "Which tells us how peculiar she is."

"What is your grievance against Mrs. Harper?" Henderson asked.

"I say he dislikes her because she doesn't tolerate his churlishness," Pratt said.

Hurst turned and glared at Pratt. He would see to it that Pratt would be walking night duty in Nichol Street, rounding up the

Romany and sending them to the workhouses. It was bad enough he might have to work with the uppity Violet Harper; he certainly wouldn't take beetle-headed insults from his underling.

"A woman should be more reserved and . . . elegant than Mrs. Harper is."

"I hardly think we are trying to evaluate the situation based upon our ideals of feminine womanhood, Inspector," Henderson said. "She has brought us a credible threat to Her Majesty's person, or at least to others around her. I think it wise that we cover the queen's Drawing Room. You have both worked with Mrs. Harper before, so I want you to take care of this."

"It seems to me that a regular bobby could handle this, since it isn't as though it concerns an actual murder or anything that Scotland Yard typically handles."

"And it seems to *me*, Inspector, that you will do this because it involves the safety of Her Majesty the Queen."

Hurst swore inwardly at his own stupidity. What kind of dunderhead refused an opportunity to serve the queen because he didn't like Her Majesty's undertaker? He was turning himself into a three-pointed, bell-tipped fool's cap. Not his usual standard for his position as a detective chief inspector, and most definitely not a standard by which to attract a potential wife.

"You are right, of course, Commissioner. My apologies."

"Pride is our enemy, Inspector. Don't let it fog your judgment. It has prevented you from picking up on the obvious."

"The obvious, sir?"

Henderson shook his head, as if explaining something to an errant boy at Harrow School. "What might a possible threat to the queen—realistic or not, whether reported by someone you respect or not—have to do with your own case?"

"Our letter writer, you mean."

Henderson nodded. "How is your search coming along with the War Office's records?"

Hurst snorted again. Good Lord, he really needed to stop producing such obnoxious noises. What woman would marry a man who sounded like a bull about to make a charge?

"About as quickly as investigating a murder in the Old Nichol."

"Perhaps you will have your man in the next three days. In fact, imagine the queen's appreciation if you could nab him before he does something nefarious at an important event at Buckingham Palace. There could be quite a reward in it for you. It wouldn't hurt Scotland Yard's reputation, either."

"If he's there, we'll find him," Hurst said.

He and Pratt left Henderson's office and went to find something to eat from a street cart. Pratt said nothing but continued looking at him with such inquisitive eyes that Hurst finally turned to him and said, "Oh, do be quiet, will you?"

There was nothing worse than an officer who could ask thousands of personal questions without saying a word.

Violet had never seen the queen so angry before. Unfortunately, it was all directed at her.

"Mrs. Harper, we were quite specific about wanting you *personally* to see to whatever danger lurked about the palace. We will not have our Drawing Room turned into a policemen's *Zirkus* under a tent, which the press will turn into weeks of sensationalism. Now our servants will have to be briefed on how to handle these officers, we will undoubtedly have to feed them, and they will be crawling about as though they are in ownership of our *Haus*. We cannot think of a more ghastly and loathsome way to spend the afternoon, other than hosting the Drawing Room itself, of course." The queen paused, closed her eyes, and drew a deep breath. A little fleck of spittle lingered at the corner of her mouth.

Violet braced herself for more.

"Just imagine how these young women being presented to us will feel. Yes, Scotland Yard will give us all assurances that they will be discreet and careful, but they won't be. The *Offiziere* will ogle these ladies of society, and come up with excuses to be near them, and will walk across the palace's fine carpets in their *schmutzig*, unpolished boots. Honestly, might it not be better to postpone than have to endure such distress?"

"Your Majesty, please allow me to explain—"

"As though there isn't enough disorder in the household, what with Louise and her refusal to take a husband. Then we have Bertie's peccadilloes and his boorish attitude toward dear Mr. Brown. Not to mention *wir haben Angst* over Leopold's health. If our darling Albert were here, he'd take it all well in hand, especially Bertie. Instead, we must suffer on alone, with no guide and no comfort—"

"Your Majesty, I apologize abjectly; however—"

"—to assist us through our troubles. We have so many national problems to which to attend, with only an inadequate prime minister to rely upon. . . ."

Violet took her verbal beating with patience, imagining she was being set upon by a newly widowed woman who was thoroughly unhappy with both the engraving on her husband's stone and the size of the boxwoods planted to either side of it. It was the same sort of lashing Violet had received many times.

When the queen was worn-out and panting from the exertion of it all, Violet said, "Yes, Your Majesty, you are right to be so upset. May I suggest, though, that I instruct Scotland Yard to be as discreet as possible, lest they risk royal displeasure? Their respect for Your Majesty is great, and I am certain they will wish to honor your wishes."

"Well, yes, we suppose it's possible to be done without total catastrophe. You may do as you suggest, but we will expect your presence for the Drawing Room to ensure nothing is disrupted as a result of their endeavors."

"You may rely upon me, madam."

Violet fled as soon as she could. Who knew that managing royals was more difficult than managing the grieving?

Louise and her friends sat again at tables, subdued and bleary-eyed, as Violet taught them a new technique in creating mourning jewelry.

"Today we will learn how to make a hair bracelet, or a gentleman's watch chain if you prefer. This is table work, as opposed to the pallet work of the brooches you made earlier. You will complete all of your work at one of the three braiding tables you see here."

Violet pointed to one of the tables, which was about two feet in diameter and stood thirty-two inches high, for someone to stand before while braiding hair. A finger-width hole was bored into the center of the table. Standing was much preferable to sitting in order to get steady pressure on the work.

"Notice that the table is perfectly smooth. If there was even the slightest rough edge in the surface, the hair would quickly break while working on it, and destroy the beauty of your creation."

Silence from her patrons.

"I have brought with me bundles of virgin hair from northern European peasant girls, of no older than age twenty-five, to ensure the hair has not been too damaged by sun, wind, and rain. This hair has never been bleached or stained, and, as you can see, was grown to more than thirty inches before being cut. It is the most exclusive of hair, much more valuable than horsehair from China or yak hair from Tibet.

"Because a hair bracelet requires so much volume of hair in the plaiting of it, we will use a quantity of this hair, interspersed with some of Lady Marcheford's. I believe the effect will be very pleasing."

She may as well have been talking to people who were dead themselves, so vacant and disinterested were their stares. She plowed on doggedly.

"Observe as I remove about half the hair from this bundle, add in some of Lady Marcheford's clipped lock, dab a tiny amount of gum arabic to the tip, then roll about half the hair around a very thin bobbin, as such. The gum arabic will prevent the hair from falling off the bobbin. I will drop this weighted end into the hole in the center of the table. Now I will spread the hair out around the tabletop, counting out twenty-five strands at a time and securing each end to another bobbin."

She worked painstakingly on the hair to an unappreciative audience. Losing two friends in such a short amount of time had to have been devastating. Perhaps it was just too soon for these women to do anything but grieve.

By the time she was finished, she had sixteen bobbin-weighted locks dangling off the table, divided into groups of four, each bobbin numbered from one to four. The hair was ready to be worked.

"Your Highness, would you like to be the first to try?" Violet said, holding up a knitting needle.

"I suppose." Louise dragged herself to the braiding table and listlessly wove together some strands around the needle under Violet's guidance. The room had the air of a mausoleum.

Desperate to cheer the women up, or at least distract them, Violet said, "The queen wears a lock of her husband's hair in a brooch over her heart. She will probably be most envious of what you create here today." More silence ensued.

"It looks a bit like the old bobbin lace weaving," Lady Julia said.

Finally, a crumb of interest. "Yes, madam, it is very similar, except that we do not pin the hair down to a pillow as we weave it."

"Lottie would have been awful at this, wouldn't she? She was all thumbs," someone else said.

There was laughter, and even Louise broke into a wan smile of agreement. "I imagine Lottie would have this in a complete knot by now. Am I still doing it properly, Mrs. Harper?"

"Yes. Remember, though, that for this design bobbins numbered one and two will move to the left, and threes and fours will move to the right."

Violet set up the other two braiding tables and set two other women to work while the remaining women called for tea. As she assisted the hairwork efforts, the tea drinkers eventually relaxed and chatted among themselves, about reports from Lady Marcheford's funeral ("dignified," "just how she would have wanted it") and then about her husband.

"What do you think, Hazel?" Lady Julia said. "Do you think Marcheford drove her to a quick end?"

"It wouldn't surprise me if he had a hand in her death," Lady Hazel said. Her bodice was close to releasing its captive body parts as she nibbled at a slice of lemon cake. "He's always struck me as quite unkind."

"But quite well proportioned," said one of the hair weavers, joining in with the conversation.

"And fashionable," added another.

"Don't forget his rakish smile," a woman drinking tea said.

"The man is a louse," Louise declared bluntly. "Hazel is right. He probably had a hand in her death."

"Did he know about Charlotte's work with the repeal group?" This, too, came from someone in the tea klatch.

"Of course he did," Louise replied. "He despised her for it, but it didn't stop her."

Did this have something to do with what Lady Marcheford mentioned at the tarot reading, which Louise hushed down? Violet stepped out of her proper social place to ask a question.

"Pardon me for asking, but what sort of work did Lady Marcheford do?"

Several of the women looked to Louise, as if for approval. Louise dropped her handful of hair bobbins and joined the tea klatch, accepting a cup of oolong and sitting down. The other braiders followed her, so now the hair jewelry session was quickly turning into a social visit.

"I suppose you would eventually find out, Mrs. Harper. Have you ever heard of Josephine Butler?"

"I don't think so."

"Your husband would be pleased to know that Mrs. Butler and her husband were great supporters of the Union during your Civil War. She is older than those of us here, probably close to Mother's age, but has been active in her work for nearly twenty years."

"Her work?"

"Yes, for women. Two years ago, she helped establish the North of England Council for Promoting the Higher Education of Women."

"Very admirable."

"Yes. She is also a passionate Christian, and simply abhors the sin of prostitution."

"I have buried more than one prostitute in unconsecrated ground, Your Highness. They usually come to terrible ends."

Louise's eyes brightened for the first time since Lady Marcheford's death. "Then you understand. But Mrs. Butler takes it a step further. She says that the prostitutes are exploited victims of male oppression. It is this double standard of sexual morality that must be confronted, not just the behavior of the prostitutes. It is for this reason that she has started the campaign to repeal the Contagious Diseases Acts."

"That has to do with the health of prostitutes, if I'm not mistaken."

"You are correct. These odious laws were intended to control venereal disease in the army and navy, but all they do is commit these unfortunate girls to workhouses."

"Your Highness, I confess I don't know specifically what the laws do."

Louise seemed only too happy to discuss the subject, signaling to Lady Hazel for another cup of tea and settling in for a discourse on it. "The laws were passed five years ago. Because military men are discouraged from marrying, prostitution is viewed as a necessary evil. To shield soldiers and sailors from the social diseases, a prostitute can be arrested at any time and subjected to any manner of personal inspection. If she is declared to be infected, she is confined to a lock hospital until deemed cured. She might be there months."

"What is a lock hospital?"

"A hospital established specifically for the treatment of social diseases. Many naval ports and army towns have them. Mind you, only the fallen girls are sent there, not the men, who are equally responsible for spreading disease."

"Does it work?"

"How can it? The police are only gathering up half the problem."

Violet nodded. "So the disease spreads, but only half the infected population is treated."

"If that. What's worse, the conditions in most lock hospitals are dreadful, and there are too few beds, so many of these women are forced into workhouse infirmaries."

Violet shuddered. She'd experienced enough of what a workhouse was like to know that it was a place to avoid. The thought of them reminded her of Susanna's early plight in one of them.

"Mrs. Butler recognized what a terrible injustice this was, where women must endure humiliating examinations and be subsequently thrown into a hospital no better than a prison, yet the men, who are themselves responsible for the demand for prostitutes, suffer no inconvenience at all. A group, the National Association for the Repeal of the Contagious Diseases Acts, was formed, but they wouldn't permit women to join. Ridiculous!"

"Indeed," Violet murmured.

"That's why she formed the Ladies National Association for the Repeal of the Contagious Diseases Acts, and we are all members, aren't we?"

The other women nodded their heads vigorously.

"There are over five thousand prostitutes working in London alone, and another twenty thousand or so working through England and Wales. Will all of these women end up dying in workhouses? The men involved must also be subject to examination and treatment, else the laws must be repealed. Repeal is Mrs. Butler's goal."

"How do you help her?"

"Of course, none of us can demonstrate or write letters, lest our families hear of it. But we donate clothing and shoes and other items for the girls. You see, Mrs. Butler says that if we are going to stop prostitution at all, we must provide a way out for them. She helps them get factory jobs, and we provide them with what they need to look presentable until they can provide for themselves."

Violet cleared her throat. "Pardon me, Your Highness, but does the queen know about this?"

"Of course not. To even mention prostitution around her would send her into an apoplectic fit. We are moralists of a high order, Mrs. Harper, but we are not fools. My mother would banish me to Canada if she knew what we were doing. She believes her daughters have two good uses: to serve as secretary and eventually make a marriage that suits the Crown. Everyone here would suffer if she knew, for she would undoubtedly go straight to Their Lordships and Ladyships to demand an end to their daughters' activities."

It was a plea for secrecy.

"I understand completely, Your Highness. You may trust that your secret has the confidentiality of the grave."

"Charlotte's secrets weren't so private, though, were they? Ripley knew, and I'm certain he is connected with her death."

Violet didn't reply to this. How could Louise be so certain? Instead, she changed the subject.

"You meet in the mews."

"Yes, how did you know?"

"I'm afraid I overheard your voices one day, although I was unable to discern what you were discussing."

"We were probably arguing over who was going to make protest flags with Mrs. Butler," Lady Hazel said.

"In fact, why don't you join us for our next meeting, since you know where it is held, Mrs. Harper?" Louise said. "We can use other sympathetic women, and perhaps you might be helpful to our cause, since you are a commoner who passes freely in and out of the palace."

Violet hesitated. "I don't know, Your Highness. I am in your mother's employ."

"She won't find out. I do things without her knowledge constantly and here I stand to tell the tale. One meeting won't despoil you, and you may find that you want to do something to help."

Violet agreed, against her own better judgment. But when a princess of the Royal House of Saxe-Coburg and Gotha asks charmingly for a favor it is nearly impossible to refuse. Violet realized that Princess Louise was far more complex than she'd ever imagined.

Violet returned to St. James's Palace that night too lost in thought to even care about eating. *Did* Lord Marcheford have a hand in his wife's death? If so, did that make Lady Maud's death completely unrelated? But what about the fabric she found at both death scenes? The bite marks? Didn't that link the two women in a manner beyond their mutual friendship? If Lord Marcheford was involved in his wife's death, for what reason might he be involved in Lady Maud's? And if he was involved in the deaths of two women surrounding Louise, was he interested in killing more? But *why?* Just because his wife was involved with a women's moralist group? No, it was inconceivable.

Moreover, it was obvious now that Mr. Brown's secret knowledge was of Louise's dealings with Mrs. Butler, something of which Victoria would heartily disapprove. Of course, it wasn't clear how much he knew, other than the obvious, that the women were meeting in private. In fact, he probably knew very little beyond that, which was why Violet was dragged into the situation. Did he expect her to report this to the queen? If so, was he mad? Violet was too entwined with Louise now to report her to her mother.

Yet wasn't it the queen she was responsible to, not Louise? What unholy mess had she just gotten herself into by agreeing to attend a meeting of the Ladies National Association for the Repeal of the Contagious Diseases Acts?

Speaking of the queen, there was her Drawing Room to endure soon, too. What trouble might come with that?

She wished Sam were home again. When he returned from Wales, she was determined she'd never let him out of her sight again.

She decided to open up the book she'd been reading, *The Humbugs of the World,* by American showman P. T. Barnum. She was amused—and not just a little reminded of Mr. Brown—in reading of Barnum's encounters with medical quacks, hoaxsters, adventurers, and other "humbugs."

The morning sky was sending pink rays of light through the draperies of her room by the time Violet had finished the book and finally nodded off to sleep.

Queen Victoria called together another tarot card reading, so once again Violet sat in the queen's private rooms, waiting for the cards to be shuffled, given the queen's touch, and spread out.

Louise, Beatrice, and the sickly Leopold were all present. The boy seemed pathetically eager to be in the room, and given that he probably had few companions besides tutors and nurses, it was understandable. His sunken eyes were bright with curiosity as he peppered Mr. Brown with questions about the deck. Finally, Victoria called for quiet so that the reading could begin. Leopold wrapped his arms around himself, but whether this was because he was actually cold or because his mother was shushing him Violet wasn't sure.

"Mr. Brown," the queen said. "Please, can you tell us whether there will actually be danger at our next Drawing Room? Others seem to think so." She shot Violet a dark look as she reached next to her to stroke Beatrice's hair.

No, it was impossible to think that Violet was going to tell the queen about Louise's activities.

"Wumman, I will do my best, but you know how reticent the cards have been of late."

"Yes, Mr. Brown, we know you will." The queen was all sunshine for her favorite servant.

Louise sat out of her mother's sight, nervously pulling at her sleeves and fingering the buttons on her bodice, her mind clearly elsewhere. Was she bored with the proceedings or nervous that Brown would make some sort of accusation toward her?

Of course, the woman had lost two friends in the space of mere days. She probably preferred to sit quietly in her rooms, lost in thought, rather than be bound to her mother's social activities.

Mr. Brown exuded spirits this evening, and not the supernatural sort, although no one seemed to notice except Violet. Or perhaps the queen chose not to notice it and Louise, Beatrice, and Leopold didn't notice it for their mother's sake.

He gazed at the overturned cards, "hmming" and "ohhing" at them. Victoria and her two youngest children sat forward, rapt, as they waited to see what pronouncement Mr. Brown would make.

"I hope ye won't cast me off, thinking I'm a fraud, but once again I cannae give ye good news."

"Is it terrible, Mr. Brown?"

"Yes. Look, here as our subject card we have a Queen of Swords. That represents ye, Your Majesty, but in your capacity as a mother. There is tension between the Queen of Swords and that of her spiritual situation, shown here in the five of swords, which represents spite or sabotage. Someone is nae safe for the Drawing Room, although I don't think it's ye, Your Majesty, but someone near you. Someone close."

Victoria hugged Beatrice to her. "Baby, perhaps we will have you stay up in your rooms that day."

"No, Mother, I'm not afraid."

Stirred from her own bleak contemplations, Louise said, "Do you not want to lock up Leopold and me that day, Mother?" Her voice was incredulous. "Will you allow us to come to doom?"

"It isn't proper for Leopold to attend, and we will need you nearby to attend to any note taking we'll need. Mr. Brown said we are not in danger, so surely you won't be, either, if you remain at my side."

Louise clamped her lips and returned to picking at her sleeves.

"However, we do now see that perhaps it is best if Scotland Yard sends men to protect the day's proceedings, especially now that Mr. Brown sees misfortune ahead. Can you tell us what might happen, Mr. Brown?"

Brown pursed his lips between a thumb and forefinger. "The cards are not specific, wumman. This card is a ten of cups. It is normally a sign of harmony, but observe: It is reversed. Therefore it represents conflict and rebellion. I believe it suggests someone who is angry."

"Why, anyone who would wish to do someone harm would by necessity be angry, wouldn't they?" the queen said.

"This is a different sort of anger. It is passionate and righteous. That's all I can say."

When Victoria declared the reading to be over, Louise stormed out with hardly a word to anyone. Violet rose to leave, but the queen requested that she remain.

"So, Mrs. Harper, it seems you were correct about needing Scotland Yard here."

"I am only trying to help, Your Majesty. I'm afraid I make a blunder of things sometimes, as I am only a mere undertaker."

The queen appraised her silently, finally saying, "Indeed. We shall meet again at the Drawing Room."

Violet went to Mudie's Lending Library on Oxford Street, turning over the myriad of questions in her mind as she browsed the latest selections of mystery stories from Mr. Wilkie Collins and others. She supposed that if she was to regularly solve puzzles for the queen she may as well know how detectives think, even if they were fictional.

As she passed a hand over the leather bindings, she wondered, had Mr. Brown's latest card reading just smoothed the path for Violet with the queen? Did he truly know something about the Drawing Room event? Or was he playacting, and were all of these readings simply pretty little tricks used to entertain the queen? Tricks that Violet had somehow managed to twist into all manner of association with real events?

She wondered what help Mr. Collins could offer, handing over her borrowing slip to the clerk for a half dozen of Collins's novels and taking them back to St. James's Palace.

It was obvious that Mr. Collins either was a rank optimist or had no idea what he was talking about, since his stories, despite their complexities, always ended with a tidy resolution. Violet was finding real life to be far more opaque and frustrating.

She sighed and closed the book. It was time to go to the Ladies National Association for the Repeal of the Contagious Diseases Acts meeting. Such a long name, almost as bad as the London Master Bakers' Pension and Almshouse Society she'd once seen advertised in a newspaper.

Violet returned to Buckingham Palace mews and this time was completely ignored by the staff, which by now must be used to her presence. She rapped lightly on the door where she'd overheard Louise talking before.

She heard: "Enter." Was that a snuffle behind the command?

To Violet's surprise, Louise was the only person in the sparsely furnished room, which looked as though it served as a gathering place for the groomsmen, with several rough tables and chairs on the unfinished wood floor, and a corner with several broken mounting blocks in it. Louise sat at a table in the middle of the room, agitatedly working a handkerchief through her fingers, her eyes swollen and red.

Where were the other women?

Louise looked at her bleakly. "I suppose I forgot to send you a message. The meeting has been canceled."

"Did your mother find out?"

"Yes, and what an uproar there was. I thought the chandeliers would come crashing down. I suspect the servants were too frightened to even put their ears to the door. It was awful."

"So the Ladies National Association for—so the meetings are now canceled permanently?"

"What? No, no, Mother knows nothing about our moralist group."

"But you canceled—"

"She found out about Ducky and me."

Ah.

Violet sat down next to the princess. "What happened?"

"Some stupid cow of a maid was cleaning my rooms and came upon a note he'd written me. He always cautioned me to burn them, but this one had the sweetest poem in it and I couldn't bear to get rid of it. She ran straight to Mother with it. God help the maid if I ever find out who it was."

"The queen does not approve." This was a statement, not a question. Of course the queen didn't approve. Duckworth was a clergyman, not a foreign prince. He was of no use to the monarchy and England's future.

"No, she does not. After she was done shouting the plaster off the walls, she summoned Ducky and summarily dismissed him. So I have lost my love and Leopold lost his tutor." Louise blew into her handkerchief. "One disaster after another occurs to me, all of it involving the loss of those I love. First Maud, then Charlotte. Now, worst of all, Ducky."

"Perhaps Her Majesty will change her mind once she calms down."

Louise laughed sharply. "Mrs. Harper, surely you have known my mother long enough to know that where she loves, she loves completely, and where she hates, well, God has created a special purgatory for those unfortunate souls who have experienced her wrath. She is especially unforgiving of those who she deems have committed moral offenses, particularly those of the, um, romantic kind. No, the Reverend Duckworth will not be back."

"I am so very sorry."

"I canceled our meeting because I couldn't possibly concentrate, and I look like a bedraggled cat. I was so committed to carrying on with the committee, not only for the good we do, but to honor Maud's and Charlotte's memories. Now, though, I'm just—I feel—I don't know. How has everything gone so wrong so quickly?"

Violet put out a comforting hand but yanked it back. She couldn't touch a member of royalty as though she were a doll to hug.

"Your Highness, there is always hope—"

"It got even worse. Mother said she would start working in earnest to find an appropriate husband for me. She's having a list of all available princes across Europe drawn up, including Russia. She said I will pick from them." Louise's eyes narrowed dangerously. "But I will have my revenge."

Violet felt the hairs on her neck stand up. "Please, you aren't planning anything that would be considered . . . treasonous, are you?"

"Actually, it might be an offense against the monarch. I suppose no one has gotten away with it since Henry the Eighth's sister Mary. Unless you count that misalliance of my granduncle, George the Fourth."

"Your Highness?"

"I told her that if I must take a husband who isn't Ducky, then it will be a British subject. I'll not submit myself to some foreign state, with foreign food and a foreign language I'll never learn and foreign servants who will laugh at me behind my back. Why should I leave London? Mother has plenty of other children to marry off to royal kingdoms and duchies. I wish to stay here and marry someone of my liking."

"What did the queen say?"

"Oh, she was sufficiently outraged. There was more storming and wailing, but I'm determined to have my way. I don't want to be trapped in a marriage where I'm merely my husband's adornment. I want to be *useful*. Like Mrs. Butler is. Her husband supports her activities. In fact, he has suffered in his own career because of what she's doing. Can you imagine such devotion? That's the sort of husband I want."

A rather improbable scenario for a princess of England.

"Yes, Your Highness. Perhaps you will be blessed with such."

"Not blessed. I demand it."

Louise's bravado was overshadowed by the twisted handkerchief in her hand.

Violet was as nervous as a child heading off to boarding school as she awaited Scotland Yard's arrival in a rear anteroom at Buckingham Palace. She wondered at her own surprise, though, when it was Detective Hurst who arrived to coordinate police and detectives about the palace.

"I should have realized it would be you here, Inspector Hurst."

"Mrs. Harper, you seem to be turning up in all of my cases these days."

"I'm not following you, if that's what you're thinking, sir."

"No, I expect you're too busy listening for the peal of mourning bells to wonder about me."

"Hmm, I thought we were friends now."

Hurst sighed. "Madam, we are not colleagues, but, rather, occasional associates. As such, we can work together politely and effectively. I doubt, though, that I shall be visiting you and your husband at home for dinner anytime soon. A woman with your royal favor shouldn't be seen associating with a mere Scotland Yard man." Hurst was unable to veil his sarcasm.

"I don't believe I hold much royal favor, but since I have no home to call my own at the moment, perhaps your plan is best. Tell me, when will your men arrive?"

"They are already posted discreetly around the palace. You needn't fear. Nothing and no one will get past them."

"Yes, of course, Inspector." Violet walked to the door that would take her farther inside the palace, then turned back to him. "Inspector Hurst, there's something different about you. The style of your beard, perhaps? Your hair?"

Hurst reddened. "Oh, that. I was merely on a little holiday recently. Probably got too much sun on my face."

Violet frowned. "No, it's not that. You seem a little more . . . humble, I think."

"You're imagining things, Mrs. Harper. I am no such thing." He picked up a newspaper and opened it, leaning against a wall for support as he read.

"No, you don't carry humility particularly well, Inspector. I'm sure it will wear off." She smiled and waved as she went inside to witness the Drawing Room.

She felt like a mouse skulking along the floor molding, trying to avoid anyone as she made her way up the Grand Staircase and through a drawing room decorated in green—how royalty seemed to love to decorate in tracts of a single color—and then into the regal throne room. This room, in rich, scarlet red with gold trimmings, today contained a dais at the opposite end from the doorway, with two thrones upon it. One was embroidered with "VR" and the other with "A."

As in all other things, Victoria kept her husband near her always.

Bewigged, liveried servants moved deliberately about the room at last-minute preparations, moving this vase a quarter inch to the right on the mantelpiece and shifting that table back and forth until it was precisely centered under the window.

Violet looked down at her dress, a black crape with a periwinkle stripe in the bodice. It was hardly worthy of such an event. She wished she were more conscious of her appearance at times like this, but living a life of daily black gowns meant she'd long ago lost concern for fashion.

Good Lord, she was just like the queen.

There was virtually nowhere to remain discreetly in the background of this room. To Violet's great disappointment, there was no way for her to witness the presentation of the debutantes, each with her full court dress, tall ostrich feathers in her hair, and butterflies in her stomach. Violet had seen engravings of previous proceedings in *Harper's*. The terrified young woman would walk slowly across the room toward the dais, perform a curtsy that she'd practiced in front of her mother for weeks, receive a kind word of acknowledgment from the queen, and, in a move that must have been invented by a circus contortionist, walk backward without breaking her focus on the dais, maneuvering her dress train and executing yet another curtsy.

Violet found her way down the Ministers' Staircase and back down to find Inspector Hurst. He and Inspector Pratt were conferring outside the Ambassador's Entrance. In their long brown overcoats and tall furred hats, they looked like giant beavers—such as those she'd seen along the Colorado River—hovering over a freshly built dam. Fancy, gleaming carriages were now pulling up, discharging their glittering passengers into the hands of waiting footmen, to be escorted into the palace, followed by their sponsors, older women of suitable rank and unimpeachable reputation who had also been previously presented.

Hurst and Pratt quietly observed each of the carriages unloading and driving off, with Pratt making notes in his worn leather notebook. "Why aren't you up there with the queen?" Hurst asked her.

"There was nowhere for me to watch without being noticed myself."

"There are officers posted everywhere now except in the throne room itself. I figured you would be alert for anything up there. I suppose it's all right, though. No one suspicious will get past us or the men around the staircase. Let's just hope it's not your female sensibilities causing you to see goblins behind every corner that have brought us here."

"Of course, Inspector. The goblins I saw behind every corner in the Raybourn case were merely wisps of my imagination."

Hurst bowed. "I apologize, Mrs. Harper. I must admit that you've been right before when I was certain you were wrong."

Violet nodded acknowledgment of Hurst's statement, which must have been a bitter powder for him to swallow. "I trust you and Inspector Pratt will have a pleasant afternoon, with hopefully no disturbances. Good day."

Leaving Hurst and Pratt to their review of opening coach doors, Violet walked down the line of waiting carriages, wondering about each of the nervous girls sitting inside. Lady Maud was once one of them, as was Lady Marcheford. Did they stumble walking away from the queen? Did their feathers droop or their sleeves tear?

No matter now. There was no stumbling, drooping, or tearing for either woman. How did they die? Was Lord Marcheford culpable? Perhaps in the death of Lady Marcheford, but why Lady Maud? To take away suspicion from his own wife's death? If so, he'd done some considerable advance planning to find a distraction for the police.

The cold-bloodedness of it was horrifying.

What if it wasn't Lord Marcheford? Who else might it be? And for what reason? Because he despised lovely aristocratic young women? It was unthinkable, positively ludicrous.

Violet paused in her walk. A hansom cab was in the line. That was strange. Every other conveyance in line either had a family crest on it or was at least adorned with gold lanterns and plumed horses. What debutante would come to the queen's Drawing Room in a cab?

Violet stepped back as the cab's door opened, despite it being at least fifteen carriages back in line. A red-haired woman around Violet's age leaped out of it, carrying a crudely drawn sign on a post. "Repeal the Contagious Diseases Acts NOW!" it proclaimed.

The woman hoisted the sign up, and Violet realized she intended to march into Buckingham Palace with it. Was Louise behind this? Impossible. Despite Louise's current battle with her mother, surely she wouldn't endorse one of her compatriots doing such a thing.

Up the line Violet could tell that Hurst and Pratt were much more focused on whatever carriage was emptying passengers at the entrance and were paying no attention to what was happening this far down. She would have to stop this herself.

"Madam," she called out. "Where are you going?"

The woman turned, but Violet realized it was to brush something away from her dress, not because she'd noticed Violet.

"Please, madam, stop." Violet picked up her own skirts and scurried to where the woman was. "You cannot go into the palace. It's for debutantes only."

The woman looked Violet up and down disdainfully. "And who, exactly, are you?"

"I am—" Violet glanced down at her simple black gown. "I am a friend of the queen's."

The woman raised an eyebrow. "You may be dressed in mourning, but you are no aristocrat."

"No, and neither are you. I, however, have business here. You are . . . ?"

"May Fisher. I also have business here. I'm here to make Her Majesty aware of the great injustice of the Contagious Diseases Acts. Do you know of it, Mrs. . . . . ?"

"Harper. Yes, I know what the laws are."

"Then you know that they are terrible for those unfortunate young women, as exploited as they are by the men who visit them, then terrorized by the men who arrest them. I'm sure if the queen really understood what was happening, she would be as outraged as many of us are. She's surrounded by all of those brainless windbags in Parliament who, I'm sure, tell her it is having the effect of turning them all into virtuous ladies."

"They probably do not speak to her of such a subject at all. The queen is very proper."

"Well, you needn't worry yourself about me. I am perfectly peaceable."

Mrs. Fisher hoisted her sign and walked toward the palace.

Violet ran after the woman again, this time grabbing her shoulder. "Mrs. Fisher, as I said, you cannot—"

She didn't expect what happened next. Wrenching herself away from Violet, the woman drew the sign back like a cricket bat and swung it furiously at Violet. It connected with her right shoulder with a loud crack, sending her sprawling to the ground.

Violet had injured this arm several years previously in a train accident, which had resulted in steam burns all along it. It occasionally twinged to remind her that it would never be healed. Now, though, she was in agony. Still, she couldn't let the woman race past Hurst and enter the palace. They wouldn't be expecting a woman as the source of trouble.

Using her other arm for stability, Violet lifted herself up. Her crinoline wasn't much protection from the hard ground and she'd undoubtedly have a nasty bruise on her hip by morning. Grabbing her skirts again, she ran after the woman once more and, with an agility she would have sworn she never possessed, leaped onto her back, knocking them both back to the ground.

As Violet went down a second time, she saw Hurst and Pratt running over, pure astonishment on Hurst's face. Within moments, Mrs. Fisher was in Inspector Pratt's custody, and he quickly hauled her away from the scene so as not to upset the proceedings.

"What the devil just happened?" Hurst asked.

"Well, you see, Mrs. Fisher wanted to march up to see the queen to protest some unjust laws. I know she was quite harmless, but obviously I couldn't let her—"

Hurst held up his hands. "Don't tell me anything further. Mrs. Harper, how is it that Mr. Pratt and I have been doing duty for well over an hour without coming across anything suspicious, but the moment you walk outside, trouble manages to find you?"

"I didn't mean—"

"Also, your hem is torn and you have a little smudge right here." He pointed to his own cheek. "Good afternoon, Mrs. Harper."

Violet limped back to St. James's Palace, ignoring the stares of the debutantes still waiting in carriages for their moment to enter the palace. She was too consumed with worry to think about her disheveled appearance. What was it Mr. Brown said at the last tarot reading? That trouble would come from someone who was angry. She supposed Mrs. Fisher was that. What else had he said about the trouble? Oh yes, that it would be in the form of someone passionate and righteous.

Mrs. Fisher was definitely both of those things.

But how did Mr. Brown know that Mrs. Fisher would try to disrupt the queen's Drawing Room? She wasn't a member of Louise's personal circle of moralist friends as far as Violet could tell, and certainly her clothing marked her out as middle-class.

More important, did Louise know about this in advance? Was she angry enough at her mother to encourage it or even plan it? But if that was true, did that mean that she and Mr. Brown were somehow in collusion?

No, that made no sense at all. If they were conspiring together, Mr. Brown wouldn't be leading Violet—and therefore the queen—to Louise's questionable activities.

Why did every day seem to make things more confusing, not less? Violet hoped the next day would bring at least one answer.

Instead, it brought more death.

7

"Thank you for coming, Mrs. Harper; I wanted you to know right away." Louise was pacing back and forth inside her secret meeting room at the mews. Violet sat down at a table.

"Know what, Your Highness?" Violet braced for the news about Mrs. Fisher's arrest. How would Louise react when she told the princess that she had a hand in it?

"It's terrible, just terrible. I've told you about my friend Mrs. Butler?"

"Yes, she leads your moralist group."

Louise nodded. "The worst thing has happened. I can hardly speak of it."

Surely Mrs. Fisher's arrest wouldn't cause so much distress for the princess. Or perhaps this was a sign that Louise was becoming unhinged from all of the tragedy around her.

"Perhaps you should sit down."

Louise sat momentarily, then stood and paced again. "Why is the world falling down around me? I just don't understand it."

"Your Highness, I don't understand, either. Perhaps you could share with me what happened . . . ?"

"Of course." Louise sat down once more. Her movements were dizzying. "I told you about my friend Mrs. Butler, who heads up the Ladies National—"

"Yes, I remember."

"She has been so influential in my thinking about life and the lives of others in Great Britain. I've always admired her way of—"

"Yes, Your Highness. Did Mrs. Butler commit a crime?"

"Oh no. No, no, of course not. Worse, it was a crime committed against her. Why has the angel of death taken so much interest in those around me?"

Violet leaned forward across the table, horrified. "Are you saying that Mrs. Butler has been killed?"

"No, one of her associates has. Her name is Lillian Cortland. She is—was—the second daughter of a baron who was tossed out when her parents discovered her work with Mrs. Butler. She made visits to parliamentary members for Mrs. Butler and was critical to our group's mission. There is no doubt this time, Mrs. Harper. It isn't possible that three women I know personally just coincidentally died within two weeks of each other, is it?"

At the princess's age, it was only likely if there was a cholera outbreak. "It does seem strange," Violet said. "Was Miss Cortland ill at all?"

"I don't think so. I promised Mrs. Butler I would send you to tend to her. Mrs. Butler is contacting the family, but doubts they will care. Can you go right away?"

"I must go to the undertaking shop first but will go there as soon as possible."

"I'll provide you with a driver and carriage."

Violet demurred. "Please, no. It would only serve to shock people to see an undertaker alighting from a royal carriage unaccompanied by a royal family member."

Violet hired a cab to take her to Morgan Undertaking so she could replenish her bag with supplies. As it rumbled and clattered along to Queen's Road, she wondered: Was it really Miss Cortland's death Mr. Brown was speaking of at the last reading, not the near catastrophe of Mrs. Fisher descending on Buckingham Palace? Although Miss Cortland had nothing to do with the Drawing Room, had she?

She needed to see Miss Cortland's body right away.

* * *

Will Swift helped Violet repack her bag with supplies, once again talking over his personal troubles as they worked.

"I've given Harry a definite date by which I'll be leaving, in two months. We've not put up my interest for sale because we're still waiting—hoping—Mrs. Harper, that you'd like to purchase back in."

"Maybe. I don't know, Will. Susanna still expects to see me in Colorado for her wedding."

"So, return to the States for your daughter's wedding and then come back. Harry will be fine for a couple of months by himself. He'd like to have you back, and I'd feel much better knowing the shop was in the hands of someone proper."

"I'm so tempted, but I'm not sure what the future holds."

"Haven't you talked to Mr. Harper about it?"

"Yes, but I haven't heard back from him. I'm sure he would agree with it, but—"

"You know Harry prefers to work in the back of the shop, moving coffins and such. Morgan Undertaking needs someone expert in the front of the store. It needs you, Mrs. Harper."

Violet looked around the shop that had once been hers, at the walnut counter she'd bought from an old cabinetmaker, at the shelves full of samples she'd always kept fully stocked. There was still a stain along the front of the counter from where she'd overturned an inkwell. She smiled, also remembering a terrible row she once had with Sam in the shop.

"Sam is still in Wales, but should be home, I mean, back in London, very soon. I will discuss it with him first thing, I promise. It would be nice to have a permanent shop again."

"He'll agree; I'm sure of it. Let me find Harry to discuss terms."

Violet left the shop an hour later, pleased with the bargain struck. Although she still needed to discuss it with her husband, she knew Will was right and that Sam would be comfortable with it.

It was soothing to think about a permanent location again in London. Perhaps she and Sam could move in above the shop, if the flat above was unoccupied. Then there would be the question of Susanna, as she was in Colorado on account of Sam and Violet. How nice it would be, though, to move out of St. James's Palace.

She laughed as she stepped up into a cab headed for the edge of Spitalfields, just outside the City of London. Most people would be overjoyed at the thought of living in a palace, but Violet couldn't wait to be gone from it. If there was anything she'd learned from her work with the queen and members of the aristocracy, it was that their lives were just as miserable as those of London's poor, except that no one cared about the misery of the rich. They had no charities or churches to help them, no prayers to sustain them, and most certainly they could never show their misery to the outside world.

Violet far preferred her own world of dead bodies, dark crypts, and mourning wear. Which brought her mind back around to the problem at hand. Would Miss Cortland possess any obvious signs that she'd been killed? Or that she'd died of illness? Violet planned to take extra-special care of her, especially if her parents didn't care about their daughter.

So far, everything was progressing smoothly and he could declare it perfect if only he didn't get caught during his current mission. Reese had donned his best uniform and was now finding his way through the palace via the servants' staircases and hallways. He needed to figure out where the queen's personal rooms were. Thus far, no one had questioned his presence.

What was down here? This hallway was much like the others, except the wall lanterns were less ostentatious and the carpets were plain. Was this where the family lived, or was this where they stored unwelcome relatives?

"What are you doing here?" came a voice from behind him.

Reese whirled around, so startled that he forgot the lie he had invented before entering the palace. "Pardon me. I—ah—I'm afraid I'm a bit lost."

"I should say you are. Who are you?"

"Reese Meredith, sir, a coachman."

"I've seen you before. How the devil did you get lost inside the queen's private rooms?"

Ah, so he'd found them.

"I—I was told that the Princess Beatrice wanted to drive

through Hyde Park, and when she didn't appear at the usual loading place, I tried to find her and a maid told me to look here."

The man before him was tall and pinched looking, as though he'd just encountered a side of moldering beef. He scowled down his nose at Reese. "The princess asked for no such thing. She is scheduled for a painting class with me today."

"So you are . . . ?"

"Her art tutor, of course, Owen Caradoc. You may call me Mr. Caradoc."

Reese knew the type. Someone hired on because his third cousin was school chums with a distant relative of the queen's, hence affording him an introduction to the royal household. Now he was cock of the walk. Unlike Reese, whose position at the palace was due to his exertion and suffering as a cavalryman, one of a few experiences that qualified one to work in the mews. And his experience hadn't even been able to earn him this position until now.

"Of course, Mr. Caradoc. It must be a great pleasure to work up here."

"The Princess Beatrice is a good student."

"So that's it? A little girl is your master?"

"Don't be arrogant, Mr. Meredith. Serving the princess has given me stature. When I am no longer needed here, I'll be able to set up my own school, and parents will flock to me from all over the kingdom to place their children in my classes."

Reese crossed his arms. "So you will be forever dependent on the gratitude and good words of the sovereign. Don't you chafe under the bonds of servitude? Don't you look at them and think, 'They are no better than I. Why do they presume to be lords and masters of my fate? Why aren't they subject to the same rules that I am?' "

Caradoc looked at him in horror. "I have an excellent position here. I serve the Royal House of Saxe-Coburg and Gotha, have a good stipend, and room and board. As, I'm sure, do you. Why are you intent on destroying your good fortune?"

"Yes, you do indeed *serve*. Like an ass carrying panniers full of gold goblets that don't belong to him."

"And you do not carry the same panniers over your uniform? What is your name again? I hear distant Welsh in your voice."

Someone else who had figured him out. "Reese Meredith. And, no, my position is due to the sweat of my brow, not connections to the royal family. I'll never be beholden to the upper crust. Mr. Marx says we proletarians have nothing to lose but our chains once the bourgeoisie are overthrown."

"We are all beholden to someone. Young man, if you believe you are going to make your mark in this world by destroying the aristocracy head-on, then you are a fool. The French have already tried. There are always other means to resolve these types of problems."

Reese shook his head in disgust. "You are a typical slave. Your mind is poisoned."

"And you are a typical member of youth. Rash and bold. You may have a noble goal, but your methods are foolhardy. You know you could be thrown out of the palace—or worse—for such treasonous talk, and without getting a good character from the superintendent of the mews, either."

"When I have accomplished my goals, a reference will be the least of my concerns. Tell the princess that when she's ready to go out, I'll have a carriage waiting for her."

Reese stalked off, pleased at the look of disbelief on the art tutor's face. Once Reese had reached the stables again, though, he wondered if perhaps he hadn't tipped his hand too far. He'd need to make sure that if that Caradoc fellow went tattling it was he who looked the fool, not Reese.

Violet could only describe Josephine Butler as having a commanding presence. She was ordinary in most ways: of average height, brown hair neither light nor dark, unremarkable brown eyes, plain—if not downright drab—clothing. Yet when the woman opened her mouth it was as if the forces of heaven were gathered together there to conduct divine business.

Her welcome at the association's quarters was warm and inviting. "Mrs. Harper, thank you for coming. The princess was good to send you. Miss Cortland lived upstairs once her family abandoned her. It was of great fortune to us to have her here to keep an eye on it, as we've been broken into more than once. Not everyone appreciates what we do."

Violet could see that this might be so. Most of the furniture was old and dilapidated, and paint peeled from cabinets. A large coal stove sat on broken blue tiles in a corner with various kettles and pans resting on it. She could just make out an obscenity on one wall, bleeding through several layers of whitewash.

"See the gouge in this cabinet?" Mrs. Butler said, observing Violet's appraisal of the place. "It's from some young lout who thought destroying the premises would earn him huzzahs from his fellow troublemakers."

Did Louise ever actually venture over here? Perhaps this explained why she was willing to risk meetings at the palace mews.

"Your work must be very dangerous," Violet said.

Mrs. Butler shrugged. "I am a cousin of the second Earl Grey, the prime minister who worked so hard at slavery abolition and Catholic emancipation, so I suppose it is in my blood to care about such causes. God has purposed me for just such a moment and I am grateful to do this duty each day, no matter the cost."

Violet had to admire the woman's strength and could see why Louise respected her so. "Do you think you'll be able to influence a repeal of the laws?"

"I do, but it will take time to change the hearts of the weaklings in Parliament. And even once they are repealed, there is so much more work to be done. Prostitution itself is not only a sin, but a blight upon all of society. It must be eradicated, but only men can accomplish this, for it is they who control everything about the practice.

"It is men, and only men, who determine a prostitute's fate. Men police lay hands on these prostitutes. By men they are examined, handled, doctored. In the hospital, it is a man again who makes prayer and reads the Bible to them. They are had up before magistrates who are men, and they never get out of the hands of men until they die." At this, Mrs. Butler's otherwise nondescript eyes flared with righteous wrath. Violet wouldn't have been surprised if the archangel Michael made a sudden appearance.

Mrs. Butler continued, visibly incensed. "Why this double standard? Why do only women endure humiliating medical examinations? Why are only women held captive in lock hospitals if found to be infected? Why are only women's reputations threatened? These questions must be answered, and they are a key part of our campaign to repeal the acts. Her Highness speaks well of you and thinks you would be valuable to our cause. Would you like to join us, Mrs. Harper?"

"Mrs. Butler, I am but a simple undertaker and must tend to my craft at all hours of the day and night." Violet patted her undertaking bag. "And my charitable causes run more to that of Mr. Booth's Christian Revival Society."

"Yes, I know his wife, Catherine. We all serve God in our own ways, Mrs. Harper. Today, you are a blessing to this cause, whether you realize it or not."

Violet nodded. "Thank you. Now, perhaps, I might ask you some questions about Miss Cortland?"

"Of course."

"Was she ill?"

"Only recently she'd been complaining of a cough, but it was minor. She'd bought some cocaine drops and was feeling better. That's why I was so surprised when she . . . departed . . . so suddenly, as if for no reason. I summoned the coroner, but he did no more than hold a lantern over her face for several seconds and declare her to have died of natural causes. A twenty-two-year-old woman, dead of natural causes? Either the man is incompetent or lazy."

"Or, more than likely, uninterested in someone associated with your movement, Mrs. Butler. Not every coroner is well trained, and there is little to compel them to find a criminal intent behind an unusual death that doesn't interest them. Had she mentioned a recent animal bite, or perhaps an insect sting?"

"Not that I recall."

Violet followed Mrs. Butler up a narrow flight of stairs to a shabby, warped door. Behind it was a small, dark room that must have served as a private office with its wooden desk, one missing leg substituted with the cracked head of an old plaster bust, and a rickety chair behind it. The walls were papered with old posters and notices of everything from ship sailings to theater performances to pages torn from *Illustrated Police News*.

Tucked away in a corner was a cast-iron bed. Upon the bed, in a nearly angelic pose, lay Miss Cortland.

"How did you find her?" Violet asked.

"Nearly like she is now. I simply rolled her a bit more upright. Her Highness said it was best to let you lay her out."

Violet nodded. "Have her parents been notified?"

"Yes. I received a note back that her remains were my problem. I hardly know what to do."

"You may rely on me, Mrs. Butler. Did they not even offer to pay for her funeral?"

"They offered nothing. Do you wish to see their letter?"

"No, I can imagine its contents. Did the princess indicate if she might be willing . . . ?"

Josephine Butler pressed her lips together grimly. "The princess doesn't have her own money, and certainly could not explain this situation to the queen and expect a contribution."

"You're right, of course. I suppose, then, that I should plan on a very simple affair. We'll rent a coffin and use a simple wagon with just a single pair of horses. She can be buried in the gown she's wearing. Was she a congregant somewhere nearby? Is there room in her church's yard?"

"I'd been taking her with me to Christ Church lately. I'll see if we can bury her there."

"I'd like to take her in two days' time, if convenient for the minister. Also, do you wish for me to cut locks of hair for mementos?"

"Yes, please. Well, shall I leave you with her?"

Mrs. Butler walked to the bedside, bent over, and kissed Miss Cortland's forehead. "Rest well in heaven, little angel. It's hard to imagine that God needs you more than we do, but who are we to question His ways?"

Once alone with the corpse, Violet felt more nervous around the woman than she had around any other dead body in a long time. What would she find this time?

"Miss Cortland, I'm here to take care of you. I'll need your help, though. Can you tell me what happened to you?" Violet put her hands to either side of Miss Cortland's head, willing an answer from her slackened face.

"I hope you don't mind, but I need to inspect you." Violet turned the deceased's head from side to side. No bite marks were visible on her neck.

Violet took both of the woman's hands in her own and rubbed them. No welts or bite marks there, either. "Forgive my personal intrusion, madam," she said, pulling up Miss Cortland's gown to inspect her legs, running her hands up and down them to feel for welts or protrusions. Nothing.

"I can hardly believe you died of natural causes. Yet you lie here so peacefully. What secrets are you hiding?"

Violet sniffed the air. There was no sign of the very strong odor she'd noticed in both Lady Maud's and Lady Marcheford's rooms. Perhaps Louise's imagination was in full bloom and Violet was allowing herself to be too influenced by it. It was certainly *possible* that Miss Cortland had died of an illness, but . . .

On a whim, Violet rolled down one of the woman's stockings and removed it from her foot. Grasping Miss Cortland's foot in one hand, she examined it. "You have the heel of a hard worker, madam," she said. "Already so rough and calloused. And your large toe so bent. I'd say you've been wearing shoes that are too tight, although whether that was for fashion's sake or afford—wait, what's this?"

Between that bent toe and the next one were exactly what she was looking for. Two tiny bite marks.

Who or what in heaven's name was running around London biting the knees and toes and necks of the city's aristocratic young women? Besides being aristocratic, all three of the bodies Violet had inspected were of women involved with Josephine Butler as well as Princess Louise. Was one or the other of the two women the reason behind these deaths? But why? Both were involved in the moralist movement behind the repeal of the Contagious Diseases Acts, but why would anyone care so much about those acts that he would unleash some deadly insect over them?

Violet ran to the edge of her own imagination about the possibilities as she carefully washed and prepared Miss Cortland for burial. Was it a military man, mad with syphilis and fearful that he might be discovered if Mrs. Butler's reforms took place? Or perhaps someone in Parliament who wanted to prevent a repeal vote? But again, why such drastically morbid measures?

Her mind drifted back to Lord Marcheford. Lady Marcheford said he had a mistress. Would he have had the will to kill Charlotte, either over his mistress or because of his disdain over her activities with the other moralist women? Would his disdain extend to killing the rest of them, one by one?

Perhaps it was time to have a conversation with His Lordship, if she could do so without becoming a victim herself.

8

Violet was pleasantly surprised to receive a note from Princess Beatrice asking if she wished to come to the palace to paint with her the following morning. She accepted the young royal's invitation and was curtsying before the girl soon after breakfast.

"You may sit here, Mrs. Harper," Beatrice said, opening the door to her art room and indicating a prepared spot in front of a canvas. "I've assembled all the paints and brushes you might need. I thought you might copy Peaches while I work on another eye portrait."

Beatrice pointed to a cockatiel with bright orange cheeks in a gilded cage in one corner of the room. Someone had skillfully placed a length of damask around the cage, and it puddled on the floor around the base of the birdcage stand.

"After we paint a few hours I will call for luncheon, and after we dine I thought we might walk in the gardens."

Once again, Violet was struck by how lonely the poor girl was, despite her mother's cloying attentions. "Princess, I am a willing student, but I know very little about oil paints. My only experience with a brush is as it pertains to mourning jewelry."

"I will show you. Here are your pigments, which you will mix with—"

They were interrupted by the arrival of Beatrice's art tutor, who entered the room drying several long horsehair brushes with a cloth. "Ah, Mrs. Harper, isn't it? We are glad to have you back. Are you here for a lesson?"

"The princess was just about to demonstrate—"

"Yes, Her Highness is becoming quite proficient in her craft. Perhaps we will leave her to finishing her current work while I tend to the mundane details of showing you what to do."

Beatrice sat down at her own table, her expression crestfallen as she picked up her own brush, dipped it in a sepia-toned mixture, and applied it to a partially finished sliver of ivory. The girl would probably be quite talented at creating a mourning piece, such as what Lady Hazel Campden had made. Undoubtedly, Beatrice's mother was ensuring her daughter had an unending stream of work to do in homage to Albert, so it was no wonder she was a talented eye portraitist.

"Here, Mrs. Harper, you see we have several containers filled with powders. They are your pigments. We shall sprinkle some ochre down like this. . . ." Mr. Caradoc tipped a container forward and tapped some into a small ceramic bowl.

"Now we will add in some linseed oil." From a thick brown bottle he poured a slick substance. The odor was exactly that of a finished canvas, so Violet now knew where the smell came from.

Mr. Caradoc used a glass pestle to grind the pigment powder into the linseed oil. After a few twists with the pestle, he handed the apparatus to Violet. "Now you try."

Violet continued the blending until the art tutor was satisfied.

"If you were truly my student, I would spend weeks teaching you how to draw. But as I suspect this is mostly a social call, I encourage you to experiment freely."

Violet certainly couldn't argue with his assessment, except that Mr. Caradoc was interrupting the social visit.

"I presume you are painting Peaches, Mrs. Harper?"

"Yes, it was what the princess recommended." Beatrice's back stiffened at the mention of her name.

"Then you should probably learn how to gild, so that you can paint a more realistic birdcage. First, I will draw a couple of the wires of the cage with a charcoal pencil, as such. . . ." Mr. Caradoc quickly sketched on her canvas and almost immediately had made a reasonably good outline of the cage on it.

"We will gild a small part of the bottom rim of the cage. Every line that I have drawn should be gilded, and so we apply bole, a clay and glue mixture, to it first." Mr. Caradoc opened up a squat, dark jar and dipped a stiff brush into it.

"Dear me, we seem to be completely out of bole," he said.

"Shall I make more, Mr. Caradoc?" Beatrice said, leaving her own work to join her art tutor and Violet.

"An excellent idea. Most appreciated, Your Highness. You'll find everything on the top shelf in the supply room."

Once Beatrice was gone, Mr. Caradoc dropped his voice. "Mrs. Harper, it is most fortuitous that you are here. I've been in a quandary since yesterday, unsure whether to pass a message about this to the queen or wait for you."

"A quandary about what, sir?"

"I try to mind my own business about the palace, indeed I do, but this is something that bears repeating."

"What bears repeating?"

"I just don't like to be known as a tattler, especially of those whose place is not perhaps as good as mine. Of course, I was most fortunate in the recognition I received while still a student at the Royal Academy and have parlayed it into a tidy position that will carry into my own private studio one day. Nevertheless, if something happened to Her Majesty I'd never forgive myself."

"Mr. Caradoc, please speak plainly to me."

"Yes, of course. Yesterday I happened upon a coachman loitering in the hallways. Said he was waiting for Princess Beatrice. He goes by the name of Meredith."

Violet frowned. "I know of whom you speak."

"You do? How are you on speaking terms with the stable workers?"

"One day I was in the mews looking for—never mind, what were you saying?"

Caradoc cleared his throat and dropped his voice further. "He said the most terrible things to me about the princess."

"I don't understand. What evil could anyone possibly speak against Princess Beatrice? She's an innocent young girl."

"It was more his opinion of serving a young girl. He told me that I was a slave and beholden to the upper crust. He quoted that Karl

Marx fellow. Have you heard about him? Many would say Marx talks treason."

Violet remembered seeing Mr. Marx once in the reading room at the British Museum. "I have. He wants the poor elevated above the rich, and recommends abolishing religion, property ownership, and capitalism in order to do so."

"Yes, and Meredith is quite enthusiastic about Mr. Marx, to the point of being rabid. He made some talk about accomplishing his goals here, although what those are I hesitate to even hazard a guess. Meredith is much more radical than is warranted."

"Was that all he said? He didn't say anything specific that he planned to do?"

"No, Mrs. Harper, and that's why I've been in a quandary. I think he may be a dangerous young man, yet he's done nothing untoward. What would I tell the police? Or Her Majesty? That's when I thought perhaps you could do something about it, given your friendship with the queen."

Violet had discovered Mr. Brown in the stables one day, and now this coachman appeared to be engaging in treasonous talk, if not treasonous activities. Was this what Brown knew and was trying to convey to Violet?

Before she could ask Mr. Caradoc another question, Beatrice returned with the mixture he wanted. He nodded at her.

"Thank you, Your Highness. Now, Mrs. Harper, as I was demonstrating, we will apply a bit of bole to the line I've drawn. You see that it is a reddish brown, from the clay. I will burnish it against the canvas with this stiff brush . . . as such . . . yes, very good. Now we take this jar of size and apply it atop the bole. Size is a weak glue solution and will cause the gold leaf to adhere. Next I will show you what gold leaf looks like. . . ."

The art tutor was moving so fast Violet could hardly follow him. It didn't matter, though. Her mind was on Mr. Caradoc's revelation about the coachman.

When she was finally able to break free from the art lesson and say her farewells, she glanced at Beatrice's eye portrait in progress, and it struck Violet that the eye being painted was very much like her own.

*   *   *

"Mother, have you seen this week's *Illustrated News?*" Bertie asked as he and Alix entered Victoria's private sitting room. He knew it always raised his mother's hackles when he applied blunt force like this, without couching things in delicate terms, but he couldn't help himself. Mother could be so blind where that idiot man was concerned.

"No, you know it upsets our digestion to read the paper with breakfast. We suppose something is troubling you?" She used a napkin to cover the remains of her breakfast and picked up her cup of tea.

Alix sat down, a hand to her swelling abdomen. Soon she wouldn't be able to wear a corset and would retire from any public appearances.

"Yes, Mother, and it should be troubling you, as well." Bertie waved the latest edition in the air and snapped it open. "Listen to this.

" '. . . and so we have on good authority that Her Majesty is not only a devotee of the spirit world, which is common knowledge, but that her Highland servant, Mr. Brown, is the sole medium through which she contacts her long-dead husband, the prince consort. Through tarot card sessions and séances, the queen's ghillie contacts the prince consort so that the queen may ask his advice on personal matters and those pertaining to her sovereignty.

" 'Does the queen disgrace herself by secreting herself away with Mr. Brown exclusively? Are there no other mediums who can communicate with those who have gone to the Beyond, that she must be in private with this man who is not her husband? Surely London teems with female spiritualists, who would be more fitting for the situation.

" 'Is there a reason the queen holds this particular servant in such high regard? Is there more to this relationship than that of mistress–servant?

" 'We wish Her Majesty many years of good health and an ever-expanding empire, but kindly suggest that she consider her standing and reputation on the world's stage.' "

Bertie threw the paper down in disgust. "It's appalling."

"Yes, the papers say the most dreadful things sometimes. They've always done so, as you well know."

"Mother, this is more than merely 'appalling.' You are the queen, and the newspaper is all but suggesting you and Brown are lovers."

"Bertie, language!"

"I hardly think that pointing out the truth is cause for reprimand, and it is hardly the point. Mother, you must dismiss that man, lest this grow into an unmanageable scandal."

Victoria slammed her teacup against its saucer. "And we hardly think that you are in a position to lecture us on the *Klatsch* and *Skandal*. You know more about the gossips than I do."

"The press has merely noted my high spirits. I have never—"

"Let us remind you that Mr. Brown tends to our needs, both spiritual and domestic. He has been devoted to our person for many years, and was likewise devoted to your father before he passed on. If your dear *Vater* were here now, how pained he would be by your attitude. But he was taken from us by an illness he never should have had."

Now Mother would thrash him with the thinly veiled reminder that Father's death was all Bertie's fault. He had to stop her before she flayed his back open with that verbal cat-o'-nine-tails again, as she'd been doing for the past nine years.

"You're changing the subject. At hand is what you will do about Mr. Brown and his increasing stain on this family."

"We will not *do* anything about our faithful servant. He gives us great *Komfort* in times of distress, and those moments occur more and more frequently." She gave Bertie her iciest stare.

His mother was summoning up the stubbornness for which she was so famous. It was best to slightly change subjects.

"Has the undertaker discovered whatever it is Mr. Brown said was lurking about in the palace?"

"Not yet. Mr. Brown recommends a séance, which we will have tomorrow. Perhaps you and Alix could join us. He says we are sure to make contact with your dear papa, to seek his advice on the situation."

"After everything I just said, you still insist—"

"Darling," Alix said. "I do feel a bit of discomfort. Might we return home so that I can nap? Perhaps we can return later to continue our visit."

"There's nothing wrong, I hope?" he said.

"No, no, I think I just need some quiet time."

As they walked arm in arm downstairs, it occurred to Bertie that Alix was making up her pain to end the quarrel between his mother and him. She was quite skillful about it, too. *Hmm.* Perhaps he hadn't given Alix enough credit for her diplomatic abilities.

Maybe it really was time he ceased his dalliances and became the devoted husband his own father once was.

He gazed fondly at Alix, who was chattering sweetly about donating baby clothes to an abandoned mothers' charity, her face flushed with the exertion of walking down the staircase to pick up their carriage. Such a gracious and beautiful princess deserved a constant and steadfast prince.

Yes, the minute he tired of Lady Vane-Tempest he would devote himself wholeheartedly to his wife.

St. James's Palace, London

"Madam, you have a visitor."

The servant bowed and left Violet to figure out that whoever had come to see her was in one of the receiving rooms downstairs. The staff was still very uncomfortable with the undertaker-in-residence who had been foisted upon them, especially with the knowledge that she was preparing for a third burial in less than two weeks.

To her surprise, it was Lord Marcheford who awaited her, anxiously anticipating the whiskey being poured for him by one of the hundreds of liveried servants who roamed the palace. They all had very specialized roles in a hierarchy that was unfathomable. For all Violet knew, this man's entire role might be to make guests comfortable inside this room.

"My lord," she said, dipping into the smallest of curtsies. She was learning quickly how far down to dip, depending upon the rank of the lord or lady she was addressing and upon what point she was trying to make.

On seeing her, Lord Marcheford took a huge swallow of the swirling brown liquid in his glass. "Mrs. Harper."

He then stared at her expectantly.

What? Was there something on her face? Then Violet remembered that she was the hostess in this situation, even though she was just an undertaker temporarily occupying palace space.

"Please, won't you be seated?"

They sat across from each other on matching striped settees of pale pink. Violet's black gown was a stark contrast to the elegant, soft surroundings she sat in.

Ripley stared moodily into his glass, saying nothing.

"My lord, is there something I can help—"

He looked up. "I understand you are investigating my wife's death."

"Who told you this?"

"Princess Louise, who else? What I want to know is why you are doing so. What is with all of you harpies, pursuing the idea that Charlotte was murdered when you know positively well that she died a natural death?"

"You seem quite convinced."

"Of course I am. I'm her husband. I knew my wife was ill, a fact she tried to hide from others. You are disgracing her death by supposing someone may have murdered her."

Violet folded her hands in her lap to remain as calm as possible. "But aren't you the least bit curious, my lord? What if someone may have had a grudge against Lady Marcheford?"

"A grudge? Over what?"

"Perhaps over her moralist activities with Princess Louise and Mrs. Butler."

"Good Lord, that Butler woman is depraved. Charlotte must have lost her senses to get involved with that harridan. Wait, what are you implying?"

"I am implying nothing, sir. I merely find it curious that a loving husband, distraught over his wife's sudden death, should make it a priority that no one investigate the peculiar circumstances surrounding her demise."

Lord Marcheford swallowed what remained of his whiskey and

slammed the glass down on the table next to him. "There are no peculiar circumstances! Lottie was ill. She was coughing up blood and losing stamina. You moralists are running about acting as if no one ever died of consumption before. It's embarrassing my family and me."

"I am not a member of the moralists. I am only—"

"But you will be. You've been poisoned by that Butler woman, and soon you'll be prancing up and down Whitehall, carrying signs and protesting the lot of a bunch of fallen women. At least you aren't a member of society, because then your husband would have to pack you off to the country until you learned a lesson."

"Is that what you attempted to do with Lady Marcheford? Send her away to the family estate? Were you perhaps unsuccessful at that and needed to take more drastic measures to stop her activities? Or were they measures to ensure you could marry elsewhere?"

Lord Marcheford reddened. "You've no idea what you're saying, you deranged crow."

"Believe me, my lord, I've been called a crow more times than I can count. You'll not frighten me with your name-calling and brute force." Violet stood to end the conversation, and so did he.

"Listen to me," he said. "I'll not have this preposterous rumor stain the earldom. I've idled away many years for it, and when I inherit, there will not be a cloud of innuendo hanging over me. Do you understand me?"

He grabbed Violet's damaged arm and shook her, bringing his face close to hers so that she smelled the sourness of his whiskey-laden breath. "I will do whatever it takes to ensure I am a respected peer of the realm. No simpleminded, gullible little undertaker will ruin what I've waited so long for. You may be assured of that, Mrs. Harper."

"You may not be aware of it, my lord, but you are touching my person. Remove your hand from me at once."

"Yes, well." He shook her away from him. He went to the sideboard and poured himself another whiskey, downing it in a single gulp. "I'll take my leave now. Don't forget what I've said."

After he stormed out, Violet sat back down, rubbing her arm. It hurt where he'd seized her, and she hoped she wouldn't be bruised. What pained her more than her arm was her own thoughts.

What was the real reason for Lord Marcheford's visit? To simply scare her? Did he genuinely believe his wife died of consumption, or did he wish for everyone else to believe it?

What might the heir to a title do to ensure his succession went smoothly? Murder his wife? Violet shook her head. Despite his boorish character, she couldn't quite accept him as a callous wife killer. Besides, if he'd killed his wife to smooth the path for his inheritance, for what reason would he have killed his wife's friends? To throw suspicion away from Lady Marcheford's death?

Something just wasn't right with that theory.

Then there was Mr. Meredith, a sly and undoubtedly shrewd member of the mews staff. But how could someone who chafed against the royal family possibly have been hired at the palace? It was highly unlikely. Was Mr. Caradoc perhaps mistaken in his assessment of the young man?

Who was guilty? Lord Marcheford, the future Marquess of Salford and despiser of moralists; or the newly hired groom, Meredith, who was agitating against the aristocracy?

She'd spent enough time with Lord Marcheford. Perhaps it was time to visit Mr. Meredith.

It had required all of Violet's skills to ensure that Reese Meredith was her driver for the short ride to Buckingham Palace to attend yet another of the queen's desired séances. Violet intended to use the time to ferret out a murderer.

"Good evening, Mrs. Harper," Meredith said as he held out a gloved hand to help her into the enclosed carriage. A groom stood on the rear boards. "How fortunate I am to escort you back to the palace."

The man was all smiles and charm, but Violet shivered inwardly as she recalled Mr. Caradoc's report of the man. "Thank you," she said.

Meredith shut the door and jumped onto the driver's box while Violet leaned back to decide how to corner Meredith in conversation once they arrived at their destination. They'd barely left St.

James's courtyard when Meredith pulled the carriage off the road. Why, he was entering the drive to Marlborough House. Were they picking up the Prince and Princess of Wales?

It didn't seem likely that they would be forced to share a vehicle with an undertaker.

The carriage stopped well before the house's main doors, and after some commotion and discussion from above Meredith opened the carriage door and hopped in to sit across from her, as the groom took over driving back out of Marlborough House.

"Pardon me, what are you doing?" Violet said. She was no refined lady, but she knew that Meredith's unseemly behavior was not only startling but also unnerving. However, he'd certainly taken care of her problem with how to corner him. He'd cornered her instead.

"Don't worry, Mrs. Harper; I mean no harm. I just wanted to talk to you, and I figured you wouldn't mind a bit of company. I'm Reese Meredith."

She nodded once at him. "I remember who you are, and I certainly hope you intend me no harm, since we are in a royal carriage, positioned between two royal palaces."

He grinned. "Harming you would be most unwise. I'm just very curious about you. You're an undertaker, yet you seem friendly with all of the women in the palace. Do they have you around in case a body drops?"

"Are you of the impression that people in palaces simply drop dead for no reason?"

He considered this. "No, they always die for a reason. I just don't understand why an undertaker would be around all of the time. Isn't it bad luck for the queen to be around you?"

Violet sighed. "No, the queen isn't permitted to be around death itself; hence she doesn't attend funerals. There is no rule against her being near an undertaker."

"But there must be some reason why you've been able to get near her. Does she like you because you both wear black all of the time?"

"Why are you so curious about my relationship with the queen, Mr. Meredith?"

"Why, because I'm new around here, and you seemed to be in the best place to tell me how to make my way in with my employer."

"Your employer is the superintendent of the mews, and the crown equerry above him."

"That he is. But it doesn't hurt to get the notice of those at the top, does it?"

Had Meredith actually just winked at her?

"Is there anything else you wish to know, Mr. Meredith?"

He didn't seem put out by her rebuffing his question. Instead, he changed subjects. "When I drove you and the queen to Cumberland Lodge, I heard you talking about your husband. He's planning to build a dynamite factory?"

Violet didn't like this turn in the conversation at all.

"Perhaps. What of it?"

He shrugged. "Nothing. I'm just a curious fellow. How is dynamite usually used?"

"My husband sees its greatest application in the opening of coal mines. He believes it to be safer than the current method of pouring black powder into paper cylinders inside drilled holes and igniting them."

"Most coal mines are in Wales, aren't they? Do you think the miners will be safer underground because the mine is blown up with dynamite?"

Violet remembered the article she'd read about the Mold riots. "Mr. Meredith, you have no accent, but are you by chance Welsh? Have you visited Flintshire before?"

The color drained from his face. "Why would you suggest that?"

So the art tutor may have been right about Meredith. She tried another question.

"Did you know Miss Lillian Cortland?"

He was recovered by this point, a cheeky grin on his face once more. "Can't say that I did. Who was she?"

"A young woman involved in the moralist movement. I buried her this morning."

"Is that right? Sounds tragic."

"It was, Mr. Meredith. Some think she may have been murdered."

He stared steadily at her, his expression not flinching. "Very tragic, Mrs. Harper. Why do you ask me?"

It was time to disengage herself from his presence. "No reason. Look, we've arrived."

Meredith looked out the window. "I must be quick." He scrambled out the door of the still-rolling carriage and somehow clambered up and over the roof to the groom's stand. As the coach came to a stop, Meredith hopped down once more and helped Violet out as composed as though he'd been nothing more than a dutiful servant the whole time.

As she removed her hand from his she whispered, "You think you are clever, Mr. Meredith, but you aren't that clever."

He smiled cryptically. "Oh, but I am, Mrs. Harper. You have no idea."

9

Violet was shaken by her encounter with Reese Meredith but wasn't sure what to make of him. Had he somehow been impacted by the events in Mold and was now seeking revenge on the queen for it? But how would killing two of Louise's friends amount to revenge? And how did Miss Cortland work into it?

More important, what did Violet have to take to the queen? That Meredith was saucy and insolent? So were half the staff at any royal palace when not around their sovereign. That he'd been in the family's private rooms uninvited? He wouldn't be the first servant to take a peek inside an area where he had no business.

No, Violet would have to catch him at something, although it had to be soon, and before he did something truly dangerous.

Once inside, Violet, the queen, Beatrice, Louise, Bertie, and Alix were seated around the large, round table with Mr. Brown, who introduced Frawley, another outdoor servant who would be assisting with the evening's event. Mr. Frawley didn't look much like a ghillie to Violet, with his soft hands and skin pale from lack of sun, but the queen seemed to know him and welcomed him warmly.

Violet hadn't been in this particular room before. It was cozy by palace standards, despite its high and gilded ceiling. The furniture was more modest and the draperies less formal, although, like every other one of the queen's personal rooms, it was filled with Albert memorabilia. Dominating this room was a marble bust of the man on the fireplace mantel. Near the fireplace was an easel containing a photograph of the queen and all five of her daughters gathered around the bust, gazing longingly at it.

As Brown explained what was to happen, Violet drifted off into her own thoughts again. Mr. Meredith certainly had mischief on his mind, but what about Lord Marcheford? He seemed a malevolent man, who had quite possibly killed his wife.

Was that it? Had Lord Marcheford killed his wife, while Mr. Meredith had been responsible for Lady Maud and Miss Cortland? Was Violet dealing with two or more killers and it only seemed like one? She shook her head. None of it made any sense.

"And now we will dim the lights, so that when the spirits enter the room they will nae be blinded. Mr. Frawley, will ye take care to extinguish the lamps? Ah, also, I seem to have forgotten my pocket watch. If ye would be so kind as to retrieve it. While he is gone, we will all join hands, to provide the energy for the spirits to join us."

How very perfect. Violet had paid no attention to Mr. Brown up to this point, and now she had no idea what to expect. She wished she could retreat back to St. James's. She needed to coalesce all of her thoughts into lists that she could mull over.

She tucked her right hand into Alix's, while her left hand enveloped Princess Beatrice's.

The lamps were dimmed one by one, and soon there was only the glow of candles in the center of the table. Utter silence dominated the room, except for Bertie's low sigh, which was quickly shushed by the queen.

"Forgive us, spirits, for disturbing ye," Mr. Brown said, his voice now a remarkable baritone. "We are a pitiful group of wanderers on this side who seek answers to difficult questions. Ye dinnae know how anxious we are to know your opinion on many matters."

Brown cleared his throat. "But we seek one of ye most specifically, His Royal Highness, Albert. Are ye there, Your Highness?"

A few moments of silence were followed by a cool breeze passing over the table. Several of the candles went out, leaving only the barest glow of light in the room. Muffled gasps broke through the quiet.

Violet shivered—from the cold, she hoped—and as the seconds ticked on, her mind wandered again. Should she go to Inspector Hurst and tell him about Mr. Meredith and Lord Marcheford? But how would Hurst react any differently than the queen? Violet had nothing concrete to tell either of them. Did she have the mettle to catch out the criminal herself? She'd done it before—

Several short raps startled Violet back to the present. Next to her, Beatrice tightened her grip on Violet's hand.

Where had the raps come from? They seemed to fill the room.

"Your Highness?" Brown asked, his voice low.

Two more raps and a distant rattling.

"Your Highness, thank ye for troubling yourself for us. Are ye aware of your dear wife in the room?"

Two raps. Were they coming from beneath the table?

Victoria sighed contentedly.

"Your daughters Princess Louise and Princess Beatrice are here."

Two more raps. No, the sound was from above somewhere.

"Do you see your son and his wife, the Prince and Princess of Wales?"

The same two raps.

"Your Highness, ye may also recognize Mrs. Harper."

Silence.

"Your Highness, she was your undertaker."

Two sharp raps.

Brown raised his voice once again. "We seek your wisdom, sir. The spirits wish for Mrs. Harper to uncover a certain foul and nefarious plot brewing in the halls of the palace. But she has nae been able to do so and your beloved wife grows worried. If you please, Your Highness"—Brown's voice dropped to just above a whisper—"help Her Majesty push the undertaker in the right direction."

Violet was reminded of a minister she'd once heard, who could modulate his voice up and down so well that the congregation was taken for a verbal voyage through stormy waters and left exhausted by the time they docked for communion.

She braced for rough seas.

A series of raps filled the room again. It was impossible to tell where they were coming from. It was as though they came from everywhere at once.

"Yes, yes," Brown said, his voice barely audible.

The room went silent again and Violet supposed they might be done, but then the rapping began again. This time it was erratic: a few quick raps, silence, a single rap accompanied by that odd, distant rattling again.

"Yes, I understand ye. Yes, I will tell her. What of—" The rapping increased in tempo, and so did Brown's voice.

"Your Highness, I feel your agitation. I cannae follow you. Ye must give me more time."

The noises dropped to a few intermittent knocks.

Violet saw Brown nodding sagely in the candles' glow. Once the knocks stopped entirely, he said—once again much more quietly—"Thank you, Your Highness, for this informative news. I will pass your greetings on to the queen and your children."

The rattling started again and faded away. They all still sat at the table, hands clutched in the near darkness. Beatrice's hand was moist in Violet's own, although Alix's was ice-cold.

Were they to stay posed like this forever? Did the queen have no idea that Mr. Frawley was Brown's accomplice in this?

Mr. Brown grunted, and both Beatrice and Alix released hands with Violet. Mr. Frawley returned, sweating but holding up the brass watch by its chain. "My apologies, Mr. Brown. I had difficulty finding it."

"As it turns out, we did well enough without it. Kindly relight the room."

The gas lamps soon came on again and Violet blinked to regain focus in the light. The queen's face was practically beatific.

"Mr. Frawley, you missed Mr. Brown's connection with the prince. It is always such a comfort to everyone to sense his presence. If only the entire nation could benefit from it."

"Indeed, madam," Mr. Frawley said as he stepped into the background like a footman waiting upon a dinner table.

"Now, Mr. Brown, do tell us what the prince said. It isn't fair to keep us in suspense."

The queen's ghillie smiled and inclined his head. "As you wish. The prince extended his felicitations to his children, cautioning them to be respectful of their mother and to be ever mindful of their positions in the world.

"He had special words for you, madam, but I dinnae dare repeat them, lest they shock the ears of young Princess Beatrice. Suffice to say that your husband misses you."

The queen brought a hand to her mouth as if to cover her shock, but her sparkling eyes spoke delight at what she'd heard.

"All of that in a couple of noisy bangings? How very clever," Bertie muttered.

Brown continued as if he hadn't heard the prince. "He also reassured me that Lady Maud and Lady Marcheford are at rest and at peace. Justice, though, must be found for them. Mrs. Harper, it is someone in this room who has the answers you seek. Ask and ye shall receive. He also makes a request of you, that you remember that those who hide in the open are often the most concealed."

"What does that mean?" Violet asked.

"I don't know. Those that live in the Beyond can sometimes phrase things in a way that is difficult to decipher."

"What nonsense," Bertie said.

Did Brown mean Louise? Himself? Violet knew better than to ask him directly, since all she would receive would be a veiled, obscure response.

"That's all?" Victoria said. "We had so hoped to learn more about what the spirits inside the palace want."

Brown spread both hands in his defense. "Madam, I can only repeat what the spirits tell me."

Bertie stared at the queen incredulously. "Seriously, Mother? You believe this to be the work of a true medium? He obviously used Frawley to conduct this trickery."

"Hush, Son. You have no understanding of Mr. Brown's deeply empathetic connection to the other world."

Alix comforted Bertie, who glared at Brown so murderously that Violet would have believed him guilty of Lady Marcheford's and Lady Maud's deaths, if he'd had any reason to want them dead.

Bertie abruptly rose with such force that he nearly knocked

down his chair behind him. "I believe we have concluded our little séance. Mother, how nice that you've had a chat with Father. Beatrice, Louise, we will see you again for Mother's birthday." He nodded stiffly at Violet, and he and Alix took their leave.

His abrupt departure resulted in Victoria's lengthy exposition on her willful and unloving son and what Albert would have done if he were not relegated to the spirit world.

Now, though, everyone else in the room was looking at Violet, as if waiting for her to make some pronouncement about how she would fulfill Albert's request.

It was proving to be a very long afternoon.

Violet folded up the note she'd been handed, a request from Mrs. Butler to meet her at a coffee shop near the moralist's headquarters. She assumed Mrs. Butler wanted to discuss some aspect of Miss Cortland's funeral expenses or perhaps the installation of a gravestone.

Since this was a business-related call, Violet once again donned her tall black hat with its trailing black ribbons, one of the hallmark symbols of her trade. Peering between the drapes of her room, she saw that it was raining, the drops pelting the hot granite blocks of the street and hissing in steam. At least the rain washed away some of the coal smuts that perpetually floated through the air.

She'd intended to walk part of the way to the coffee shop, but perhaps not. Grabbing her wood-handled umbrella, she joined the other Londoners in the street who were darting to and fro, trying to stay dry.

The cab stand was crowded and few cabs were available, making Violet late to her meeting with Mrs. Butler. Nevertheless, the woman greeted her enthusiastically with a kiss to the cheek.

They sat before a window and ordered cups of chocolate and a plate of shortbread to share. They talked pleasantries until the white-aproned server placed steaming cups and a platter of sweet biscuits before them.

"So, Mrs. Butler, did you wish to discuss Miss Cortland? I trust you were pleased with her funeral and have no complaints? Perhaps you are interested in adding—"

"Please, call me Josephine. And actually, no, I wished to see you about something else. I understand from Louise that you are investigating Miss Cortland's death as a murder. Please, don't look surprised. The princess and I are closer friends than anyone knows, for obvious reasons.

"It seemed to me that if you are looking further into Miss Cortland's death, there is something you need to know." Josephine paused.

"Yes?"

"I am loath to say anything about my associate that could be misconstrued, or could add to the pile of grievances her parents had against her."

"I understand. Whatever you say will remain confidential with me, Josephine. And you must call me Violet."

"Thank you. I thought you'd be discreet. Miss Cortland was stepping out secretly with a young man."

Violet frowned. "That's not so unusual. Young women sneak out with young men behind their parents' backs all the time, despite their parents' best efforts to preserve their daughters' virtues."

"Yes, but this particular young man was wholly unsuitable for her."

"Was he in a lower class?"

"Not at all. That's the problem. He was in society."

"Then why was he a problem?"

"He was married."

Violet dropped her pastry. It fell into her lap and rolled to the floor, leaving a trail of buttery crumbs on her dress.

"You say he was married? To whom? Who is he?"

"I don't know. As I told Louise, Miss Cortland never offered a name, so secretive was she about it. I didn't want to pry into a distasteful situation. I just knew that—according to her—he was desperately unhappy in his marriage, but then, they always are, aren't they?"

"You never met him?"

"No, he never came around to the association headquarters, but why would a man of his class do so? She always met him in parks and other places. It's a tragedy the sin that people commit in their marital unions, Violet, whether it be with willing partners or if they pay for the opportunity."

"I suppose in that case it was rather ironic that Miss Cortland was trying to help prostitutes, yet allowed herself to fall prey to a man."

Josephine nodded sadly. "In my work, I have chosen to focus on the poor girls who are paid for their services, since, despite the money, they are often the least willing and most abused."

As Mrs. Butler went on to talk about some of the tragic cases she'd seen, Violet was connecting several things together in her mind. If she was right, there was a definite link between Lady Marcheford and Miss Cortland, and Violet didn't like where it was pointing.

What could she even do about it? Confronting Lord Marcheford was out of the question, and Inspector Hurst would only laugh at her supposition.

How confident was she of her theory, anyway?

"Have you ever seen a lock hospital, Violet? Let me take you to the London Lock Asylum in Kensal Green. It's near the St. John the Evangelist chapel, so that the women can be ministered to there. Their customers, of course, receive no spiritual counseling."

They took a train to the hospital. It was located across the street from Kensal Green Cemetery, a public burial ground where Violet had overseen many interments. How ironic that the women who died inside the lock hospital would not have been permitted burial in the cemetery.

The hospital itself had around a hundred beds, filled with women wearing tattered gray gowns, beneath tattered old bedcovers. The decrepit fabric looked right at home with the cracked plaster walls whose dull green paint was peeling off in dismal sheets.

Some beds contained two women, each barely hanging on to her side. Several patients looked as though they were burning up with fevers. One woman was hunched over a bedside commode, rocking back and forth and groaning as she expelled waste. A few bored physicians sat at bedsides or stared apathetically out of windows.

On another floor was a men's ward, housing about a dozen men who had submitted themselves voluntarily for treatment of their sexual diseases.

"That is the difference, Violet," Josephine said. "The men come and go as they please and get medical care if they so choose. The women are forced into the lock hospital. Both have the same problem; why such substantially different treatment?"

"Why are they called lock hospitals?" Violet asked. "Because the women are locked in?"

"No, it comes from the old leprosy hospitals, which came to be known as lock hospitals because of the 'locks,' or rags, used to cover the lepers' lesions."

Violet had visited a workhouse once before and was hard pressed to decide which conditions were worse: those of the workhouse or the lock hospital. Surely as many people died in each.

After Violet and Josephine completed their tour of the hospital the sky was still pelting the streets, so the two women agreed to take a cab together to Josephine's headquarters, whereupon Violet would take it back to St. James's Palace.

The rain had been steady since Violet left the palace, and now the piles of horse droppings in the roadway were crumbling into the swirl of water on the granite.

A steady rain usually resulted in a mucky mess in the streets, followed by a human stampede to laundries.

Violet lifted the hem of her dress. She would undoubtedly be in the stampede.

As was true earlier, the cab stand nearest the hospital was crowded with Londoners looking for dry passage to their destinations, so Violet and Josephine decided to try their luck finding a cab elsewhere. With umbrellas up and offering little protection, they plodded through the crowds to a side street, hoping it would be less busy.

It wasn't.

"Let's try one more block up," Josephine said.

They pushed on through the thronged street, but it was no less crowded in another block. "Let me try to hail a cab here," Violet said. She stepped away from Josephine and looked both ways up and down the street.

"Oh, I believe I see an available one coming from—" Violet didn't finish, for someone came from behind and shoved her violently onto the pavement, into the path of an overloaded furniture delivery truck. She landed on her right cheek and felt an agonizing burn from the street scraping up her face. Frozen in pain, she was unable to move as she saw the oncoming truck bearing down upon her. Four horses scrambled to obey their master's command to stop. Violet saw the panic in their rolling white eyes and heard a woman scream.

The driver stopped, but not before the horses had scattered pebbles and wet dung into Violet's face.

"What in the name of—?" the driver bellowed, jumping down from his box as Violet struggled to get up. Other passersby, seeing that Violet had a rescuer, continued on their way as if nothing had happened. The driver offered her an arm, which Violet gratefully accepted.

"Are you ill?" he asked.

Violet shook her head, still too shaken to form words.

"It's not often that women go tumbling into the street," he said. "And if you'll pardon my saying so, you look a fright. You're bleeding, madam."

She touched a gloved hand to her face and it came back wet, but who knew if it was blood or rain? "My umbrella," she said weakly.

"Here." He retrieved it, along with her hat, from where they had each flown several feet away. "Do you need me to take you somewhere? A hospital?"

Violet was too wet at this point to be saved by an umbrella, although at least it had made it through unscathed. "No, I'll be fine. My friend . . ." She looked around. Where was Josephine?

The driver nodded and resumed his trek, guiding his horses carefully past her.

Violet finally saw Josephine, huddled nearby in the doorway of an abandoned shop and clutching her left arm in her other hand.

"What happened to you?" Violet asked.

"Nothing. I'm fine. You're injured, though."

"It's not serious. I'm sure I look—and smell—worse than it is. Did you see who pushed me?"

Josephine shook her head as she stepped out of the doorway. "Come, we must get your face attended to."

They walked together slowly, as Violet had sustained what would surely end up as many purple bruises. Josephine, she noticed, still clutched her arm. "Tell me what is wrong," Violet said.

"I'm quite all right. I just bumped my arm."

Violet stopped and tugged on Josephine's hand. It came away smeared with blood and Violet inspected the other woman's arm. "Good Lord, you've been stabbed."

Josephine snatched her hand away from Violet's and continued walking. "I said it's nothing."

Her own injuries forgotten, Violet said, "How can you say this? You're the one who needs attending to. You might bleed to death. You need help."

"You don't understand. In what I do, there is a certain element of society that not only doesn't approve of what I'm doing but is willing to go to certain lengths to stop me."

"Are you saying that you know who attacked us?"

"No, I'm saying that if it gets out that I was stabbed, no matter how minor the injury, then men and women will be afraid to join my cause. I can't allow that, and so we will keep this matter to ourselves."

"I was nearly killed so that some unhinged lunatic could attack you?"

"Probably. I must apologize. I should have warned you that association with me can have terrible consequences, as poor, dear Miss Cortland learned. God has always protected me in this righteous cause, but I can't say that everyone else has so much insulating cover."

As they continued walking in silence, it occurred to Violet that Josephine wasn't necessarily the target. It may have been she.

Worse, perhaps the attacker actually meant harm for both of them. But other than planning a funeral for the recently departed Miss Cortland, what did she and the great moralist leader have in common?

Friendship with Princess Louise.

But why would that result in an attack in the middle of the

street? Did someone hate Louise so much that he was willing to kill everyone around her? It simply made no sense. The more Violet dwelled on it, the more confused she became.

Surely there must be an answer right in front of her, one that she was unable to see.

Violet dropped Josephine off at her headquarters, ensuring the woman made it inside safely. Josephine paused in the doorway and turned back.

"Violet, if you've no plans on Tuesday, would you like to accompany me to Parliament? They are having a discussion over the Contagious Diseases Acts that you might find interesting."

Violet was about to politely decline when she realized there might be others in attendance who disliked what Josephine and her compatriots were doing. Might this be a chance to discover who had attacked her and Violet?

"I would be delighted."

Reese was nervously excited as he left the meeting, his senses on alert, as though he'd been given supernatural powers and was unsure when to use them. It proved a much better feeling than mourning for Margaret, and he thought maybe he was on the verge of doing something truly remarkable that schoolchildren would study centuries from now.

Mr. Marx had thoroughly whipped up the crowd tonight. The man's eyes blazed when he spoke, so impassioned was he about his arguments, arguments that made so much sense it was amazing that they'd never been implemented in society before.

Marx envisioned a new society, populated with men who would be devoid of selfishness, greed, laziness, hate, fear, or any other undesirable trait. They would be utterly healthy, of great intelligence, hardworking, and infinitely talented.

Reese saw that potential for himself.

This new man would, through his industry and talents, develop a society of such abundance that any individual could partake of all that he needed just as easily as today's man partakes of oxygen in the atmosphere. His near perfectness meant that there would be no need for governments or armies or police or courts or taxes. Each man would voluntarily minister to the well-being of others.

What was Marx's slogan that they had all chanted? Oh yes: "From each according to his ability, to each according to his need."

Thus there would be no need for anyone to own land or any property and instead it would be redistributed for everyone to work upon. No land ownership meant a classless society, and Reese would be the equal of men such as Lord Christie. Men like those who owned *The Times* would be swept away. If only the revolution had come sooner, perhaps Margaret wouldn't have died at the hands of soldiers answering to the bourgeois mine owners.

"Bourgeois" and "proletariat" were two words Reese had learned to love and use regularly. The bourgeois were those who owned everything and used the wealth thus created to oppress the proletariat, or working class. He rolled the word "proletariat" around on his tongue again. It was an exciting word, full of significance and opportunity. Too bad he couldn't use it on any of the other stable workers, lest they become suspicious of him.

More than anything, though, Reese approved of Marx's means to achieve this perfect society. To establish equality, the proletariat must overthrow the bourgeois by riots or the creation of unions or by any other means necessary.

Hadn't this been Reese's own plan all along? To eradicate those who were responsible for the wanton destruction of life? To create long-lasting change in society?

Marx had further expounded on his critique of a capitalist economy, but Reese's mind was too full of possibilities to listen to the man go on about the abolition of religion in society to make his plan work or his confidence that the miracles of science would eventually change human nature itself.

No, Reese was confident that he'd found someone who could eloquently express precisely what he himself thought. If the enthusiasm of the crowd was any indication, Marx's communist revolution was coming to England, and Reese's actions would propel him to the forefront of the movement, maybe even earning him public recognition from Marx himself.

Perhaps he should consider expanding his plan even further. What were one or two more deaths when it meant a brand-new world?

He whistled as he made his way back to the mews, unaware that another member of Marx's audience observed his departure with interest.

To get away from all of the madness surrounding Buckingham Palace, Violet made plans to visit with her old friend Mary Cooke, a mourning dressmaker of some renown. The two women had become friends years before Violet had moved to the Colorado Territory, through their respective occupations in funeral work.

Mary was twenty years older than Violet, yet her face was still youthful, this despite marriage to a man who was feckless and weak and caused Mary no end of heartache.

They met for a light luncheon at a hotel near Mary's dressmaking shop.

"Violet, my dear, what happened to you?" Mary jumped up from the table at the sight of her.

"I had an unfortunate encounter with some street gravel. First, tell me about yourself. How is business? Have you heard from George?"

Mary's eyes immediately clouded over. "He is still in Switzerland. I begin to despair of him ever returning home."

"He always does."

"Yes, I suppose so." The women ordered carrot soup and larded fillets of rabbit. "Would you like to go with me to Morris, Marshall, and Faulkner?" Mary said. "They sell decorative work. Stained glass, furniture, embroideries, that sort of thing. I want to look at their fabrics. Mr. Morris is a designer and is known for his interior fabrics."

"Are you planning to redecorate?"

"Yes, my—our—bedchamber. I think George would be pleased to see it redone on his return."

Violet could believe that. George Cooke was quite fond of spending money. His latest disappearance had occurred after he lifted some jewelry and money Mary had hidden underneath a floorboard of her shop.

"I'm thinking of perhaps having the room repapered. The firm was hired to do some rooms at St. James's Palace, you know."

Which meant that they were probably very expensive and beyond Mary's budget. Yet what wouldn't the woman sacrifice for her wayward husband?

"I would be happy to accompany you. I'm considering buying back into Morgan Undertaking, and Sam and I will move into the rooms above the shop if I do. I might need some wallpaper and draperies myself."

Mary smiled. "We will have a lovely afternoon. Now, you must tell me why you hurled yourself into the street."

Violet recounted everything in detail for her friend, from the queen's initial summons to Miss Cortland's funeral yesterday. By the time Violet was done, she and Mary had polished off their meals and tasty servings of gooseberry tarts and were halfway through a bottle of sherry. Mary didn't utter a word during Violet's tale, only asking a question when she was certain Violet was done.

"So you think that this Lord Marcheford may have murdered his wife, as well as his mistress?"

"That's just it. I'm not sure. There is something very dark about him. Being dark isn't much to go to Scotland Yard with, though, is it?"

"No. And anyway, the heir to a marquess would never commit a murder on his own, unless he was in a fervor of madness. He would hire someone to do it for him."

Violet contemplated Mary's opinion as she poured a final glass of sherry for herself. Was she right? Was a lord above sullying his hands? But whom would Lord Marcheford have hired?

Reese Meredith, the coachman, flashed through her mind. Was he the type who was willing to commit murder for the right price?

She shook off the thought. Impossible. How could Lord Marcheford be acquainted with Meredith?

Perhaps it was time to find out exactly how Mr. Meredith had acquired his job.

Violet and Mary left the hotel for Mr. Morris's shop, located in

Red Lion Square. The expanse of windows at the front of the shop was brimming in a joyful kaleidoscope of color and patterns covering tables, chairs, and wall hangings, with lengths of brightly tinted fabrics draped over everything. The two women stood outside, gazing in and trying to catch their breath over the profusion of styles, unlike anything they'd ever seen.

"Shall we go inside?" Violet said.

"In a moment." Mary took a deep breath. "I've been thinking," she said, "of going to Switzerland to retrieve George."

"You mean, like a package?"

Mary laughed, despite the tears welling up in her eyes. "Yes. I need to know what he's doing when he runs off on all of these buying trips for watch parts. I worry that things aren't what he says they are."

Violet squeezed Mary's hand sympathetically. "My friend, you may not like what you find."

"You're right. But I have to *know*."

"Perhaps you should hire a detective to track him and report back to you."

"I've thought about that, but no, I must do it myself. If I go, then I will just be a wife surprising her husband. If all is well, and then he comes home to a newly redecorated bedchamber, he will be doubly surprised. I never need tell George that I was suspicious of him. If I hire a man to spy on him, and he discovers anything . . . dubious . . . about George's activities, I will have to admit that I was having him followed. It makes me look as if I was mistrustful."

"You *are* mistrustful."

"But if my fears amount to nothing, I wouldn't want George to know I doubted him."

Violet didn't think Mary's plan would have good results, but she understood her friend's desire to simply know. "Well then, we'd best get your room redecorated so you can be on your way."

They spent the afternoon in the company of Mr. William Morris himself, who unrolled bolt after bolt of richly dyed wallpapers for Mary's inspection. For a few hours, Violet forgot about death.

* * *

The next morning, Violet stepped into the superintendent's tiny office inside the mews. Unlike the spotlessly maintained stables and courtyard area, this cramped room was dusty and heaped forlornly with broken harnesses, torn box blankets, cracked carriage lamps, and stacks of books on horse care. The horses themselves worked in better conditions. Despite the slovenly appearance of his office, the man himself was painstakingly groomed, his thinning hair combed and oiled and his nascent paunch well controlled with a waist cincher.

"Yes, madam?" Mr. Norton said, with an air so bored he might almost be an aristocrat.

"If you don't mind, I'd like to ask you a couple of questions."

"We've been instructed to help you whenever possible."

"Thank you. I was wondering how it is that the staff here, particularly the grooms and coachmen, obtain their positions with the palace."

"That's an odd question. Why do you wish to know?"

"If you could perhaps just help me . . ."

Norton cleared his throat. "Of course. Our men come with impeccable credentials. Many have served in Her Majesty's cavalry, and have distinguished service in the Crimean War, the Indian rebellions, or the Opium Wars."

He opened a desk drawer and pulled out a folder. "Others come with unimpeachable references from quality people."

"Quality people?"

"Usually a peer. Certainly no one less than a baronet. Is there someone specific you want to know about?"

Violet wanted desperately to ask about Reese Meredith, but there was no point in tipping Norton off that she was suspicious of him.

"No, you've answered my question. Thank you, Mr. Norton."

She didn't see him frowning and scratching his carefully arranged hair as she left.

Bertie was making a final attempt to convince his mother of Brown's unsuitability to serve in the palace, appalled that not only was he having to supplicate himself over that donkey, but also his mother, the Queen of England for heaven's sake, was too blind to see that Brown was undermining her reputation.

Bertie had come alone this time, to spare Alix what was sure to be a frightful row. He was glad he did, for when he stepped into Victoria's private sitting room his mother looked braced for battle. Undoubtedly, he, too, looked prepared with his own verbal arsenal.

"May I join you for tea?" he asked, trying to keep himself at a low simmer.

A maid poured for them both; then Victoria waved her away.

"We don't have long. Mr. Brown is in the stables preparing Lochnagar for our afternoon ride."

Bertie swallowed his irritation with his first gulp of tea. *Mother rides out nearly every day with that drunkard leading her.* "I'm sure you will enjoy the fresh air."

"It's hot outside."

"I imagine many people must see you when you go on your afternoon jaunts."

"The people like to see their sovereign."

"They also like to gossip. What do you imagine they say when they see you riding with your ghillie every single day?"

"Don't be ridiculous. Everyone knows that we are devoted to your father and would never consider such a thing. Besides, Mr. Brown is a *servant.*"

"It's not ridiculous, Mother. There are people who call you Mrs. Brown now. Do you understand? They think you are intimate enough with him that you could be his wife. You must dismiss him."

She stirred two cubes of sugar into her tea. "Son, your jealousy makes you petty."

"Jealousy? What have I to be jealous of?" Had he just snorted again? He must temper that, lest someone bridle him and escort him to the mews.

"Your mother's crumb of happiness."

"You are happy with that whiskey-swilling, arrogant dung collector, who shows you no more respect than a sailor shows a prostitute?"

"Your language, Bertie, is really quite atrocious."

"Not as atrocious as all of the rumors that follow that sot around.

Do you know what I heard about him yesterday? That he is a fol-lower of that Marx fellow, that Brown is a communist."

Victoria snorted. "Of all the foolish things you've said before, Bertie, this must be the silliest. Of course Mr. Brown isn't a com-munist. Anyone who gave off even a whiff of revolutionary ten-dencies would be dismissed instantly."

"Except that you can't smell him out through the bottle of Begg's Best that he keeps on him. I tell you, Mother, no good will result from this unseemly attachment you have to Brown."

"Bertie, the Bible says to attend to the plank in your own eye before pointing out the speck in another's eye. Need we remind you of your own troubles with Sir Charles Mordaunt?"

"Nothing will come of it. It's all idle gossip."

"Is it? Sir Charles has accused you of improprieties with his wife, Harriet, and will probably drag your name through his in-evitable divorce proceedings, and you believe that nothing will come of it?"

"Sir Charles is a little put out by his wife's . . . private adven-tures. She isn't walking through Hyde Park every day on the arm of some other man."

Victoria pushed her teacup and saucer away from her and leaned forward. *When did Mother become so pudgy?* "No, she is merely dallying with the Prince of Wales, whose wife is carrying their fifth child."

"Those are unsubstantiated rumors."

"Perhaps we should refer to Lady Mordaunt as the Princess of Wales, eh?"

"You're changing the subject, Mother."

"And you are forgetting that we are the queen. As your mother, we are sorry to have this conversation. As your queen, we demand that you stop and never bring it up again."

Bertie threw down his napkin and pushed back his chair. Why did every discussion with his mother end up like this? "It may be over for now, but, assuredly, your adoring people will remind you of it over and over."

He stalked back to Marlborough House. How could he ever make his mother see reason?

*   *   *

Violet accompanied Mary to Charing Cross station, with a final plea to her friend not to go. "No good will result from surprising him like this," she said.

Mary, however, had developed a will as strong as that of the iron steam carriage that would carry her to Dover before she boarded a ship to Calais and then another series of trains across the border of France to the city of Lausanne in Switzerland.

"I must know, and this is the only way to be certain of his fidelity. I will be fine, Violet, I promise."

Violet nodded in resignation and kissed Mary's cheek. "When you and George return, we will visit Madame Tussauds to celebrate your happiness. I hear they have an exhibit on the upcoming opening of the Suez Canal that I would love to see."

Mary smiled and boarded her train, waving through her window as she sat down. Violet kissed her gloved fingers and waved back. How she hoped Mary would still be smiling when she returned home.

Back at St. James's Palace, Violet had two letters waiting for her, one from Sam and one from Susanna. She opened Sam's first. He was back in northern England, dejected over his meetings with Nobel and the officials in Pembrey.

> *They have refused to permit the building of a dynamite factory. The site Mr. Nobel had located was ideal, but it is of no use to purchase it. I don't know what to do next. Should you and I return to Colorado, where I would try to build a factory to service gold and silver mines in the West, or continue to stay here in Great Britain in hopes of eventually changing minds in either Wales or the North?*
>
> *I confess, my love, that I see that thousands of miners' lives might be saved through the use of dynamite. I saw terrible things in Wales. Mining is a dangerous business. Could I be of help here? Should I stay until I am absolutely certain dynamite will never be used? I know you have a desire to formally reopen your undertaking activities—should we stay?*
>
> *But if we stay, what of Susanna?*

He then offered an admonition:

> *Now, my darling wife, I expect that you will keep out*
> *of trouble until I return. No chats with murderers, no*
> *tumbles over bridges, and most certainly no near accidents*
> *with trains.*

Had all of those things really happened over the past few months? It was hard to believe that life was more adventurous here than even in Colorado.

> *. . . and when I do return, I'll not go anywhere without*
> *you again. Whether we stay in England or return to*
> *Colorado, it will be together. I'll brook no arguments.*

Violet smiled and kissed the letter, in which her husband agreed with her own thoughts. How she missed him, especially as someone of good reason with whom to discuss things. Sam would have insights into Mr. Brown, Mr. Meredith, Lord Marcheford, and the host of spirits supposedly waiting for her to do something about it all.

She didn't dare write to him about it, though, lest someone else—accidentally or otherwise—open the letter. No, she would have to figure it out for herself.

She opened Susanna's letter and threw it down in frustration and dismay after reading the first two lines:

> *Dearest Mama, I hope you and Papa won't be angry,*
> *but Benjamin and I are married. We just couldn't wait*
> *another day for each other. You do understand, don't you?*

Susanna hadn't waited for Violet and Sam to return. Violet would have none of the pleasures of preparing her daughter to be wed. Sam would be so disappointed, too. Violet shook her head at the impetuousness of youth.

Of course, with Susanna already married there was now little impetus to rush back to Colorado for a wedding. So was it a blessing in disguise?

Violet retrieved the letter from the floor and continued reading. Susanna and Benjamin were planning to take a honeymoon by traveling to London, so that she could show her new husband the home of her youth, ". . . and because I don't foresee you ever returning, Mama."

Her daughter was beginning to sound like Will Swift.

The letter closed with Susanna jokingly suggesting that Violet present her to the queen.

Based on the date of the letter, Violet predicted that Susanna and Benjamin would arrive in another month. She looked around at her disheveled room. This was no place to entertain guests. Nor did she have permission from the queen for guests beyond her husband.

Perhaps it was time to meet with Will and make a commitment to owning the shop once again. Surely she could have the rooms above Morgan Undertaking ready by the time Susanna and her new husband arrived. Violet spent her evening writing a long letter to Sam, telling him about Susanna and her plan to buy back into Morgan Undertaking.

They would stay in England.

Violet didn't expect the House of Commons to be so hot and crowded. She was sweating by the time she and Josephine secured spots on the long, green leather-covered benches on one side of the viewing gallery. There were quite a few women in attendance today, and most were vigorously waving fans at their faces.

Another viewing gallery faced Violet and Josephine. Beneath each gallery were four rows of pews facing each other across a center aisle. The aisle was dominated by a desk and a tall altar chair behind it. What wasn't covered in green leather was done in paneled wood. Enormous gas chandeliers hung imposingly from the ceiling. The entire effect was dramatic and dignified.

Until the members entered. Hundreds of men in their finest

black frock coats began filing into the pit, taking seats on either side of the aisle, already arguing among themselves. Once they were seated, an older gentleman with a large, hooked nose and a florid face, wearing a judge's wig and black robes, walked ceremoniously up the center aisle and took his place in the altar chair.

"Who is that?" she whispered to Josephine.

"Evelyn Denison, the Speaker of the House. He's a Whig. I like him, as he's working to have a plain but complete commentary of the Bible written for the public."

Violet nodded. The Speaker would need considerable cosmetic attention one day. However, for now he projected determination. Denison opened up the session and recognized the honorable member for Cockburn to speak.

A middle-aged man, whose somber dress was relieved by a bright scarlet waistcoat, rose and spoke at length about the addition of more gas lampposts in heavily populated areas.

When he was finished, Denison recognized someone else, who also spoke tediously, this time about British rule in Ireland.

Violet might have found it all more interesting if it weren't so stuffy in the building. She was struggling to stay awake.

And so the next couple of hours went. Various members were recognized from either the Tory or Whig side of the aisle to discuss a variety of issues, measures, and reforms. Some generated wild debate; others were politely ignored.

Finally, the Speaker brought up the Contagious Diseases Acts, asking for opinion on them. This caused the most uncontrolled arguing of the day until the Speaker finally intervened. "Gentlemen, be seated once more. Members, I ask for your attention. I say, *SILENCE!*"

The members all sat down noiselessly, the only sound now the whirr of ladies' fans waving back and forth.

"We will now recognize Sir Charles Mordaunt, the member for South Warwickshire."

A man in his early thirties, who might be described as handsome if not for an expression so bitter it was as though he had a mouth full of ginger root, stood on the Tory side. He was trim and finely dressed, however, and moved with the lazy assurance of someone whose primary occupation was pleasing himself.

He also quickly proved to be an effective orator.

"As my distinguished colleagues are aware, there is a movement to repeal the Contagious Diseases Acts, a movement populated by derelicts, reprobates, and headstrong women. These acts, which not only protect our sailors and soldiers from disease, but also keep the health of these prostitutes in check, do not need to be repealed. No, I say the laws should be strengthened."

There were murmurs of both approval and disagreement. Next to Violet, Josephine sat as still as a statue, although her darting eyes were indicative of her total concentration on the proceedings. Violet worried that the woman might have a raging outburst if Sir Charles continued in this vein.

In this vein he indeed continued.

"The acts, passed easily in 1864, have had no deleterious effects on prostitutes. How could they, when all they do is seek out those that are infected and attempt to treat them? They are put in hospitals at taxpayer expense for this treatment for up to three months, then released to continue plying their trade. Why so much worry over it?"

Violet put a calming hand over Josephine's as a warning not to interject. She didn't need to, for another member jumped up.

"We recognize Mr. Walter, the member for Berkshire," Denison said.

This member was as corpulent as Mordaunt was thin and with as placid a countenance as Mordaunt's was churlish.

"While I appreciate Sir Charles's sincere beliefs about the Contagious Diseases Acts, he is quite mistaken about the effect on prostitutes. Despite his claim that the British taxpayers are paying for these treatments, in truth there is little funding for the lock hospitals. In fact, there are fewer than four hundred beds for these patients—when our prostitute population numbers in the thousands—and only about two hundred beds are actually funded for use. So what happens? These female venereal patients must resort to workhouse infirmaries. We all know the condition of such institutions. These unfortunates are lucky to survive the infirmaries, much less be in condition to 'continue plying their trade,' as Sir Charles states."

Josephine smiled, nodding in approval. She leaned over to Violet. "Mr. Walter publishes *The Times*. We might see a favorable article on our cause in tomorrow's paper."

But Mordaunt wasn't finished.

"The member for Berkshire might speak true, and is it any wonder that the government is reluctant to spend money on treating prostitutes when there are so many problems across Her Majesty's empire that need attention and money. Regardless, this allotment for the lock hospitals will certainly be in flux over time. What we are debating is the value of the acts themselves, which are clearly of use to a great and moral society like that of Great Britain. Why, in times past, the Bishop of Winchester himself regulated prostitution, to ensure the cleanliness of the girls. Are we not at least as concerned about it as the church leaders of the medieval period?"

Mordaunt templed his fingers together in front of his face, as though deep in thought. He spoke again.

"I'm of no doubt that Her Majesty approves of what the acts do—"

Josephine leaned over and whispered, "More than likely, Her Majesty would refuse to even have it discussed in her presence."

"—and so what we have is a small faction attempting to destroy the good work being done. What should be of no surprise to anyone here is that there are several women—moralists, as they are known—who claim to know better than their husbands, their government, and their God what is best for the unfortunates who walk the streets providing attentions to our military men. Of particular arrogance is Mrs. Josephine Butler, who formed her own organization to protest what are surely some of the most valuable pieces of legislation this body has passed in some years."

At this reference to her, Josephine visibly stiffened.

"She sends out unsuspecting women, whom she convinces that they are unsatisfied in their domestic duties, to create disturbances at public events. These women embarrass themselves by parading around, carrying signs and exhibiting the most unseemly behavior. These moralist women would be of more benefit to society if they returned to their preordained station in life."

There were several nods of agreement among the other members. Having pressed his advantage, Mordaunt managed to use it to make another point.

"In fact, so deeply do I believe in the Contagious Diseases Acts that I submit to this august body that my own wife could surely do with a stay in a lock hospital."

Scattered laughter broke out on both sides of the aisle. Denison glowered and hushed them once again.

Violet was shocked that a member of Parliament would say such a thing to an audience. Why was he doing this?

"I say this, gentlemen, to prepare you for the suit of divorce I intend to lodge against Lady Mordaunt."

The word "divorce" had everyone's attention and Mordaunt knew it. His soured face almost looked happy.

"Yes, I plan to divorce her. I was charmed by her beautiful face and charming words, but now realize I married a viper. A viper who has slithered into many other nests, including some that are perched up very, very high. So high that I dare not—yet—speak their names."

Even the viewers in the gallery gasped. Who had ever heard a baron speak so vilely of his wife in public? And in Parliament, no less. His insinuations were breathtaking, and the newspapers would undoubtedly print no end of speculations in the next day's papers.

"Therefore, yes, so confident am I in the wisdom of passing the Contagious Diseases Acts that I would recommend my wife be forced into a lock hospital for treatment, for surely her activities have resulted in a disease of—"

The Speaker stood abruptly. "We believe that no further conversation is necessary of private matters, nor of the Contagious Diseases Acts, for the day. We will continue on with the rest of the day's agenda."

Violet and Josephine left, the moralist too angry and discouraged to continue listening to the posturing and bickering of the men below.

Despite the heat of the day, it was refreshing compared to the inside of the House of Commons. Violet patted her face with a handkerchief. "Your injuries are much improved," Josephine said.

"What of you? How is your arm?"

"It is bandaged under my sleeve. It will heal, although probably not without a scar."

Violet thought of her own right arm, scarred by burns. "As long as it heals well, you will eventually not notice the scar anymore. Are you sure you don't want to report—"

"I'm quite certain. I'll not worry about what happened any further. God will preserve me to work another day, and when He has exercised all of His will through me, then perhaps some deranged man might be more successful than whoever attacked us the other day."

Violet had to admire Josephine's courage.

"And you? Have you reported that you were pushed into the street?"

"No. I didn't see him, just as you did not see your attacker."

Josephine nodded. "Perhaps God has much more for you to do, as well."

That evening, Violet contemplated what she'd heard at Parliament that day. Mordaunt had implied that his wife was dallying with men who moved in the highest circles. The Prince of Wales had a less-than-stellar reputation, but surely Mordaunt wasn't implicating Bertie, was he?

Even if he was, so what? It had nothing to do with Lady Maud, or Lady Marcheford, or Miss Cortland.

Did it?

Violet couldn't even begin to put together a connection between a cuckolded husband and the deaths of two aristocratic women and a moralist.

Except that the two aristocratic women were like his hated wife, and the moralist represented a hated viewpoint.

Violet shook her head. No, it was just too fantastic an idea and completely impossible. Lord Marcheford was a far more likely suspect.

Whoever it was, had he ceased killing? If not, could Violet search him out before he tried again?

Sleep did not come easily that night.

10

Will retrieved a bottle of champagne and passed out glasses to Violet and Harry before holding up his own and offering a toast.

"To Morgan Undertaking's previous and new co-owner! May you have an unending flow of customers who have died peacefully in their beds of old age."

"Huzzah!" Harry said, grinning.

Violet could hardly believe she'd actually secured the deal with Will and Harry and was going to be running the shop again. It was all so familiar yet all so strange and foreign. Much like working for the queen again. Could she really just step into her old life again?

Harry put down his glass, which he probably could have crushed in his lion's paw of a hand. "So, Mrs. Harper, will you and Mr. Harper be moving in upstairs?"

"That's my plan, although I know it will need renovating."

Harry nodded. "It will be good for someone to live over the shop, I think, to watch over it. Will Mr. Harper mind living above a stack of coffins?"

"Sam saw his share of bodies during the American Civil War. I doubt a few empty coffins will rattle him."

"I suppose you will want to review this first," Will said, going behind the counter and bringing forth an enormous old leather-bound ledger. It was the one she'd started years ago when she first came into the shop.

"There's a ribbon in here marking the funerals coming up in the next few days. I figured I would handle those and you can start fresh with anything new."

Violet accepted the ledger and ran her hand over it lovingly. Despite the coal fogs, the decrepit buildings, and the abundance of cutpurses, she was happy to be residing here again.

After she finished her celebration with Will and Harry, she went upstairs to look over her new lodgings. They ran the length and width of the shop and included a sitting room, study, dining room, kitchen with a reasonably new coal stove, bedroom, and small washroom with, happily, a flushing toilet.

The wallpaper was old and peeling, and discarded pieces of furniture, broken and with upholstery torn and stained, littered the rooms. There was a peculiar odor, as though a dozen cats had taken up residence. It was lucky she wasn't superstitious, or the cracked mirror hanging at a precarious angle over the fireplace mantel would have her worried.

Was Violet even remotely capable of turning these rooms into a proper living space? As soon as Mary returned from Switzerland, Violet would enlist her help in making these rooms right again. She would wait for Sam's return to move into them.

His return would, she hoped, be very soon.

Must all *of my children be unmanageable?* Victoria wondered. Of course, darling Beatrice was never a moment's trouble. And Leopold was in bed most of the time. And although Helena was constantly complaining of phantom illnesses, at least she was agreeable to her mother's wishes. The queen ran down the list of her other children, who were all either successfully married off or distinguishing themselves in military careers.

No, when it came down to it, it was just Bertie and Louise who caused so much grief. Bertie had always been wayward, but when had this rebellious streak appeared in Louise? It must have been after Albert left them. The poor girl just couldn't cope with the loss of her father, and now she ran wild, proposing all sorts of unsuitable matches for herself, like the Reverend Duckworth. What *was* Louise thinking, nearly ruining her reputation by dallying with a commoner like that?

True, he might have brought her some much-needed spiritual guidance, but how much assistance could he actually have been in that realm, given that he was conducting himself in a most undignified manner with a royal princess?

Ach ja, the tears the girl shed when Duckworth was, naturally, dismissed. Victoria hadn't heard such wailing and dramatic threats of self-destruction since, well, since Albert died.

But *that* was understandable.

And here Louise was again, bemoaning the dreadful fate to which her mother wanted to consign her, insisting that she was much more valuable to England by remaining at home, the way Helena had, and demanding to know the reason why she couldn't be treated the same way.

"Little Miss Why," Victoria said, reverting back to an old pet name for Louise that was inspired by her overly inquisitive nature as a child, "we would like it if all of our children remained at home, but most of you have a duty to me and to your country to marry one of our allies. Look here, we have a list of eligible and handsome princes, each of whom would be only too happy to call you his wife."

"I won't do it, Mother. I have too much important work to be done here."

"What work? You perform secretarial duties for us, but you know that both Helena and Beatrice will take over for you."

"I have to—" Louise stopped.

"You have to—what?"

Louise bit her lip. "Never mind."

What was the girl hiding?

"It would please us greatly if you chose an eligible prince. Your sister-in-law, Alix, has proposed her brother, the crown prince."

"You would send me to Denmark? Never to return?"

"It is a princess's duty to her country to make a marriage that will form an alliance with another country. It establishes peace among the European nations. Vicky, Alice, and Helena have all done so."

"Helena remains here, though."

Victoria sighed. "Helena is a special case."

"She isn't. You simply prefer her company."

"Don't be ridiculous."

"I'm not ridiculous, Mother. I have no desire to leave England, nor do I wish to be a smiling puppet on the arm of some popinjay. I'll marry an Englishman of my own choosing, or not at all."

"Of your own choosing? Like Reverend Duckworth? As well you should blush, girl. And what Englishman is qualified to marry into our house? No, put your childish fancies away and obey your mother."

Arguments, it was always arguments with Louise and Bertie. Yet niggling in the back of Victoria's mind was the dearth of eligible princes in the houses of Europe with whom to attach Louise. Truth be told, Victoria had already married her children off into the important ones and the dynastic alliances necessary for Great Britain's preeminence were already formed. Was it just tradition that caused her to compel Louise into a foreign marriage?

And yet even the most noble duke of the land was steps beneath a princess. Victoria would be the laughingstock of Europe if the most beautiful of all her daughters was given over to some commoner, for anyone *not* of a royal house was, ultimately, common.

Louise's misery, though, was palpable. In these moments, Victoria was never sure if she was mother or queen. What was she to do now about Louise, without Albert to advise her?

Violet looked up at the majestic façade of Buckingham Palace, apprehensive about her meeting with the queen, who had summoned her just an hour ago. Did the queen want to know her progress with the spirits? She had nothing to report.

Violet was unprepared for the real reason the queen had summoned her.

"You have become close to our daughter Louise, have you not, Mrs. Harper?"

If Violet had been summoned to the palace to answer this question, then this was not a casual visit. What did the queen know? Had she discovered Louise's activities with the moralists? Did she want Violet to spy on her daughter? Or worse, was she about to accuse Violet of conspiring to hide Louise's activities?

"I believe I am in her good graces, Your Majesty."

Victoria nodded. "Our daughter Beatrice also seems quite fond of you. I am in possession of a problem, Mrs. Harper, one that you might be able to help me solve."

Violet braced for whatever it might be.

"You see, we are both queen and mother, and, as such, sometimes we command and sometimes we persuade. It has been our experience that commanding is of little use with family members. Certain situations require tact and persuasion."

"Yes, Your Majesty."

"Sometimes, though, we employ both approaches. Unfortunately, our efforts using both command and persuasion have been unsuccessful with our daughter the Princess Louise."

Violet was silent. Did the queen expect an undertaker to intervene in a situation where the queen's command had been ignored?

"Our situation is a delicate one. Louise is an eligible princess, and a quality marriage must be made for her. We have presented her with several potential matches, but she has refused them all."

"Are the men objectionable?"

"Only in that they are not British. Louise wishes to remain at home."

"Like Princess Helena."

"You are perceptive, Mrs. Harper. Yes, like Helena. Only Helena is a special case. Louise is quite beautiful and would be happily accepted by a foreign house whom we would wish to be friendly to our interests. Furthermore, no one in the kingdom is of sufficient rank to marry into our family. It hasn't been done in centuries."

Violet cringed. Why was she being put in the middle of a family squabble?

"We do not wish to involve any of the princess's friends, who will go off tattling to their parents and ensure all of society knows of our difficulties. You have proved yourself discreet in the past, and we expect that you will be so again. Therefore, we command you—we wish for you—to talk to our daughter, to encourage her to make a proper marriage."

Violet would rather climb into a centuries-old coffin containing a plague-ridden corpse than do this. Yet she couldn't refuse the queen. What was she to do? Louise would never forgive her for appearing to side with Victoria, but didn't she know what was best for her daughters? Nevertheless, Violet had developed a certain loyalty to Louise and felt she owed it to the princess to support her.

"Your Majesty, if I may be so bold as to say this, it might be good for your kingdom to permit the princess's marriage with a duke or earl."

The queen frowned, never a good sign. "And why is this?"

"Craving your pardon, madam, but an outsider, someone not of royal descent, might introduce new blood into the family. Many royal houses have suffered from too many . . . close . . . marriages, have they not?"

"What you say is true. But is introducing common blood the correct answer?"

"I do not claim to understand how these things work, Your Majesty, but is there not a special title or rank you could confer on such a man that the Princess Louise might choose? Such as that which was conferred upon the prince consort upon his marriage to you?"

"The prince consort was a prince of the House of Saxe-Coburg and Gotha!"

Violet bowed her head in deference.

"And yet, Mrs. Harper, there may be truth to what you say. We shall think on this."

"As you wish, ma'am."

The queen was silent, not dismissing her, so Violet waited. Finally, the queen spoke, more to herself. "We had hoped that sending Louise off to the Continent, to busy herself with begetting heirs, would not only get her over the deaths of her friends, but cure her of the need to dally about with the moralist women."

"I—I—Your Majesty, you knew about this?"

"Mrs. Harper, we are not queen without some ability to monitor our children's activities. We had hoped if we ignored it long enough, Louise would tire of it, much as she did her dolls and other playthings. We have also been too worried about Bertie's transgressions to give much thought to it."

Violet didn't dare ask how long the queen had known, nor how she knew. Had Beatrice told her mother what they'd overheard in the mews that day? Or had Mr. Brown told the queen in the first place and was using the story about the spirits as a way of amusing the queen? Was Violet just a pawn in some foolish game? If she was, she'd personally cane Mr. Brown with a mourning stick.

"You are perceptive, Your Majesty."

"Not entirely. What we weren't sure of was whether or not you knew, Mrs. Harper, but we have our answer now."

The queen was much smarter than her perpetual mourning suggested. Violet wondered what else Victoria knew.

"You may be wondering about my conclusions regarding Lady Maud's and Lady Marcheford's deaths, Your Majesty. It is my opinion that both were murdered."

Victoria didn't act shocked at all. "Does Scotland Yard agree with you?"

"I don't think Scotland Yard is particularly interested in the deaths of two sickly young women."

"We see. And how did you come to your conclusion about Louise's friends?"

"Ah, yes, well, I was moved to believe so by what I saw—"

"You were moved? Did the spirits finally visit you, Mrs. Harper?"

"Oh, the spirits, yes. I suppose I would say that I have been visited by someone whom I could not see."

Victoria clasped her hands together. "This is marvelous in our eyes. Mr. Brown will be so pleased to hear it. To think that our dearest Albert has been guiding them into your path. Perhaps it is time for another séance, so that you can report to the prince consort on your discoveries and receive more guidance."

Again? The plague-infested coffin was once more looking attractive. "Your Majesty, might I suggest that if the spirits wish to continue their, ah, interaction with me, might it not be better for me to communicate privately with them, to obtain all of their secrets and thus resolve their mysteries for myself?"

"We suppose that makes sense." The queen was crestfallen. "But if you have not figured things out within a week, we will definitely call on Mr. Brown to conduct another séance."

One week. Violet would most certainly have everything solved by then, come plague or pestilence. Anything to avoid another one of Mr. Brown's conjuring tricks.

Violet's mind was thoroughly muddled as she left Buckingham Palace. She stopped at a stationer for writing paper and a new pen. She picked a hefty fountain pen made of elm, a wood she thought made the most elegant coffins.

She headed back to St. James's to sit and think in the calm of her own rooms. Not that her rooms were that calm. As usual, she had clothes and documents piled everywhere, as though a whirligig lived here. How did she feel qualified to call the lodgings over Morgan Undertaking messy? At least Mary would help her take those in hand.

First things first. She requested some dinner be sent up, then moved her dresses and underclothes into a single pile on the bed and arranged the documents into three piles: letters, newspapers, and funeral records. At that point, her dinner arrived and the aroma of roasted goose caused her stomach to grumble with anticipation, making her realize that she hadn't eaten in many hours.

Before lifting her fork, though, she decided it was time to organize her thoughts with some lists. She pushed aside her untouched food tray and drew out some paper, her new elm fountain pen, and a bottle of ink. She made two lists, drawing a long, vertical line to separate them. She titled them "Why" and "Who."

Inspector Hurst undoubtedly had far more sophisticated terms, she thought, but it was a start. Under "Who," she listed her suspects, such as they were, with guesses as to what motives they might have under the "Why" column:

Lord Marcheford—to get rid of his wife for another woman; anger at moralist movement

Sir Charles Mordaunt—revenge for his wife's infidelities; anger at moralist movement

Reese Meredith—revolutionary tendencies

Mr. Brown—?? (seems impossible)

The problem with Violet's list of motives was that they didn't seem to fit across all three women. Lord Marcheford's anger at his wife's involvement in the moralist cause didn't justify Lady Maud's death. The same was doubly true for Sir Charles: Why kill Lady Maud and Lady Marcheford, two women not associated with his wife at all?

Mr. Meredith had done nothing specific, but his anger seemed directed at the queen. What could Louise's friends and a young woman in the moralist cause have to do with him? Didn't revolutionaries tend to things that were, well, showy and exhibitionist? Like when royalist plotters planned to kill Napoleon Bonaparte in 1800 with their *machine infernale*, which exploded but missed its target. That sounded more like what Reese Meredith would plan if he was truly a revolutionary, not just a few random murders.

As for Mr. Brown, he was just behaving peculiarly, as if he smelled something afoot other than his usual spirits. There was no reason to think he'd actually done anything.

But who else might be interested in these three women?

Once finished with her fruitless examination of who and why, Violet made a third list on a separate sheet. This one she titled "Puzzles." Here she hurriedly wrote down the torrent of questions that confused her.

Why is Mr. Brown so wrapped up in this? Why is he so sly about what he knows?

Bite marks—what insect are they from?

Soiled cloths?

What do Lady Maud, Lady Marcheford, and Miss Cortland all have in common?

Why is the killer after both aristocratic young women <u>and</u> moralist young women?

Was it possible that the murders of Lady Maud and Lady Marcheford had nothing to do with Miss Cortland?

Who attacked Josephine and me in the street? Why? Was he after her . . . or me?

With that done, Violet settled down at the table with her dinner and a stack of unread newspapers, determined to get caught up on the news while she ate. Undoubtedly, her mother would admonish her that she'd get indigestion by reading about the country's tragic events while she ate, but Mother didn't understand the iron stomach of the average undertaker.

My, she was more than two weeks behind on reading. She decided to start with the most recent edition of *The Times*. It was filled with articles about the upcoming Henley Royal Regatta rowing event, the latest additions to the Royal Academy's summer exhibition, as well as death notices and the usual assortment of dressmaker, ironmonger, and hair tonic ads. There was also a touching tribute to an ancient naval officer, Darden Hastings, who had recently died. The captain had served bravely with Lord Nelson at Trafalgar, the magnificent victory against the French fleet that every schoolchild was intimately familiar with now.

Violet shifted uncomfortably. She'd been wearing her corset for too many hours and was feeling strangled. She removed her dress, wriggled out of her corset, and resumed her position in her chemise. Much better.

She picked up other papers and skimmed them. Wait, what was this? It was an article detailing Sir Charles Mordaunt's outburst in Parliament. The writer was clearly sympathetic to Mordaunt's viewpoint about the Contagious Diseases Acts and his outrage over his wife's perfidy.

It must be said that our interview with Sir Charles was revealing. A man of great honor and high scruples, he was wounded to his core to learn that his wife was behaving as a common trollop.

"It is these moralist women," the member for South Warwickshire said, "who are sowing discord at the highest levels of the feminine realm. These moralists convince our wives, our mothers, our sisters, that they belong somewhere other than the domestic sphere. But what woman can be happy away from the warm fires of the hearth and the innocent babble of her children, children she is certain belong to her husband?"

A delightful picture Sir Charles paints of the beauty of womanhood and all its glory. It is in our great nation's best interest that we encourage our females to once again embrace and cherish the mantle that God has so graciously bestowed about them.

Oh, poppycock. Did Sir Charles mean to say that Lady Mordaunt had no hand in the running of their estate, managing servants and ensuring bills were paid and supplies were delivered? Could he not see through the fog of his outrage that the sovereign of Great Britain was a woman? And the man would surely have apoplexy if he met Violet, whose hands had been sullied by the handling of thousands of corpses and who couldn't tell the difference between a turbot and a tureen.

However, the article made Violet pause. Sir Charles was angry at the moralists, whom he perceived as having influenced his wife into perfidy. Did he think all noblewomen had been so influenced?

Furthermore, were there other men, like Lord Marcheford, who felt as Sir Charles did? Exactly how angry were they, and might they be moved to do something about it? Of course, this number of men could run into the hundreds, if not thousands, and chasing them all down would be a fruitless task.

Violet stayed up late into the night turning things over in her mind. If only Sam were here to discuss it. With only a gas lamp for company, she paced the floors, reading aloud from her lists, hoping something might reveal itself in her spoken words. Nothing did.

However, she kept turning Lord Marcheford and Sir Charles over and over in her mind. Was it time to call on each of these men? First, though, it was time to see Mr. Brown. It was time that man told her what he knew, and this time she would not shrink away from his posturing and chicanery.

Violet caught up with Mr. Brown in the Buckingham Palace gardens, where he was bent over in the morning sun, examining the foreleg of a horse he must have been exercising. She hoped they were far enough away from the palace not to be noticed and that the queen wasn't in one of her morose moods, staring out the windows.

"Mrs. Harper, have ye come to fix Angus's shoe, or do ye prefer to put him straight into a casket?" Brown laughed at his own joke.

Good Lord, it was only nine o'clock in the morning and the man reeked of spirits.

"No, I have come to have a frank discussion with you, sir."

"Have ye, now? Well, you'll have to walk along with me, then. Angus needs to return to the mews so I can wallop the farrier in his bean for such a sloppy job on him."

What an incongruous sight they made: the prim, black-garbed undertaker and the unkempt ghillie in plaid, walking together on a path bordered by a profusion of summer blooms in clumped riots of purple, red, and pink, as Brown coaxed the gelding along.

"I'll have the truth from you this morning, Mr. Brown, with no double-talking, no smirking at my ignorance, and above all else, no suggestions for tarot card readings, séances, or chats with spirits."

"My, you've got a burr in your saddle this morning, don't ye?" He said it mildly, further irritating Violet.

"Tell me what it is you know, sir. What supposed treachery lurks behind the palace walls that frightens you so much that you resort to tricks and chicanery to convince the queen that I need to investigate whatever it is. Furthermore, why me? Why is it that you do not tell her yourself?"

Brown stopped, and Angus snuffled in protest behind him.

"Bear in mind, Mrs. Harper, that the queen enjoys the readings and such. Ye deal with the hard, cold facts of the dead. The queen likes to stay in the world of the living, even imagining that the dead are still with her. I help her with it, it comforts her so she can manage her daily life, and that, madam, is that. Besides, your unbelief in spiritualism makes ye a hard wumman."

"It makes me practical."

He shrugged. "As ye say."

She pressed him further. "Still you are not answering my question."

Brown glanced about to be sure there was no one nearby and resumed walking. "What I know I cannae tell the queen, for to be deliverer of the news would make her question how I came by the information. And that answer would cause an anger I dinnae care to witness. She might be angry enough to dismiss me."

"Dismiss *you?* That is hardly likely."

"You do not know the reason."

"Then tell me, Mr. Brown, what do you know and how did you come by the information?"

Brown patted Angus's nose, reaching into his pocket for a sugar cube and feeding it to him. "Just a little further, laddie, and we'll have you fixed in a tick. Now, Mrs. Harper, I suppose ye'll plague me to my grave unless I tell you, but ye must swear not to tell the queen.

"Her daughter the Princess Louise has been involved with a woman named Josephine Butler, one of these new moralists who propose to seek rights for prostitutes. The princess meets with these moralists in the mews, which is where I was trying to guide ye."

"Well, I have some news for you, Mr. Brown. She already knows about Louise's involvement with the moralists."

"So ye finally told her?"

"No, she told me."

For once, Violet had the upper hand over Brown. His mouth fell open. "Ye make a jest. She'd of told me something like that. She'd 'ave banished the lass, or married her to the first hunchbacked foreign prince who came along."

"Blood is thicker than water, Mr. Brown. Her Majesty has problems enough with her child—in other areas—that she decided not to banish her or condemn her to a marriage sight unseen."

"She told you this?"

"Not directly."

They had reached a rear entrance to the mews courtyard. Brown put a finger to his lips. "Follow me, Mrs. Harper."

He led her to the stables, where he handed Angus's reins to a stable boy, then led her through the building into the carriage house, straight to the coronation coach. He pulled out the elaborately carved steps, opened the door, and offered Violet his arm.

"I—we—cannot sit in here. It is the queen's coach."

"'Tis the only place private enough on the palace grounds that I can tell ye this."

He shut the door behind him. Now Violet was locked up with Brown and his foul breath inside this glorious, regal coach, with its crimson velvet seats, thick and tufted, and matching velvet draperies hanging along the sparkling glass.

"This is the rest of it, Mrs. Harper. You think that I must have stumbled onto the moralists' meetings because I am always in the mews, preparing for Her Majesty's afternoon rides. Nae, I learned of it another way." He leaned closer. Violet tried to keep from looking revolted.

"Ye know the queen doesn't like it when her unwed servants find their hearts' desire. They end up marrying and then leaving Her Majesty's service. If I told her how I came by my information, she would nae understand my . . . disloyalty."

"Are you saying—"

"Yes. I'm quite taken with the Lady Hazel Campden, and I think she is fond of me, too. She told me of the princess's involvement with the moralists, but if I told the queen that I learned this while caressing one of her daughter's friends, I would nae be long of this world."

Violet digested this information carefully, while trying to remember exactly who Lady Hazel was. Had she been at one of the mourning jewelry sessions? Violet couldn't remember. No, wait, Lady Hazel was the tightly corseted, barely breathing young woman who was so talented at painting the mourning scene on ivory.

She was involved with the crude, imbibing Mr. Brown? Utterly inconceivable.

"I see," she said slowly. "So you concocted your plan about the spirits to let the queen know while also protecting yourself."

"And to protect Lady Hazel. She's society, of course, and cannot be seen with a servant. I'm nae merely a servant, but I'm nae society, either. A sticky situation, ye see, to be untangled before I could think about telling the queen about us."

"Lady Hazel is not a member of the moralist group?"

"Nae. She is just an innocent. It was nae my desire to tattle on the princess, but the queen needed to know the sort of trouble her daughter was finding for herself. I devised my plan around the tarot card readings, guiding Her Majesty to seek your assistance, knowing ye'd figure it on your own. Lady Hazel thought my plan was brilliant."

Violet nodded, still startled to learn that Mr. Brown was dallying with one of Louise's friends. He must be in his mid-forties at least—and his dissipation made him look older than that—while Louise's friends were in their twenties. Of course, who could understand the desires and longings of men and women for each other?

"I knew that a bunch of hens meeting together over the problems of prostitutes could nae lead to anything good, and might eventually cause terrible problems for Her Majesty, so I had to figure out a way to let her know. But now, it seems as though she knew all along. I still dinnae understand why she had no reaction, why she dinnae say something to me. I am her most beloved servant."

Brown shook his head, bewildered.

Everyone keeps secrets, Mr. Brown, both the dead and the living.

"Your secret is safe with me, sir, but I must ask: What do you know about the deaths of Lady Maud and Lady Marcheford?"

"They were sick, weren't they? Tragic, the young lasses dying like that. I can't imagine losing Lady Hazel so soon."

It was so strange to hear Mr. Brown going on like a lovesick calf. Stranger still was the thought that Lady Hazel didn't mind his foul habits.

"Did you know Miss Cortland? She was a worker in Mrs. Butler's moralist movement."

"Nae, I don't know this name."

Could she believe him? His story certainly rang the bell of truth, but even liars had been known to pick up a hammer and strike a true-sounding note.

Finally released from the coach, the miasma of Brown's foul breath dissipating in the air around her, Violet left back through the stables while Brown went to tend to the lamed horse. As she entered the courtyard, she encountered Mr. Meredith. He was in drab, loose-fitting clothing that was covered in dust. Pretending to doff the cap he did not wear, he bowed exaggeratedly to Violet.

"Forgive my appearance, Mrs. Harper. I've been training a new gray today and am not fit to be in your presence."

Why did the coachman always seem to be mocking her?

With one piece of the puzzle solved—she hoped—Violet went on to capture her next prey. From Buckingham Palace it was but a short walk to her next destination. Mounting the steps of the Tate residence, a stately affair in Belgravia that was surely on tourists' lists of places to gape at, Violet hoped her strategy of showing up unannounced would unsettle Lord Marcheford enough into revealing something.

She told the rigid, bored butler who answered the door that she was one of His Lordship's deceased wife's friends, come to pay her condolences. It wasn't too much of a fib, since the relationship between a corpse and an undertaker was a very personal one.

She was escorted up a flight of stairs whose balusters were gold leafed and whose newels were shaped like leopard heads. The Marchefords were lords of the manor and made sure every visitor knew it.

Lord Marcheford's mouth dropped as Violet entered his study, a room full of photographs, engraved trophies, and leather-bound books all attesting to Marcheford greatness. He was standing next to an antique globe housed in an elaborate wood floor stand, an amber-filled glass in one hand and a cigar in the other. His guard was lowered for mere moments before he quickly resumed his usual sardonic and caustic demeanor.

"Mrs. Harper, have you come to secure another body? Not my own, I hope. Jeffries said you were one of Charlotte's friends. A clever façade."

"It is not a façade in that I am your wife's advocate in discovering who killed her. If she were alive, she would no doubt call me a friend for that."

"If she were alive, you wouldn't be here, and I probably wouldn't be enjoying this bottle of Pernod Fils absinthe I had imported from France. Do you drink absinthe, Mrs. Harper?"

"No."

"A pity. I find it calms my temper. I've no doubt you could use a glass or two yourself."

Lord Marcheford was attempting to wrest control from Violet, and she wasn't about to let that happen. "My lord, I've come to resolve our last conversation."

The earl drew deeply on his cigar and leisurely blew a great cloud of smoke upward. "I wasn't aware that a resolution was needed."

"It is." Violet noticed he wasn't inviting her to sit down. Very well, her point could be better made standing, anyway. "When we previously spoke, were you aware that one of Mrs. Butler's associates had been murdered?"

"No, why should I take note of anything that woman does?"

"Do you deny now that you hated her?"

"Of course not. I only deny that I know anything about her and whoever her associate was."

"Had you ever met Miss Cortland?"

"No, I can't say that I have ever met Miss Cortland." He tapped the cigar into a silver ashtray on top of the globe's wood enclosure. It was a slow, deliberate, and, Violet thought, practiced move, designed to give him time to think.

"I'll ask you another question."

"Are you preparing to join Scotland Yard, Mrs. Harper?"

"Sir, do not mock me."

"Is that what you think I'm doing?" He tossed the half-smoked cigar into the ashtray. "Perhaps I'm just tired of this discussion."

And Violet thought dealing with Mr. Brown was difficult.

"I think you may have killed Lady Marcheford because she was involved in the moralist movement. It embarrassed you, my lord, a man so proud of his family's reputation. Miss Cortland was probably one of Lady Marcheford's friends and you were outraged at her influence over your wife, so you murdered her, too."

Marcheford stared at Violet for several long seconds, then burst into laughter. "My dear Mrs. Harper, I don't know what sort of fumes a dead body puts off, but they must be toxic indeed to give you such ludicrous ideas. Charlotte's involvement with Mrs. Butler was the least of her problems. She was meeting secretly with another man, and I was considering divorcing her for it. And indeed, if I were to have committed these supposed murders, your boldness would find you requiring your own services."

Violet ignored the jibe. "Did you know her paramour?"

"Of course I did. Lottie thought she was clever, but there was little she did that wasn't done in an obvious manner. She was running about with Henry Cape, Lord Blevins's younger brother. Not a shilling to his name, will never have a title, and always mooning about with his lines of poetry and his silly Pre-Raphaelite paintings. I'm sure it was all very romantic for Charlotte."

Was Lord Marcheford truly insensible to his wife's affair, or was he covering up rage over it?

"Is Mr. Cape in London?" she asked.

"Not anymore. I made it clear that he wasn't welcome at Lottie's funeral, so he scurried back to the family home in Dorset. I doubt London will be darkened with his presence again anytime soon."

"Did Lady Marcheford know of your plans to put her aside?"

"Yes, and she frequently threatened to shoot me over it, although I knew she never would. Charlotte was always so full of feelings. When she loved me, she loved me passionately. When she decided she hated me, it was with hellish vigor. She was as mercurial as the Greek god Hermes."

"But you yourself were having an affair. She told me."

He lifted a shoulder. "I am the future Marquess of Salford, and as such would have lifted Charlotte far above her station, something for which she should have been grateful. I didn't interfere with her private affairs, and she stayed out of mine. Her dealings with Mrs. Butler were public, and humiliating, and had to be stopped."

"What did you do to stop them?"

"What every husband does. Ordered her to do so. Charlotte was terrible at obeying, though."

"And you, Lord Marcheford, are a terrible liar."

"And I'll remind *you*, Mrs. Harper, that you are in my home, so have a care."

A delicate throat clearing behind her alerted Violet that they were not alone in the room. She turned to see a petite but elegant woman rise from a chair, her dress of pale gray and naval blue accenting eyes of liquid aquamarine. Why had Lord Marcheford let their argument go on as long as it had without making Violet aware of this woman's presence? Was he hoping for Violet to embarrass herself? Did he want a witness for some reason? Or perhaps Violet was to be the source of amusement later.

"Ripley, won't you introduce me to your friend?" she said, her dulcet voice the whisper of butterflies.

"Of course, my love. Lady Henrietta Pettit, may I present to you Mrs. Violet Harper? She is an undertaker of some renown, and was present for Charlotte's—ah . . ."

"How very curious, a woman undertaker," Lady Henrietta said, airily holding out her hand, which Violet clasped. "I suppose there is no end to what common women can accomplish these days. Another drink, please?"

Ripley reached behind him for a decanter on his desk and poured Lady Henrietta a full glass. "Thank you, darl—Ripley," she said, sipping delicately at her glass as though she were a hummingbird dipping into a foxglove bloom.

"Lady Henrietta is an old friend of the family, Mrs. Harper, and as such comes to visit for dinner from time to time. We were just having a drink before our meal. I'm sure you understand that I'll need to wish you a good evening."

"One more thing, my lord. Why did you threaten me over my investigation into your wife's death?"

"When did I do such a thing?"

"A week ago, when you visited me at St. James's Palace. Surely you were not so far into your cups that you don't recall it."

He gave Lady Henrietta a guilty glance. "I-I can hardly remember—oh yes, I was passing by and thought I'd stop in."

Stop in to a royal palace?

"You thought you'd stop in to harangue me over your wife?"

Lord Marcheford drained his glass and put it down. Another measured move? "No, of course not. I was out of my mind with grief. Grief and worry. Not only had I lost my wife, but I was in a precarious situation. I had widely disseminated my dissatisfaction with Charlotte, and I knew that some suspicion might fall upon me, especially with you poking around acting like she'd been murdered. I'd no desire to be falsely accused of doing away with my wife. Now, if you're quite finished, Mrs. Harper, Lady Henrietta and I are famished."

Violet's own stomach was grumbling as she left Lord Marcheford's home. She decided to stop at the Grosvenor Hotel at Victoria station, one of the many new hotels popping up in London to serve the city's growing railroad network, for her own dinner before going back to her rooms at St. James's to freshen up for a trip to see Sir Charles Mordaunt. As with Lord Marcheford, she intended to drop in unannounced, hoping it would startle Mordaunt into some sort of confession.

Full and drowsy from turtle soup, salmon cutlets, and apricot tart, Violet strolled lazily back toward the palace, trying to ignore the feeling that her corset was strangling her. The sun was just beginning its drop in the sky. She needed to revive with a splash of water to her face before heading out to confront Sir Charles. Perhaps she should also consider a change of dress.

Meanwhile, the air was pleasant and the redolent fragrance of freesia in nearby window boxes wafted over her. The profusion of blooms filling every window and doorstep was another reason Violet loved London, despite its grime and dust. It was just another one of the city's many contradictions, the way it—

"Pardon me, madam, I was wondering if you can tell me where the London Lock Hospital is. I'm trying to find my sister."

"You're some distance away, sir. You'll need to take a train to—" She turned to see who inquired but was stopped by a strong hand clamped over her mouth, a piece of rough cloth between her teeth and her attacker's fingers. Violet tried to jerk away violently, but she was no match for her attacker's powerful arms. A strange and horrible odor overcame her, and she felt herself floating, as though she were a tiny coal smut, drifting away to soar over buildings and parks.

The smell was familiar, though. Yes, it was what she smelled on the fabric she'd found in Lady Maud's mouth and near the other two bodies. Now she knew the fabric had been soaked in some sort of poison. Whoever had murdered those three women was about to murder her, too.

Struggling to keep her eyes open as the man was pulling her in one direction—did he plan to throw her in the street again?—her feet stumbling along uselessly, she still maintained a few vague thoughts. Such as, if this was poison to kill her, then what were the bite marks from? Was she to have bite marks that no one would ever notice? Would he continue killing women? Was Violet destined to die without knowing the truth?

No, of that one fact she was sure. It was important that she not die today.

Summoning her last reserve of strength, Violet managed to open her mouth beneath the cloth. As he pulled the cloth tighter against her mouth, his fingers slipped in between her lips.

Violet bit down as hard as she could but was near to losing consciousness and so was certain her bite was no stronger than the butterfly whisper of Lady Henrietta's voice.

Somewhere far in the distance above her—or was it below her or next to her?—Violet heard an angry shout followed by a string of curses. The cloth was whipped away from her face, and she felt herself being pushed to the street, as when she'd been with Josephine.

Except this time she had no idea if there was an oncoming cab, omnibus, or other vehicle that would cause her death faster than the poison. She yielded to unconsciousness.

11

Reese was burning with anger. Having just returned from his errands, he was berated by Mr. Norton for not being available to take Prince Leopold's doctor to and from the palace. Reese was used to the occasional cuffing and ear boxing, although it was getting harder and harder to tolerate it.

He shook his head. He couldn't let his irritation get in the way of what was important. Mr. Norton was nothing but a flea, to be picked, crushed by a thumbnail, and wiped on Reese's pants. He must keep his eye on the goal, the mission, what was important.

He shut the door to the room he shared with Roy Beckham, another groom. Beckham was training a new Cleveland Bay, which would eventually be used by the queen's guard, and would be gone until sundown for certain. Reese examined his purchases, not easily obtained.

He hefted the detonator in his hand. Such a small item for the power it could unleash. Was it too much? Was his plan too great, too spectacular? No, he must not allow fear to overcome him now, not when he was so close.

Margaret, you will be avenged, and I will be responsible for changing the course of history as a result.

He'd considered seeking a private meeting with Mr. Marx to explain his plan to him, to seek his approval and blessing, but changed his mind. If Mr. Marx was waiting for the event to happen and Reese somehow failed to make it happen, he would look like a fool before the great man. No, better to execute his plan and have Mr. Marx admire him afterward.

Who knew what position Marx might offer him as a result of his successful daring?

Reese unrolled a package containing several cylindrical sticks wrapped in paper. How remarkable to think that such innocent-looking rods could be responsible for utter devastation, were they only placed properly.

Despite all of her prudish airs and prying nose, Reese supposed he should have been grateful to Mrs. Harper for her assistance in the matter, for it was her talk about her husband's involvement in dynamite that gave Reese the idea in the first place.

He rewrapped the gelignite sticks and the detonator. He'd tried to find dynamite, but it wasn't available anywhere in Great Britain, so this coal-mining explosive would have to do.

He buried his treasure deep inside the chest at the foot of his bed, which contained all of his worldly goods. It was an unwritten rule in the mews that no one ever bothered another man's chest, so he had no fear that Beckham would go snooping inside it.

Now he needed to check the schedule for the queen's birthday celebrations, coming up in just four days. It would be a splendid moment to make a bold display against the tyranny of both the bourgeoisie and the Royal House of Saxe-Coburg and Gotha.

He'd managed a feat that required no other soul for assistance, just a bit of luck and careful planning. He also needed there to be no last-minute changes to the queen's plans. That was the problem with the rich; they could do whatever they wanted, when they wanted, no matter the inconvenience to anyone else.

What were all of these faces hovering over her own? Violet shook her head to clear her mind and immediately regretted it. Her head clanged like a church bell tolling a death.

"Madam, you're alive!" exclaimed a woman's voice.

All of these people, crowding her, staring at her. "I cannot breathe," she whispered.

"Everyone, away," came a commanding male voice, followed by a strong arm around her shoulders. "May I help you up?" he said.

Violet nodded and soon found herself upright, facing a kindly older gentleman who wore a dusty apron over his rotund belly. "I was pulling my evening loaves from the oven and setting them out to cool when I saw that man attack you."

Violet leaned gratefully on the baker's arm. Her legs were wobbly, although she supposed she should be used to being shoved into the street. "Did you see who it was?" she asked.

"Alas, no. It all happened so quickly that by the time I threw down my loaf board and made it outside he was gone."

"Did you notice anything about him at all? Was he tall or short? Well or poorly dressed? Anything at all?"

The baker shook his head. "I'm sorry, madam. The only thing I noticed was that he wore a hat pulled low over his brow, as though it didn't fit him properly. It made it impossible to see his features. He also wore a long cloak—strange in this weather—that covered anything else he was wearing."

"Thank you, anyway."

"I'll fetch a bobby," said a young boy wearing a telegram delivery uniform.

"No, please, I'll be fine. I don't want to cause trouble. I can just walk from here."

The baker laughed gently. "You are in no condition to walk, Mrs.—?"

"Harper. Violet Harper. Thank you for your assistance, sir. My lodgings are but a short distance from here."

There was nothing more to see, so the onlookers drifted away, back about their business. The baker, however, held firm to Violet's arm.

"I will hail a hansom cab. I insist."

In moments, it seemed, a carriage had pulled up and a driver was tipping his hat at her, pretending not to notice her undoubtedly frightful state. "Farewell and God bless you," the baker said as he handed her into the cab and gave the driver some coins. He slipped a card into her reticule. "Here's where you can find my wife and me when we're not at the bakery."

As the horse ambled off, she realized she'd not even gotten the man's name. She searched through her reticule for the card:

MR. AND MRS. ZACHARIAH MERRILL
CHRISTIAN REVIVAL SOCIETY
SERVING MEALS TO WIDOWS, ORPHANS, AND
THE UNFORTUNATE AT THE CEMETERY
ON WHITECHAPEL HIGH STREET
TUESDAYS, THURSDAYS, AND SATURDAYS
"BUT WHEN THOU MAKEST A FEAST, CALL THE POOR,
THE MAIMED, THE LAME, THE BLIND:
AND THOU SHALT BE BLESSED; FOR THEY CANNOT
RECOMPENSE THEE: FOR THOU SHALT BE
RECOMPENSED AT THE RESURRECTION OF THE JUST."

Violet laughed in delight. When she'd worked on the mysterious situation involving Lord Raybourn, his grandson, Toby, had worked for the Christian Revival Society and Violet had passed a peaceful afternoon helping to serve soup to the East End's poor. How ironic that the man who helped her in the street was part of the Society, especially after she'd just mentioned it to Josephine.

Violet also remembered that she'd promised Toby that she would return to do more work for them. Perhaps she should plan to go back soon, on one of the days listed on Mr. Merrill's card, so that she could thank him properly at the same time.

By the time Violet arrived back at St. James's Palace, she felt better, despite garnering raised eyebrows among the staff, who considered her no better than an unwanted cat they couldn't get rid of because she caught an occasional mouse, She took a Beecham's powder for her throbbing head, changed out of her dress—it would need Mary's expert needling to make it acceptable again—and into her nightdress, then went to work on her hair, pulling out all of her pins, brushing it out, and tying it up for sleep.

As she went through these motions, she considered all that had happened today. Why had she been attacked again? It was much more likely now that the attack upon her and Josephine was intended for Violet, but if so, why did Josephine seem to be hiding something?

Furthermore, how did Violet's attacker know where she was to be on both occasions, both on a visit with Josephine and on her return from Lord Marcheford's home? The only human being who knew of her visit to Lord Marcheford was the earl himself. Had he followed her from his home, then waited for her outside the hotel?

What was it that Mary had said? A lord would hire someone to do such foul work. Was that what he had done? Sent someone after Violet? Had he somehow learned of her visit with the moralist and sent someone there as well?

There was a difference in the attacks, though. The first time, whoever it was had merely pushed Violet into oncoming traffic. This time, he'd tried to poison her. Which reminded her, did she have the soaked cloth? In all of the aftermath, she'd not had presence of mind to think about it. She went through her reticule. Besides Mr. Merrill's card, there was nothing new in it. Yet she did still have the fabrics she found with the other women's bodies. Perhaps it was time to get an expert opinion on them.

Chief Inspector Hurst looked at Violet with distaste. "Mrs. Harper, if you don't mind a frank opinion, you look as though you've been knocked flat by a coffin sliding off a bier. What happened to you?"

"I can always rely on you to speak your mind, Inspector. Your assessment is not far from the truth." She described for him the two attacks.

"Have you a suspect in mind?"

"Yes, but I can hardly believe it to be true." She then told him her suspicion of Lord Marcheford, leaving all of her other notions unspoken until she could explore them further.

"An accusation against a peer, or the son of one, is serious, Mrs. Harper."

"I make no formal accusation yet. In fact, there is something else I wish to investigate." Violet produced the cloth she'd found near Lady Marcheford. The odor was nearly faded but still there.

Hurst sniffed at it and shook his head. "I don't know what this is, but I know of a surgeon who is an expert on poisons. You should show this to him."

"A surgeon?"

"I realize he does not carry the stature of a physician, but this man knows his business."

"Very well, I will see him." He couldn't possibly be any worse than some of the coroners she'd encountered as an undertaker. Most of them were arrogant fools and from such unlikely professions as barber, butcher, and politician. Few had any idea what they were doing. If Inspector Hurst thought this surgeon competent, she would trust him.

Finally, Violet might get an answer to all that clouded her mind.

The ironically named Mr. Leech looked as though he belonged in robes at Oxford, not in a sweaty surgery removing limbs. He wore wire-framed glasses containing thick lenses and moved nervously, as though fretting about being on the verge of discovery of some great sin. His tousled hair suggested he spent large amounts of time worrying his fingers through it.

However, he was as informed as the inspector said he was.

"Chloroform," he said, after taking a gentle whiff and handing it back to her.

"What is that?"

Mr. Leech went to a bookcase groaning under the weight of books that were heaped on the shelves in an utterly disorganized fashion and pulled out a book buried under four others. He flipped inside the book until he found the page he wanted.

" 'Chloroform: a clear, colorless, heavy, sweet-smelling liquid, used as a solvent and sometimes as an anesthetic.' "

He snapped the book shut. "You weren't poisoned; you were anesthetized. The queen employed chloroform during the births of her last two children, Prince Leopold and Princess Beatrice, thus giving it social acceptability."

What? How was this possible? Violet's mind reeled. So the other women also weren't killed by poison but were anesthetized. How, then, did they die?

Furthermore, whom did she know who had access to chloroform?

The bites. The bites must have been poisonous and killed the women once they were already unconscious. More questions rose in Violet's mind. "May I ask you one more thing? Is there an insect or other small animal that makes a bite mark like this"—she took pen and paper from his desk and drew two tiny circles—"that would have enough poison to kill someone?"

Mr. Leech spread his hands. "Mrs. Harper, I am a surgeon; I know nothing of entomology. The thought of spiders and wasps and beetles is enough to send me diving into the Thames."

"You? A man who cuts off gangrenous feet and probes diseased intestines?"

"I admit it sounds peculiar, but I've never been able to stomach tiny creatures with multiple legs or wings. So . . . unnatural. I'm sorry I cannot help you. Perhaps you should visit the Royal College of Surgeons."

Mr. Leech referred her to a surgeon there, but he in turn was of little help, telling Violet that any number of insects and rodents prowled the homes of London and could be responsible for biting an unwary victim and causing death.

All Violet was left with at the end of these visits was the knowledge that she was looking for a clever killer, one who had access to a sophisticated opiate and who wasn't afraid of crawling creatures.

Violet greeted Mary at the train station but was distressed to find an entirely different Mary than she'd known before. The first hint that something was dreadfully wrong was Mary's letter letting Violet know of her return train and that she would be unaccompanied. The letter had offered no explanation for that.

The second hint was that the letter had arrived far too quickly to be from a woman enjoying a reunion with her husband.

Mary was pale and thin, her eyes bleak from either crying or lack of sleep or perhaps both. Violet did not press, and Mary did not offer to say anything until she and Violet had returned to Mary's lodgings, located over her shop just as Violet's would soon be.

With Mary's luggage back in her bedchamber, which now had pale blue acanthus scroll wallpaper on the walls and vivid green draperies adorning the window and bedcoverings, as well as an unusual spindle-backed bench in one corner, Mary sat heavily on the bed, her brown-and-black-striped dress making her look like a plain little sparrow among the riotous field of flowers that dominated the bedspread.

Violet quickly assembled the makings for tea and brought the tray back to Mary's room, encouraging her friend to drink.

"Now, what happened? Where is George?"

Mary sniffled and pulled a handkerchief from her sleeve. "He is—he was—" Mary shook her head.

Violet sat next to her and took her hand. Mary was showing all of the signs of a terrible grief. "Tell me everything, but start from the very beginning. Did your travels to Switzerland go well?"

Mary nodded.

"Did you find it to be very beautiful there?"

Another nod. "There is Lake Geneva to the south, the Alps to the east, and the Jura mountains to the west and north. Breathtaking."

"You were able to find your husband without too much difficulty? Where did you find him?"

Mary dabbed her eyes with her handkerchief. "I checked with some clock shops, and discovered he was working at one of them. I didn't understand. Why would he be employed there, when he was only in Lausanne on a buying trip? Had he run out of money? And then when I found out, oh, Violet, it was too much to bear."

Violet squeezed her friend's hand. "What happened when you confronted him?"

"I'm sure I picked the worst possible moment to do so. I lurked outside the shop until he left for the day, then stepped into his path. I'd planned it to be very dramatic, so that he would be astounded to see me. I thought his expression would tell me everything."

"Did it?"

Mary nodded her head miserably. "He wasn't happy at all about my presence. He took me back to his lodgings and we had a terrible row. George told me that he—that he—" She sniffled again. "George said that he had no desire to return home, that he wanted to be free of the burden of marriage. Can you imagine it? George called me a burden."

Violet could well imagine George saying that. She put her free arm around her friend's shoulder. "Then what?"

"I told him that he must come home, that I would be a better wife and he would learn to love me again. He refused. We argued for what seemed like hours. I made a terrible fool of myself. It was what happened next, though. . . ." Mary stared off in the distance. Violet stepped away to pour more tea and pressed the warm cup into her friend's hand. Mary took a few sips and handed the cup back, shaking her head. Violet returned the cup to the tray.

"I heard a key in the lock, and in walked this woman. She was dark haired and frumpy and there were wisps of hair on her upper lip. She was from Italy, working in Lausanne as a maid in the hotel where George stayed when he first arrived. They took up together and moved into rented lodgings. I had been too blind to notice the marks of a woman living there as we were arguing."

"What did you do?"

"The first thing that popped into my head. I ran. I ran out of his rooms, out of the building, and back to the safety of my own hotel room. I lay on the bed all night with a cold compress on my head, but it was of no help whatsoever to my aching mind and heart."

"So you started for home the next day?"

"No. I'm afraid I'm a terrible glutton for punishment, devouring it like it's hazelnut cake. I went back to the clock shop, imagining we could have a calm discussion and that I could talk reason to him. After all, he was my husband, and this woman—Vanozza was her name—was merely some harlot that had put a veil of lust over his eyes."

"Did he speak to you?"

"He wasn't there. The owner said he hadn't shown up that morning. Concerned that I had made such a scene that he took ill, I recklessly went back to his lodgings, not caring whether Vanozza was there."

"Was she?"

"No. The door was open and I found George, found him—" Mary sobbed into her handkerchief while Violet wrapped her arms around her, murmuring words of comfort until Mary was ready to continue.

"I found him on the floor, his head bleeding. Oh, the blood, it was everywhere. And he was quite dead. I don't know how you do undertaking work, Violet, dealing with the dead and talking to them in the way that you do. Anyway, I ran back to the clock shop, and the owner summoned the *Polizei*. In short order, Vanozza was arrested. She readily admitted to it, too. She seemed almost proud of it."

"How terrible for you, my friend."

"Yes, I am utterly, irrevocably heartbroken. Twice a widow and I'm only fifty-six. This was the end for me, Violet. I'll take no other man into my life."

"Don't say that. Someone else will appear who will love you dearly, who will recognize your fine qualities just as your friends do."

Mary sniffed again. "I don't think it's possible. And this dreadful wallpaper will have to come down."

That gave Violet an idea. "Before you get to work on destroying your bedchamber, why don't you help me with my new lodgings? I haven't had a chance to tell you that I've bought back into Morgan Undertaking, so I'll be around the corner from you again, and Sam and I will be living above the shop."

Mary's eyes opened wide. "Truly? Why, that's wonderful. Of course I will help you with decorating."

"I'm afraid it will require more than mere decorating, and I'd like to have it finished before Sam returns."

As she diverted Mary with talk of renovations and a promise to bring her to see it the next day, Violet's mind wandered, as it was wont to do these days. There was something Mary had said, about Vanozza almost seeming proud of what she'd done. It made Violet wonder: Was the killer she was seeking cowering in the corner over his actions, or was he proud of them and Violet was ignoring the signs of that open pride?

Violet took a deep breath inside Sir Charles Mordaunt's drawing room. His home was a shadow of Lord Marcheford's, yet the man's insufferable ego was equal to any earl's. She wasn't sure whether to snap at him or cringe in fear. Was he one of Parliament's greatest bags of wind or a dangerous murderer?

"I suppose you are another of my wife's friends, dressed in black to show mourning for Harriet's imminent demise as my wife? Your cut of cloth is not that fine, though."

"I come on behalf of the Princess Louise."

"Does she plead my wife's case? I'll not be swayed in this, even by royal begging."

"The princess made no mention of supplication to you, sir. I am here on an entirely separate matter."

"It wouldn't have mattered. It's the prince who owes me satisfaction."

"Do you propose challenging the Prince of Wales to a duel?"

He had enough grace to lower his eyes. "Of course not. Are you sure you're not a messenger from the prince himself? No? So if this has nothing to do with my wife, why, exactly, are you here, Mrs. Harper?"

From her reticule Violet brought out a folded sheet, torn from a newspaper. "This is from a recent edition of *The Times*. It details your performance inside the Commons."

"So you *are* here about my wife."

"No, I am here about your antipathy for repeal of the Contagious Diseases Acts."

He narrowed his eyes. "Are you one of those moralists?"

"I am an undertaker who has been involved in the deaths of Lady Maud Winter, Lady Marcheford, and Miss Lillian Cortland."

"Lady Maud and Lady Marcheford, yes, I know of their deaths. Sickly creatures, I understand."

"Did you also know Miss Cortland?"

"Doesn't strike a memory. Was she also ill?"

"No, she was one of the moralists working with Mrs. Butler."

"What has she to do with Lady Maud or Lady Marcheford?"

"A question I thought you might be able to answer, Sir Charles."

"I? Why should I be on speaking terms with one of those wretched moralist women?"

"You seemed to be very passionate in your disavowal of their work."

Mordaunt grunted in disgust. "Because they are wretched women,

as I said. Worried about things that have nothing to do with them."
He eyed her suspiciously. "Who did you say you are?"

"Violet Harper. I am an undertaker who—"

"I am expected to permit an interrogation by a coffin hauler?
What joke is this?" Mordaunt laughed, but the sound rang hollow
against the wood-paneled walls.

"You are welcome to inquire about me at Buckingham Palace.
Meanwhile, I must ask you: Who among your colleagues who despise the moralists might be so angry about them that he would
seek to murder one of them?"

"Murder! You said she was ill."

"Actually, I didn't. I'm investigating her death as well as Lady
Maud's and Lady Marcheford's."

"Why you and not Scotland Yard?"

"I am cooperating with Scotland Yard." Was that too much
stress on the truth?

Mordaunt's lips went flat as he appraised her. Violet was glad he
hadn't invited her to sit down, so that she could flee if necessary.

"So both the princess and Scotland Yard endorse your presence
here. What is it you truly want, Mrs. Harper?"

Violet realized she was going to have to learn more finesse and
diplomacy if she was going to be successful at puzzling out these
sorts of situations. Neither trait was an especial talent of hers outside of undertaking. She decided to confront Mordaunt like a
matador with a cape, to see if he would charge.

"Lady Maud and Lady Marcheford were secret moralists. I am
wondering if you are passionate enough about the Contagious Diseases Acts that you would do away with those who want to repeal
them."

"Preposterous!" He was pawing at the ground.

She lowered her voice. "And might these murders just be a re-
hearsal for the prime target, Lady Mordaunt? Your blustering
about a divorce might just be a cover, an excuse for when her body
will be found, attacked by some exotic insect that just happened
to fly into her dressing room. And there will be Sir Charles, claim-
ing that he had intended to divorce her—the lowliest of chimney

sweeps knows of your intentions by now—but he never, ever wanted his wife's death. What do you think of my theory?"

She slowly bunched her skirts in both hands, ready to bolt if he put his head down to attack the scarlet cape she'd just waved before him.

To her surprise, though, Sir Charles sank to his knees in front of her, covering his face with his hands and sobbing wretched, deep guttural sobs, such as only a man can do.

Was this a trick? "Sir Charles?" she said, still holding her skirts and taking an imperceptible step backward. What if he reached out and grabbed her and—

"No one understands my grief, Mrs. Harper, but you're an undertaker, so you must be familiar with all forms of it."

"Yes."

"My marriage has died from humiliation. Cuckolding me as she has, with all sorts of men, has been my death. At least all of them are highborn, thank God, but my devastation is complete."

"Can you not reconcile with her, if she is not totally unrepentant?"

He shook his head sadly. "No one knows this truth yet, but Harriet is expecting a child. That she-devil doesn't even know whose it is. I was never cruel to her. I let her buy whatever she wanted. She was the wife of a prominent citizen. How could she do this to me? I'll not have some bastard foisted upon me. No, my wife must be put aside. My God, I've even been cuckolded by the Prince of Wales."

Sir Charles rose, passing a hand over his reddened eyes. "And avenging yourself on the Prince of Wales is no easy feat, as you can imagine."

"Which reminds me of my last question, sir. Are you acquainted with Reese Meredith?"

"No. Another moralist?"

"In his own mind, perhaps." Violet unclenched her fists and smoothed down her skirts. "Thank you, Sir Charles. This has been an enlightening visit."

"I trust you will not share my confidences."

"You need not worry, sir. I'm not interested in divorces, only in murders."

Violet felt talons of fear clawing at her back as the cab pulled up near the Christian Revival Society's tent in Whitechapel. Even the horse was fearful, shaking his head back and forth until the driver commanded him to move on.

Somehow, the vacant, hollow expression on a dead person wasn't nearly as frightening as seeing it repeated on all of these barely living creatures.

Catherine Booth, wife of the Society's founder, William Booth, was assisting her husband in handing out loaves of hard-crust bread when Violet arrived at their tent in Whitechapel. They hugged her like a family member, with William booming out his gratitude for her presence.

"My dear lady, this is the time of our most critical need. Everyone in London shows up to help on Christmas Day, then forgets the Lord's work the other three hundred and sixty-four days of the year."

Violet looked down to hide her embarrassment. She'd given no thought to time of year. In fact, the only thing that had nudged her to come was seeing the baker's calling card, a reminder that she'd promised to return to help soon and never had.

She had no more time to think about it, for Catherine tossed her an apron and set her to work ladling out cups of clean water to those who had gathered there.

The baker, Mr. Merrill, and his wife were also working on the opposite side of the tent, distributing clothing and shoes. Mr. Merrill acknowledged Violet with a wave.

Violet's stomach was all butterflies as the first group of people gathered around her, holding out battered tin cups in hands so filthy they might have belonged to coal miners. Of what was she fearful? She'd done this once before and survived.

Yes, but that was when her mind was on pursuit of someone working at the Society, someone she thought might be a murderer.

Today she was here purely for charitable purposes, and somehow that was different. Her entire focus was on the destitute people clamoring in front of her. Would someone paw at her? Demand money? Shout an obscenity at her? The dead never did that.

She splashed water into the first cup presented to her, belonging to a young man whose face had the line traces of someone who'd been on the losing end of a knife fight. He accepted the cup, shrugged, and walked away.

That wasn't so terrible. The man wasn't necessarily grateful, but he hadn't fulfilled Violet's fears, either. Her stomach quelled and she went to work with vigor. She had been scooping out generous servings of water for about a half hour, with varying degrees of reaction by the recipients, when a painfully thin woman, dressed in the garish colors of a prostitute, gulped down three cups before lunging for a loaf of bread. She had open, oozing sores around her mouth. Violet had seen these sores before, at the lock hospital.

She was drawn to the woman. Taking a fourth cup of water to her at the bread table, Violet said, "Miss, are you in trouble? Are you ill?"

The woman's eyes were fearful. "No. Not anymore. I'm as clean as they come. I won't go back."

"Back where?"

"To the lock hospital. You aren't one of their nurses, are you? I'll not let you take me."

Violet held out a hand. "Please, miss, be calm. I'm not—"

The woman flung her cup at Violet, splashing its contents down the front of her apron, and, picking up her shabby skirts, ran erratically out of the tent, pushing aside a mother and her crying infant in her haste.

Violet was stunned into numbness by the woman's reaction to her question, nearly forgetting that others clamored around for a cool drink of water.

William Booth appeared at Violet's side in an instant. "Cheer up, Mrs. Harper. Not everyone can be reached. We just try talking to one soul at a time and let the good Lord do the rest."

"I must have scared her. She thought I was . . . someone I'm not."

Booth's eyes twinkled as he stroked his wiry beard. "I doubt that, dear lady. Some folks are frightened of a great deal in this world, some of it real and some imagined. I trust she'll come back one day."

Initially upset, Violet finally settled back into her routine of handing out cups of water to the destitute residents of Whitechapel, some of whom were grateful, some of whom were tetchy, and some of whom just stared at her vacantly as though "hope" was not a word that had ever been whispered into their ears.

The image of the prostitute stayed with Violet, though. Had she been mistreated at the lock hospital? Was she really a workhouse escapee? What humiliations had she endured?

Perhaps Josephine's work was as righteous as she claimed it to be.

Violet arrived back at St. James's Palace to find two important pieces of mail. One was an engraved invitation to attend the queen's private celebration for her fiftieth birthday, to be held at Cumberland Lodge following the public displays on July 5.

Violet tossed that aside for the far more critical envelope, addressed in Sam's familiar hand. He wrote to tell her that he would be arriving at the Victoria station within a week. What a blessed relief it would be to have him home.

It also meant she had very little time to finish preparing their new quarters, and it was nearly impossible to think she could resolve the deaths of three women before Sam returned.

Violet met Mary at Morgan Undertaking, and together the two women went upstairs and set to scrubbing, straightening, and cobweb cleaning with fury under Mary's direction.

With both of them dressed in black mourning, they were soon covered head to toe in a gray film of dust. Mary was especially disheveled, cleaning with great vigor as though she was erasing the memory of her dead husband. She refused to speak of him, instead only making suggestions along the way for furniture ("you definitely need a walnut curio here"), pictures, lamps, and rugs. Violet was certain her home would be ready for display in Mr. Morris's shop window by the time Mary was done.

"I'll make you some heavy, fringed draperies that we'll do in, say, three layers. That should keep the smuts out," Mary said as she chased a plump, long-legged spider with her booted foot. The spider escaped through a hole in the wall where a heating pipe entered.

Mr. Leech would have fainted dead away to see this place.

"Have you considered hiring day help, Violet? Or that room off the kitchen could be converted from a pantry to a bedchamber for a live-in."

Violet smiled. "Tactfully stated, my friend."

"Oh, I didn't mean—"

"It's quite all right. I know I'm a terrible chatelaine, but I'm even worse at hiring domestic help. Do you still have day help? Perhaps I can use the same girl."

"An excellent idea. Now, before we visit Mr. Morris's for fabric, didn't you have a dress that needed repair?"

Violet showed her the dress she'd been wearing when she was attacked. Mary examined the rips with her expert eye, testing seams with her thumbnail and pulling the fabric gently to determine its give.

"Well, it will never be quite the same, but I think I can make it serviceable. Here, let me see this on you." Mary held the dress up against Violet and frowned. "My friend, what have you been eating?"

"What do you mean?"

"You'll need a new corset soon. Violet, you don't think you're . . ."

"No, there are no symptoms of that condition. I'm afraid it's from the palace food, which agrees with me too well."

Violet ran to the cracked mirror over the fireplace, standing a distance away to examine herself. Why, her cheeks *were* filling out a bit, weren't they? And her upper arms were straining against the sleeve seams.

What would Sam think when he saw her?

"When did I become a stout, middle-aged woman?" she asked.

Mary smiled. "You're hardly stout, my dear. Maybe a little plump. Like a sweet little partridge."

That was it. No more treacle tart or creamed dishes. Violet needed to move out of St. James's Palace, soon.

Several sharp raps on the door interrupted their discussion over Violet's wardrobe.

"Inspectors Hurst and Pratt, this is a surprise. How did you know I was here?"

"You weren't at either palace, so naturally I came to your place of business. It didn't involve much investigative work," Hurst said as the two detectives entered, taking in the disheveled appearances of both women and the flat.

"How did you know this was my place of business again?"

"Ah, now that was a bit of detective work, at which I am expert. Who, may I ask, is this lady?"

"Your detection skills have not yet informed you of my friend Mary Cooke?"

"A great pleasure, I'm sure, Mrs. Cooke." Hurst swept off his hat and bowed over Mary's hand like a practiced gentleman. Where had that come from? Pratt also removed his hat and shook her hand.

"Mary, this is Chief Inspector Hurst and Inspector Pratt. I worked with them on the Lord Raybourn situation."

"Yes, I do remember. Didn't you say that Inspector Hurst saved your life?"

"Well, he found me—"

"'Twas nothing, Mrs. Cooke. Just the sort of work a man does every day." For heaven's sake, was Hurst's chest swelling up?

"Mary is recently in mourning for her husband," Violet said. "As a detective, you probably already noticed her black garb."

"Of course I did, Mrs. Harper." His voice said he didn't care.

"How may I help you? As you can see, we are busy with preparing my new quarters before my husband returns from a trip."

Hurst smiled, but it was directed at Mary. "It is a good friend indeed who will help with such difficult chores."

"Your duty here today, Inspector?" She had to save Mary from Hurst's attentions.

"Ahem, yes. We've been investigating a man who has written threatening letters to *The Times*. Perhaps you've read about the recent riots in Flintshire?"

"In fact, I have."

"The man's half sister was killed during the riots, and this lunatic blames the queen for what happened. We think he may truly be of danger to her. We have reason to believe he may actually be working at Buckingham Palace. His name is—"

"Reese Meredith."

Hurst stared at her. "How the hell did you know that? Oh, pardon me, Mrs. Cooke, I apologize for my crudeness. Your ears shouldn't be subjected to such talk. Mrs. Harper, what travels have led you to Meredith?"

"He is a coachman at the Buckingham Palace mews." She told Hurst of the peculiar things Meredith had said to her, while Mr. Pratt took out his familiar worn notebook from his jacket pocket and began taking notes. She concluded, "But he never said anything specific that seemed to warrant your attention."

"We are certainly attentive now. I didn't want to alarm Her Majesty by invading the palace without reason, but now that we know where he is, we'll arrest him without delay." He replaced his hat and nodded at Violet. "Good day, Mrs. Harper. Mrs. Cooke, I do hope I will encounter you again."

Mary nodded but said nothing.

If this was Inspector Hurst as an infatuated puppy, Violet was terrified to know what the man in love might look like. At least Mary was in mourning, so his attentions would probably drift elsewhere before Mary would ever have the chance to be interested in him.

After the detectives left, Violet blew out a great sigh of relief that not only were her instincts about Reese Meredith correct, but also he would soon be in custody and unable to harm anyone.

She and Mary went to Morris, Marshall, and Faulkner to examine more fabrics and wall coverings for Violet's new lodgings. She was glad she had Mary along to advise her, for the dizzying array of colors and patterns made her numb. By the time they were done Violet wasn't sure what her new place would look like, but Mary assured her it would be spectacular.

It was good to see a shadow of a smile on Mary's face after what she'd been through. Perhaps she'd ask Mary to supervise the workmen as they installed everything in a few days' time.

The two friends parted ways and Violet returned to St. James's Palace to change dresses and freshen up. Another, much more pleasant, surprise awaited her, for Sam was exiting a cab in the courtyard just as Violet was. In salute, he touched his eagle-headed cane to his right eyebrow, the one with a scar cut through it. Unlike many dandies who carried canes as fashionable affectations, Sam relied on his heavily from injuries taken during the American Civil War.

Violet loved him all the more for his imperfections.

"You're a sight for sore eyes, my love, although you do look a bit dusty," he said.

"You're early. I had so much preparation to do before your return. I want to show you—"

"You are beautifully prepared. Let's go inside."

Several hours later, the pair emerged from St. James's Palace in search of a confectionery shop, as ice cream was Sam's greatest weakness and he'd expressed a need for it to rejuvenate him after— well, Violet still blushed to think upon her pleasant afternoon.

With burnt filbert ice-cream cups before them, they finally settled down to talk. Sam told her of his and Mr. Nobel's frustrations in Wales. "As I wrote, I was confused as to whether to return to Colorado—and Susanna—or to stay here in Great Britain in hopes that Mr. Nobel and I will eventually convince the authorities in Wales or the North to recognize the wisdom of dynamite. I received your letter stating that you wished to buy back into Morgan Undertaking, so I figured that was God's way of telling me that a Colorado mine was not to be."

"Don't forget that Susanna has already married and we have the opening of the Suez Canal to attend in November."

"Yes, Wife, I don't need any further convincing. I took the train as far as Nottinghamshire with Mr. Nobel, with the intent of parting ways there, but we ended up scouting the area there for possible mine locations. We found a colliery there that went bankrupt when the original owner died and his son abandoned any pretense of interest in his father's business. There are new tunnels to be opened up, we are sure of it, and believe that many of the men who used to work there would be interested in returning. In fact, a reopened mine might rejuvenate the town."

Violet blinked. "But—are you saying you want me to move from London all the way to practically Scotland so you can run a mine? I've already agreed to buy back into—"

"No, although I'd like you to visit there at least once. I'll need to be on hand on occasion to open it, as will Mr. Nobel, but we'd planned to bring on some of the previous foremen who know the mine best to hire the best workers and get everything reestablished. If we can prove the value of dynamite to this mine, it will serve as proof to mines around the country that it is the safest way to open their tunnels. My goal is not to be a mine owner, but a seller of dynamite. Mr. Nobel, though, intends to also have a mine in Wales someday."

"So you'll leave again."

"Only for a few days at a time, and only a few times, I promise. I must confess, I have another thought in mind with regard to the mines." Sam pushed aside his finished dish, clean except for a few drops at the bottom. "In the mine in Mold, they use children as laborers."

Violet nodded. "Don't most poor families send everyone to work?"

"Yes, but these children were in terrible condition. There was one girl . . . I actually thought she was a boy, she was so . . ." Sam stared off, unable to finish. "I tried to imagine Susanna working there. She might not be alive today if she had. These mines aren't safe, especially for children. I want to build up a colliery that protects its workers. I think it can be done, and it will be an example to other mine owners."

"I'm sure you will do what's best."

"Enough of me—tell me what skullduggery you've been involved in with the queen."

Violet relayed all of her adventures, ignoring his outrage over the two attacks on her and ending with the tale of Reese Meredith. "Inspector Hurst believes Meredith intended to harm the queen, and I think he may have been responsible for the deaths of Lady Maud, Lady Marcheford, and Miss Cortland."

"What was his motive?"

"His anger at the queen spilled over into hatred for all aristocrats, so he began killing friends of Princess Louise."

"But what of Miss Cortland? You said she was one of Mrs. Butler's moralists?"

"Yes, but she was the daughter of Lord Sadler, a baron. She was an aristocrat turned out by her family, but an aristocrat nonetheless, and Louise knew her."

Sam shook his head. "It seems as though Miss Cortland wasn't quite as prominent as Lady Maud and Lady Marcheford. Perhaps someone else killed her and you've erroneously linked the three together."

"I suppose the three also link together not only because they were aristocrats, but because they were moralists. But Meredith wouldn't have killed them for that, would he? At some level, their work was as revolutionary as his. Unless he viewed them as competition against his own work? I don't know; it sounds too fantastic."

Sam reached his spoon into her dish to take the last melting morsel of ice cream from it. Setting it aside, he said, "Nevertheless, I think you'll need to interview him in his prison cell to learn his true motives before calling a conclusion to your work."

Had she been too hasty in thinking this was finished? Meredith was on her list of suspects, but hadn't she suspected Lord Marcheford and Sir Charles far more than him? Was her duty really over? Besides, she hadn't even figured out what the bites on the women's bodies were from.

She changed the subject. "I have an invitation to the queen's private celebration for her fiftieth birthday tomorrow."

Sam grimaced. "Another royal entertainment. Wouldn't you rather stay at St. James's alone together for our own private celebration? I'm sure we can find a moment to hail Her Majesty."

"Sam! You wicked man."

He raised an eyebrow. "I'm full of cream and sugar. You have no idea my powers of evil right now."

Violet blushed at her husband's brazenness in the middle of a public place. "You're incorrigible," she mumbled.

"A man who has been too long away from his wife might be excused for releasing his uncivilized side for a while, eh? I'm like a parched man in the desert, and you are my oasis."

Violet was both horrified and delighted by her husband's manner. He said he didn't want her out of his sight again. Indeed, she had no desire to be anywhere else.

"Well, there is another oasis you need to visit. I've started to renovate our new lodgings over Morgan Undertaking, but I warn you, they are far from habitable yet."

"As long as the rain can't get in and you're there, it's habitable enough for me. Let's go see it now."

In the joy of having Sam home again, Violet chose to forget about murder for the rest of the day.

Hurst knew he was ruffling the feathers of the man before him, but that was no concern of his. This was why he detested dealing with palace staff. They had an opinion of themselves so elevated as to think they were royal family members themselves.

Which they were, in a way, since many of them could trace service to the reigning King or Queen of England back five or more generations.

The sight of Hurst and Pratt undoubtedly made Mr. Norton nervous, for the arrival of Scotland Yard detectives implied that he had somehow failed in his duties.

Such a failure used to be cause for execution, Hurst thought, *but you needn't worry about that anymore.*

"This is the second time I've been asked about my staff this week. Previously it was a lady undertaker Her Majesty favors."

Hurst rolled his eyes.

"Who is it you say you're interested in again?" Mr. Norton said as he opened up a large ledger book.

"Reese Meredith. 'M-e-r'—"

"Yes, I have him here. He came to us by way of Earl Baverstock, but he was previously in the King's Dragoon Guards, with service in the Second Opium War."

Hurst nodded. "How is he in his duties?"

"Competent. He has proved himself to have talent in training horses, so I've let him work with our new stock at times."

Hurst knew that sort of response. Mr. Norton was complimenting Meredith without saying he actually liked him.

"Did he ever displease you?"

Mr. Norton huffed. Palace staff shouldn't be gossiping about one another. It was undignified and reflected badly on the queen herself if staff were behaving badly.

Hurst almost smiled to see Mr. Norton in so much mental anguish. The man could prevaricate all he wanted; Hurst would have the truth out of him eventually.

While the superintendent pretended to look at his ledger, Hurst's thoughts turned to Mrs. Harper's friend Mary Cooke. What a reserved beauty. So dignified. She was beyond childbearing years, but perhaps that was beyond his care now. After all, he was no young cock of the walk anymore, either. Mrs. Cooke had a very fragile look to her—from mourning, presumably—that made him instinctively want to shield her from the cruelties of the world.

He wondered if Mrs. Cooke would entertain his attentions once she was finished with her first year of mourning. The thought of a courtship with her sent pleasant, unfamiliar sensations through him.

He had to face reality, though. Mrs. Cooke had one serious drawback. She was close friends with Violet Harper, the most aggravating woman he'd ever met.

"Mr. Hurst?" Pratt was looking at him strangely.

"What?"

"Mr. Norton wants to know what else we want."

"Right, yes. Bring us Meredith, and have a mind not to tell him we're here."

The superintendent huffed once more but did as he was bid. He returned some time later, wide-eyed in shock. "He's gone."

"What do you mean?"

"No one has seen him since yesterday, and his chest is cleaned out. No one ever gives up their position at the palace willingly, and one certainly doesn't leave in a way that would prevent receiving a good character. Something is wrong."

Something was certainly wrong. And now the queen was in grave danger. It fell to him and Inspector Pratt to make sure no harm came to her.

Reese congratulated himself on being smart enough to lift a set of mews keys from Mr. Norton before departing. The superintendents for each palace's mews shared keys to ease the transfer of coaches between royal residences. Mr. Norton's sloppiness was fortunate; it meant he wouldn't notice the set was gone until Reese was far away from Windsor.

The queen had nearly ruined everything with her decision to have a second, private affair at Cumberland Lodge in Windsor, which had altered the schedule for her public appearance. It required some nimble rethinking, but Reese finally had decided that the private event was much easier to infiltrate and changed his own plans accordingly.

Several coaches and their pairs were lined up in the courtyard on the day of the queen's celebrations, waiting to be driven to the royal apartments in the upper ward. Otherwise, there was no activity. By now, the Windsor Castle mews staff would be indoors, washing up and donning new uniforms.

He knew the routine. The coachmen would drive the carriages in a single file around to the entrance to pick up passengers. A groom would step down from the back, hand in the ladies, then jump onto the rails again to accompany the coach to its destination. Even a family event such as the queen's private birthday celebration required pretentious ceremony.

The queen would most likely be in the first coach. Yes, that was one of her broughams at the front of the line. He must execute his plan carefully; this was the moment when everything could go wrong. He fingered the knife handle beneath his waistband. Reese always carried one belted under his shirt these days but thus far hadn't had to use it. Would he have to use it today?

He peered into the queen's brougham. A velvet-covered box had already been placed upon the floor for the queen's feet to rest upon. A mere ten-minute ride, and the queen still needed to ensure that she didn't have a moment's discomfort.

What would Mr. Marx say to that?

Reese opened the driver's box and threw in his supplies, glad that they fit among all of the tools and spare equipage stored in it.

"Meredith, what are you doing here?"

Reese whirled around. It was Dudley, one of the Buckingham Palace coachmen. He must have been commissioned for this evening's event. Why wasn't the fool in stable quarters, dressing in his livery?

"I, ah, was assigned to this event at the last minute."

"I heard you ran away. Why did you do that?"

"Is that what you were told? You know what a rummy old cove Mr. Norton is. I told him I needed to go back to Wales for a short time. A funeral. My uncle."

Dudley frowned. "Why would he lie about that?"

Reese laughed. "You know how he's always disliked me. He probably hoped to replace me before I returned. He's the one who's kicked up a shine now, isn't he?"

"Which carriage are you driving tonight?"

"This one, the queen's."

"You're the liar, Meredith. Mr. Norton assigned me to Her Majesty's coach."

"He must have forgotten to tell you he'd replaced you with me."

Dudley took a step forward. "How did you even get inside the mews? The gates were locked."

"It sounds like you're accusing me of trespassing. Are you? I won't take kindly to it." Once again, Reese felt for his knife. Should he withdraw it? The threat of it would make Dudley back off, but he might then run straight to other palace staff and report him.

Reese had no more time to contemplate the situation, for Dudley grabbed him by the arm. "I'm taking you to the stable manager."

Not likely. Instinctively Reese shrugged out of Dudley's grasp, and instead grabbed the other man's neck. With both thumbs on the other man's Adam's apple, he squeezed. Dudley's eyes bulged. "What . . . you . . . doing . . . stop."

Reese felt power surging through him, as he had on so many other occasions, but somehow this was wrong. It wasn't part of the plan. Besides, it was too easy to get caught. He released Dudley, who stepped back, panting, and pointed at him.

"You're a devil, Meredith, and I'll see your name blackened from Richmond to Greenwich."

No, not when Reese had so much to accomplish. "I'm afraid I can't allow that."

Dudley turned to run, but Reese was quicker. He grabbed a fistful of the coachman's shirt, which stopped him, then put his arm around Dudley's neck, pulling him closer. In a moment that was full of pure rage—or was it fear?—Reese removed his arm from around Dudley's neck and instead used his hand to slam the groom's head against the side of the queen's carriage.

Dudley slumped down the side of the brougham, leaving a small trail of blood along the shiny black surface. There was something symbolic in it, but Reese wasn't sure what it was.

He gazed down at Dudley's crumpled form. Things weren't going according to plan. He knelt and examined the man. Still breathing. Reese looked up. No one rushing out of their quarters yet, so he'd not been observed. Quickly he dragged Dudley's body outside the mews gate and left it along the stone wall that enclosed the courtyard. He'd eventually be found and would report his attacker, but by then Reese's goals would be accomplished.

He raced back to the queen's brougham, opened the driver's box, and found a rag to wipe down the side of the carriage. That done, he hopped onto the box and slid his wig as far over his forehead as he could. The sun was setting, so as long as no one was specifically looking for Dudley on this carriage Reese wouldn't be noticed.

Dudley, he thought, *as stupid as you are, you are my own kind, and that's why you still live.*

Now, where was the queen?

12

The queen and Beatrice stepped into their carriage and rumbled off as the next carriage pulled up for Violet and Sam. "Such pomp," Sam whispered as the groom jumped off the back of their coach and helped her in. With a lurch, they, too, were on their way to Cumberland Lodge, several hundred feet behind the queen's carriage.

"The queen shows me high esteem by inviting me to her family celebration."

"I suppose you're right. You know I'm not comfortable with all of . . . this. I'm like a fish out of water, as your Mr. Chaucer once said."

"It's just for a few hours. Perhaps you'll witness one of Mr. Brown's tarot card readings."

"How entertaining. Is the queen satisfied that the spirits have completed their mission?"

"Not quite. With Mr. Meredith having left London, she thinks they might still have something to say about his whereabouts."

The carriage left the inner castle walls and traveled along the Long Walk toward Cumberland Lodge. Flaming torches had been set along the darkened path to illuminate the way, yet Violet could barely make out the gas lamps on the queen's carriage up ahead of them. Bertie, Alix, Louise, Leopold, and Mr. Brown rode in carriages behind Violet and Sam, creating an intimate cortege.

"How far?" Sam asked.

"Not very. The queen installed Princess Helena at Cumberland Lodge to keep her very close by. It's the official residence of Windsor Park's ranger, a title the queen bestowed upon Prince Christian to keep him happy with living in Great Britain."

"Why doesn't he develop a hobby or work on an invention?"

Violet smiled indulgently. "Oh, Sam, you're such an American. He's a prince. If he's not assisting with the ruling of his own country, he can only undertake gentlemanly pursuits."

"Such as?"

"Well, he can hunt, or host house parties, or go riding, collect art, that sort of thing."

"How boring. The man must want to fall on his own hunting knife."

"You haven't met Prince Christian yet. I believe he is quite content in his circumstances. I think we will be coming up on Cumberland House in—"

"Dudley, what are you doing there?" The carriage came to a sudden halt as their coachman shouted at the driver of the queen's brougham, which had stopped in front of them. "Damn you, get back on your box. What are you fooling with?"

Violet frowned and opened the door to their coach, craning her neck to see what was going on. "He can't be . . ." She pulled her head back in and spoke, her tone even but urgent. "Sam, the queen's driver has some sort of explosive."

"You mean a bomb?" Sam, too, looked out of the coach. "Oh, hellfire, he's got sticks of gelignite. Run away from the coach as far as you can. Get everyone out of the coaches behind you. Run!" Without further explanation, Sam jumped out of the carriage, stumbled upon landing heavily on his bad leg, and righted himself before running faster than she'd ever seen him go.

She clambered out as well, completely ignoring his direction. "Go to the coaches behind us," she said to the driver. "Get everyone away from here, now!"

The man jumped down from his box without questioning his passenger's command. Violet picked up her skirts and ran after Sam. She was faster than he was and reached the door to the queen's carriage just as he clambered onto the driver's box and grabbed the driver. The two men tumbled off to one side, a burning object between them.

With no time to consider Sam, Violet yanked open the door to the queen's carriage. The queen looked horrified by Violet's presence, and Violet was certain she looked like a Bedlamite. Without a thought to royal propriety, she said, "Your Majesty, come with me."

"I'm not sure I understand—"

"I have no time to explain it to you. Now!" With a show of force she hoped wouldn't land her in Newgate later, Violet reached in and yanked on the queen's arm.

"Well, I—" the queen protested, but suddenly tripped out of the carriage and, without the steps pulled out for her comfort, landed with an undignified thud onto the gravel path. Beatrice exited the brougham, hopping down easily and nodding at Violet before grabbing her mother's other arm.

"Come, Mother, you must run on your own."

Violet and Beatrice each held on to one of the queen's hands, and the trio ran together, skirts flying, for Cumberland Lodge. Just as they reached the entry, where a bewigged and puzzled butler stood waiting, they heard a loud explosion.

Or, rather, they felt it, as the ground rumbled violently beneath them as though it was about to split apart. In the distance, Violet heard Alix screaming. Or was it Bertie? The screaming was cut off, and Violet realized she'd been deafened by the sound of the explosion. Where was Sam?

Victoria twisted out of Violet's hand, and she realized that the queen was huddled over Beatrice, who had fallen to the ground. Beatrice's lips were moving wordlessly. No, wait, Violet couldn't hear her.

Where was the butler? He must have run into the house to find his mistress, for soon he returned with Princess Helena and Prince Christian on his heels. All of them were shouting something, but it was impossible to know what it was.

Where was Sam?

Princess Helena pointed, and Violet followed the line of her arm. The carriage the queen and her daughter had occupied moments ago was obliterated, as was the one Violet and Sam had ridden in. The most complete part was a spoked wheel that lay smoking in the carnage. The rest of the family ran toward Cumberland Lodge, their faces white with shock.

Where was Sam? Her thoughts flew back to a time when his death was falsely reported to her. *Please, Lord, I cannot take this a second time.*

The queen and Beatrice tugged on her, ushering her into the house. She shrugged them off and instead walked toward the wreckage. There were no bodies anywhere.

Had Sam been annihilated in the wreckage? No, it was too much to consider. She sank to her knees, coughing, crying, and threatening to utter curses at God if he'd abandoned her by taking Sam away.

13

❧❧❧

"Sweetheart, what are you doing out here?"

Had Violet just heard something? Was her hearing recovered? She looked up. "Sam!" She jumped up and flung herself at him, covering his face with kisses and not caring who was watching from Cumberland Lodge's windows.

"Whoa, I'm a bit too filthy for such attentions."

"I thought you were—that you had—" She pointed helplessly at the wreckage.

"I've faced cannon fire and been a prisoner of war, and you thought a simpleton carrying a small bomb would stop me?"

"But how did you escape the explosion?"

"I wrested the bomb away from our little friend and threw it back just as he was detonating it. I only hoped you'd followed my instructions to run. I grabbed him and he put up quite a good struggle, but you can't win against a lame, scarred old billy Yank. Come inside."

She followed him into Cumberland Lodge, where she found Reese Meredith bound and in the custody of Inspectors Hurst and Pratt. When had they arrived? Had they seen Violet mourning outside? The queen and her family were chattering anxiously about what had happened.

Everyone except Princess Helena, that is. She was in a faint on a settee with Prince Christian hovering over her.

"Mrs. Harper," Victoria said, stopping all other conversation.

"We wondered where you were. As you can see, Scotland Yard has our perpetrator in hand. This is not the first time we have been attacked, but God has preserved us to reign another day." Far from being cowed, the queen looked positively exhilarated from her experience.

Hurst yanked Meredith forward. "Is this him? We learned from the superintendent of the mews that Meredith had fled Buckingham Palace. We figured he followed the queen to Windsor, and finding an unconscious coachman outside the mews here confirmed we were right."

Violet nodded. "Yes, this is Mr. Meredith."

"So what do you say for yourself, boy?"

Meredith was no longer the cocky young man of the mews. Beneath his torn, disheveled clothing and bloodied nose lay a boy whose rage was palpable. "Nothing. All of you are in on destroying the working class. I should have known you were really one of them, Mrs. Harper. So many slaves in our society lap at the puddles the ruling class make, not realizing a perfect society is within their grasp if they would just throw off the shackles of the bourgeois."

By this point, Princess Helena was finally rousing and starting to whimper, so a call was made for tea, as well as a sedative for her.

"Was it your aim only to kill the queen and Princess Beatrice, or were you aiming for the entire cortege?"

"Didn't matter to me. The more the better."

"How did you get the explosive material?"

"I'm clever."

"Damn you, you little—" Hurst swung a brawny fist out, and Violet had no doubt that Meredith would be unconscious if it landed true.

"No!" she said. "No violence in front of Her Majesty."

Hurst had the good grace to look sheepish. "We have to get his story somehow."

Violet shook her head. "His face needs cleaning. Here." She removed a handkerchief from a pocket of her dress. "You cannot appear before a judge looking like this." To the openmouthed horror of everyone in the room, including Sam, Violet dabbed the cloth against her tongue and wiped his face of the smeared blood and dirt that made Meredith's face unrecognizable. At first Meredith resisted her, but he soon settled into her ministrations, although his scowl didn't diminish.

"Where is your mother?" she asked.

"Dead."

"Your father?"

"Also dead."

"An orphan, then; that explains much. Any other relatives?"

"I had a half sister, but thanks to the queen, she's dead, too."

"What happened to her?"

At this, the groom's bluster finally broke. "She was murdered during the Mold riots. My defenseless little sister, Margaret, minding her own business for certain, shot and killed like a doe in the forest."

Something clicked in Violet's mind. Hadn't Sam written about a young woman dying in his arms during the riots? It must have been Meredith's half sister. She exchanged a look with Sam. He'd realized the same thing.

Hurst shoved Meredith in the shoulder. "And you thought that was reason enough to kill the queen? I'll see to it that you regret it long before you're pronounced guilty and sent to the noose at Newgate."

"Inspector, please," Violet said. "Mr. Meredith, why do you blame the queen for your sister's unfortunate demise?"

"Because she doesn't care about the poor or the downtrodden."

"Who is this—this—*person*, and how does he dare accuse us of no feelings for the poor?" the queen said. "We would have you know, young man, that we give alms to the poor each year, a tradition much encouraged by our beloved husband, the prince con—"

"So it was your anger over your sister's death that caused you to attack the queen?" Violet said.

"Mostly. I wanted her to pay for her disregard for her subjects."

Tea arrived, but everyone ignored it except for Princess Helena as well as Bertie, who was exceptionally solicitous of Alix's condition and made sure she was served a hot cup as well as a selection of pastries. The remainder of the room was riveted on Violet and Meredith.

"You would have thrown the entire kingdom—if not the entire world—into chaos had you been successful."

"Yes." A smile flitted across Meredith's face, quickly replaced by a look of regret.

"Mr. Meredith," Hurst interjected, "your plot was an abysmal failure, and now you shall pay the ultimate price. You've thrown your life away for the gain of nothing."

Violet ignored Hurst and continued. "If your target was the queen, why did you find it necessary to murder the friends of Princess Louise?"

Meredith responded with a glare.

"I'm referring to Lady Maud Winter, Lady Marcheford, and Miss Lillian Cortland."

"These highborn folk got their comeuppance."

"So you don't admit to killing these other—bourgeois, I believe you call it—members that were close to the queen?" Violet said.

Hurst yanked Meredith's arm up behind him. "Treason, murder . . . shall we add perjury to your list of charges, my boy?"

"You're hurting me."

"This is nothing compared to the rope. You won't be eligible for the silk noose, either. It's all hemp for you."

Violet saw a glint in the coachman's eyes as he relaxed in Hurst's tight grasp. His next words were chilling. "My execution will make me a martyr. The proletariat will remember me for all time, and will move forward with Mr. Marx's great plans. And I will be reunited with Margaret. And yes, that's right . . . yes, I killed all of your fine ladies, and enjoyed watching them suffer."

Hurst wrenched Meredith's arm upward again. "We'll take it from here, Mrs. Harper. Rest assured he will have a quick trial and conviction."

The two detectives dragged Meredith out of the house.

"Well! That was quite the birthday surprise, wasn't it, Bertie?"

"Yes, Mother. How many attempts on your life does that make now?"

"We believe we have lost count. So terribly frightening when it occurs," Victoria said, patting back strands of hair that had escaped her widow's cap.

"At least it happened inside the privacy of Windsor, so we won't see the presses churning out extra editions to cover it," Louise said. "Shall we call for new carriages to take us back, Mother, or do you want to proceed with this evening's event?"

"This is a time for the family to be together, we think, so we will carry on as we have done so many times before. This has certainly been one of the most . . . stimulating . . . days of our reign, has it not?"

"Mother, you were almost killed," Bertie said. "As were we all. We owe thanks to the undertaker's husband."

All eyes turned to Sam, who reddened as the royal family spoke their thanks all at once. He looked to Violet, a plea for help in his eyes. She smiled to see him drowning in praise.

The queen resumed what she was saying. "Yes, it has been a day of surprise and revelation, but now we wish to express what joy we have as we turn fifty years of age. So much has happened since we took the throne: the expansion of our glorious empire, numerous marvelous inventions, the births of our nine children, as well as their own marriages and children. We still face distress, though, in our son's involvement in that distasteful Mordaunt affair, the ridiculous rumors of Mr. Brown, and, of course, the loss of our dearest—"

"Mother, you were talking about your joys," Louise said.

"Yes, of course. We are joyful that our subjects love us dearly, as we are the most loving of monarchs, despite the disturbance with that young man. What was his name again?"

"Reese Meredith, Your Majesty," Violet said.

"Hmm. We may have to see about the mews superintendent, Mr. Norton. He showed very poor judgment in hiring Meredith. But as I was saying, it is our hope that happiness will once again cover England when we see our daughter Louise successfully married. We have agreed to let her find an Englishman of her choosing, as we always want the utmost happiness for our children. . . ."

As the queen droned on, Beatrice tugged on Violet's sleeve.

"Mrs. Harper," she said quietly, "you haven't been back to paint with me."

"You're right, Princess. I'm sorry for it."

"You'll come back soon, won't you?"

"I will."

Beatrice grinned, reminding Violet of how very young and tender the girl still was, despite her maturity. Yes, Violet would visit Beatrice again soon.

Violet and Sam joined the royal family for an informal meal, and the queen opened token presents from her family, smiling and chatting as though all were right in her kingdom, now that the perpetrator of the murders had been captured.

Violet, though, wasn't so sure. Meredith admitted to the killing of the three women, but how could he have enjoyed watching them suffer when they were made unconscious first?

No, it didn't seem possible that Reese Meredith was the culprit, despite Hurst's swaggering confidence in it.

It was time to plan another confrontation with Lord Marcheford and Sir Charles.

Violet opened the note, written on Buckingham Palace stationery. It was from Beatrice, asking Violet to come for a private visit that evening and requesting that she come through one of the rear entrances, so that Victoria would not be aware of Violet's presence.

> *I fear Mother might think I prefer your company to her own, and I shouldn't like to face the wrath of that accusation.*

Beatrice wanted to have tea together and play with her pet cockatiel. Again, Violet's heart broke over the girl's obvious loneliness. So many family squabbles to endure, with no girls her own age for friendship and comfort.

Violet ordered a light supper with Sam first, and over their meal they discussed what to do about her two suspects. Sam suggested that Inspector Hurst accompany her on her interviews for safety and to make an immediate arrest if she should wrest a confession from one of them. Violet thought Sam was neglecting the subordinate role this would place on Hurst, not to mention the inspector's resulting consternation, but didn't argue with the basic logic of her husband's idea.

Thus satisfied that she would have her killer within the next twenty-four hours, she headed over to Buckingham Palace alone to visit Beatrice.

The palace staff were now used to her frequent coming and going and hardly gave her a cursory glance as she came in through a servants' entrance and went up a rear staircase. There was no activity sounding from the royal apartments. The thought flitted through her mind that perhaps Alix was in distress in her pregnancy and everyone had abruptly departed for Marlborough House to attend to her. Perhaps they'd left in such a hurry that Beatrice had forgotten to send her a note.

Beatrice was not in her own bedchamber, so Violet went to her art room. That room was also dark. Violet entered and lit a couple of the oil lamps in the room. One lamp was near the birdcage by the windows, which energized the cockatiel into a few chirps and peeps.

"Hello, Peaches, why aren't you covered for the night?" she greeted the bird. "Did your mistress leave in a hurry and forget? I think she forgot me, too."

Violet sat next to Beatrice's art table to wait. Surely the princess would be back soon to keep her date with Violet. With Peaches quietly whistling in the background, Violet leaned back and closed her eyes, trying not to drift off to sleep after her filling supper.

Really, she thought, as she put a hand over her mouth to cover a most unladylike belch, *it will be good for me to stop the palace meals*.

She rested for only a few moments when she smelled something pungent and familiar. What was it? Rousing herself, she attempted to find the location of the odor.

What she saw next stilled her. On the floor was a rag, very similar to the ones she'd seen at the death scenes.

Oh no, not the princess, too. . . .

With alarm welling up in Violet's throat, she ran into the hall-way, rapping on doors and opening them. All of the rooms were un-occupied.

She stopped a maid who was closing drapes for the evening. "Where is Princess Beatrice?" Violet asked.

The maid stared wide-eyed at her, no doubt noticing her pan-icked appearance. "Most of the family went out earlier, ma'am, to Windsor, to dine with Prince Christian and Princess Helena."

"And Princess Beatrice? Was she with the family?"

Now the maid was frightened. "I suppose so. She must have been. I don't know, ma'am; no one told me to keep an eye on her." The poor girl had tears in her eyes.

"Never mind," Violet said. "I'm sure she'll be back soon."

Violet dashed off before the maid could ask her another ques-tion. As she fled the palace, she tried to think. Who had Beatrice, Lord Marcheford or Sir Charles? Who was the more likely suspect?

Sir Charles was an embittered man with a vendetta against the opponents of the Contagious Diseases Acts, even calling out Josephine Butler by name. His wife's indiscretions had thrown more fuel on the fire of his hatred of the moralists. But he was a man of Parliament. Would he really resort to murdering these women when he could just have easily legislated them out of the way?

Unless he was stark raving mad from his wife's peccadilloes.

What of Lord Marcheford, another man resentful of his wife's activities with the moralists? But in Marcheford's case, he had an-other motive, which was to be free to marry Lady Henrietta Pettit. Such desire could make a man do strange things.

But why take Princess Beatrice? She was just a child. She had nothing to do with the moralists.

Except that Beatrice was often in Violet's company and cer-tainly Violet might be accused of being a member of the moralists. Had the girl's note been faked to lure Violet to a place where she would join the princess in her fate? If that was the case, Violet had been left with no clues.

Where was the girl? With Sir Charles or Lord Marcheford? *Think, Violet, think.*

Sir Charles had more political connections to see his goals accomplished. Lord Marcheford, though, was vain, arrogant, and condescending, with no love for his wife's social circle.

Violet ran from the palace, hailing the first cab she saw. She should go to Scotland Yard to fetch Inspector Hurst, as she'd promised Sam. There was no time, though. Every second was precious if she was to find Beatrice alive.

Her mind was made up. She would risk seeing Lord Marcheford alone.

Lord Marcheford's irritation exuded from him like a noxious gas as he stood primly inside his study. "I hardly believed it when the butler said it was you again, Mrs. Harper."

"Sir, I have no time to exchange barbs with you. Where is the princess?"

"Who?"

"Do not attempt to delude me. I know that you have taken Princess Beatrice from Buckingham Palace. Is she here?"

"From Buckingham Palace? I had no invitation to go there. Why would I take a twelve-year-old girl? I've no interest in tea parties and dolls. What is this madness of yours? First you accuse me of causing my wife's death; now you blaze your way into my home with nonsense of my having kidnapped a royal princess."

Violet regretted her methods. Perhaps it would have been better to go to Inspector Hurst first. He would have known how to handle this. Besides, now that she was here, seeds of doubt were sprouting inside her head. Had she been rash in coming here? Should she have thought this through more?

Violet's only choice was to think it through now. She decided to approach Lord Marcheford more tactfully.

"My apologies for my brusqueness. If you will humor me, I wish to ask you something, sir."

He reached for a decanter and two glasses, pouring himself one and then tipping the bottle toward Violet as if in question.

"No, thank you," she said.

"Suit yourself. I find that a finger or two of whiskey helps settle the nerves when faced with hysterical women. The women are usually in more need of it than I am." He put aside the second glass and sauntered to a high-backed chair, its upholstery so perfectly plush that it might have just been covered yesterday.

"Now, what is your question, Mrs. Harper?" Lord Marcheford said, occupying the chair with aristocratic boredom while not inviting her to sit down.

Something was dancing at the edges of her mind, if only she could grasp it. Something to do with Lady Marcheford's affair.

"Tell me, what was the name of Lady Marcheford's paramour?"

"Why? Do you think Cape was involved?"

Violet tapped her foot impatiently. Lord Marcheford responded with an eye roll.

"Very well, it was Henry Cape, Lord Blevins's younger brother."

"You said he was involved in activities of which you did not approve. What were they?"

Lord Marcheford took a long swallow from his glass. "Would this be a second question, Mrs. Harper? Very well, you need not thrust a mental dagger through my heart. It wasn't so much that I didn't approve, just that his activities were laughable. How he ever thought he was—"

"Lord Marcheford, *please*, I haven't much time and lives hang in the balance."

"How very dramatic of you. Cape thought himself a poet and a painter, in both of which he demonstrated himself little more than a dilettante."

A man of the arts. Mr. Cape didn't sound like a man interested in murdering women, but she had to be sure.

"Was Mr. Cape angry about anything that you know of?"

This elicited a self-satisfied smile from Lord Marcheford. "He was probably angry at his own stupidity. He has been in and out of debtors' prison for months. His brother refuses to assist him. It's another reason why I couldn't fathom what Lottie saw in him."

So not only was there no decipherable motive on Mr. Cape's part, but also most of his time had been occupied in a cell.

"Your wife was friends with Lady Maud Winter. There was a rumor that Lady Maud had recently found a beau. Do you know who it was?"

Lord Marcheford emptied his glass. "Lottie never mentioned

anyone, and she and Maud were quite close in their shared love of that dratted moralist movement. Are you sure you aren't confusing her with Miss Cortland?"

Violet caught her breath. "What do you mean? You told me before that you'd never heard of Miss Cortland."

"To the contrary. You asked me if I knew her. I'd never met her, but knew of her from Lottie."

Violet felt the same urge to fling the man from a window that she'd experienced with Mr. Brown. She clamped her lips together to avoid saying something she might regret, allowing Lord Marcheford to continue.

"Miss Cortland was involved with a man. Someone Lottie said was highly inappropriate. He and Cape knew each other, I believe. In fact, Lottie probably introduced Miss Cortland to her beau."

Violet blinked as a thousand jigsaw pieces clicked together at once. She suddenly knew, without question, what had happened. As she continued silently arranging the puzzle her host continued his usual rant.

"These moralist women will come to no good end. Why they won't stop their activities I'll never understand. Why didn't Lottie listen to me? She should have never—"

Violet left Lord Marcheford, his complaints barely registering in her mind.

She arrived back at Buckingham Palace, returning to Beatrice's art room after verifying with palace staff that the royal family had not yet returned.

She picked up the rag she'd seen earlier. It didn't smell of chloroform. Yet the odor was unmistakable in the room. It seemed to be coming from Beatrice's desk. Hoping she wasn't violating too many rules of propriety, Violet looked in the drawers below the expansive table, lifting out tubes and pots, opening them, and sniffing their contents.

Nothing.

Violet was determined to find it. Dropping to her hands and knees, she went under the table. Yes, the smell was much stronger here. She ran a hand along one side of the table support. Still nothing.

As she ran her hand along the other support, though, her fingers found a depression in the wood. She pressed into it, heard a latch click, and a slim, upright drawer popped open.

Inside was a bottle of liquid. Before she even unstoppered it, she knew what the contents were.

Chloroform.

Violet heard a noise. She crawled out from under the table and set the bottle on the table, then went to the expanse of windows to look down, thinking that perhaps she'd heard the royal carriages pulling up. The courtyard was empty.

The door slammed behind her. Violet whirled around.

"Mr. Caradoc, you startled me. The princess asked me to meet her, but she isn't here."

"No, the family is off to Windsor to dine with Prince Christian and Princess Helena. It would seem congratulations are in order, Mrs. Harper. You listened to me regarding Mr. Meredith and now he is in custody for the tragic deaths of those young women."

So the princess was safe. "Yes. I'm not quite sure he is the culprit, though."

"Really? Yet he stands accused. And he admitted to their murders."

"Mr. Meredith was certainly guilty of attempting to murder the queen, but as for the other women . . ." Violet instinctively took a step backward.

"You think someone else is responsible for Lady Maud, Lady Marcheford, and Miss Cortland?" Caradoc said.

"Yes."

"And who might that be?"

"I believe you may already know who it is, Mr. Caradoc." If she screamed, were there staff close enough by to hear her? What weapon was at hand? There were brushes and paints nearby, but none were likely to injure him. She took another step backward.

"Me? How should I know? I'd like to hear your theory, though, Mrs. Harper." He grinned, and Violet knew the sinister mind behind that smile.

"It was you, of course. I admit you had me fooled when you reported on Mr. Meredith to me. I believed you to be a devoted royal servant."

"Interesting. Please, continue."

Violet went on. "I realized that I kept looking for what the murdered women had in common, without looking for what the men in their lives may have had in common."

"And what is it that they have in common?"

"Art. For some reason, you have built up resentment as Princess Beatrice's art tutor. Lady Marcheford's paramour, Henry Cape, already knew you—"

"Of course, we met at the Royal Academy. But knowing a fellow artist doesn't make me a murderer. Have you gone mad from corpse vapors?"

"—and Lady Marcheford was friends with Miss Cortland because of their moralist activities together. You took up with Miss Cortland. You were her secret inamorato."

Caradoc crossed his arms. "And so you say I killed my sweetheart and two of her friends? For what reason would I do that?"

"It does seem puzzling on the face of it. At first, I thought you were murdering aristocratic women. Then I thought their commonality was the moralist movement. Finally, I realized that you killed them for entirely different reasons."

Caradoc stared at her for a moment, then brought his hands together, clapping slowly three times. In a more hushed tone he said, "How very bright of you, Mrs. Harper. Do tell me what strange story you have concocted."

"It's not so strange. Because I couldn't resolve the type of victim you were choosing, I overlooked some clues, the most obvious being that Lady Maud more than likely had hired you as her art tutor. When I taught Lady Marcheford how to make mourning jewelry, I remember her discussing Lady Maud's interest in china painting. Once I recalled that, it was easy to see that a young woman of Lady Maud's position would more than likely hire a tutor, and that she would go to the most prestigious tutor she could find—that of the royal household."

Caradoc laughed. "So now you have established that I gave Lady Maud a few painting lessons? What of it? She was quite terrible, you know. I broke up every pot and bowl she put her hand to, lest anyone see them and ask who her tutor was."

"You're right." Violet nodded. "What crime is there in your serving as Lady Maud's art tutor? None. But I thought back on the day you came to me, confidentially reporting on Reese Meredith. You said something curious, that Mr. Meredith was much more radical than was warranted. What did that mean? I thought nothing of it at the time, but realized today that you were expressing sympathy for Mr. Meredith's Marxist ideals."

"A simple poor form of speech." Caradoc waved a hand at her. "It meant nothing."

"I wondered," Violet continued. "Was it possible that you had let slip some of your Marxist leanings to Lady Maud, a proper lady who would never countenance such thoughts? Did she, perhaps, threaten to report you to the lord chamberlain of the queen's household?"

"This is a very preposterous theory, Mrs. Harper. One for which you have no proof. After all, Lady Maud is dead."

"I had to make the connection between you and Lady Maud myself, but Lord Marcheford provided the clue about your relationship with his wife. When I arrived at the palace earlier, I saw this cloth on the floor." She pointed down. "It was just like the chloroform-soaked ones I found on or near two of the bodies. I mistakenly thought Princess Beatrice had been kidnapped, and rushed to judgment against Lord Marcheford.

"I went to his home to confront him, and he revealed to me that Henry Cape and Lady Marcheford had introduced Miss Cortland to a friend of Mr. Cape's. A friend who was another man of the arts. You, Mr. Caradoc.

"Miss Cortland had been tossed out by her parents yet still had an aristocratic background. A servant in the royal household might have seemed a good match. It was clever to have her tell Josephine Butler that she was dating a married aristocrat. No one would suspect a thing."

"There is nothing to suspect." Violet noticed that Caradoc's protests were weakening.

"These women must have done something that angered you,

but I'm not sure what it was. All I'm certain of is that you are a murderer and deserve to hang."

Caradoc went to the rear of Beatrice's art table and bent down, popping open another secret drawer. He withdrew two small, cylindrical tubes.

"Do you know what Karl Marx advocates, Mrs. Harper? The proletariat throwing off the bourgeoisie, creating a perfect society, and all that rot. I've attended Marx's meetings, just like Reese Meredith, and I realized that he doesn't go far enough.

"No, Mrs. Harper, if we want society changed, we need more. Meredith's plan of self-glory, assassinating the queen in a violent explosion, only means that her son becomes king. What does that do? Nothing. I tried to stop Meredith, so that my own plans could move forward, but the idiot didn't pay attention to me."

Caradoc pocketed the two tubes into his apron and picked up a tightly stoppered bottle from the table. He examined the label, nodded, and, with some exertion, opened it.

Whatever it was Caradoc was planning, Violet was absolutely certain she wouldn't like it.

"What is it you think should happen, sir?" she said, hoping to distract him while she figured a way out of the room.

"Anarchy, my dear Mrs. Harper, is the only answer. You may be wondering how I came to this conclusion. Don't worry, we have all evening, and what I have for you won't be painful at all as long as you don't struggle. You struggled when I met you in the street, and it ruined everything. You were fortunate that the baker ran into the street, although I knew I would create another special moment for us. Sending you that note was brilliant, wasn't it? You thought it was in the princess's handwriting."

Could she get to the birdcage, remove it from its hook, and fling it at Caradoc? Would it injure him or at least startle him enough to give her time to run from the room?

The odor from the open bottle floated over to Violet. "What is that?"

"Turpentine. Helpful for cleaning brushes and other things. A bit offensive to the senses, isn't it?"

Violet stood still, hoping he wasn't aware that her heart was struggling to leap from her chest. Did he intend to make her drink the turpentine? To shove a cloth soaked in it into her mouth? How was it related to the chloroform?

Remain calm, Violet Harper.

"So why did you kill Lady Marcheford and Miss Cortland?"

Caradoc withdrew one of the tubes from his pocket and dipped one end into the turpentine bottle, making Violet realize what it was: a hypodermic needle.

"Mrs. Harper, it may interest you to know that I have not always been the benign, polished royal tutor of oils and pastels. I have quite humble origins in Wales, where so many of my countrymen have been abused by callous colliery owners. Some of us who fled that brutal life learned to lose our Welsh accents, but never what it means to be a Welshman. My *tad*—my father—was a shot-firer, and his leg was near burned off when he slipped into one of the holes packed with explosives that he'd set. The head of the mine refused to pay for a doctor, and by the time he got treatment, the infection was so bad there was nothing to do but amputate his leg. He could no longer work, and turned to drink. My *mam* went to the mines to take his place—"

"Women aren't permitted to work in mines."

Caradoc looked at her condescendingly. "That law is routinely ignored. The mine owner wasn't willing to help my father, but he was happy to send my mother down into the depths as a bearer, carrying heavy baskets of coal away from the coal face and handing them off to putters, who put the lumps of coal into coal wagons. My *tad* died two years later, when I was but a mere boy of eleven, and my mother followed him shortly thereafter, a completely broken woman.

"My brothers and sisters and I were shuffled around to various relatives and lost touch with one another. I ended up with an aunt and uncle who found me to be a nuisance, although they claimed I was difficult, and I finally ended up with an elder brother in Cardiff when I was fourteen. This was my first truly good stroke of fortune in life. Drystan was very bitter over what had happened to

Tad, but he taught me that it was not just the company I should hate, but those who rule in government. Drystan had anarchist notions; he just didn't know it."

Caradoc tucked the filled needle back into his pocket and withdrew the second one, again dipping it into the turpentine bottle and pulling back the metal plunger. He put the second filled needle into his pocket and closed up the turpentine. He frowned. "Now where is my . . . ah, yes, I see you already found it."

Caradoc picked up the chloroform bottle. "Hidden right among the princess's things, yet she never noticed. She's a very obedient child and never touches anything unless I tell her to. I'm afraid I wasn't quite so amenable as a student.

"When I expressed interest in sculpting and painting, my brother saved up to send me to the Royal Academy to learn art properly. I thought it was my second stroke of luck, although I admit I didn't enjoy taking chemistry, anatomy, and ancient history alongside my drawing and painting classes. Don't think I don't see what you're doing, Mrs. Harper. Lady Marcheford attempted something similar and you know how she fared by struggling."

Violet halted from backing up imperceptibly—or so she thought—toward the birdcage.

"Where was I? Oh yes," he said, opening the bottle and taking only a quick whiff before stoppering it up again. "My work attracted a very wealthy benefactor, who I soon discovered had a very beautiful daughter. Dora was a flawless diamond kept hidden away and unable to sparkle. As her father obtained more and more lucrative commissions for me from his aristocratic friends, I was falling more and more in love with Dora.

"She was the rock upon which I based my sanity during those years of serving the vapid ruling class. I eventually suggested that she and I run away together, that my talent as an artist was enough to support us. I realized then that she was no better than the rest of her father's cronies."

"She left you?" Violet asked.

"She said that she'd been enamored of my rebellious nature, but she'd discovered that I was not really the romantic figure she thought I was, just a commoner in a nice waistcoat."

Caradoc sat down in Beatrice's chair, casually crossing one leg over the other. Did he think they were having a social visit before he murdered her?

"I'd already become interested in Mr. Marx's ideas, although, as I said, I knew his plan was weak and would never bring about the revolution he claims it will. My experiences with the colliery and Dora and her social circle taught me that aristocrats can never be trusted and amount to nothing more than a boil on the rump of society that must be lanced in order for people to be happy and free."

The more comfortable Caradoc became in his conversation, the more likely it was that he might delay fulfilling his intentions with Violet. She endeavored to keep him distracted by his own story, which he so smugly enjoyed.

"You still haven't explained why you killed Princess Louise's friends and Miss Cortland," she said.

His eyes narrowed. "Kindly do not interrupt me. Working at the palace neatly coincided with my plans to undermine the aristocracy. Dora's father knew nothing of our relationship, and was only too happy to recommend me for the job when it became available. It's always an extra feather in the wings of those stuffed birds when they can say that they obtained a royal position for one of their protégés.

"Once I was lodged here, I overheard Princess Louise talking to one of her friends about the burgeoning moralist movement, intent on repealing the Contagious Diseases Acts. I knew that these moralist women, bent on breaking down society as we know it, were a perfect fit for my own goals, and I determined to join forces with them."

"So you *approve* of the moralists."

"Your mind is getting more proficient, Mrs. Harper. Of course I do. They had much to teach me in terms of protesting, disturbing the peace, and so forth. What a magnificent marriage it would have been, the moralist and anarchist movements."

"But the moralists don't want society to break down. They simply want prostitutes treated humanely, with basic dignity."

"It is their methods, not their goals, that are attractive. In time, they will agree to my own goals."

"How did you pursue this marriage with the moralists?" Violet had a glimmer of an idea but needed time to work it out.

Caradoc smiled. "It was brilliant and should have worked nicely. I went to Mrs. Butler and offered my services, but she turned me down. Lillian was too afraid of exposing our relationship to the world to intercede with Mrs. Butler on my behalf.

"What a harridan that moralist is. All of her pious bleating about what God did and didn't want her to do, and that I wasn't part of The Plan. I could have wrung her neck and dropped her to the ground at that moment, as much as she reminded me of Dora's rejection, but I figured she just needed more convincing first." He tapped the pocket in his apron.

"You attempted to kill us both in the street."

"I attempted nothing. I wanted to scare you both and was quite successful."

"Did you also attempt to frighten Lady Maud?"

Caradoc's smile turned into a smirk. "So we are back to the Lady Maud again, eh? No, I wasn't interested in merely scaring her, because you are right, she had reacted in a most unseemly way to my explanation of Marx's teachings, except it wasn't the lord chamberlain she threatened to tell. It was the queen herself. I couldn't have that, could I?"

The man exuded evil. Violet knew she was in danger, but she pressed on. "What of Lady Marcheford? Weren't you practically friends, what with having Mr. Cape in common?"

"An aristocrat friends with an art tutor? You are delusional, Mrs. Harper. No, she found me an amusing appendage to her beloved Henry. Believe me, when she discovered I was attending some of Mr. Marx's meetings, she, too, wasted no time in seeking me out with a direct threat to report me if I didn't stop."

Violet felt as though she were receiving multiple blows to the face. First to one side, then to the other. "Why didn't you simply resign your post? Why was it necessary to kill Lady Maud and Lady Marcheford?"

"Resign? Didn't I just say that I needed my post for now?"

His rationale was that of a madman. Violet knew she was in serious trouble, yet she still wanted the entire truth of the matter.

"How did you manage to break into Lady Maud's and Lady Marcheford's homes?"

"You don't need to force entry when you are the royal art tutor. Servants happily admit you to their masters' residences."

Violet could only imagine the women's terror, believing they had an innocent appointment with an art teacher, only to discover the appointment was with death.

"Surely they didn't invite you into their bedchambers."

"You'd be surprised how trusting a young lady is with a palace servant."

"Lady Marcheford tried to shoot you." Violet was rapidly putting more things together in her mind.

"Yes, that was foolish. Once I got the chloroform on her, she collapsed."

His explanations accounted for the aristocratic women, but what about Miss Cortland? Violet grasped for an answer. "So it was your anger at Mrs. Butler that caused you to turn on your sweetheart, Miss Cortland."

"Lillian was amusing and we had many interests in common. But she was another Dora, disguised in homespun. One day she decided I was not an appropriate match for her. How dare she, a society castoff, think I was too low for her?"

Poor Miss Cortland, her only crime a sound decision that Owen Caradoc was not a suitable match.

Violet saw the absurdity of Caradoc's crimes. "So Reese unsuccessfully attempted to kill the queen to further his Marxist ideals, and you actually murdered three women for reasons unrelated to furthering those ideals?"

"I suppose that's ironic, yes, but all five women—I include you and Mrs. Butler, of course, Mrs. Harper—were just inconvenient detours as I develop my bigger scenario. Events were proceeding well, except that Princess Louise was overcome by Lady Maud's death and dragged you into it. Until you started prying, I was convinced that no one would be the wiser. In fact, once Meredith took the blame, I was in the clear, but you had to continue your pursuit. You can see how you have burdened me."

Indeed.

"How did you obtain the chloroform?" she asked.

"Did I not mention that my brother, Drystan, is a surgeon? No? You can imagine the thriving practice he has among those who are routinely crushed, burned, and cut working in collieries, although most can only pay him in food and running errands for him. It is easy enough to pilfer the supplies I need from him on periodic visits."

Violet eyed his pocket. "Such as hypodermic needles?"

"Among other things. Chloroform comes in handy for a variety of situations. It's been all the rage since the queen used it to help her through two of her births."

"Which is what you used to send me and three other women into unconsciousness, too, before killing them."

"Bravo, Mrs. Harper, perhaps you are mildly brighter than I gave you credit for. Yes, it calms down my intended victim so that I can complete my task in peace."

"And an injection of turpentine is how you complete your task."

"Brilliant, isn't it? Very effective, yet leaves no cause for suspicion when used on the right victim. Two injections behind the knee, between the toes, under the arm, or at the back of the neck, and the unconscious woman is quickly and painlessly sent to her death."

So what Violet thought were insect bites were two consecutive hypodermic injections.

"But why two needles? Surely one is sufficient."

"I like to be thorough, Mrs. Harper. One injection makes me confident; two makes me absolutely certain. Fortunately, tonight marks the end of my troubles. Once we are done here, I'll give Mrs. Butler her final minutes of life, then I'll run both the anarchist and moralist movements. The world will change beyond anything you can imagine, Mrs. Harper. The monarchy and everything surrounding draconian rule and law will disappear—poof!"

Violet realized that Caradoc was completely insane. Who in his right mind could possibly think he could overturn society like that?

He pulled one of the hypodermics from his apron pocket and, with the needle in the air, depressed the plunger slightly, sending a bit of the turpentine upward for effect. It sprayed backward onto his apron, but he seemed not to notice. He tucked the needle back in next to its mate.

Violet knew she didn't have long remaining. She edged closer to the birdcage.

"You understand, sir, that I am no weak miss to be easily overcome."

"You may not be weak, but you will certainly be dead soon. You are the one vulnerability in my plan, what with your investigations on Louise's behalf."

"How do you possibly expect to inject me with turpentine—in Princess Beatrice's art room—and think no one will suspect you?"

He smiled again. "Do you listen to nothing? A couple of needed piercings—perhaps under your arm this time—will never be noticed, and I will carry your body elsewhere. Perhaps I toss you down the Grand Staircase so that it looks like you tripped and fell. A tragic accident. The royal family would mourn you, no doubt."

He pulled the syringes from his pocket once again and stood. "Enough nattering. The family will be home soon."

This time, Violet didn't hesitate. She stepped deliberately to the table that held one of the lit oil lamps, picked it up, and threw it with all of her might at her target.

"More stupidity, Mrs. Harper," Caradoc said. "You missed me by at least—what? Oh! You dreadful little—"

Violet had hit what she intended, the turpentine bottle. It shattered, and the vaporous liquid met the lamp's flame, igniting in the air in a blinding firework. Flames landed on the art tutor's apron, already damp in spots from turpentine. He patted at the flames but must have inadvertently pushed the syringe plungers again, for his apron erupted in golden heat.

"How dare you?" he sputtered, moving backward. One of Beatrice's many canvases was now on fire, and the flames, enjoying their meal of paint and horsehair brushes, threatened to spread farther. Violet could only imagine what would happen when they had a taste of the carpets and draperies. If she didn't get past Caradoc quickly, she'd be trapped in an inferno.

She had to do two things first. Running to the birdcage, she opened the door and shouted, "Go!"

Peaches didn't hesitate, jumping off his perch and flying past the gilded door, over Caradoc's writhing, flame-engulfed body, landing on the heavy brass doorknob of the room's door and beating his wings wildly.

Violet raced to the heavy draperies and tugged on them. They were tightly affixed to the wall. She pulled again, harder. She heard a faint tear, despite the sound of the growing fire, which both crackled and roared in an unholy alliance of destruction. Rivulets of sweat ran down her face into her collar, making it itch against her neck, but there was no time to think about it.

She managed to rip off a large section of a drapery panel. It was preposterously heavy, and Violet had the rambling thought that she needed to tell Mary not to use this fabric in her new lodgings, lest she be unable to tear it down in case of a fire.

Between her long skirts, her drenched skin, and the unmanageable drapery in her hand, she nearly tripped twice as she made her way toward the door, coughing as the smoke swirled around her, making it difficult to breathe. Caradoc was howling as he attempted to rip his apron from his body. Violet used the curtain material to smother most of the flames around her as she made her way out. Caradoc reached his arms out to her in a blazing inferno of supplication.

She threw the drapery over the man and wrapped her arms around him, holding him as the fire died out. When he fell limp against her, she laid him on the ground, still careful not to let her dress touch any burning embers nearby. Once he was resting on the ground, she quickly removed the drapery from his body to finish beating out flames and embers until she could no longer see anything glowing red.

Had none of the staff heard what was happening up here?

Utterly exhausted, she sank down next to Owen Caradoc. "Are

you all right?" she asked, but immediately saw that he was not. His eyes stared vacantly at her, and the stench of his burnt flesh was far worse than that of turpentine.

A man's own evil never ceased to turn on him like a rabid dog.

She shut his eyes. "I'm sorry, Mr. Caradoc," she said quietly. "But I'll not serve you in death. I'll send you back to your brother on the funeral train, and he can have you buried in Wales."

Trembling and nauseated from the exhaustion of her ordeal, Violet covered Caradoc with the piece of drapery with which she had beaten out the flames from his body, then dropped heavily back to the floor again next to his remains.

Violet was finished with the death surrounding Buckingham Palace.

As Violet wearily rose from Caradoc's stiff body, she again coughed violently from the smoke that still filled the room. As her heaving subsided, Peaches appeared from nowhere, landed on her shoulder, and offered her a loud and belligerent chirp.

"My apologies, Peaches. I was only doing my best to save you."

The door banged open. Two footmen and a young maid, followed by Louise and Beatrice, burst in. They all froze, utterly mystified by the scene before them. Beatrice's spate of coughing set them in motion again. The footmen and maid, trained to clean and straighten whatever was before them, went right to work. While the maid futilely attempted to right the blackened room, the footmen lifted Owen Caradoc's body to carry it out.

"No!" Violet said. "Scotland Yard must see him first."

"Mrs. Harper," Louise said, "what has happened here?"

Violet shook her head. "An unfortunate end to a man's unfortunate plot."

"Is that Mr. Caradoc?" Beatrice asked.

"I'm afraid so."

The girl frowned and bit her lip. As if sensing her distress, Peaches flew from Violet's shoulder onto Beatrice's and whistled softly in her ear. The girl and her bird chirped quietly at each other.

"Was he . . . ?" Louise said.

"Yes."

"I can't believe it."

"Nor could I." Violet explained to Louise what had happened as more servants entered the room to cover any evidence of destruction, as good servants do, making a wide berth around the art tutor's body.

"I'm thankful you're safe, Mrs. Harper, but you do look a fright. Thank God Mother is staying at Cumberland Lodge tonight. Hopefully, this room can be made to look somewhat normal by tomorrow. I dread her finding out that another palace servant has been disloyal."

Beatrice had Peaches on her finger. She kissed his beak and said, "Did Mr. Caradoc do something bad?"

"I'm afraid so, Princess."

"He's dead, isn't he?"

"Yes."

Beatrice nodded solemnly. "I didn't really enjoy my art classes, anyway. Perhaps now Mother will allow me to learn to play the piano."

14

Inspector Hurst shook his head as he entered Beatrice's damaged art room, Inspector Pratt at his heels. He took charge of the room, ordering the servants out and inspecting Caradoc's body. Finally, Hurst joined Violet, who was despairing of her soaked clothing and the smell of smoke permeating every pore of her skin. She needed a mirror and a bath, just not in that order.

"Given your condition, I suppose you're responsible for this," Hurst said.

"Indirectly, yes."

He sighed. "Mr. Pratt, take notes. I'm sure this will be an enlightening explanation. Now, Mrs. Harper, do tell us what sort of mischief you've been up to."

With Inspector Pratt furiously scribbling away, Violet accounted for the past few hours. When she was done, Hurst shook his head. "Just a moment. You're saying that Meredith, the man we have in custody, had nothing to do with those deaths?"

"No. There have always been two minds at work. Both were followers of Karl Marx, but Mr. Meredith was after the queen in order to destroy the monarchy, while Mr. Caradoc had varying motives, with an overall goal of taking over the moralist movement."

"Were they working together?"

Violet shook her head.

"But surely they knew each other as servants of the palace."

"Yes, but that was coincidence. Mr. Caradoc witnessed Mr. Meredith at some of Marx's meetings, and the two once spoke in the corridor, but they weren't confederates."

Pratt looked up from his notes. "A lesson to us, sir, that it isn't always just one perpetrator on a crime, even if it isn't a gang."

"Heaven forbid I should take crime-breaking lessons from an undertaker. You were fortunate, Mrs. Harper, that you didn't get yourself killed on numerous occasions throughout this case."

"In fact, Inspector, I agree," Violet said. "I am far more competent at managing corpses than criminals."

Mollified that he'd won the point, Hurst softened. "All's well now, I suppose. Which reminds me, ahem, speaking of all being well, how is your friend—Mrs. Cooke, isn't it?"

"As well as can be expected. She is, of course, still in mourning and will be so for many more months, Inspector."

"Yes, yes, of course. I mean nothing untoward. My concern was merely for a lady in distress. I am an agent of the law, concerned for all of the kingdom's citizenry." He puffed his chest at his vaunting self-description. "Please give Mrs. Cooke my regards."

"I will."

"Don't forget, Mrs. Harper."

Oh dear.

After returning to St. James's Palace to bathe and tell Sam what happened, Violet felt an immediate need to visit Josephine, so that the moralist would know she was now safe. Sam argued against the lateness of the hour for visiting, and Violet eventually agreed to wait until morning.

Before dawn, though, Violet was dressing and urging Sam out of bed so that they could hurry to the moralist's headquarters. Josephine was unlocking the front door when they arrived and invited them in to share in some poached eggs, oysters, and bacon she'd just picked up.

Over their morning repast together at the repeal headquarters' largest table, a round oaken affair that wobbled on its base, Violet relayed to Josephine what had happened with Owen Caradoc.

The moralist nodded sadly. "I wondered if he might be involved, but didn't want to accuse him if he was innocent. He came to me months ago, seeking to join our movement, but his words and manners told me that he saw us as a way to glorify himself, not God. There was no spiritual fire in him, so to speak, just a self-consuming desire for power. He was here several times to press his case, but I always rebuffed him.

"I was also suspicious that it was Mr. Caradoc who had followed us into the street, simply because he was the most volatile human being I'd ever met. Had I known he worked for the queen, I would have reported him immediately. If only I had known!"

Josephine speared the last remaining oyster and put it on her plate. "Poor Lillian, to have been caught up with him and then suffer such a consequence for his attentions. I pray she is at rest now. I suppose my next task is to inform her parents, even though they let her be given a pauper's burial."

Violet and Louise strolled privately in the palace gardens. Louise was particularly animated, which Violet took to be due to her relief that her friends' murders had been solved.

"Your husband must be so pleased by your bravery," the princess said, plucking a stem of lilac and inhaling deeply from its heady fragrance before twirling it between her fingers. Violet noticed that the princess was wearing her bracelet made from Lady Marcheford's hair, as well as her mourning brooch commemorating Lady Maud.

"Yes, except he worries now that he cannot leave my side to buy a newspaper without my becoming embroiled in a life-threatening circumstance."

Louise laughed for the first time since Maud's death. "I must admit, I always thought it was Marcheford who was guilty."

"I thought so, as well. I also had my suspicions of Sir Charles Mordaunt."

Louise gave an unladylike snort. "That fool. He's got no more brains than a donkey. First he marries a giddy little debutante, then expects her to mummify up in Warwickshire while he spends his days running down deer and blasting grouse. He didn't even bring her to London while he sat in Parliament. If she sought a little entertainment, who can blame her? Now he's bruiting it about that Bertie had a dalliance with her. What good does he think will come of pursuing a divorce from Lady Mordaunt and naming my brother as a corespondent?"

Violet had no answer.

"Mother is furious with Bertie over it, but she'll defend him; you can be sure of that. Did you know that she's also furious with Mr. Brown?"

"No, and it surprises me."

"She told me privately that his handling of things with you—falsely calling upon the spirits to lead you to me—was unconscionable. Naturally, she's too afraid of falling out of his graces to actually confront him. She just railed at me for it. Imagine if it had been Bertie or me who'd used you so carelessly."

Violet had no answer for this, either. She'd witnessed how little Victoria tolerated indiscretions in her children.

"What Mother doesn't know is that Mr. Brown was carrying on with Lady Hazel. Oh, how jealous she would have been to learn of it. I should have tattled on him, but I couldn't bear to hurt Mother that badly, especially now that I'm, well, in a better position with her. So instead I talked to Hazel, and convinced her that a dalliance with a servant—even if he is the queen's favorite servant—could only end in ruin for her. She broke it off with him a few days ago and, to his credit, you'd never know his heartbreak except by the thicker fog of spirits clinging to him, although I guess even that is no indicator of anything amiss with him.

"Speaking of dalliances," Louise continued, "have you heard the news? Marcheford is engaged to marry Lady Henrietta Pettit. Everyone is aghast, what with poor Charlotte hardly cold in her grave. A double injustice for my dear friend. He'll be ostracized for a while, but he's the heir to an important marquess, so he'll be forgiven. I hear Lady Henrietta has a velvet viper's bite, so it is my greatest wish that she use it on him regularly."

For this Violet had a ready reply. "Lady Henrietta is sure to have the upper hand with Lord Marcheford. It may be that in time he is the one who carries a pistol to protect himself."

Louise nodded. "What do you think will happen to the coachman?"

"Mr. Meredith? I see no happy end for him. I suspect he will quickly be found guilty of treason, attempting to murder the queen, and a variety of other charges, and sent immediately to the gallows at Newgate. I'm sure he'll enjoy the sensationalism of his trial, though."

"A more painless end than Mr. Caradoc's, I'll warrant. That's fitting. Mr. Caradoc deserved intense, hellish pain, since he murdered dearest Maud and Charlotte, as well as Miss Cortland."

"I wonder," Violet said, "how Her Majesty is coping with what has happened? Does she particularly blame anyone?"

"You mean for hiring Mr. Caradoc and Mr. Meredith in the first place? Mr. Norton received a serious dressing-down, but he'll survive in his position. Truthfully, I think she was more agitated over whatever evil influence Mr. Caradoc may have had over Beatrice than upon any danger she herself was in. Beatrice is her favorite, you know. Mother will never let her marry, a fate I don't intend to share. Which reminds me."

Louise paused at a bench and invited Violet to sit with her.

"I must share something with you," Louise said, tucking the lilac stem above her ear. "I've met someone, someone I think I might marry."

"Truly? Princess, that's wonderful. Who is it?"

"John Campbell, the Marquess of Lorne. He's the heir to the dukedom of Argyll. He's very handsome and debonair, and I believe he is quite taken with me, too."

Undoubtedly any peer of the realm would be quite taken with a princess.

"Congratulations, Your Highness. Does Her Majesty approve?"

Louise wrinkled her nose. "I've not told her yet. I want to be sure before I suggest such a thing. Mother has come around, but she will have to battle Parliament on my behalf should we reach the point of a proposal. Speaking of proposals, I understand

Mother offered you permanent quarters at St. James's Palace as a reward for ridding the world of Owen Caradoc."

"Yes, but my husband and I intend to start over in London in our own way. I've bought back into my old undertaking shop, and we are fitting out the quarters over it."

"It won't be as prestigious as living at St. James's."

"No, Your Highness, it won't."

"I bet Mother had apoplexy when you refused her."

"It wasn't quite that bad. My husband and I are still invited to attend the Suez Canal opening in November."

"Then you are still in her good graces. I doubt I'll be allowed to travel there. Mother will require that I stay behind to write boring thank-you letters and notes of condolence and invitation refusals. You must be sure to tell me what Egypt is like."

"I would be most pleased to do so, Your Highness."

"I believe I shall count you among my friends, Mrs. Harper."

Violet wasn't sure she could survive much more royal friendship.

Violet returned to St. James's, where Sam was tightening a strap around a trunk. "For heaven's sake, woman, how many geegaws have you collected since I've been gone?"

"My notes and papers probably take up the most room. Oh, and I suppose I've been dragging undertaking supplies into the palace. That will all go into the shop. Don't worry, Sam, I won't have you shaving among bottles of embalming fluid."

He stroked his face. "Perhaps I'll grow a fuller beard and avoid any risk of encounter with your concoctions. I've just read about Professor Modevi's beard-generating cream. He promises that my resulting thick and silky whiskers will add to my strength and virility. What do you think?"

Violet was saved from a retort by a palace servant, who said that they had an *unannounced* visitor in one of the reception rooms. His emphasis on "unannounced" was to let Violet know that people did not simply come and go as they pleased on royal property.

She bit her lip to hide a smile, glad that today she would be leaving stuffy royal etiquette behind. She and Sam walked together downstairs to greet their visitor.

Violet gasped at who awaited her, then smiled. "My sweet girl, you are the perfect ending to a troubled time," she said to her daughter, Susanna, who stood next to her new husband holding a fluffy cat in her arms.

"How did you arrive so quickly?" Violet asked, enveloping daughter and feline in her arms while Sam shook Benjamin's hand and offered congratulations on their marriage.

"Both trains and ships were very efficient, much to Mrs. Softpaws' relief," Susanna said, scratching the cat behind the ears.

"We are so pleased you are here," Violet said, standing back from Susanna just to drink in the fact that her daughter was really here, in front of her. "Both of you. Benjamin, I am delighted to call you my son-in-law."

"It is my honor to be a member of the Harper family," he replied.

"How long will you stay? We must plan to go to the British Museum, and to a pantomime show in Drury Lane, and I hear there is a traveling circus in the city—"

Susanna laughed, the tinkling sound a balm to Violet's soul. "Oh, Mother, I don't know if there's time for all of that. Benjamin and I are here mostly to check on you."

Violet was puzzled. "To check on me? I'm quite fine."

"Father says otherwise."

Violet looked at Sam, who made it a point to inspect a piece of sculpture on a pedestal nearby.

"What does my husband say?" she asked.

"He writes that you have been involved in all manner of murder and mayhem and pandemonium. We don't want to visit any tourist sites until you sit down and explain to us in great detail what has happened these past few months."

Violet did so, leaving out nothing. As she explained everything to her family in great detail, it occurred to her that perhaps she was indeed becoming a bit of an amateur detective.

Not that Inspector Hurst would agree.

But what did it mean for Violet, being an amateur detective? Thus far, she'd been close to her own demise on several occasions. What if next time she wasn't as fortunate as she'd been thus far?

Yet Violet had helped to bring justice for several people callously murdered in London. Wasn't that worth the perils involved?

The dead deserve justice as much as the living do, Violet Harper, and you know more about the deceased than anyone.

Yes, it was worth it. It was worth all of the possible danger, risk, and tribulation to protect the dead.

The **Mold Riot of 1869** occurred as described in this novel, with a group of angry townspeople attacking the policemen escorting a pair of convicted miners to the train station for a month's hard labor at Flint Castle. Soldiers arrived and fired into the crowd, killing several, including a nineteen-year-old housemaid named **Margaret Younghusband**. Her half brother, Reese Meredith, is a figure of my own imagination.

Feminism was in its nascent stages in the Victorian era. In fact, the term "feminist," coined by utopian socialist and French philosopher Charles Fourier, did not appear until 1872. I have chosen to call members of this early group moralists. Largely an evangelical movement, it was concerned primarily with basic human rights and dignity, hence their concern with the Contagious Diseases Acts, which placed humiliating burdens of examination and potential imprisonment upon prostitutes, while exempting from any such burdens the men who hired them. The suffrage movement also began in 1872, although the Victorian woman's activist probably wouldn't even recognize the feminist movement of today.

As a passionate Christian, **Josephine Butler** (1828–1906) abhorred the sin of prostitution but also regarded women as exploited victims of male oppression. After the death of her only daughter, Josephine sought solace by ministering to people at a workhouse and had her first encounter with the despair of prostitutes. Her husband, George, encouraged her activities, so when a national campaign was started in 1869 to repeal the Contagious Diseases Acts she set up the Ladies National Association for the Repeal of the Contagious Diseases Acts and became actively involved.

The **Contagious Diseases Acts** were passed by the Parliament of the United Kingdom in 1864, with modifications made in 1866 and 1869. The legislation allowed police officers to arrest prostitutes in certain ports and army towns, then subject the women to compulsory checks for venereal disease. If a woman was declared to be infected, she would be confined in what was known as a lock hospital until "cured," generally a period of three months. By 1869, the acts expanded to allow for interment in lock hospitals for up to a year.

Lock hospitals were seriously underfunded and did not have enough beds for the number of prostitutes being confined. Thus many of these women ended up in workhouse infirmaries, which were ill equipped to handle these cases.

The level of prostitution was high in Victorian England, and it was predominantly a working-class profession, common in commercial ports and pleasure resorts. The nature of it makes it difficult to establish the exact number of prostitutes operating in the Victorian era, but judicial reports from 1857 to 1869 estimate the number to be between 50,000 and 368,000.

Regulating prostitution was not an attempt to protect the prostitutes themselves but to control the high level of venereal disease in Great Britain's armed forces. By 1864, one out of every three sick cases in the army was caused by venereal disease.

The issues surrounding the Contagious Diseases Acts and venereal disease created significant controversy within Victorian society, as debate erupted over the double standards between men and women. It was one of the first political issues that led to women organizing themselves and actively campaigning for basic human rights. There was a great deal of energy behind the repeal of the acts, led by people such as Josephine Butler. After an active campaign involving hundreds of meetings and petitions totaling more than 2 million signatures, the acts were finally repealed in 1886.

The notion of the **Princess Louise** (1848–1939) as a feminist (or moralist) is not far-fetched. The sixth of Victoria's nine children, Louise was considered the most beautiful of the queen's four daughters. Always interested in the advancement of women, she was a regular correspondent with Josephine Butler and other women's rights activists. Louise knew that she could best serve her causes by remaining in Britain, instead of becoming the consort of a foreign prince.

She demonstrated a rebellious streak early on, by falling in love with her brother Leopold's tutor, the **Reverend Robinson Duckworth** (1834–1911), whom Victoria dismissed in 1870, a year later than I have it occurring in this story.

Princess Louise then set her sights on John Campbell, the Marquess of Lorne and heir to the dukedom of Argyll. Victoria had arranged dynastic marriages for her children with royal houses throughout Europe, making her known as the grandmother of Europe. After a minimal amount of argument from her mother and Parliament, Louise was permitted to marry her commoner, so considered although he was a British aristocrat. Such a marriage was nearly unprecedented, having not occurred since Charles Brandon was permitted to marry the Princess Mary, Henry VIII's sister, in 1515.

Albert Edward or "Bertie" (1841–1910), the Prince of Wales, had an acrimonious relationship with the queen's favorite, **John Brown** (1826–1883). In fact, after the queen's death in 1901 Bertie had destroyed as many of Brown's letters and other mementos as he could possibly find.

The prince was also implicated in the divorce proceedings of **Sir Charles Mordaunt** (1836–1897) against his wife, Harriet Sarah Moncreiffe. Sir Charles was a country squire primarily interested in hunting and shooting expeditions. Unfortunately, he married Harriet, an empty-headed beauty. She caught the eye of the prince, and while Sir Charles was away in Parliament or off killing foxes she was entertaining Bertie and many other aristocratic lovers.

In 1869, Harriet gave birth to an illegitimate daughter and confessed all to her husband. When Sir Charles discovered his wife's perfidy, he went on a rampage, threatening to name the Prince of Wales as a corespondent in his divorce case. He never did so, mostly because his father-in-law announced that his daughter was mad and had her incarcerated in a series of locations.

It should be noted that I have Mordaunt loudly decrying the Contagious Diseases Acts in Parliament in 1869, whereas in reality he'd left Parliament by 1868.

Bertie's wife, the **Princess Alexandra of Denmark**, or "Alix"

(1844–1925), endured the Mordaunt scandal during a pregnancy and indeed spent years gracefully surviving her husband's many affairs. Ironically, Alix and Bertie had a very affectionate relationship. Things were not so affectionate with her mother-in-law, as the queen was very fond of the Prussians and Alix was not.

Queen Victoria (1819–1901), Queen of the United Kingdom, despite her Christian piety became acutely interested in the occult, especially after the deaths of her mother and husband in 1861. Victoria had several spiritual advisors, including John Brown, who became her spiritual medium through whom she contacted her dead husband, Prince Albert. Interest in spiritualism and the afterlife was widespread during the Victorian era, understandable given their serious attitudes toward death and dying.

The queen's interest in death and dying must have been acute, since she was not only permanently bereaved by her husband's death, but she also survived no fewer than seven assassination attempts in her life. Three of her attackers went into mental asylums, two were transported to Australia, one received an eighteen-month sentence, and one was given a one-year sentence and a caning. Less than pleased by the light sentences, Queen Victoria insisted that laws be changed so that defendants could be found both "insane" *and* "guilty."

Despite the numerous attempts on her life, the one I portray in the book is completely fictitious.

Queen Victoria regularly held Drawing Rooms at Buckingham Palace. Their purpose was to permit aristocrats to present their marriage-eligible daughters to the queen. The young woman would be dressed in her finest and would curtsy before the queen, who would exchange a few innocuous pleasantries with her before turning to the next girl to be introduced. Thus "presented," an aristocratic young woman was a far better catch in the marriage market. An invitation to a Drawing Room was a singular event in a girl's life. Drawing Room receptions could also be used for the presentation of foreign diplomats to the British sovereign.

Although the mourning jewelry that Violet helps Louise and her friends make was extremely popular in Victoria's reign, the eye portraits that the **Princess Beatrice** (1857–1944) paints had fallen largely out of fashion after the eighteenth century, when they were called lovers' eyes and given as romantic gifts. Eye portraits did experience a short resurgence of popularity in the Victorian era as mourning pieces.

An able actress and dancer, as well as a keen artist and photographer, Beatrice was the queen's favorite child, and in fact Victoria referred to her as "Baby" for most of her childhood, an unusually affectionate nickname for the queen to use. Victoria kept Beatrice at her side almost constantly.

Because the queen kept the young girl from experiencing life outside the privileged confines of the royal palaces, Beatrice spent considerable time in John Brown's company, working with him to carry out the queen's wishes. Beatrice was also a devout Christian, fascinated by theology until her death at age eighty-seven.

Prince Leopold (1853–1884), the second-youngest of Victoria's offspring, was a sickly child, having inherited hemophilia through his mother. Hemophilia is a blood disorder that decreases the body's ability to create blood clots and thus causes the sufferer to bleed severely from even a slight injury. He was nearest to Beatrice in age, but he was often confined and she spent little time in his company. Leopold died in 1884 at the age of thirty, after a brief two-year marriage.

In 1869, **Karl Marx** (1818–1883) was on the General Council of the International Workingmen's Association and regularly gave speeches encouraging his viewpoints. Originally from Prussia, Marx moved to London from Paris in 1849 and remained there the rest of his life.

William Morris (1834–1896) was a textile designer, artist, writer, and libertarian Marxist who was well known for his wallpaper and furniture design in the English Arts and Crafts style. Along with several partners he founded Morris, Marshall, and Faulkner at Red Lion Square in London, offering a range of stained glass, carpets, furniture, wall hangings, and tapestries.

John Walter III (1818–1894) was the proprietor of *The Times* as well as a member of the House of Commons.

Evelyn Denison (1800–1873) was Speaker of the House from 1857 to 1872. He was raised to the peerage after his retirement and became the First Viscount Ossington.

William Norton held his position as superintendent of the mews for over thirty years.

Henry Peach Robinson (1830–1901) was an English photographer best known for his work in joining multiple negatives together to form a single image, an early example of photomontage. The reader should note that by 1868 Robinson had relocated from London to Tunbridge Wells, yet I have chosen to have him still working in London in my story's time frame.

Postmortem photography was common in the Victorian era for two reasons. First, because photography was still fairly new in the late 1860s, most people did not have such portraits routinely made. If someone died unexpectedly, a picture made after death might be the only one that the deceased's loved ones would ever have.

Second, the Victorians considered an after-death photograph a very sentimental keepsake, much like mourning brooches. Hence the subjects would be posed in various ways with their loved ones, with the photographer often employing techniques to make the subject as lifelike as possible.

Most postmortem photography would be done fairly quickly after the deceased breathed his last, since the Victorians did not typically embalm their dead and so burial happened within a few days of death.

Queen Victoria's fifth child, **Princess Helena** (1846–1923), was never in very good health, although her mother claimed she was a hypochondriac. Like Louise, Helena enjoyed a healthy flirtation with a palace employee, librarian Carl Ruland, who also taught German to the young Prince of Wales. And, as with Louise's infatuation with Reverend Duckworth, Ruland found himself dismissed in 1863 the moment the queen discovered their relationship.

Following Ruland's departure, the queen searched for a proper husband and found him in **Prince Christian of Schleswig-Holstein** (1831–1917). Schleswig and Holstein were two territories fought over not only by Prussia but also by Denmark, Princess Alix's homeland, hence making the match politically awkward for the princess. However, Helena and Christian were devoted to each other and Victoria was delighted because Christian was willing to live in nearby Cumberland Lodge, thus keeping the princess near her mother, even if Victoria did scoff at her daughter's many illnesses, real or imagined.

A final note: History can be inconvenient for a fiction writer when its events do not line up properly for a story. I have already mentioned a few date shifts I made for the sake of the story. In addition, I also point out to the reader that Queen Victoria's birthday was on May 24. The public celebrations for her fiftieth birthday were held on June 2, 1869, the same day that the Mold riots were occurring in Wales. I have moved the date of her birthday festivities to a month later, to fit with the pacing of the novel.

SELECTED BIBLIOGRAPHY

Griffiths, Jenny, and Griffiths, Mike. *The Mold Tragedy of 1869.* Llanrwst, Wales: Gwasg Carreg Gwalch, 2001.

Louis, Anthony. *Tarot Plain and Simple.* Woodbury, MN: Llewellyn, 1996.

Packard, Jerrold M. *Victoria's Daughters.* New York: St. Martin's Griffin, 1998.

Underwood, Peter. *Queen Victoria's Other World.* London: HARRAP, 1986.